Ace titles by Deborah Chester

THE
KING
IMPERILED

DEBORAH CHESTER

ACE BOOKS, NEW YORK

THE BERKLEY PUBLISHING GROUP
Published by the Penguin Group
Penguin Group (USA) Inc.
375 Hudson Street, New York, New York 10014, USA
Penguin Group (Canada), 90 Eglinton Avenue East, Suite 700, Toronto, Ontario M4P 2Y3, Canada
(a division of Pearson Penguin Canada Inc.)
Penguin Books Ltd., 80 Strand, London WC2R 0RL, England
Penguin Group Ireland, 25 St. Stephen's Green, Dublin 2, Ireland (a division of Penguin Books Ltd.)
Penguin Group (Australia), 250 Camberwell Road, Camberwell, Victoria 3124, Australia
(a division of Pearson Australia Group Pty. Ltd.)
Penguin Books India Pvt. Ltd., 11 Community Centre, Panchsheel Park, New Delhi—110 017, India
Penguin Group (NZ), Cnr. Airborne and Rosedale Roads, Albany, Auckland 1310, New Zealand
(a division of Pearson New Zealand Ltd.)
Penguin Books (South Africa) (Pty.) Ltd., 24 Sturdee Avenue, Rosebank, Johannesburg 2196, South Africa

Penguin Books Ltd., Registered Offices: 80 Strand, London WC2R 0RL, England

This is a work of fiction. Names, characters, places, and incidents either are the product of the author's imagination or are used fictitiously, and any resemblance to actual persons, living or dead, business establishments, events, or locales is entirely coincidental. The publisher does not have any control over and does not assume any responsibility for author or third-party websites or their content.

THE KING IMPERILED

An Ace Book / published by arrangement with the author

PRINTING HISTORY
Ace mass market edition / December 2005

Copyright © 2005 by Deborah Chester.
Cover art by Aleta Rafton.
Cover design by Judith Murello.

ISBN: 0-441-01353-8

ACE
Ace Books are published by The Berkley Publishing Group,
a division of Penguin Group (USA) Inc.,
375 Hudson Street, New York, New York 10014.
ACE and the "A" design are trademarks belonging to Penguin Group (USA) Inc.

PRINTED IN THE UNITED STATES OF AMERICA

10 9 8 7 6 5 4 3 2 1

PART I

Chapter One

❧

In the last slanting rays of sunlight, King Faldain of Nether drew rein atop a low rise and gazed northward, watching the two distant specks that were his trackers casting back and forth in ever-widening swaths. At his back stood an army of two thousand men—knights, Agya warriors, and archers trained in the new style of Mandrian longbow—reinforcements urgently requested by General Borenskya weeks ago. Ahead stretched this strange, empty land, reaching toward a distant horizon smudged with twilight.

No maps charted these open plains beyond the northernmost boundaries of Dain's realm. The closest hold lay a hard five days' march behind them. There were no roads to follow, no caravan trails. No settlements or villages to aim for. Only rolling, featureless plains unfolding in all directions, rendering two thousand men as insignificant as a speck of chaff in a field.

And where in all this, Dain wondered, squinting against the cold wind, *am I to find Borenskya?*

The trackers were out of sight now, for although the treeless plains looked open, the land folded into gullies, ridges, and shallow valleys, offering a plentitude of hiding places. Dain's men stayed alert, watching in case of ambush.

"It's nearly dusk, sire," Sir Chesil Matkevskiet said quietly beside him. Devoted and utterly loyal, the chief aide had served Dain a long time. Clad in the crimson and blue favored by most Agyas, Chesil wore his cloak fastened tightly to his throat and his numerous, shoulder-length braids tied back in a thick club. His swarthy face was pinched with cold, and white breath streamed from his nostrils and mouth. "Shall I give orders to make camp?"

Still gazing across the vista, Dain did not immediately answer. The idea of enduring another long night in bedrolls on the stony ground did not appeal. He was worn by the hard pace he'd set, as were the men. According to their sketchy information, they should have reached Borenskya's position two days ago. Instead, there they were, still searching, while the trail grew ever colder and harder to follow.

"Sire?"

"Wait," Dain murmured and held up his hand for quiet. A faint tracery of sound teased the very limits of his hearing. It was too distant for recognition, and yet something about it made him frown.

A gust of wind cut through his fur-lined cloak and made his horse swing around and stamp. His efforts to curb the animal distracted Dain, and he found himself unable to catch the sound again. Frustrated and unsettled by the lack of trees and forest, he wondered if the wind was playing tricks with his hearing.

How he loathed this country, finding it a miserable place. Very little game other than rodents made hunting futile. He smelled no water, no running streams nearby. The very scent of the hard, thin soil was of minerals, not fertile life. This ground would grow no crops. It barely supported the sparse tufts of weeds and scrub, and there was no indication of recent rainfall to soften it. As darkness gathered, the cold increased, rendered harsher by the dry winds that sprang up at midday and blew ferociously until dawn.

Nights were eerie and unwholesome. The rising moon was a useless sliver, and the stars sparkled large and unfamiliar in a sky too vast to comprehend.

An army could lose its way out here, Dain thought uneasily, *and perish while wandering, never to be found.* If they could not forage or hunt, how much longer would their rations hold out? And if Borenskya had left them no mark to follow, how could they ever hope to find him?

Another gust of wind buffeted him, and Lord Omas's horse bumped into Dain's mount.

Omas reined it back. "Your pardon, sire," he rumbled, his voice muffled beneath the hood of his cloak.

The animals were trying to turn their rumps to the wind, and Dain felt tempted to let them drift southward, abandoning the quest. Only he never would. In the thirteen years since the Grethori had murdered his son and he'd declared perpetual, blood-soaked war on them in revenge, the brutal atrocities had only escalated. But Grethori savagery against the Netherans had kept the cause hotter than any persuasion Dain could have used, and the entire kingdom was united in driving the tribes out forever. Years of merciless persecution and dispersion had accomplished the breaking of all the tribes save one, the one Dain most wanted, the one Borenskya had promised to corner that spring and defeat.

Now, Dain wondered if the general had perished instead. Instead of voicing such doubts, however, he said, "The wind's colder tonight."

"Aye," Omas agreed hoarsely. "There's a bank of clouds coming up from the west. We'll lose the light quicker this eve. Do we ride on or make camp in yon gullies?"

The sound of galloping hoofbeats distracted Dain from answering. Moments later a horse and rider topped the rise and reined up as close to Dain as his Agya guards would permit. Through the fogging dust, the rider saluted and dismounted.

"One of the trackers," Chesil said eagerly.

The man was allowed to approach Dain's stirrup. "We've found them, sire!" he said.

Grins broke out all around. Swept with relief, Dain leaned forward in his saddle. "Borenskya's army?"

"Aye." The tracker pointed northeast. "We found a scout on patrol. He says they're camped less than a league in yon direction and will be sore glad to see us."

Dain's youthful aides laughed and began to chatter excit-
edly but Chesil swiftly quelled them. Still, already the word
was being passed back into the ranks.

"Have they had much trouble?" Dain asked the tracker.

"Aye, I think so. Been mauled pretty bad, with heavy
losses. The man wanted to know if we've brought food."

Dain and Omas exchanged troubled looks.

"And the Grethori they were following?" Dain asked.

The tracker shook his head. "Not far off. We could hear
their drums now and then."

Dain nodded to himself. "Aye. I think I heard them, too."

"War drums mean they are not ready to run away," Chesil
said quietly. "They will be planning to attack Borenskya's
camp soon, *neya*?"

Dain set his jaw. "Then we'd better be there to give them
a surprise. Chesil, pass the word. No trumpets or fanfare.
We'll go in quietly."

Saluting, Chesil wheeled his horse away, passing instructions to the most junior aides. Two of them were Omas's twin
sons, as identical as podded peas. Nearly as tall as their father, but not as broad, they had grown up into fine young
men, possessing merry, mischievous faces and their father's
twinkling brown eyes. The only way to tell them apart was
that Trin sported a narrow brown mustache while Fordra
went clean-shaven.

As they galloped away, Dain beckoned to Lutmalyin.
"Fetch Vaunit. If he will not come, send a priest to me."

"Sire!" Lutmalyin hurried to obey.

Omas's dark brown eyes met Dain's. "It could be a trap
awaiting us."

"Aye, but we'll give them more than they counted on."

"If they're close enough for us to hear their war drums,
they'll have spies watching everywhere." Omas shifted his
large bulk in the saddle. "Could be they've already seen us."

"Perhaps. Unless Vaunit makes our arrival invisible to
them."

A wide grin spread across Omas's face, and his eyes
began to twinkle in the fading light. "Now that would be a
fine trick to serve."

Dain nodded. "I've seen a bellyful of burned-out villages

and dead peasants on this journey. I've no mind to find a massacred army at its end. Come on!"

It was well after dark, the tired horses held to a cautious walk as the men followed the faintest intermittent glimmer of soft green light cast from the fingertips of Vaunit and two other battle *sorcerels*. Obedient to orders, no sound did the men make among themselves, and under Vaunit's masking spell even the thud of hooves, the creaking of saddle leather, and the soft jingling of bridle bits and spurs seemed muffled.

The wind gusted against them, so cold Dain felt sure it must be blowing off snow somewhere. *Did thaw never come to this land?* he wondered.

His body was so tired and numb he could no longer feel his fingers inside their gloves. He rode with his face buried in the folds of his cloak, its hood pulled up over his helmet, and fought to stay alert. Unlike civilized people, the Grethori had been known to attack in the dark.

Yet they did not. Between gusts of wind, Dain could hear the drums plainly now. *Too close for comfort,* he thought.

His horse stumbled, jolting Dain in the saddle. He pulled hard on the reins to bring up his mount's head, and there, straight ahead, shone orange torchlight. The camp stretched before him in orderly rows, the tents moth-pale and tenuous, their canvas a frail barrier against the clawing wind. He found it a most welcoming sight.

Shortly thereafter, the sentries were throwing open the makeshift gates and saluting while Dain, his entourage, the pennon bearers, and men entered the camp.

A command rang out, and a hastily assembled ragtag of knights and foot soldiers—some of the latter still clutching their supper bowls—pulled themselves to attention. A short man, wrapped to the eyes in a hooded cloak worn over his hauberk, came limping up through the gathering crowd.

"Your majesty." He pushed back his hood to reveal a worn, pale face in the torchlight. His hair, cropped short, was disheveled, and the wind ruffled it yet more as he dropped to one knee and pressed his fist to his opposite shoulder in salute. "I am Commander Kostrinki. Thod be thanked that you have reached us here. 'Tis almost a miracle I can scarcely believe."

The raw emotion in the man's voice made Dain glance at the assembly in rapid assessment. The men looked dirty and cold, their hauberks in poor repair and their eyes hollow. Although they were cheering and saluting in warm welcome, the desperation behind their smiles pricked Dain's senses. The men had been frightened, he realized, and were frightened still.

"Welcome, your majesty," Kostrinki was saying over the noise. "I am to convey the compliments of General Borenskya and offer you the hospitality of his tent."

"My thanks to the general." Dain wondered why Borenskya hadn't appeared. "My men and their horses must be seen to immediately. We've traveled long and hard, and had no easy task of finding you."

Kostrinki looked troubled. "Please, if your majesty's knights will follow this man," he said, gesturing to an individual in a torn cloak, "he will show them where to pitch their tents. Has your majesty brought food and supplies?"

Ignoring the question, Dain beckoned his commanders forward.

Adyul, a seasoned veteran in charge of the Agya forces, looked as wiry and slender as a boy, although his braided hair showed gray beneath his fur cap. Equally experienced, Commander Tolumin was a gruff, heavily scarred man of few words and tremendous efficiency. Both officers worked well together, could handle their men, and needed scant direction in getting things done.

Tolumin eyed the guide Kostrinki had pointed out, saluted Dain, and wheeled his horse around to face the knights. "Knights and archers, fall out!" he bellowed.

Adyul turned to Dain and said, "We'll see the men quartered and the horses foraged without delay, your majesty."

With a nod, Dain dismounted, obliging his command staff to do the same. Omas stood close, wary and alert. Handing over his reins to a groom, Dain resisted the temptation to stretch his aching joints.

"Where is General Borenskya?" Dain asked Kostrinki impatiently. "And why does he not attend me?"

"He lies wounded." Kostrinki's gaze darted nervously about. "He is with our camp physician at the moment, having the wound re-dressed, but soon he will attend your majesty to express his greetings. That is why I thought perhaps your majesty would prefer to get settled, with wine and a good fire, rather than remain chilled outdoors. Please, if your majesty will consent to follow me, I will—"

"If the general is wounded, still even less reason for me to displace him in his own quarters," Dain said. "My people will see to my shelter while I speak to Borenskya."

Kostrinki's expression looked defeated, but he bowed in silence.

Dain glanced at his aides. "Chesil, you and Lutmalyin will accompany me. Lord Ivar?"

His night protector came forward, a tall, rawboned man with a jaw and brow like granite. "I'm ready to go on duty, sire."

"Good." Dain glanced at Omas. "Thank you, Lord Omas. You are relieved."

Omas did not look happy, but he stepped back, permitting Ivar to take his place.

"Where is Rof?" Dain asked.

His adjutant emerged from the mill of people. "Sire?"

"Find a courier and brief him. Give him the dispatches already prepared."

"Yes, sire," Rof Krelinik said. "Do you want the man to wait until after you've spoken with General Borenskya?"

"Yes. I may have additional letters to send to Nabov Hold and onward to Grov. But I'll decide when I return."

Rof Krelinik was a younger brother to Archduke Vladno Krelinik, a powerful member of Dain's court. Only nineteen, Rof had served as adjutant for only a few months, but already he'd proven himself adept at his post, both competent and dependable, possessing far more of a courtier's polish than the rest of Dain's young staff.

Now he inclined his dark head. "I'll see that the courier is ready when your majesty wants him."

Satisfied that his people had plenty to do, Dain turned back to Kostrinki. "Commander, please take me to the general. 'Tis time Borenskya and I had a council."

"Would it not be better if the lord general came to your majesty?"

"Perhaps, but we are not at leisure here." Dain gestured. "If you please."

As a reluctant Kostrinki limped forward, the onlookers parted to let them all pass. Lord Ivar stayed close to Dain's left side, and some of the Agya guards brought up the rear. Dain could hear Borenskya's veterans murmuring as he strode past them. Obviously they had not expected the king to walk anywhere.

Dain thought he would find the trek across camp to be informative. And it was. Although from its outer sections the camp had looked to be very large, the inward sections showed long gaps where no tents were pitched at all. Boys in livery were running about, keeping the wind-guttered torches lit along the intersecting roadways. Too many of the men huddling around campfires were too quiet. In Dain's opinion, they should have been talking and gambling, joking together. The smell of lentil pottage without meat came to Dain's nostrils, and if that was all they had, he no longer regretted not getting to share camp food.

When he reached the center, he saw a long tent lit within with lamps. Shadows silhouetted against the canvas moved back and forth. The stench alone told Dain that it was the camp infirmary, filled with wounded. He turned in that direction, but Kostrinki blocked his path.

"No, your majesty," the commander said quietly. "The lord general is not there."

Dain studied the man, shivering under his cloak, so wrapped in despair and exhaustion he was almost swaying on his feet. "Kostrinki," Dain said in a low, firm voice, "don't you think it's time you stopped lying to me and spoke the truth?"

Chapter Two

❧

The commander froze with his head bowed before he slowly lifted it and looked at Dain like a kicked dog.

"Is Borenskya dead?" Dain asked. "I command your answer."

"Not here, sire. Not where we can be overheard."

Beside Dain, Chesil drew in an audible breath, and Lord Ivar moved his hand to his sword hilt. But Dain calmly followed the limping commander to a large, square tent, where the general's pennon streamed in the wind. Armed men stood on guard at the entrance.

At a quiet word from Kostrinki, they saluted and stood aside. Within, Dain found the two-room tent pleasantly warmed by blazing cressets. He saw a campaign table and a couple of chairs. A map case of tooled leather lay atop the table, and a servant was busily setting a tray of food beside it.

Frowning, Dain strode to the door flap at the rear of the room.

"No!" the servant cried out, and rushed over to stop him. "The lord general is resting and not to be disturbed."

Lord Ivar slung the lackey out of Dain's way, and Dain stepped into the second room. It was very small, clearly intended only to serve as the general's sleeping quarters. Outside, the wind gusted and clawed at the sides of the tent, sending icy drafts through the confined space.

A single candle flickered, its yellow flame feeble against the shadows. The general lay on his bunk, ashen and very still. Dain remembered Borenskya as moody, temperamental, and a brilliant military leader. Now the man's keen eyes were shut and sunk deep into his skull. The wounded general's mouth hung slightly open, and bright pink blood frothed on his lips with every struggling breath. Dain knew that wet, sucking wheeze of air indicated a mortal wound.

An impassive physician huddled in a long, fur-trimmed robe at the bedside.

Dain gently clasped one of the general's hands. Borenskya's flesh felt cold and clammy, with little life force remaining. A bitter longing—one he had not felt in a long time—surged through Dain. Most of the eld folk were healers or had the ability to cure in some degree. Dain had nothing. At the moment, he would have given much to be able to do something to help this valiant man.

Borenskya's eyes dragged open and focused themselves hazily on Dain's face. His mouth opened wider, and he gasped as though trying to speak.

"Quiet, lord general," Dain said gently. "Your eyes do not deceive you. I have come, bringing the men you asked for."

Borenskya seemed to understand. "Lost . . . battle," he whispered, and turned his head to cough up blood.

Dain waited while the physician wiped the general's mouth, then he said, "No, the battle is not lost. Your men are safe. They are eager to fight the Grethori again."

Borenskya tried to smile, but a spasm of pain contorted his face. His hand clutched Dain's hard as he coughed and wheezed.

"He is suffering," Dain said to the physician. "Give him something for the pain."

The physician stood at Borenskya's head and met Dain's gaze with a helpless shake of his head. "We have no more," he whispered so quietly even Dain's keen ears barely heard him. "So many wounded . . . the medicine is gone."

Dain turned to Lutmalyin. "Fetch our physicians at once, with all their supplies."

Gratitude flashed across the physician's face, but Kostrinki seemed overpowered by grief and did not lift his gaze from his general's countenance.

Dain sighed quietly. Borenskya the Butcher might drive his men ruthlessly, risk their lives with scant regard for casualties, and take them beyond the ends of the known world; but he was a general with more victories than losses, one who aroused fierce devotion from those who served under him. The men were subdued and worried because obviously they sensed something wrong despite Kostrinki's assurances.

Such loyalty as Borenskya commanded had made him a great leader. It would also create a terrible problem when he died. The men, Dain realized, might well be terrified of fighting without him.

Dain began to sing a quiet little song of ease and comfort. He sang of warmth and quiet and serenity. He sang of soft-flowing streams and the gentle rustle of trees. He sang of home and family, of strong walls and secure roofs. He sang of fields heavy with harvest, and of a brave man returning home in triumph, to be honored and paraded through the streets of Grov. He sang of glory and success, and saw Borenskya's drawn face relax into a little smile.

And when the general slept again, Dain gently released his hand and backed away, feeling compassion for the dying man, who would never experience his triumphal parade except in the little fantasy Dain had woven for him.

Wearily Dain returned to the other room with Kostrinki, who was shaking.

"Thod forgive me for lying to your majesty," he burst out. "For the men's sake, I had to. They mustn't know! We lost half our force to Grethori ambush. They were on us before we knew it, and when Borenskya fell the men panicked. We were nearly lost. I got them this far, but the Grethori have followed us, gathering to attack again. Our scouts say we're three times outnumbered, and those savage devils mean to finish us, probably come the dawn."

"How know you when they'll attack? By the drums?" Dain asked.

Kostrinki nodded and passed a hand unsteadily across his brow. "Forgive me," he said, trying to regain his composure. "We thought we had them this time. We chased them into this wasteland, intending to cut them off and finish them, but it was a trap. We—we didn't know all the Wind Tribe clans would be here. We didn't know there were still so many of them. We thought . . . we . . ."

His voice trailed off, and he sank to the ground in a heap before Chesil could catch him.

Dain pointed at a chair, and Chesil lifted the commander into it, steadying him as Kostrinki blinked dazedly and tried to come to.

"Physician!" Dain called.

The man emerged, blinking against the stronger light in this room, and hurried over to Kostrinki. He held a small vial with an evil stench beneath the commander's nostrils, and Kostrinki coughed, choked, and revived.

Chesil was busy untying the strings of the commander's cloak and pushing it back off his shoulders. A bloodstained bandage showed at the throat of his hauberk, revealing that he'd sustained more wounds than just an injury to his leg.

Dain frowned, worried by the crumbling chain of command here.

"*Aychi,*" Chesil said softly, shaking his head as he came over to stand close to Dain. "This is bad, sire. Very bad. Borenskya had three thousand men when he set out from Grov a month ago. If he's lost half—"

"Possibly more," Dain said thoughtfully.

"If there are as many Grethori as this little one claims, then all the men we've brought do not even the numbers."

"We have elite fighters, archers, and the very best of my cavalry," Dain said. "Not common foot soldiers. I know the way Borenskya liked to fight. Methodically, according to rigid plan, sustaining heavy casualties. But there are other ways to meet the Grethori. The Agyas alone are two to one better than any savage."

"Your majesty speaks truth there," Chesil agreed, with a fleeting grin. "But still—"

"I know," Dain said grimly. He did not like it either. "There's more to this than we've yet learned. Kostrinki!"

The commander lifted his wobbling head and tried to focus.

"Please, your majesty," the physician said in protest. "He needs to rest. He's been trying to do too much, despite my urging him to—"

"Kostrinki!" Dain said harshly, ignoring the physician. He did not wish to be unkind, but he had to have answers. "Commander, pull your wits together and talk to me!"

"S-sire?"

"What are the men afraid of?" Dain asked, bending down so that Kostrinki could see him better. "I know they're afraid. Valiant, well-trained Netheran knights should fear nothing. What haven't you told me?"

Kostrinki's face contorted, but he managed to straighten and even meet Dain's eyes. "D-deliverer," he gasped out. "All the clans . . . whole tribe in uprising . . . like the old days."

"I remember," Dain said grimly. "What else? What about the Deliverer?"

"Here," Kostrinki said.

"Rubbish," Ivar burst out as though he couldn't stop himself. He caught Dain's eye on him and turned bright red.

"He's here," Kostrinki insisted. "To lead them. Spies c-confirmed it today. Spell-fires on the ridges. The drums never stop. Last night we could hear them yelling, working up some kind of magic. They've gathered all their *shedas*, too. When we fought them, it was different than anything I've ever experienced. Like wading through mud, moving too slow, thinking too slow, missing the planned maneuvers. I never believed in their foolery—all those rituals and magic paint and chants—but there must be something to this Deliverer. We couldn't beat them. We barely managed to retreat in disorder, and now we're trapped here."

"Nonsense," Dain said crisply. "I've just brought two thousand reinforcements—"

"Forgive me, your majesty, but with their Deliverer leading them, they're six times as fierce as I've ever found them." Kostrinki colored up, and his gaze dropped. "I know I sound like a craven coward. I—I've never questioned my valor before. But we are trapped. They have us cut off."

"We got through," Dain snapped.

"They let you." Kostrinki's eyes were dark holes, his face pale and sweaty. "We were the bait that lured you in. I'm sorry. There was no way to warn you."

Dain drew back from him with a frown. "What are you saying? You knew this was going to happen? Borenskya knew? How long ago?"

"The general suspected something days ago, after we left Nabov behind. It's been a game of cat and mouse in these damned ridges and gullies. To our north is a very small valley. Beyond it is a sort of ice wall."

"A glacier?" Dain asked.

Kostrinki nodded. "I advised the general to turn back one day past the border, but he wanted to get them so bad. He wouldn't listen. He kept pushing them, and they kept retreating. It wasn't until they turned that we realized what they'd really been up to."

Dain clasped his hands at his back and began to pace back and forth, letting Kostrinki ramble.

"We're cut off to the south," Kostrinki said. "Your majesty got through from that direction, but only because they let you. To the east are gullies—"

"We saw them."

"They're a maze of dead ends, impassable. To the west, we're cut off by more Grethori. I think that's where their big camp lies. The only direction we can go is north, into that valley, and it's another dead end because of the ice wall. We're trapped. I'm sorry, your majesty. It was bad enough when we were hoping for reinforcements, certain they'd be trapped with us or ambushed. I never dreamed that you would come yourself. Damne, but it's—"

"Steady yourself, Kostrinki, for the sake of Thod," Dain said with a frown. "You've got to pull yourself together and take charge of your men."

The commander nodded. "Yes, your majesty. Forgive me." He rose shakily to his feet. "I am ready to serve your orders."

Dain pointed at the tray of food. "Is that for you? Eat

some of it and regain your strength. I'll need a list of the names of your surviving, able-bodied officers, and some idea of what forces you have."

"Yes, majesty."

"How certain are you that they mean to attack at dawn?"

"Pretty certain. The signs are there, and they tend to stick with their rituals."

Lutmalyin returned with a physician in tow. Carrying a soft leather pouch, the man vanished into the general's bed-chamber.

"We've work to do," Dain said. "Lutmalyin!"

The aide stepped forward. "Sire?"

"Send word to Adyul and Tolumin that I shall want a war council with them immediately. We've strategy to plan. And then I want to talk to Vaunit."

Lutmalyin hurried out.

"You'll join us, Kostrinki," Dain said, and the com-mander's nondescript face lit up a little.

"I'm honored, your majesty."

"Don't be a fool," Dain said gruffly. "We're all in this to-gether. You'll be leading part of the attack—"

Kostrinki looked startled. "Sire?"

"If you're up to it."

Determination filled the man's face. He nodded.

Smiling, Dain touched him lightly on the shoulder. "Good man. You have your orders. I'll see you anon."

"Thank you, sire. But the Deliverer?"

As Chesil lifted the tent flap, Dain glanced over his shoul-der. "That rumor, or legend, or myth—whatever it is—stops here and now. There's no such person, nor will there be."

"But—"

"Have you seen him?" Dain demanded.

Kostrinki shook his head, looking confused. "No."

"Nor will you. The *shedas* have been working on your mind."

"But the spies are so sure."

"The spies are paid informers and will always work one advantage against another if there's coin to reward them," Dain said dismissively. He drew himself to his full, impres-sive height, looming over the smaller man, and smiled at

Kostrinki with all the charm and reassurance he possessed. "Is not your king more than a match for these blood-drinking barbarians?"

Light kindled in Kostrinki's eyes. He straightened his shoulders and lifted his chin. "Aye, sire!"

"I have fought this Wind Tribe before," Dain said with confidence. "They are full of more trickery than any other kind of Grethori, but I am sworn against them, and I am to be reckoned with. Go and tell that to your men, Kostrinki, and let us set about what I intend to *deliver* to these savages."

He left the little commander saluting, bright-eyed and filled with hope. But outside, where the brutal wind and cold nearly took his breath, Dain knew it would take more than a few bold words to rebuild the army's broken morale. And he prayed to Thod for the strength of leadership required.

Chapter Three

Dain's tent, set up and supplied, was not yet warmed by the fires newly kindled in the braziers, but Dain threw off his cloak, mail coif, and gloves, allowing his squire to unbuckle his heavy breastplate. He wished he could sit down and kick off his boots as well. But there was no time to take his ease.

He ate standing, listening to reports from nervous sergeants and shifty-eyed scouts, and studying the marks Chesil was mapping out on a large piece of vellum. His officers arrived, looking grim, but digging into the problem without hesitation. Kostrinki came later, still haggard but calm and coherent as he explained the situation in greater depth.

Then Dain began to outline his plan. The commanders contributed their ideas, and a strategy was finally agreed on. It was rough, but Dain thought it would do.

"Certainly this will give the Grethori a few surprises," he said with a grin.

His officers chuckled, going out to pass along the necessary orders. Suppressing a yawn, Dain called for his cloak and gloves.

Chesil frowned at him. "Let me or the commanders do inspection for you, sire. You're weary."

"Thank you," Dain said coolly, drawing on his gloves, "but I think the men need to see me tonight." He glanced at Rof. "Pen a very brief report of our situation to the commander of Nabov. I'll look it over and sign it when I return."

Rof bowed. "As your majesty commands."

"In the circumstances, the courier had better wait with my dispatches until daylight. I don't want him riding into a trap he can't see."

"Yes, your majesty."

Bracing himself, Dain ducked out into the cold. A fresh horse had been saddled for him, and he climbed up, settling himself against the icy cold leather with a wince. With Chesil and Lord Ivar mounted, Dain kicked his horse into a slow amble through the camp, going up and down the long rows of tents, watching those of his army who wanted it taking salt and wafer from a priest, seeing the mead boys ladling out the warming drink from wooden kegs, listening to the men grumble at having to stop their gambling and turn in, smiling at those who scrambled to salute, pausing here and there to talk to an archer carefully checking his arrows and fitting them into a quiver one by one, or to a squireless knight whistling while he polished spurs and helmet.

With his men settled, Dain turned his horse and rode through the rest of the camp, talking to the listless men until they looked heartened.

The torch boys reappeared, dousing most of the lights that had been burning all evening. Out in the darkness, sentries rotated off duty, exchanging their gruff passwords. A priest in pale robes hurried by, a shadow that did not stop. The lamps went out abruptly inside Borenskya's tent. Sensing that the general was dead, Dain bowed his head in prayer for the man's soul. Best to tell the general's men tomorrow, Dain decided, when the battle was finished.

With the camp bedded down uneasily, he returned to his quarters. Vaunit still had not responded to his summons. Dain shrugged it off, knowing that at the best of times *sorcerels* did as they pleased and could not be commanded. Outside, the wind gusted and moaned, sobbing like a thing demented. And in the distance, the war drums began to throb anew.

The sound sent a shiver up Dain's spine. Frowning, he tried to ignore them. Stripping off his boots and hauberk with a sigh of relief, he entered his tiny prayer closet. Although Lord Ivar stood on duty outside, it was the first time all day that Dain had truly been alone, and he found the privacy welcome.

Element candles burned atop the small altar, flickering as the wind buffeted the tent in a ferocious gust and set the icons to swaying on the paneatha. Dain knelt alone in worship, his heart and body weary, and shed his mantle of kingly confidence for the worry that filled his heart.

He prayed for strength for himself and his men. He prayed for victory. But most of all, he prayed for an end to this war of revenge.

Rising, he pulled back his sleeve and exposed a narrow bracelet of eldin silver coiled around his wrist.

It had been fashioned from his son Ilymir's circlet of royalty—not the one stolen so long ago by Choluk, the barbaric chieftain who had slain the boy, but another circlet kept in the nursery for ceremonial occasions.

Dain thought of Ilymir, who would be seventeen had he lived. He would be a tall, straight, pale-eyed boy on the edge of manhood. A boy in training to take the throne after Dain.

Instead Ilymir was only a tiny collection of bones entombed in Grov, and in whose name so many had died. For Ilymir would these sleeping soldiers fight on the morrow.

"Blood for blood," Dain whispered. It was the age-old cry for vengeance, but his eldin side knew it to be but false comfort. There was no bringing back Alexeika's favorite son, the boy whose name still brought wistful melancholy to her lovely eyes. Dain could no longer remember Ilymir's face; memories of the child passed, ghost-thin, through his mind, layered over with images of Niklas winning an archery contest or the merry peal of Syban's laughter.

Dain's living sons were sturdy, fast-growing boys—the future of Nether—and he was proud of them both. It was time, he told himself, to let Ilymir lie in the past while the rest of them went forward. He'd waded through enough Grethori blood for a lifetime.

Had the Grethori vanished forever into uncharted lands, he would have let them go, glad to be rid of them. But they kept coming back, attacking villages and trade caravans, wreaking any destruction they could.

The tribes had to be destroyed, for the sake of his realm. With Gant forever prowling at his eastern border, Dain understood how vital it was to keep the interior of his kingdom as peaceful as possible. Nether was vast and unwieldy, filled with bickering factions and corruption—complications enough for any ruler. He wanted no more Netheran infants abducted in Grethori raids, no more accounts of Grethori brutality and massacres. He wanted the mysterious power of the *shedas* destroyed and forgotten. Above all, he wanted to end all rumors of this Deliverer, an individual who was supposed to come and unite the bickering Grethori tribes into a great force that would smash the kingdom of Nether to pieces.

With all the tribes dispersed save one, there had been talk in the Privy Council and Kollegya of letting them go, of letting them bide there in a land no one wanted or cared about. But of course the Wind Tribe would not stay settled. They constantly stirred up trouble. And the *sheda* of one of the clans of the Wind Tribe was a mortal enemy of Dain's. He could not let her go, nor could he show clemency to her followers. Even if his soul was going to be forever soaked in blood and hatred, never again to be cleansed, he wanted her caught. He wanted her to pay dearly for all that she had done to him and his family.

"Sire?" Ivar said, startling him. The protector stood on the threshold. "Forgive me, sire, for interrupting you. Vaunit has come." Stepping aside, Ivar revealed the *sorcerel* standing behind him.

Hoping to get some answers, Dain met Vaunit's cold yellow eyes ever so briefly, and then flicked his gaze to one side from long-established habit to evade having his thoughts sifted and read. "Thank you for coming, Vaunit," Dain said, while Ivar resumed his position at the doorway, muscular arms crossed over his chest, his deep-set eyes dark and liquid in the lamplight. "I have questions to ask."

The *sorcerel* retreated in silence. Aware that he disliked such close proximity to the prayer closet, Dain was pleased to see evidence that Thod remained supreme over the most potent forces of magic. He joined the *sorcerel* on the opposite side of his sleep chamber, as far away from the altar as Vaunit could retreat.

"I need omens for tomorrow's battle," Dain said softly. This was no conversation for sleepy aides or servants to overhear. "I want information about the Grethori Deliverer."

Although far older than any living man, Vaunit was considered young for a *sorcerel*. He possessed dark, leathery skin, a body elongated from countless years of wielding magic, and gnarled, misshapen hands with nails as dark and thick as talons. Gray tufts of hair grew from the tips of his ears, and his hair and fur robes smelled of ashes and magic. He was the quickest, ablest battle *sorcerel* in Dain's service, aside from the great Samderaudin himself. And if his powers were not quite as strong as Samderaudin's or his knowledge as deep, still he was often easier to talk to, inclined to fewer riddles and mysteries, and patient with the mortals around him.

Vaunit stared at Dain for a long moment, hissing quietly through his teeth. "Many questions."

"The omens first," Dain said.

"Faldain hunts Grethori the way a ratter hunts vermin. What portent is needed for that?"

"I hoped for something to hearten the men. They fear this so-called Deliverer."

"With cause perhaps."

"Explain."

Vaunit said nothing.

Dain drew a deep breath and tried again. "Is he myth or real?"

"Faldain believes him to be myth," Vaunit said slyly.

"Yes, but if I am mistaken, I need to know it. Do I fight a real man on the morrow or a legend?"

Vaunit spread apart his hands, and tiny spheres of golden light, like miniature glowstones, appeared. They floated and bobbed between his fingers and around his hands, shimmering bright or falling dim in irregular patterns of radiance. Their light glowed upon Vaunit's dark face and made his heavy-lidded eyes glitter.

"Myth and legend are real," he said. "He is as an eagle. He circles and hunts, awaiting his time to strike."

Startled, Dain blinked. Outside, the wind dropped for a moment, and he heard the Grethori war drums. They stirred his blood in a primitive way that made him uneasy and cold.

"You're certain," he whispered.

"Certain."

"Then they'll fight like fiends possessed. We must be prepared for that. Can you part the veils of seeing and show me this man?"

"The *shedas* have joined to make strong battle magic." Vaunit wiggled his fingers and set the tiny light globes spinning before gathering them in his palm. He held them out for Dain to see. "Five clans. Five chieftains. Five *shedas* drawing on the power of *Adauri*. Their magic is woven together well. Where does one power end and another begin?"

"Are they shielding him?"

"Which among them is the Deliverer you seek? They are calling on his power to make themselves stronger. Hear them."

As he spoke, he curled his fingers over the small globes. And Dain found himself listening to faint shouts and the harsh babble of the Grethori tongue emanating from the little spheres in Vaunit's hand. Although Dain had learned the rudiments of Grethori dialect, he could not understand what was being chanted, except that words of power were being uttered. Primitive, raw, elemental power . . . old and very dark.

His heart felt squeezed, unable to beat as it should. He remembered a time of imprisonment inside a Grethori tent, and the fiery tendrils of foul *sheda* magic working on his body.

With a muttered oath, he flinched back from Vaunit and turned away. His temples were throbbing, and his breath came short and fast. For a moment he rubbed his forehead, feeling the old scar beneath his hair.

Ivar approached him in concern, but Dain waved the protector back and faced Vaunit again. "Can you break through
their shielding and find this Deliverer? Will you show him to
me?"

Vaunit held out the globes once more, but Dain averted
his gaze sharply.

"I know the past," he said with more harshness than he
intended. "'Tis the present, the future I want to understand."

Vaunit slowly lowered his hand, and the globes vanished.
"The *shedas* conceal him well. If Faldain wishes to find the
Deliverer, he must look where he most fears."

"I know what lies beneath this battle, this war," Dain said
through gritted teeth. "Hatred and the desire for vengeance
burn long and deep in this matter. Is it one of the chieftains
selected now to be given power by the *shedas*?"

"Vaunit has answered."

"But if he—"

"When prophecy is true, what is foretold will come."
Vaunit's yellow eyes narrowed. "Unless Faldain tricks destiny."

"How?"

"By leaving now. This night."

Dain felt as though he'd just been buried under rock.
"Leave?" he choked out. "You mean, run away from this battle?"

"It is Faldain's choice."

"Are we that overmatched? Can there still remain that
many Grethori warriors?"

"Faldain has already considered leaving the Grethori
here. As I brought your men into this camp, so can I take
them forth, in the darkness." Vaunit watched Dain intently.
"It is Faldain's choice."

Hot refusal burned Dain's tongue, but he checked an outburst and began to pace back and forth. He needed to think,
for he sensed there was more to this than Vaunit had yet told
him. "Why should I flee?" he asked. "Why take a coward's
leave, slipping away under cover of darkness and magic?
Why, Vaunit?"

"Faldain has a great destiny," Vaunit replied. "The same
is foretold of the Deliverer. These destinies lie in opposition.

If these men meet, only tragedy can come. If they do not meet, tragedy is averted."

"It can't be that simple!"

"Nothing is simple. Nothing is as it appears."

"Why didn't you warn me before I set out?" Dain asked.

"I did not sense the Deliverer then," Vaunit admitted. "Much magic surrounds him, and only this close do I feel his force. It is strange, nothing I understand. His magic is very old."

"Morde!" Dain said in frustration. "Who is he? He can't have sprung from nothing!"

"The *sheda* who is sworn as Faldain's enemy intends great harm against Nether's king."

"No greater harm than I intend her," Dain muttered. "That's hardly prophecy, Vaunit."

"Her reach is long, Faldain. Be warned."

Dain shook his head. "You know what I want to do to her. We've discussed it before, and you agreed to help."

"I will follow Faldain's choice. But heed this: If Faldain lets the Grethori go, the Deliverer will fade. Such magic as his is old magic, reactive magic."

"Explain."

"It feeds on another source."

Dain frowned in bewilderment. "The *sheda's*?"

"The *sheda* is near her ending and summoning the last of her powers against Faldain. Given no opportunity to use them, she will fade."

"But will the war end?" Dain asked. "Will the Grethori stop raiding my people?"

"Grethori do what Grethori do."

Frustrated and confused, Dain walked over to one of the braziers and stared blindly into the flames. After all this time, after all the lives lost and the battles fought, how could he turn back on the eve of this fight and just give up? The Wind Tribe—in its entirety—was gathered within his reach. All he had to do was smash it, and the problem would be over. He had planned this, hoped for this, and anticipated this, for years. Why should he seek safety? Never had he avoided risks. Never had he taken the easy route.

"If we go, if we let them escape us," he said slowly, still

staring at the fire, "then my vows are dishonored, my son's memory is dishonored."

"Faldain has many sons. Which matters more? The living or the dead?"

Dain looked up sharply and found Vaunit's yellow eyes watching him. "Will I fight the Deliverer tomorrow? Are you saying one of us will die?"

Vaunit looked away.

"Answer me," Dain said.

"It has been many years since the king bade me cast the stars for his future."

"I remember. You warned me of death, then."

"More than death."

Dain nodded. "You said I would see the third world."

"And Faldain did."

"Briefly, but I survived."

"That price is not yet fully paid."

Dain's brows snapped together. Aye, he thought, thinking of his daughter Tashalya with a familiar stab of regret. Some things could not be undone.

"If your magic is strong enough to break a *sheda* of her power," Dain said at last, "then it's strong enough to break the shielding that hides the Deliverer. I want to see him. Show him to me, and let me decide after that."

Vaunit's answer never came, for at that moment a bugle blared through the night, sounding a call to arms.

Dain whirled around, his heart thumping fast, already heading for his weapons and armor.

Chesil, bare-chested, his face creased with sleep, burst inside, holding his hauberk in one hand and a sword in the other. "Sire! To arms! We're under attack!"

Drawing Mirengard, Dain felt the sword hum to life within his hand.

Vaunit glided forward. "Faldain, it is not too late to leave. I can make that possible."

Assisted by his squire, Dain was swiftly pulling on tunic and hauberk. *Thod damn the Grethori for attacking in the dark,* he thought. Although he'd expected them to try something of the sort, he'd believed it would be closer to dawn.

More bugles were sounding outside. He heard the running tramp of booted feet and shouting. Dain picked up his sword belt.

"Faldain!" Vaunit said urgently.

Startled by the *sorcerel's* tone, Dain glanced back but his decision was already made.

"No," he said. "There is no running away. Mine is the path of the sword, and I cannot change. Go and do your part in this battle, as I must do mine."

Chapter Four

Naked to the waist, daubed with paint, and screaming at the top of his lungs, Anoc ran through the smoke and confusion of the battlefield. The war drum he was supposed to be beating had been torn from him and smashed, and so he plunged through the melee of fighting warriors and knights, clubbing anyone who attacked him with his carved beater stick.

He was searching for a sword, any real weapon he could snatch from the hands of a dead man. He'd forgotten that it was forbidden for him to be on the actual battlefield. Barely twelve seasons old, small and scrawny, he had not yet been proclaimed warrior age, had not yet passed the rituals. No matter how many growth spells he attempted to work on himself, his efforts to hasten manhood remained futile. Nevertheless, he knew he was destined to be a warrior. He was, after all, the Deliverer as born and proclaimed. The song of war throbbed in his bones and ran so hot in his blood he could not obey orders. Instead of fleeing to the caves as he'd been told, he screamed the war cries of his elders and ran toward danger.

The too-close whistle of a sword sent him somersaulting

out of reach. Regaining his feet, he barely dodged a giant warhorse galloping out of the smoke and fog, sidestepped a knot of bloody, sweat-soaked men hammering at each other with sword and spiked club, and darted down into a shallow gully choked with the dead and dying.

Losing his footing on the dusty shale, he skidded and half fell across a dead man, one clad in Netheran chain mail and already denuded of fingers and ears. Cursing softly, his breath ragged and fast as he kept alert for danger, Anoc searched the man for weapons, but the scavengers had taken even dagger and boot knife.

He scrambled to the next body, and the next, but the scavengers—like wraiths unseen—had already stolen all the weapons, belts, and boots. Stumbling and skidding his way to the bottom of the gully, Anoc paused to run a filthy forearm across his hot face. His breath was steaming from his nostrils in the chilly air, and he was tired and thirsty. His eyes felt swollen and gritty from lack of sleep. Attacking the sleeping pale-eyes camp should have finished the enemy quickly, but the pale-eyes fought hard, and now in the morning fog, when the wind lay quiet and still, they were still fighting.

Frustrated, Anoc gazed across as much of the field as he could see through the fog. The only other place to get a weapon was back in the middle of pitched battle. Perhaps he could pounce just as a man fell, grab a sword, and run before the victim's comrades impaled him.

"Anoc!"

Looking up, he saw Ostur standing above him at the edge of the gully. The older boy's long blond hair hung in tangled hanks down his back. Since this was Ostur's first battle, he possessed no war trophies and instead wore sticks and rat bones braided in his hair. Streaked with grime, his jerkin ripped, he leaned over and gave Anoc a huge grin.

"Hiding?" he taunted.

Angrily Anoc jumped at the dusty side of the gully, trying to scramble up and catch Ostur's feet, but with a laugh the boy stepped out of reach and waved his rusty sword with bravado. "Get back to your drum!" he shouted. "Leave the fighting to men!"

Before Anoc could retort, an arrow thudded deep in

Ostur's back. His mouth sagged open while his eyes grew wide and vacant, then he toppled into the gully, crashing down into the dust beside Anoc.

Shocked, his heart hammering wildly, Anoc cringed back, staring at the dead boy before he regained his wits and grabbed Ostur's weapon.

It was a dull, ill-balanced thing, its blade nicked and badly cracked near the guard, but Anoc did not care. He was ready to fight, and he meant to take first blood from that archer. Gripping the sword hard, he scrambled out of the gully. An arrow whizzed past his head, and he flung himself flat, panting at the near miss.

A man's voice shouted over the din of clashing weapons. Black demon smoke roiled everywhere, making it hard for Anoc to see, but no more arrows came at him. By the time he gained his feet, the smoke thinned, leaving him exposed to the archer, who had continued to advance and now stood less than ten strides away. Laughing, the pale-eyes fitted a fresh arrow to his string and sighted it on Anoc, who froze.

The archer yelled at him, and although the man's words were gibberish, Anoc understood that he was being urged to run. Refusing to play his enemy's game, Anoc stood his ground, hollowly aware that the great destiny foretold by She Who Made Him was about to end. There was a roaring in his ears, and his breath came short and quick.

"May Shartur-god smite you!" He brandished his rusty sword in defiance. "May your enemies drink your blood hot! And when my brothers wear your bones and your scalp flies from the trophy pole of my village, my spirit will laugh and haunt yours, gnawing it for all eternity!"

The man laughed cruelly, oblivious to the curse, and drew his bow.

And still Anoc could not move. His mind screamed at his body, but his feet remained rooted. His heart thumped so hard it hurt his chest.

Out of nowhere there came the thunder of hooves and a furious shout. As though conjured from magic, a horse and rider galloped out of the smoke, bearing straight at the archer as he released that long, thin shaft of death. The rider's sword swung so fast it was a pale blur of steel as it deflected the arrow, popping it high into the air.

And all the while the rider was shouting at the archer in a voice like thunder and storm. Turning fiery red in the face, then pale, the archer dropped to his knees in supplication. Bewildered, Anoc stared up at his rescuer. Mounted on a black charger pawing sparks from the stony ground and snorting with nostrils flaring red, the rider wore armor like no other among the Netherans, with a heavy gold breastplate embossed with lightning bolts. Metal-plated gauntlets protected his arms nearly to the elbow. He carried a long, magnificent sword, with a blade that flashed and gleamed. Danselk antlers grew from the top of the rider's helmet, so that Anoc knew not whether he stared at man or beast, for this apparition's face was concealed. Two eyes as pale as steel stared through the visor slits, eyes that were not Netheran at all, but wolf fierce and strange, eyes of *sight*, eyes that saw deep truth as the *sheda* did, perhaps deeper.

Those strange eyes pierced through Anoc like daggers, pinning him with a force and intensity he'd never encountered before. Anoc felt cold, as though he'd fallen through the ice covering a stream and been trapped there.

Knight or god, Anoc could not tell, and when this apparition spoke his deep voice resonated inside Anoc's head. The boy felt the sudden urge to drop to his knees and bow low to what must surely be Shartur-god himself. Yet he remained unable to move. Scarcely could he breathe. He felt faint and exhilarated, both at once, and his heart was racing so fast he thought it might burst.

Men, pale-eyes all, galloped up to join the god. They bowed and saluted with deep respect—pleasing Anoc to see that they recognized Shartur-god's supremacy, although he'd heard it said that the pale-eyes worshiped other gods, lesser gods. The chastened archer was driven back. The god gestured imperiously at Anoc, and some of the pale-eyes hurried forward as though intending to capture the boy.

Anoc backed away, dodged the men by jumping back into the gully, stumbled, gained his feet, and ran for his life. They shouted at him, but he didn't bother to glance back. Swiftly, he scaled the other side of the gully and jumped into the next

one, followed it for a short time, and climbed out of it to cut
back across the field toward the west hills.

As he ran, taking care to avoid the fighting all he could,
Anoc found himself grinning. *It's true,* he told himself.
Everything She Who Made Him had ever said about his destiny was true. Had not a god—perhaps indeed Shartur-god, to
whom he'd prayed—descended just now to save his life?

A flash of green fire to the west dazzled his eyes and made
him flinch involuntarily. He heard the boom of magic, saw
the flames shoot through the air while men screamed in death
agony. Through the smoke he glimpsed one of the flying
demons and dared not continue that way.

Rescued by a god or not, Anoc knew he could not afford
to be a reckless fool, for such intervention might never happen again. He turned north toward the ice wall.

A rider came looming out of the fog right at him, too close
and unexpected. Anoc tried to jump out of the way, but suddenly everything was happening too fast. The horse's shoulder struck him a glancing blow, knocking him sideways, and
the rider's blade slashed across Anoc's arm instead of cutting
off his head.

Pain engulfed him. He went down hard, screaming, and
was only dimly aware of the horse going over the top of him.

He lay in the mud, writhing, his teeth gritted against the
agony in his arm. Another horse thundered past him, so close
its hooves kicked dirt in his face. It could have smashed his
skull like a melon.

He told himself to get up. Somehow he'd miscalculated
while running and had not reached the Grethori warriors. In
trying to avoid the foot soldiers, huge brutes wielding short
swords and pikes, he'd somehow found himself among
mounted knights, galloping past him. This was far from
where he should be, and there was too much danger. He had
to get away before he was trampled or killed.

Raising his head, he saw red Agya demons suddenly racing right for him, crouching low on their horses' backs and
screaming curses.

Fear and horror gripped his entrails, making them burn,
but there was no time to panic. He had to go.

Clutching his bleeding arm, he rolled to his knees and

tried to regain his feet. Bellowed commands made him spin
around, but the fog had thickened again, disorienting him.
And then the red Agya demons were on him, galloping
around him like water cascading past a stone. He crouched
low, arms and legs tucked tight, one hand over his head, his
eyes slitted against the dust and flying clods of dirt.

The riders ignored him. The horses didn't trample him, although the flying hooves brushed and jostled him in a deafening moment of rush and thunder. A moment later, they had
all vanished into the smoke and mist.

Breathing hard, he managed to stand up and take a few
unsteady steps. A lone rider passed him, looming out of the
fog without warning. Crying out, Anoc tried to dodge out of
the way, but this knight leaned out of the saddle and smote
him with a club.

The pain seemed to break his body in half. Anoc fell heavily and lay stunned and limp. His head was ringing, his shoulder felt numb and separate from the rest of him, and he could
not seem to catch his breath.

Get up! he told himself fiercely, and thrashed about until
he succeeded. Dizzy and weak, sweating with pain, he
looked around but could not see far because of the fog.
Frowning with effort, he turned about and sniffed until his
nostrils picked up the distant frosty scent of the ice wall.

Grimly he started trotting in the direction he hoped was
northwest. He'd dropped Ostur's sword, he realized belatedly, but when he looked back he did not see the weapon. His
arm was throbbing and he lacked the heart to go back and
search for the sword, although he knew his duty to his clan
was to bring home any weapon he found. He would not be
permitted to keep it; only a weapon he killed for would be his
by right. Still, he'd failed even to retrieve the weapon he'd
found. He'd also forgotten to lick Ostur's wound in respectful farewell, and he was ashamed of having been so poor a
friend.

*Perhaps I am not yet big and strong enough to be a war-
rior,* he thought glumly, *for I have done nothing brave
against the enemy at all, except curse the archer. Even a female could have done that.*

The shrill sound of war pipes reassured him. They were

played to please the gods and to strike fear into the hearts of the enemy. But then the pipes stopped abruptly. When they did not resume, Anoc stumbled to a halt and listened hard.

The battle must be over, he thought, believing that last rush of Agya and pale-eyes cavalry must have been running away.

Before he could toss back his head and scream his joy, a roar came rumbling up around him from all sides. It was a sound he did not at first understand, but when it swelled louder, he recognized the cheering of the pale-eyes. *They* were shouting victory.

At first he couldn't believe it. He thought perhaps that last blow had addled his wits and given him bad dreams. The only Netheran screams he wanted to hear were those of fear and defeat.

Besides, the pipes had stopped playing, and they would only do that if no more Grethori warriors were fighting.

Today was to be a great Grethori victory. Exactly as they had won only a few days before, only this time the enemy would not escape them. The officers of the pale-eyes were to be slain, their heads cut off and mounted on poles while the *mamsas* drained the blood from their bodies and mixed potent drinks for the most valiant warriors, who would then join with the chosen females, anointed with Adauri paint, and sprinkled with spells to enhance their fertility. And all the rest would dance and yell in the frenzy, lost in such joy as made the blood pound and the heart thunder.

But Anoc heard no Grethori victory cries. Foreign voices laughed and cheered and shouted and whooped.

How can this be? he wondered. *We outnumbered them. We went into battle with strong spells. All the portents were in our favor. And I was here, as it was foretold.*

Bitterness filled his mouth, and he wanted to scream a curse of silence on them. All the clans of the Wind Tribe had gathered there to fight, to slaughter these pale-eyes and reclaim their mountain territories. It was to have been the beginning of the greatest uprising, destined to mark a new cycle of glory for the true people. So had Chank proclaimed last night from within the circle of *ini* stones, while he and the other clan chieftains incited the warriors to a frenzy of blood-lust.

Big-eyed, swept up in the fever of war, Anoc had listened to the men, wanting desperately to be counted among their number. Only She Who Made Him failed to join in the chants and yelling. Instead, she had sat in the shadows beyond the reach of firelight, her rheumy, half-blind eyes unfocused, her toothless mouth mumbling softly. Anoc wondered now if she had been seeing a vision of failure.

If so, he thought, why hadn't she spoken up? Why hadn't she warned the warriors?

But would the chieftains have listened to her? asked a cynical little voice in the back of Anoc's mind. *They would not listen to Chank, especially with that chieftain of the Roaming Clan calling him an untried boy. And Shulig's father did not help, in trying to push himself forward to lead us instead of Chank. Did they all forget the plan to work together? Were the chieftains fools, each trying to outvie the others in garnering the most trophies?*

Overhead, sunlight chipped through the clouds. Guessing it was midday, he knew that the clouds and fog would soon clear. A light breeze blew away the battle smoke.

He had to get off the field. He ran, half-slipping at times on the trampled, blood-soaked ground. He jumped over the fallen Grethori, ignoring the moans of the wounded, refusing to look at the staring eyes of the dead.

A part of his mind refused to believe the fallen were the warriors who had chanted so valiantly last night among the *ini* stones while they were being painted for victory and the *shedas* cast spells of strength over them. The Wind Tribe was the greatest and most ferocious of all the tribes, with Dryland Clan, Scatter Clan, Roaming Clan, Thieves Clan, and Storm Clan. How could they fail with Anoc among them? The *mamsas* had chanted the call of the Deliverer last night, weaving him momentarily into a spell of victory before She Who Made Him tapped his wrist, indicating that he was to lead her back to her tent.

He'd resented going with her, resented leaving the ceremonies that stirred his blood and made him a vital part of the great magic being made. Although disobedience was not permitted, he'd come very close to defying her. Never had he longed more to be one of the men, grown and honored, independent of the commands of females.

Perhaps, Anoc thought, angry enough to blame her, if he'd been allowed to stay, the spell of victory would have been made strong enough to keep this from happening.

Veering away from a group of scavengers, he saw a sword, a wondrous, well-made, shining length of weapon almost as handsome as the one carried by Shartur-god. The weapon was lying on the ground where its owner had dropped it, and although dirt and gore had soiled the blade, nothing marred its beauty.

Anoc's heart lurched with longing, and suddenly he could think of nothing else. It was as though for the second time today his destiny was reaching out to him. He felt certain this weapon had been created for him, or it would not be lying almost directly in his path and unnoticed by the scavengers running across the field in their tattered clothing, chased and yelled at, but flocking elsewhere and stealing back, as determined in their way as the carrion eagles already sailing overhead.

A voice shouted too close. A rough, foreign-tongued voice. An enemy's voice.

Startled, Anoc jerked around and saw a pale-eyes knight dragging himself out from beneath a dead horse and climbing to his feet. He staggered, then strode forward, gesturing and shouting angrily at Anoc. The pale-eyes carried a drawn dagger in his fist, and his filthy cloak hung torn and tattered from his shoulders. He shouted again, his meaning unmistakable.

He thinks I am a scavenger, Anoc thought. Disdainfully, he straightened his narrow shoulders, then—in sudden renewal of courage—Anoc wanted to laugh. Even if those pale-eyes fools won today's battle, the war was far from over. So had it been foretold.

Determined to show his utter contempt for the knight, Anoc darted bravely forward to scoop up the shining sword. It was immensely heavy, heavier than Ostur's rusted weapon or any of the scimitars Anoc had ever touched before, and of such quality it delighted him. Yet as he curled his hand around the hilt, a tingling shock ran through his flesh.

His fingers spasmed and jerked, causing him to drop the sword.

The knight halted and leaned over to catch his breath. He started laughing, and this time when he spoke, his tone held contempt.

Ignoring him, Anoc picked up the sword again. Pain like fire shot through his hand. He jerked away, dropping it, wincing and cursing the strange demon-magic protecting this weapon.

Angry frustration filled him. What trickery was this, to lure him to something so wonderful, yet burn him in punishment for taking what should be his?

Suddenly leery of Netheran magic and trickery, Anoc broke to run but he'd lingered too long. A hand gripped his long dark hair from behind and yanked him backward. Biting off a yelp, Anoc twisted about in attack, but the pale-eyes swatted him off his feet.

When he landed on his wounded arm, a wave of agony engulfed him. He sucked in air, hurting too much to scream. Although it was tempting just to lie in the dirt and give way to his pain, desperation drove him upright. But the knight's mailed fist smashed into his jaw, driving him to the ground so hard all the breath was jolted from him. For a moment he could not tell what had become of sky or ground. The world seemed to be in pieces floating around him; and then there was only darkness.

Chapter Five

Leaning over a balcony perched high above a bottomless chasm, Tashalya, princess royal of Nether, ignored the vista of jagged, barren mountain peaks stretching before her and watched the sunrise impatiently. Time was running out, and if she intended to succeed that morn she would have to act soon.

But not just yet. Forcing back her restlessness, she made herself stand quietly by the stone railing, feeling the dew condense on her face while the chilly desert wind stirred her long black hair, left unbound in the fashion of the sorcel-folk.

She wore the unadorned black robe of an apprentice, devoid of jewels or even her circlet of royalty. Her face and hands were milky pale in contrast to her somber clothing and dark cloud of hair. Only her pale blue eyes gave her color.

Although she stood motionless and outwardly serene, inside she felt hollow with anticipation and excitement. This was her chance to prove herself, to make Bona take notice of her the way the preceptress had when a much-younger Tashalya first came to the citadel for training. Yesterday Tashalya had been passed over in the selection for cupping, forced to sit stunned and disbelieving while two other apprentices were chosen for the final step in becoming completed *sorcerelles*. Last year, Tashalya had been passed over. And the year before that. She was nineteen, too old to keep waiting and hoping indefinitely. Her life and future, her dreams and ambitions, were all fading away. If she did not demonstrate her depth of talent with enough boldness to gain attention for selection, she feared she would end up like Callyn—useless and withered—a perpetual failure whispered about by the others.

Her gaze shifted away from the horizon to the door behind her. Faintly over the sigh of wind, she could hear Bona's voice spiraling upward in song, queer and spell-laden, not to be listened to, not to be asked about. It was the only time of day that Bona's attentions were attuned absolutely away from her apprentices, the only time that Tashalya was free to attempt what she was about to do without attracting the *sorcerelle's* notice.

Such a small window of opportunity, and time trickling away in all directions, yet she must not hurry. Later today, the chosen apprentices would drink of the Cup of Nostaul and be completed. If Tashalya did not join them, it would be another endless year, and she did not think she could endure more waiting.

Yet proper timing was critical, and Tashalya told herself to bide quietly for the right moment like a huntress sighting her prey.

Before her, the orange sun lifted slowly above the farthest line of mountains. Golden light danced around her, filling the balcony with radiance. For a moment, she was reminded of the early-morning light in the royal nursery where she'd spent her first eight years. A nursery painted yellow and stenciled with flowers, a happy place that glowed each dawn and made her feel good when she woke up.

Compressing her lips tightly, Tashalya flicked the memory away. Happiness was the past. She had only the present.

And just then she wished to stay focused on her purpose, which was to defy all she had been taught and take the biggest risk of her life.

As the rising sun warmed her face, she listened inwardly,

gauging the moment when day fully claimed the land from night, when the first, second, and third worlds came together in perfect alignment for a short while. It was the perfect opportunity for seeing the future . . . or the past.

Turning her head fractionally, Tashalya said, "Callyn, now."

"No. I won't do this."

Swept with disbelief, Tashalya lost her concentration and glared at her servant, who was standing near the wall with a basin of hammered copper in her hands and a look of mutiny on her face.

"Now."

"It is wrong," Callyn insisted. "Forbidden. You know it is. You will destroy yourself out of pride and—"

Tashalya struck her with a blow of *marzea*, her inner force. Callyn rocked back on her heels, her head snapping to one side.

"I did not ask for your opinion," Tashalya said. "This is my choice."

"A wrong one. Punish me all you like, but I am here to dissuade you from terrible mistakes. And you are making one now."

"What will you do? Run to Bona and betray me?"

Callyn shook her head. "This is far more serious than you know. Terrible evil will come from what you intend."

"You don't know what I intend."

"I sense your purpose. I can still do that, even if I have no *marzea* left. I give you warning. Turn aside from this, for you will bring disaster."

Despite her annoyance, Tashalya shivered. Callyn was odd and crippled, but the authority, the *knowledge*, in her tone made Tashalya suddenly wonder if she could be right.

"Disaster for whom?" she asked.

Callyn bowed her head. She was perhaps twice Tashalya's age, petite and slender, her brass-colored hair lying lank and unplaited down her back. Her skin held the faintest tinge of green in its complexion, and Tashalya could not imagine where she came from, for she was like no one the princess had ever encountered. Callyn never talked about herself, and her thoughts were completely closed to Tashalya's probing.

She had a mossy look, like something enspelled and left too
long in the forest. Her skin was moist, her hair damp and life-
less, her eyes glistening as though she'd just emerged from a
slimy pool. At night, she glowed with an eerie radiance, as
ethereal and dim as moonlight, but by day she exhibited no
such quality.

Ghostly pale, except for the dark, ridged scars that knotted and crisscrossed the left side of her throat up across her
jaw and cheek, Callyn had one eye of piercing emerald green
and one eye milky white. She wore a shapeless white robe
that covered her from shoulder to foot, but Tashalya had seen
the other scars on her body, as well as the deformity growing
on her side. All were part of the legacy of Callyn's failure
while drinking from the Cup of Nostaul. She had not become
a completed *sorcerelle*; nor had she died, which was usually
what happened when the ceremony went awry.

From Tashalya's first day in Bona's citadel years ago,
when Callyn had been assigned to her as servant, protector,
and companion, Callyn had been a warning of potential disaster, one that Tashalya feared at first, then despised, and now
ignored. She was never going to be like Callyn, lingering on
here in this place of magic, unable fully to belong, hungering
for what she could never have.

When the servant did not answer her question, Tashalya
scowled. "You're trying to distract me with false prophecy. It
won't work. Come here as I have commanded."

"Please," Callyn whispered. "You are so close to completion. Don't risk—"

"Fie! I was passed over. Always I am passed over."
Tashalya's pent-up frustration and bewilderment came
spilling out. "I can't wait another year. I—"

Feeling her eyes sting, her throat choking up with emotions she didn't want to reveal, Tashalya broke off and turned
her back on Callyn. Blindly, her eyes awash with furious
tears, she glared at the mountains. *I can do this,* she told herself. *I am the princess royal, the firstborn of Faldain. I do not
fail at anything.*

"You must be patient," Callyn said softly. "When the time
is right, you will be chosen, then you will know completion.

Waiting is hard for you, but it is better than disaster. Do not, please, take the chance of becoming like . . . me."

"I shall never be like you," Tashalya said harshly, facing her. "Now stir the water and do not interrupt me again."

Hurt and some stronger emotion twisted Callyn's face before she lowered her gaze.

"Hurry!" Tashalya snapped.

Callyn bowed her head over the copper basin and stared into its contents. The surface of the water began to ripple and swirl.

Tashalya focused her formidable powers of concentration on the water, and her mind took over from Callyn's, brushing her weak abilities aside.

"Antiquavalla chanti," Tashalya murmured, gathering the *marzea* force around her. *"Chanti avalla antiquite."*

And it came in response to her summoning, that smooth, potent ripple of power and magic that was hers to command. It surged to her, filling her, and spread around her like a cloak—warm and heavy.

Callyn swayed and emitted a tiny, forlorn sigh as the magic she could never again possess swirled past her.

The tiny distraction renewed Tashalya's anger. Ruthlessly, she forced her emotions away, intending to deal with Callyn later, and concentrated.

And when she found the center of her thoughts and purpose, she opened her eyes.

The rising sun flared golden as it lifted above the mountain peaks. The heat and brilliance of its light filled the balcony with sudden scorching force, but Tashalya noticed only that she'd achieved her purpose just in time. She had captured the perfect alignment of the three worlds, and they were hers to command.

All she had to do next was stare deep into the mist rising off the water's surface and ask for that which she sought.

But she hesitated.

Tashalya had been parting the veils of seeing for years, but she'd never before attempted anything of this magnitude, and her natural self-confidence had been shaken yesterday when she was not chosen for completion. She had always known herself to be different and special, not as a princess

royal, but as an individual. The evil *sorcerel* Tulvak Sahm
had abducted her when she was only six years old because he
admired her precocious abilities with magic. When Samderaudin, chief *sorcerel* at her father's court, had first brought
her to Bona's citadel, the very old, very powerful *sorcerelle*
had been so impressed she gave Tashalya individualized
training. Tashalya believed that she was being groomed to
become a *magecera*, one of the strongest, most gifted, and
most rare of *sorcerelles*.

Bona was such a creature, infinitely valuable. A *magecera*
could travel into the past. She could walk in the future. She
could see all worlds simultaneously and change a man's fate
by her will. She could reweave time. She could alter the
course of history. She could create a kingdom, or destroy it.

There had been no new *magecera* known to appear in the
past century, but Tashalya dreamed of becoming the next one.
This, Tashalya was convinced, was her destiny, the reason
she'd been brought to Bona for training, the reason Bona and
Samderaudin had consulted so frequently about her.

She would possess the ability to hold her younger
brother's kingdom in the palm of her hand, and would give it
to him, or deny it, *as she chose*.

She was ready for this grand future. She'd trained hard in
preparation for it. And no one was going to hold her back
from what she wanted.

Focusing, she gazed deep, deep through the parted veils
into all that lay beyond, her mind plunging through the icy
realm of the second world, with all its strange nothingness,
that place of gray mist and shadow where illusion and reality
merged.

She drove her thoughts toward the past, through the coils
of time and the folds of history. And she poured all her will
and strength into her summoning: *"Solder,"* she called with
her mind. *"Solder First, you are summoned. I, Tashalya of
Nether, call you forth."*

At first there was nothing save the thick, gray mist.

"Solder!" she called more insistently. *"Ancient one, I am
your daughter, born of your dynasty. Come forth and tell me
that which I seek. Solder First, I summon you!"*

The mist parted before her, revealing a strange glowing

light cast by no fire. Ever brighter did it shine, until she found herself squinting. Her heart thumped eagerly. She wanted to rush forward, and yet her training held her where she was. It was vital to remain focused and in control, keeping her concentration unbroken despite the swell of intense excitement gathering inside her. She knew she must let the summoned one come to her. Never must she risk going to it.

She waited, but the light stayed where it was, bright and distant, tantalizing her. The second world did not frighten her. She'd crossed its threshold before, hiding when she needed a refuge.

A faint shudder passed through her. Surprised to feel fatigue and strain, she fought to keep her *marzea* steady. The alignment was fighting her, the three worlds slipping apart. Instead of releasing them, she held them even tighter under her control, struggling, but determined to succeed.

Abandoning all caution, she risked moving closer to the distant light.

"Solder First, come forth and answer my question," she called. *"You are summoned. You must obey!"*

A man's silhouette appeared before her. There came a rush of warm, moist air that blew against her face and brought the scents of ground in early thaw, mingled with a whiff of fruit blossoms and smoke. She heard faint sounds of battle and men crying out. The stranger seemed close enough to touch, yet too far away to see clearly.

Tashalya's heart thudded painfully fast, and her knees were weak. She dared not move, could scarcely breathe. Beneath her skilled self-control, she was quivering from the churning frenzy of her emotions. *This is Solder,* she thought in amazement. *He is actually obeying me.*

Solder was the greatest general in the history of man, the first king of Nether, the earliest ancestor of known record. His accomplishments were legendary, epic. He had known the gods, and they had rewarded his courage with sovereignty over the land of Nether, charging him and his descendants with defending it against the minions of darkness. Solder's sword hung in Faldain's palace. Solder's ring encircled her father's finger, although no longer could Faldain use its power.

To Tashalya's knowledge, no one had ever before dared to summon Solder's spirit to the very threshold of the first world.

But indeed he had left his battlefield and come to her like a dog to its master, hers to command. Triumphantly she wanted to laugh aloud. Who else but she could do this?

Three strides toward her did he take, looming larger with each one as though crossing leagues of time to reach her. As he grew more distinct, she saw that he was a broad-shouldered man wearing strangely configured armor of sticks woven together over a garment of brightly hued silk. His helm was fashioned from wooden disks somewhat in the style of the obsidian armor of Gantese fire-knights, yet nothing like it at all. How, she marveled, could such fragile wooden armor protect him?

The light behind him flared up, dazzling her momentarily before he stood revealed, no longer in shadow.

His chin was beardless; his face that of a young man, very comely. And his eyes were like crystal—clear, colorless, and bright, with fire in their depths.

She found herself mesmerized by his gaze, as though she stared into starlight, and incautiously she permitted him to look on her with sight in return. His gaze seemed to turn her inside out, and the intimacy both confused and fascinated her.

Stunned by his physical presence, she drank him in, absorbing every detail. He'd been fighting. He was smeared with dirt and blood, with male heat rising off his muscles. His nostrils flared from exertion, and his eyes . . .

Compelling, mesmerizing, extraordinary. The longer she met his gaze, the more she lost all connection with herself, and she did not care. A strange warmth filled her, and her breathing grew tangled. She could not think of anything save him. Her mind was blank, sizzling with some peculiar sensation that seemed to explode her thoughts before they could form. She longed to reach out and touch the solidness of his arm, to slide her palm against his callused one and be held by its strength.

"Solder," she whispered.

"What are you called, good lady?"

The resonance of his voice thrilled her. She smiled, trusting him absolutely. "Tashalya of Nether."

"Lovely." His gaze traveled from her face to the rest of her and back again, making the blood hum in her ears. "Long has it been since such a vision of beauty was given unto me."

His flattery pleased her. "I have summoned you, great Solder, to ask a question. By the laws of the summoning, you must answer."

"Solder heeds no call. Solder obeys no one, save by his choice."

"But you're here. You came."

"Everything for thee will *I* do." He smiled, extending his hand. "Ask *me*, Tashalya of Nether."

The sheer physical longing to place her hand in his made her dizzy. Some faint instinct warned her that if she touched him, she would forget everything else, including her reason for summoning him. She almost didn't care, but the question that had burned in her as long as she could remember drove her onward.

"Solder," she whispered, while her hand reached out to his, "where is Truthseeker?"

His fingers curled around hers. It was not spirit she touched, but flesh and bone. She felt a tingle pulse through her skin, carrying a sensation unlike anything she'd experienced before. She inhaled sharply, but already he was pulling her closer within the curve of his arm, and she did not care. Man or ghost, she wanted his embrace.

At that moment, however, a heavy force struck her from behind, seizing her and sweeping her back. Her hand was torn from his, and he vanished like smoke.

Returned to the first world, and disoriented by its vivid shapes and colors, Tashalya was knocked down so hard she went sprawling on the balcony's stone floor.

Water from the copper basin splashed over her, icy cold, and the bowl went spinning on the floor where Callyn had dropped it.

"Callyn!" Tashalya yelled, but her servant fled.

Furious, Tashalya gathered her *marzea* to strike Callyn down, but another voice spoke a harsh word of power that crackled in the air.

Whipping around, Tashalya found herself staring up at Bona. Floating in an enormous ball of blazing green-and-blue fire, the *sorcerelle* pointed an ebony power-staff at her. Although nothing visible came from the power-staff's tip, its magic pinned Tashalya to the floor.

Realizing it was Bona—not Callyn—who had interrupted her, Tashalya forgot her anger and instead lifted her hands in quick supplication. "Bona!" she called out. "Hear me! I have proven myself—"

The force from the power-staff intensified, burning through her chest. The pain sent Tashalya writhing back with a strangled cry.

"Disobedient fool!" Bona raged. "Now you will be taught a lesson you cannot forget."

Chapter Six

Standing in a low-lying section of ground with his cloak wrapped around his left arm and with screaming Grethori coming at him from all sides, Dain swung Mirengard, deflecting a mace trying to bludgeon him. As his opponent yelled and attacked again, Dain ducked his shoulder under the clumsy onslaught, knocked the man back, and plunged Mirengard deep. At the same time he fended off another Grethori with his left arm, long enough to free his sword. His blow across the Grethori's shoulder drove the man to his knees but did not vanquish him.

A scimitar slashed viciously at Dain's legs. As he twisted aside to avoid it, his foe scrambled upright and charged. Gripping Mirengard with both hands, Dain swung straight and clean, and his opponent's head toppled.

Green spell-fire flashed close by, nearly blinding him. The resultant boom staggered him, while black smoke surrounded him on all sides. Squinting and coughing, he sensed someone approaching his right side.

Dain turned and swung.

"Sire!" shouted a voice. "Disengage! 'Tis I!"

At the last moment, Dain checked his blow, and Mirengard wobbled, skidding lightly off a deflecting blade. "Omas?"

"Aye!" A tall figure loomed before him, emerging from the smoke.

Dain grinned, gulping in air, and gestured. "Stand at my back . . . together we'll fight the rest of them."

"No need, sire. 'Tis over. The fighting's over. Be at ease now."

"Nay," Dain said urgently. "Saw more coming . . . half dozen at least."

"But you've dealt with them," Omas said. "As have Tulmahrd and I."

"More—"

"No, sire. There are no more."

Dain heard the words, but they wouldn't stay in his mind long enough to make sense. Badly winded, light-headed with fatigue, and a little dazed, he frowned at Omas. Slowly he realized that no enemy was rushing at him. No longer did he hear shrieking war cries and curses. The fighting had paused, and he was thankful for a respite.

Vaguely he lifted the tip of Mirengard and let it sink down again. His chest was heaving. Sweat drenched him beneath his armor, running down his face and stinging his eyes. His arms and legs were trembling from exertion.

The smoke thinned at last, dissipated by a rising breeze. Now that he could see more clearly, he found that he and Omas were standing in a circle of slain men. The stink of death and expended magic choked the air. There came a roar of sound, incomprehensible at first before it clarified into the Netheran war cry.

"Faldain! Faldain!"

Heartened, Dain laughed a little. "Where are we positioned now? Let's fall back and regroup at yon—"

"No, sire," Omas said patiently. "The battle's over. It's won."

"Won?"

"Can't you hear the men cheering?"

The noise gained in volume, spreading from one end of the field to the other. "Faldain! Faldain! Faldain!"

"Borenskya!" came a smaller, more ragged cheer.

Dain laughed. If the men were vying against each other to honor their leaders, they were all right, he thought, more than all right.

"Over," he said, numbed by hours of hard fighting. "Great Thod. Over."

Blinking, he pulled off his helmet and wiped his eyes with the back of his sword hand. He had no idea what had become of his horse and shield, or how he came to be defending that particular spot. It amazed him to be alive and whole, and his army—from the sound of things—victorious. He couldn't seem to remember farther back than picking himself off the ground at some point and seeing a small horde of Grethori warriors rushing straight for him.

"Ivar?" he asked. "Chesil?"

"I know not, sire. I think I saw Chesil fall. That last assault pressed us hard. May I have your majesty's permission to check you for injury?"

"I'm all right," Dain said impatiently. "Search for Chesil. See if he needs help."

But by then Omas was unwinding the cloak from Dain's arm. He grunted at the sight of pale blood seeping between severed links of mail. Ripping a strip of cloth from his surcoat, he bound the wound tightly enough to make Dain wince. "Would it please your majesty to sit down?"

"No."

"How came you to lose your gauntlet?"

Dain shook his head, still unable to remember. "It's probably gone for a Grethori trophy."

"I doubt that," Omas said grimly, toeing a body out of his way. "Most likely you lost it when you were pulled from the saddle. My heart went right into my mouth, but I couldn't get to you."

A worried shout came, and Omas raised his formidable voice in answer. Moments later, Fordra came running up to join them, a bit wild-eyed, blood running down his face from a cut on his forehead.

"Father! Your majesty! Thod be praised," he gasped out, and whirled around, waving his sword high. "I found them! Over here!"

More men came on foot and on horseback to surround them. Everyone seemed to be talking and laughing at once. A pennon bearer lifted Dain's colors high.

Cheers from the field rose again. Flushed with triumph, Dain smiled back at the joyous, begrimed faces surrounding him. When someone gave him water, he quaffed it with huge gulps. Despite being weary and sore, he was filled with the glory of victory. Just then, it was enough to be strong, and alive, and a man. The war song of Mirengard still echoed inside his head, and he could have gone onward if necessary, oblivious to everything save the enemy and the fight.

But the fight was over, and there were countless details to be sorted out. Trin reached them, looking very serious. "Majesty! Matkevskiet has been found. He's wounded but alive, on his way to the infirmary."

Dain exchanged a relieved glance with Omas. "Thod is merciful," Dain said. "See that he's given the best of care."

Trin saluted. "Aye, your majesty."

By then Dain's squire had arrived, throwing a clean cloak around Dain's shoulders before taking Mirengard to polish off the gore. A horse was supplied for the king's use, and Dain was just climbing into the saddle when Lutmalyin galloped up.

"Sire," the aide said, saluting, "with Commander Adyul's compliments, I bring you report of the battle."

"Good," Dain said, curbing his restive mount. "Has he estimated how many Grethori escaped?"

"No, your majesty," Lutmalyin said blankly. "There were none."

Dain frowned. "Did I hear you aright? None escaped?"

A grin spread across Lutmalyin's face. "A complete and total victory, your majesty. Every man of them is slain, wounded, or held captured. Commander Tolumin has taken a detail to round up the women and children from their camp. And I am to report that Vaunit and the other *sorcerels* are bringing the *shedas* in from their hiding place."

"Our casualties?"

"Heavy, sire," Lutmalyin said more soberly. "But I haven't taken counts yet from the sergeants."

"Too soon," Omas commented, turning his gaze to the

section of the field where a patrol of knights and corpsmen were already searching for survivors among the fallen.

Dain nodded thoughtfully. By the angle of the sun, he guessed it to be a little past midday, and yet they seemed to have been fighting for an eternity. Despite the foul trick of the Grethori in attacking their camp last night, Dain's strategy had worked. He'd led his men into the valley, where the Grethori pursued them eagerly. No doubt the Grethori thought they had the Netherans cornered there, but Dain had turned the trap against his foes, and it had been the savages who could not escape the valley.

Thinking of Vaunit's dire prediction and warnings, Dain was grateful to find the *sorcerel* so mistaken.

Surrounded by an ever-increasing cluster of officers and men, he was heading across the southern end of the valley when Kostrinki reached him. In a tight little voice that quivered now and then, Kostrinki reported the numbers of dead and wounded.

Of the seven hundred foot soldiers remaining among Borenskya's forces, only fifteen men had survived. Three-quarters of Dain's prized archers were slain. The Agya forces had lost many horses; as yet their numbers of wounded had not been counted. Over five hundred knights lay among the dead or seriously injured. And among the officers, seven sergeants and five captains had been lost. Some men were missing and unaccounted for, either among the wounded or possibly deserters. In total, perhaps two-thirds of the entire Netheran forces had been lost. The Grethori casualties, of course, outnumbered even that.

Dain listened patiently through the long accounting, his gaze staring across the valley, his heart grieving for the dead and injured.

Thirteen years, he thought. *Thirteen long and bloody years. How many men have died to bring us victory?*

When Kostrinki at last fell silent, Dain roused himself. "A most efficient and useful report, commander. Thank you."

Looking gratified by the praise, Kostrinki straightened in his saddle. "Your majesty honors me. I am here only to serve."

"Go and see to your men," Dain told him. "I shall want you among my officers in a short while."

As the commander rode off, Dain frowned wearily for a moment, trying to gather himself for the next task. Mirengard was handed back to him, clean and shining, its song quiet as he slid it absently into its scabbard. A throb of pain went up from his wound, and he leaned forward to rest his bandaged forearm on the front of his saddle.

"Your majesty!" Lutmalyin reappeared at Dain's side. "There's a red-haired chieftain captured alive."

"Chuntok," Dain said grimly. "Have him brought to me at once."

When guards brought the prisoner, he shuffled weakly as though barely able to walk. His head hung low, so that his long red hair hid his face.

Dain's heart squeezed with memory. How long, he wondered, had he longed to be once more face-to-face with his son's murderer? At the time of their last confrontation, Dain had been too injured to give Chuntok what he deserved. *Now,* Dain thought grimly, *the circumstances are far different.*

The captain rapped out an order, and the guards hoisted the sagging Grethori erect. Although stocky, the prisoner was not as tall or as burly in the arms and chest as Dain remembered. And when one of the guards yanked back his head, a stranger's face was revealed.

Disappointment crashed through Dain. He told himself that Chuntok had probably perished years ago, perhaps in some other raid or battle, hopefully at Netheran hands. Dain knew that Grethori chieftains often led short lives, for their way of life was a brutal one. There'd always been the possibility that he would never meet Chuntok again, yet he kept the hope of making the man accountable.

"Sire?" the captain said. "Is this the man your majesty seeks?"

"No," Dain said curtly. "That is not Chuntok."

His men exchanged somber looks.

"Are there any red-haired men among the dead chieftains?" Dain asked.

"No, sire. This is the only one."

With churning emotions, Dain dismounted—Omas and

Agya guards flanking him protectively—and faced the prisoner.

This chieftain was no more than a half-grown boy with scruff instead of beard and dark eyes that held more bravado than courage. Blood was seeping from a wound in his side, and now and then a tremor passed through him, making his knees wobble. The guards were propping him up, keeping him standing respectfully before Dain, and he looked pale and weak from loss of blood.

But he still had strength enough to spit contemptuously at Dain.

The guards struck him for that, making him sag, then shook him until he roused.

Dain snapped his fingers, and a shifty-eyed translator, his jerkin reeking of beyar grease, was shoved forward.

"Are you Chuntok's son?" Dain asked the chieftain.

As the translator repeated the question, the boy's eyes flattened with hostility. He would not answer until one of the guards prodded him with a dagger, then he snarled out a reply.

"He says that he is Chank, chieftain of the—"

"Chank," Dain said, not letting the translator finish. He kept his gaze fixed steadily on the Grethori boy. "And who was chieftain before you?"

This time when Chank answered, the translator said nothing.

Dain glanced at him impatiently. "Well?"

"He spoke an insult, majesty! I dare not repeat it."

Omas growled in his throat. "Let the guards beat him into better cooperation."

Dain raised his hand to prevent the guards from following that suggestion. Although sullen and defiant, Chank was too weak to withstand much battering.

Suddenly Dain felt distaste for bullying an injured boy simply because he could not confront the enemy he wanted. "Take him away."

When the guards moved Chank aside, the sunlight glinted on a flash of silver at the boy's throat.

"Wait!" Dain said, pointing. "What is that around his neck?"

One of the guards pulled it off so roughly it left a bloody scratch on Chank's skin. With a yelp, Chank lunged at the man, snapping at his hand with vicious teeth. The guard struck him across the face, making the boy crumple while the item was given to Omas, who in turn brought it to Dain.

Crusted with years of dirt and grime, the slim metal circlet was nevertheless unmistakable. Dain felt cold inside as he closed trembling fingers around it. When he rubbed at the dirt, the pure gleam of eldin silver engraved with the royal crest was revealed.

The past rushed over him, and for a moment Dain saw a small, golden-haired boy with innocent blue eyes and a radiant smile. A boy who loved to play in the mud. How he would race, shrieking with laughter, through the palace corridors to evade his nurse at bedtime.

"Ilymir," Dain whispered.

Rousing, Chank mumbled something with a scornful smirk.

"He said it is his war trophy, majesty," the translator said nervously. "Better than wearing the skull of an enemy's baby."

Angry murmurs swelled through the ranks of the Netherans gathered close enough to overhear. Dain's aides stood white-faced and grim. Omas's hand closed on his weapon, while his brown eyes narrowed and grew cold.

Dain's pulse was throbbing beneath the tight bracelet wrapped around his wrist, the one he'd had fashioned from Ilymir's ceremonial circlet, so seldom worn. But this . . . *war trophy* . . . had adorned Ilymir's brow every day of his short life from the time he first began to walk. It was a symbol of royalty, not a piece of loot to be worn by a barbarian. Dain felt the tiniest hum within the metal, sensed the faintest thread of Ilymir's presence still contained within it. His eyes began to sting, and he felt a sudden overwhelming urge to be alone, deep in the woods, where he could cope with reopened wounds. He'd thought himself past all emotion, his grief quite sealed over after so many years, but he was wrong. *Morde*, he thought desperately, *I am unmanned.*

Boldly, eyes agleam, the young chieftain taunted Dain. "Your son dead by Chuntok's hand. A great coup for our clan.

I wear it as my legacy, passed to me when I became clan chieftain."

Dain stared at him, saying nothing, his face on fire.

"We have not forgotten you, Faldain," Chank said cruelly. "We still talk of you around our fires, and of my father who bested you in battle."

"Chuntok."

"Yes, my father was Chuntok, a greater warrior than you. He captured you and kept you chained like a dog in our camp. I saw you, pale-eyes king. I was one of the small ones then who threw dung at you."

"Sire," Omas rumbled angrily, "I'll cut out his tongue—"

"Let him rant," Dain commanded, never taking his gaze from Chank.

"My father took that trophy instead of your son's fingers," Chank continued. The silence and looks of anger around him only seemed to feed his boasting. "My father, his father before him, and all my brothers have led our clan. Now it is mine to lead. You cannot defeat us, pale-eyes king! Never can you break the Wind Tribe, for it is foretold that we have a Deliverer who will avenge this day."

"You and your people stand defeated," Dain replied. "If he exists, where is this Deliverer? Why did he not lead you to victory?"

Uncertainty cracked Chank's defiant façade. He fell silent, struggling a little for air, his face losing color.

Although it would be easy to pity him, Dain knew better. Despite his youth and evident inexperience, Chank had led men into battle today and could not be treated like a child.

"Your clansmen are dead," Dain said harshly. "Your tribe is broken. Never again will it rise. The Grethori people are vanquished forever."

"No!" Chank lunged against his restraints. "We are not finished, never finished. As long as our *sheda* shields us with her magic, the Deliverer will avenge us. This she has sworn!"

"Your crone will soon be my prisoner," Dain said. "Her magic will be stripped from her."

"You have no such power!"

"I command demons," Dain told him, using the boy's own

superstitions to confound him. "They are stronger than any *sheda.*"

Trembling, white, wild-eyed, Chank shook his head. "No demon commanded by man can vanquish her powers. She brought us the Deliverer. We will be avenged." He gasped for breath. "You cannot chant victory over us, for this is not finished. She has foretold our future!"

One of the guards moved to subdue him, but Chank was already collapsing. They lowered him to the ground, where he lay sprawled, his eyes staring in death, his words lingering in the air.

With raw emotions Dain turned the little circlet over and over in his hands.

No matter what these savages believed, it had been proven false, Dain told himself firmly. The great prediction of their evil *shedas* had come to naught. Nothing had saved them from today's ruin and destruction.

"I'm sorry, sire," Omas said very softly. "That little vermin was nothing but spite and insult . . . a waste of time. Come away now, and rest."

Dain drew a deep breath and resolutely turned his back on the last of the clan chieftains. He lifted his chin, his gray eyes clear and filled with purpose.

"Send for the priests," he commanded.

Atop the highest hill of those rimming the little valley, where all could see him, Dain performed the official prayers of thanksgiving, assisted by the priests. He offered salt, soil, blood, and ash. Kneeling, he took the sacrament of salt and wafer and sipped of the water purified within the Holy Chalice of Eternal Life. He asked for the mercy of Thod over the souls of the slain and offered his gratitude for the lives that had been spared. And he asked that the wounded might heal to return home to their families.

Silence held over victorious knights and prisoners alike. With his public prayers at an end, Dain remained kneeling a few moments longer, listening to the soft, ritualized words of the priests standing before him while his private prayers filled his heart. Bowing his head, he pulled the bracelet from his arm, as he had sworn never to do until his vow was completed. *Now,* he thought, *I can send both this coil of silver*

*and the circlet recovered today to Alexeika, and perhaps we
can find peace.*

When he rose to his feet and faced his army, they cheered
him anew. The afternoon sunshine shone on his face and
armor. He raised his arm in salute, projecting his voice skillfully as he praised their valor that day, reminding them of
what they owed to Thod for sparing their lives and granting
them victory. He promised each of them a medal and gold
chain in reward when they marched home to Grov.

The cheers went on and on, filling the grim valley and rising to the skies. He let them cheer until they were hoarse.

Then one of his aides came hurrying to his side.

What Dain read in the young man's eyes made his heart
quicken. One last confrontation, he thought. "The *shedas*?"

"Aye, majesty," Trin replied. "Word has come that they're
captured."

"All of them?"

"All, sire. They're coming now."

Chapter Seven

❧❦❧

When Bona's punishment ended, Tashalya sank to the floor with a moan of relief she could not quite stifle. Every inch of her body felt flayed. Trembling, she pressed her palms against the sun-warmed flagstones and fought back tears.

At the other end of the balcony, the blaze of green-and-blue fire surrounding Bona faded to a faint aura. Potent, dangerous, furious, the *sorcerelle's* power washed over Tashalya again, taking the girl's breath. So rapidly and skillfully did the preceptress sift through Tashalya's thoughts, there was no chance to shield herself.

Struggling, Tashalya could not gather her *marzea*. She felt as though she'd been stripped naked and left exposed.

Bona approached her. Immensely ancient, older perhaps even than Samderaudin, the *sorcerelle* possessed skin as thick and smooth as leather. Innumerable tiny plaits of her long silver hair flowed down her back and dragged the ground behind her. The end of each plait was knotted around a small, polished pebble, and these stones clattered softly against the floor when she moved.

Lowering the power-staff, Bona snapped her fingers, and the burning fire faded inside Tashalya's chest.

"Get up," Bona commanded.

Forcing back her tears, Tashalya schooled her features into a rigid, autocratic mask. She did not want Bona to know how much she hurt or how frightened she'd been.

Rising to her feet, she found herself unexpectedly clumsy and off-balance. She could hear a faint buzzing in her head, and the walls and railing tended to move at the corners of her vision.

"Proving yourself, Tashalya?" Bona asked. Her voice was an unpleasant, dissonant rasp. "Proving you can do the forbidden? Why have you defied the rules and risked your life?"

"You know why, preceptress. You have already read my thoughts."

"Impatience and stupidity make a reckless brew."

Tashalya flushed hot. "I'm neither! I've waited—"

"It is forbidden to call forth the ancient ones, especially a *ciaglo*. And you touched him!"

"What of it? He came so close, all the way to the very threshold of the first world. That's uncommon, isn't it?"

Bona wasn't to be deflected. Her pale eyes went on boring relentlessly into Tashalya. "Did you also tell him your name?"

"No," Tashalya lied, putting the truth in a small, locked corner of her mind, the way Tulvak Sahm had taught her. "I would never do that."

"Wouldn't you?"

Tashalya remained silent. No matter what Bona said, she'd accomplished something tremendous, and she wasn't ashamed of it.

Bona hissed through her teeth the way she did when lessons went awry. "Your name, your touch . . . keys into the first world that you've given freely. This *ciaglo* can find you anywhere now, perhaps even come without being summoned. Such danger!"

"But it's Solder," Tashalya said. "Why shouldn't he know who I am? He's my ancestor, the first in a line of kings that stretches from him to my father. He would never harm me."

Bona was twisting the power-staff around in her hands.

"Such a child, still," she muttered. "Sighted, yet blind. Strong, yet vulnerable. Gifted, yet so very inept."

Stung, Tashalya cried out, "I am not! I knew the risks before I started, and I judged them worthwhile. I did exactly what I set out to do, and would have accomplished even more if you had not intervened."

"You like the dark side of things, do you not? You love to tempt danger and risk, because they are within you. You should be fighting such weakness, yet you embrace it, time and again."

"Solder is *not* of the darkness."

"No one says that he is. But it is forbidden to summon the ancients. To defy that is—"

"I don't care!" Tashalya stamped her foot. "I brought him forth, something no other apprentice could do. Why can't you be proud? What do old rules matter when I've shown you how ready I am to be completed?"

"You did not bring forth Solder."

"But you saw him," Tashalya insisted. "I know you did."

"I saw a fool taking unnecessary risks."

"It *was* Solder! I called him, and he came to me. Solder First," Tashalya said, laughing a little in renewed triumph. "Who has ever before reached him?"

"No one. Nor did you."

Tashalya stopped gloating and narrowed her eyes. "You cannot deny what happened. Preceptress, that's unfair!"

"What is fair about an apprentice who will not obey the boundaries, who endangers herself and those around her for personal gain?"

"No! I—"

"What is fair about an apprentice who thinks she knows better than her preceptress, who lets pride and arrogance sway her past common sense?"

Hurt, Tashalya stared at the *sorcerelle* whom she admired more than any other. Why couldn't Bona understand her? Why was Bona making this so awful? Tashalya had expected praise and approval, not scathing condemnation.

"I just wanted to show you how strong I am," she said. "I want to drink of the cup and be completed."

A small coronet of green flame blazed above Bona's head. "Completed? You think you are ready?"

"I know I am," Tashalya said eagerly. "I can be like you, a *magecera*. I held the three worlds together. I held them! And I can—"

"No."

Stunned and bewildered, Tashalya stared at Bona. "Why?"

"Your boasting is foolish. The *ciaglo* is not Solder."

"He must be," Tashalya insisted. "Who else would come in his place? What magic has anyone—even an ancient—to resist a summons? When the veils parted—"

"You did not part the veils," Bona said angrily. "You went to meet him. Against all training! You went."

"Not far. I was reaching so hard, I just had to . . . I did not go far."

"The second world is no place to wander."

Unconcerned, Tashalya shrugged. "For most apprentices perhaps. I know it well."

"You have traveled through it as a child, with the power of the Ring of Solder to protect you." Bona shook a knobby finger at her. "That does not mean you know it well. Such arrogance, Tashalya, is why you are not ready for the Cup of Nostaul."

Tashalya stiffened with temper, although she tried to keep it controlled. "Believing in myself is *not* arrogance. I'm an adult now. Why won't you treat me like one?"

"Today you disobeyed the rules like a child," Bona said harshly. She lifted the power-staff. "Perhaps you need another lesson."

Hiding her alarm, Tashalya faced the preceptress with the hauteur of her royal background. "I think not. The rules protect the ordinary apprentices, but I'm not like them. Stop holding me back! You know I'm like you, or will be once I am completed. You command the past, and so will I. The next time I summon Solder I shall do it even better."

"There will be no next time. As part of your atonement you must admit your mistake. Admit you summoned one other than Solder."

Tashalya's mouth dropped open in astonishment. "Atonement?" she echoed. "No! I—I won't!"

"Never again will you seek to align the worlds or tamper with past fate or future destiny," Bona went on, as though she hadn't spoken. "Such is not for you."

"Why not? There was a time when you praised me for trying new things and stretching my abilities." Tashalya frowned in sudden suspicion. "But not anymore. Why? Are you growing jealous of me? Do you fear I will be stronger than you? Is that why you won't let me be completed?"

"The past is forbidden to you, Tashalya."

"No! You have no right to dictate to me!"

"I have command of you. I teach you. And learn you must, until you are ready."

"I'm ready now! You've taught me nothing for weeks!" Tashalya said in sudden rage. "Those stupid rites with the soil . . . of what use is such primitive magic to *me*? I have my destiny and a—"

"And what?" Bona broke in sharply, her eyes watchful. "What is the true purpose in what you did today? The truth, Tashalya. Not these lies about being completed and proving yourself."

Compressing her lips, Tashalya did not answer. This time, when Bona's thoughts swept across hers, Tashalya was ready and did not let the preceptress see everything. She was adept at concealing her secrets. She'd learned how from a master.

Bona studied her a moment and scowled. "Tulvak Sahm. I thought you had rid yourself of his influence."

"I have!" Flustered, Tashalya tried to sound less defensive. "You know I have. We spent all that time undoing his—"

"We spent much time," Bona said thoughtfully, "but how much did we undo?"

Tashalya glared, almost hating her. "You make it sound like I—I admire him or something. He was horrible!"

"Much evil did he do, and on days like this I see his mark on you still."

"No!" Tashalya said in a choked voice, furious with her. "No! That isn't true."

"Denial does not help you, child."

The sudden kindness in Bona's tone undid Tashalya's anger. She found herself shaken, on the verge of tears. Once she would have run to the preceptress's arms, but she was no longer ten years old.

"Heed me," Bona said. "You sought personal gain in this action. You went to the dead seeking answers the living will not give you. Such is not a valid reason for opening the past."

Stifling a gasp, Tashalya could feel her heart thudding. Bona's statements were too close to the truth, but Tashalya assured herself that the preceptress did not as yet know the whole.

"Let me be very clear," Bona continued. "Solder First did not come to you, no matter what you believe. Solder's ghost is protected under the seals of the third world. Those cannot be broken."

Tashalya said nothing.

"It is unwise to rouse entities such as *ciaglos*. They are ghost-demons and best left alone."

"Whoever he was, he was very handsome," Tashalya said, just to provoke her. "Very strong and manly. His eyes—"

"You flirted with him. You would have kissed him, kissed the dead, had I not intervened. Fool!"

"You can't hold me back forever, Bona, no matter how much you may wish it. There are things I am meant to do, and I won't wait."

Bona stared at her hard. "You wish to leave the citadel?"

"I believe it's time," Tashalya said coolly, with every appearance of confidence. "I'm nineteen, and my brothers are growing up. If I'm to be useful to them, I need my full powers. I've waited long enough."

"The span of a *sorcerelle*'s existence is long. There is plenty of time to do all that you wish."

Tashalya managed not to roll her eyes. "I'm ready now."

Bona shook her head. "Perhaps next year you will be considered for completion. But not—"

"No! That's not fair! Jesala will be taking the cup tomorrow, and she has not half my abilities. Why do you keep me here?"

"Accept my wisdom in this matter."

"I want a better answer than that. I deserve to be told your reasons."

Bona glided over to the balcony railing with her gray hair trailing the ground behind her. The sun, hot and merciless, beat down on them both. "When a woman drinks of the Cup of Nostaul," Bona began so softly Tashalya could barely hear her, "her magical powers are completed, but she loses much that is womanly. The desire to bear children, for example."

"So?"

"If I still possessed such a desire, I should have wished for you to be my daughter."

Tears welled up in Tashalya's eyes. Before she could stop herself she ran to Bona and embraced her from behind, resting her cheek on the *sorcerelle*'s shoulder. "Oh, Bona," she whispered. "You *are* my mother. Only you have been kind to me and cared about me. Only you."

"You are wrong, Tashalya. Someday you will learn that."

Bona shrugged herself free of Tashalya's embrace, and Tashalya backed away from her, conscious of the silent rebuke. Sorcel-folk did not hug or touch each other. Theirs was a lonely existence, seldom in the company of others. It had to be that way, but sometimes Tashalya found it unbearably lonely.

She drew in a breath. "Thank you for saying that to me. I—"

"You misunderstand," Bona broke in, her face quite impassive. "I tell you my reason, as you have requested. I have delayed your selection because I know you have been content here, and I wished to be kind to you."

Tashalya stared at her in bewilderment. "I don't understand."

"You will never be selected for taking the cup. You will never be a *sorcerelle*, certainly not a *magecera*. But once I declare this officially, you will be required to leave at once and return to your family. To spare you that difficult transition for as long as possible, I have made sure that you were passed over in each selection."

Tashalya could only stare, conscious of a strange roaring

in her ears and the feeling that she wasn't hearing correctly. "No," she said in a small, puzzled voice. "No."

"You have gifts, a certain degree of strength, some brilliance," Bona went on in a toneless, impersonal way that seemed to make everything worse. "When you first came here, you were astonishing. I had never seen such magical power in a child so young. Your ability to learn was equally phenomenal. In your first year here, it was suggested to me that we cup you immediately."

"Why didn't you?"

"Because I have trained apprentices a very long time," Bona said. "And I have seen the inept grow strong and the most promising ones fail. In wanting to be very sure I did not create another Callyn, I have waited and watched you with great care."

An awful feeling was spreading through the pit of Tashalya's stomach. She tried to ignore it. "How can you say I'm a failure? After—"

"Oh, don't repeat your boasting," Bona said wearily. "You are so foolishly proud of what is nothing more than dangerous error."

Tashalya frowned, unable to find words, her heart thudding too fast. She felt as though she were running hard, running for her life, and yet she could not move.

Bona bent her gray head. "Your mother the queen possesses a drop of eldin blood, enough to give her the ability to part the veils of seeing, yet she cannot command her gift. She has seen wrongly, sometimes much to her cost. When she was your age, she tried to summon the spirit of her dead father, yet Faldain came to her instead."

Tashalya went on staring at Bona.

"Your mother could have damaged Faldain with her ineptitude, could have led terrible danger to him. In later years, she tried again, and brought only grief to herself. Although she is a stubborn woman—and assuredly has passed that trait along to you—she finally accepted her limitations and attempts magic no more."

"I am not like her," Tashalya whispered, through lips that felt frozen.

"You are becoming so. Your powers are waning. You have

not yet noticed, but we who watch over you know it. Such a pity."

Fury began to build in Tashalya, something so black and terrible she could not control it. At that moment she did not care what she said or did. How could Bona tell her something like this? After all she'd endured and worked for . . . it was impossible.

"I don't believe you."

"Tashalya—"

"No!" As she screamed the word, her *marzea* lashed out, shattering the stone railing to rubble. "It isn't true! You're lying!"

Bona lifted her power-staff, and the force it unleashed knocked Tashalya staggering back against the wall.

Her head thudded painfully against the stone, and little black dots danced in her vision. She shook them off, her anger swelling too hot for prudence. "Do not punish me again!" she cried out. "You have no right! I am not some insignificant provincial but a princess of the royal house. I—"

Bona pointed at her, and fire danced through Tashalya's veins, making her writhe and nearly scream.

"You are still bound by our rules as long as you abide under this roof," Bona said. "You will not threaten or attack me."

"I'll do as I please!" Tashalya shouted, her voice shrill as she tried not to scream. The fire crawled inside her until her skin felt like it would burst. "You're just lying because you're jealous of my surpassing you! You're old and lazy, teaching me less and less. But I'll—"

Bona spoke a word of power that reverberated through the air.

Before she knew what was happening, Tashalya found herself on the ground, curled up tightly in agony. Somewhere deep inside her came the old panic and rage, clawing its way out. "You've kept me here all these years and taught me nothing!" she shouted. "Did you think I'd believe your lies forever? You aren't my preceptress. You're my jailer! How much has my father paid you to betray me?"

Bona hovered near her, staring down at her with a pity that enraged Tashalya even more. "You will go back to Grov, back to your family," she said. "I shall notify Samderaudin at once."

"No!" Tashalya panted, twisting about in an effort to grab the hem of Bona's robes. "Don't you dare!"

"Poor child. I did not want to tell you this way."

Her pity infuriated Tashalya even more. "You won't send me back to Grov! I'll break free and take the cup myself if I have to. And I'll open the door to as many ghosts as I choose to unleash because—"

Bona spoke with power again, and this time the world seemed to break. Blackness encompassed Tashalya, shutting out the world of sight, sound, and feeling. Even the fire tormenting her faded away.

It should have brought her relief, but she found none. For now she could not move. Her limbs were bound by the darkness, as immovable as though she'd been carved from wood. She tried to howl more defiance, but no words would come from her throat.

Afraid, she fought the darkness. How she hated the smothering awfulness of it. Gathering her *marzea*, she struck hard against her invisible bonds, which should have shattered, but did not. She remained held in its inky depths, lost and alone, as though she'd been struck blind and deaf, as though she'd been put to death. And she thought—unwillingly at first, then angrily, then with a rush of panic—that perhaps Bona was telling the truth.

If she could not break free of this binding, if she could not take control and escape . . . then truly she must be losing her powers.

The realization made her feel as though she'd been dropped into icy water to drown. Her magic was the only part of herself that she took pride in.

Terrified, she could not think clearly. What was to become of her? What was she to do? How fast would it happen? Would she end up a cripple like Callyn?

Failure. Failure. Failure.

No, she refused to accept it. She had survived far worse than this. Nothing frightened her. Nothing. She would bide her time in this awful darkness, and when Bona let her out all would go on as before . . . except that Tashalya would keep summoning Solder's ghost—or whoever he was—until she had the answer she sought. And if doors were wedged open to the horrors of the ancients, if demons worse than Nonkind emerged and raged across the land, so be it. Bona, Tashalya thought angrily, needed to be taught a lesson, too.

Chapter Eight

✦

It was a day of *dralaig*—a day of defeat, shame, and despair.

Crouching on one of the flinty hills rimming the battle-field with the other Grethori prisoners, Anoc sat in numb dis-belief. He'd regained consciousness a short time ago, finding himself shackled in a rope enclosure among the other drum boys, a cluster of small ones, and females moaning in grief. A few captive warriors, mostly from the Roaming Clan, filled another, smaller enclosure nearby. Pale-eyes guards armed with pikes circled them slowly, alert for any trouble.

Anoc's head was throbbing. The sword cut on his arm burned and stung, and his bruised ribs ached.

Down on the battlefield, Netheran knights—tall and pal-lid in their fur-lined cloaks and heavy boots, the sunlight shining on their armor—patrolled with grim efficiency, kick-ing the fallen onto their backs in a search for survivors.

Servants followed with carts, gathering the dead and stacking them like firewood in two great piles on the edge of the field.

Scowling, Anoc wished the *mamsas* would rise into sight along the hilltops and cast terrible curses. No *shedas* or *mam-*

sas were among the prisoners, which meant they'd gotten away. That was the only good news he could cling to.

An elbow dug sharply into his sore ribs, making him flinch. "They insult us," Parnak growled, spitting through the gap where his front teeth should have been. "Look yon! No scalps do they gather. No fingers. Are we only animals to them, Anoc, that they take no pride in killing us?"

Still scowling, Anoc let his gaze flicker across the chubby visage of his friend. Parnak's dark eyes were shiny, his mouth set in a grim line. He kept jerking at his bonds although the ropes were too tight and stout to break.

"Why?" Parnak complained. "Why will they give us no honor?"

His whining sent some of Anoc's anger spilling over. "Brave, empty words are worse than no sword in the hand. What good is your courage now, when it does not matter?"

"I am not the one who ran when they smashed our drums," Parnak retorted. "You are!"

"I went into the battle, not away from it."

"If that were true, you'd be dead."

Anoc stared at him haughtily. "I was saved by a god."

Parnak, Shulig, and the other boys laughed.

"It is true," Anoc said defensively. "Shartur-god, arrayed in great glory, came out of the fog and destroyed the arrow meant for my heart. Ostur was not saved. When he fell, I took his sword, and Shartur-god held back the pale-eyes to let me escape."

Shulig sneered, the sunlight glinting on his dirty blond hair. "Oh, hear the Deliverer speak. Tell us, Deliverer, did you see visions when the god appeared before you? Can you smite that guard over there and take his weapons, proving your greatness? Oh, yes, here is our Deliverer, who was to bring us a victory today, and instead has brought us shame and defeat."

Heat flamed through Anoc's face and throat. He found himself choked, with nothing to say.

Holv frowned at Anoc. "How dare you lie and say you saw a god? Be silent. We have no ears for what you say."

Their anger and blame was like a wall. Even Parnak's eyes held accusation as though today's defeat was Anoc's fault.

Anoc stared back, refusing to let them shame him, although inside he was a seething mass of doubt.

He remembered last night, when She Who Made Him retreated from Chank's brave talk of attack and glory, forcing Anoc to leave the gathering with her.

In her tent, she'd worked deep and private magic, the most potent kind of fire and blood. How the heated blood had smoked in the *sheda's* bronze bowl. In the steam rising from its surface, she had bent her seamed and withered face close to peer and mumble, poking here and there into the liquid with her gnarled forefinger. The scent of magic filled the air, and Anoc stayed quiet and alert while the spell woven inside their tent shimmered and glowed with power.

"A legendary king fights us because we shamed him," she said, her rheumy eyes glimmering in the firelight. "He will come and grapple hard with us, and our warriors will not prevail."

Her gnarled, palsied hand, crisscrossed with innumerably tiny white scars from ritual knife cuts, reached out and gently stroked Anoc's dark hair. Seeking comfort, he nuzzled her hand, and after a moment she cut the end of her finger and gave him her blood to suckle.

"Revenge gives this devil king strength," she murmured. "Hatred against us gives him strength. We made use of him long ago, and he cannot forgive us. But his hatred will avail him not, for destiny works against him."

"But are we to win, or lose?" Anoc had asked her in confusion, licking her warm blood from his lips. "Chank says we will win."

When she smiled at him, his senses swam, and he imagined he heard the hiss of serpents and the rattle of dead bones. "There must be an ending in order to create the beginning," she said. "And you are the beginning of this king's ending. Never forget that, my brave Deliverer. Never forget."

As he sat a prisoner, Anoc wished he'd listened more carefully to her prophecy. At the moment, humiliated by shackles, defeat, and the fierce scorn of his companions, it seemed to Anoc that everything he'd believed in was proven false. Instead of victory, there was defeat. Instead of honor, there was death. And how did those things mark an ending to the vic-

torious king, their most despised enemy? At the moment, that
king stood on the next hill, leading his people in rituals.

Suddenly, Anoc felt a jolt of pain stab through his head,
and with it came She Who Made Him's voice, threading its
way through his amazed thoughts, whispering and filling his
skull with the force and vitality of her being: *"It is time for
your destiny, my brave Deliverer. Let no one turn you aside
from your purpose. All I have told you will come to pass."*

The pain made him wince and lift his hand to his temple.
Never had she communicated with him like this since his
birthing. He'd forgotten what it was like, in the misty, barely
remembered times of *before*, when she'd crooned to him,
singing words that shaped his mind and newborn body. This
was not as gentle. Her strength overwhelmed him, threatening to crack his skull.

"Guard your anger," she commanded him. *"You stand in
danger of forgetting your path. Heed me!"*

He gasped aloud, clutching his head with both hands.

Someone gripped his wrist. "Anoc?" Parnak asked. "What
ails you?"

"He's having a fit," Shulig said. "Touch him not."

"Anoc?" Parnak asked worriedly. "Can you speak?"

The *sheda* was too loud in Anoc's mind, beating his
thoughts flat, crushing his will with her own.

"Wait for me to strike," she ordered. *"Be guided by me.
Remember all that I have taught you. Obey!"*

A shattering burst of agony inside his head made him cry
out, then mercifully she was gone. Gasping in relief, he
opened his eyes and found himself lying on his side in the
dirt, shivering and weak. He closed his eyes a moment, swallowing back tears he refused to shed, and finally forced himself to sit up.

The boys watched him.

"When dogs go mad, we kill them," Shulig said cruelly.
"Have you gone mad, Anoc?"

"No," Anoc said fiercely, grinding the heels of his hands
against his burning eyes. "The *sheda* spoke to me."

Some of the younger boys grew round-eyed.

"Oh, I see," Shulig said with a sneer. "First he claimed to
see Shartur-god. Now he hears voices that speak to no one

else. You should have been a girl-child, Anoc, and then we could make a *mamsa* of you."

Rage lit inside Anoc's chest and blazed through him with such heat he nearly lunged at the older boy's throat. As it was, the effort to control himself made him tremble.

"Look at him shaking," Shulig said. "Our Deliverer has no courage without his *sheda* to protect him and tell him what to do."

Glaring, Anoc dared not speak in his own defense, fearing that he might utter a terrible curse and use the magic forbidden to him, magic the *sheda* had taught him in secret. But he was so angry he wanted to seize Shulig by the throat and snap his worthless neck, dig out his eyes, and cut off his lying tongue.

"Coward," Shulig taunted him. "How you boast of deeds no one can see, yet when I make challenge, you fall silent."

"Shut up," Anoc said through clenched teeth. "You deserve a coal on your tongue for speaking ill of the *sheda*—"

"She is too old! Her magic is weak, and we pay the price for it." Shulig gestured violently. "Look what she has brought us."

"The pale-eyes brought this," Anoc protested hotly. "She is—"

Without warning, Shulig launched himself at Anoc and seized him by the throat.

Hampered by his bound hands, Anoc squirmed desperately to free himself from Shulig's grip. The larger boy's fingers were digging in, making the blood hammer and throb in Anoc's throat. He couldn't breathe. Tiny spots danced in his vision.

Desperately he grabbed one of Shulig's thumbs and bent it backward. Swearing, Shulig loosened his grip enough for Anoc to break free. Scrambling to his feet, breathing hard, and trying not to cough, Anoc found himself shaking from rage and reaction. He wanted to kill Shulig.

The pale-eyes started cheering in a deafening roar, all turning in the same direction, and even the guards took their gaze off the prisoners.

Scowling Shulig got to his feet and faced Anoc. Dirt smeared his face, and his eyes blazed with hatred.

"Fool," Anoc said to him. "We must stay united against our enemy, not fight each other."

"Weaklings like you deserve no life," Shulig said. "I will be—"

"We must wait for our chance of escape," Anoc broke in. "This day is not yet finished. Our defeat is not yet certain."

"No? With our chieftains dead?"

But Parnak elbowed Shulig aside. "What are you planning?" he asked eagerly. "What are we to do?"

Anoc wasn't sure the *sheda* would approve of his telling them anything, but he saw no other way to gain their cooperation. "We are to stay quiet and cause no trouble until the *sheda* is ready to strike," he began.

Shulig snorted. "The *sheda* can do nothing. She is not even here."

"Yes, she is!" Torjin cried, jumping up and pointing. "Look!"

They all turned and pressed against the ropes, straining to see.

Hope swelled in Anoc's chest, for he was eager for the *sheda* to unleash her formidable powers. She would free them all, he thought, and kill the pale-eyes king while they escaped. And then . . . and then she would surely proclaim Anoc chieftain. After that, he would form a new kind of army. One that fought together and not in disarray.

But when he saw her coming, his dreams collapsed. For she was not riding a litter borne by her attendant *mamsas*. Instead, she was being carried like a child in the arms of one of the warrior-demons. How tiny and withered she looked. As fragile as a curl of bark burned almost to ash, ready to crumble at too harsh a touch.

Anoc's heart squeezed inside him. She looked so old, so frail. Her white hair hung in its plait over her stooped shoulder. Her hands, misshapen and gnarled, had been bound at the wrists with shackles of fire that did not burn her flesh.

It was the same strange green fire that had been used in battle, spell-fire, some called it. It blazed like an aura around the warrior-demon carrying her, and it hurt Anoc's eyes when he stared too hard at it. Clearly the demon was using his magic to contain the *sheda's*. Worriedly, Anoc watched her as she went by. He wanted to call out to her, but held his tongue.

The other *shedas* and a handful of *mamsas* stumbled along in their wake, herded along by two other warrior-demons. Bonds of flame encircled the hands of all the *shedas*. Their robes were torn and muddy, their hair disheveled, their faces wiped clean of all magical symbols. Their staffs were gone, and their bells and the necklaces of tiny skulls had been stripped away. Some of them shuffled along as though they lacked enough strength to walk. They looked exhausted, and demoralized.

Staring at them in disbelief, Anoc felt certain that something terrible had happened to them, something beyond mere capture. Tears were streaming down the faces of the *mamsas*, and he'd never seen anything like that before.

How, he wondered frantically, had they let themselves be captured? Five *shedas* surely had enough power to unite against any warrior-demons. He'd been expecting She Who Made Him to arrive in a blaze of flame, not to be bound by it, not a *prisoner*.

The females held captive in the enclosure began to wail and scream hysterically. The noise unsettled Anoc even more. He wanted to vault the ropes and hurl himself at the warrior-demon that carried She Who Made Him. He thought he could perhaps free her, or distract the demon enough for her to free herself.

His mind was spinning, and he did not know what to do. Her orders had not included *this*.

"She will save us?" Shulig mocked him. "She will use her magic to free us so we can run away? Oh, yes, now I believe, for thus says the Deliverer."

Anoc turned on him, ready to fight, but just then the *sheda's* voice came into his thoughts:

"Nothing is as it seems. Be ready."

Without realizing it, Anoc nodded.

Parnak gripped his arm. "Quiet!" he whispered to the others. "She's speaking to him again. Anoc, what are we to do?"

Anoc blinked, his vision coming back into focus. He could still feel her presence strong within him, filling him with fresh determination. It was as though she'd given him fresh blood to suckle, and his mind grew clear and cold with purpose.

"Anoc?" Parnak whispered. "Speak to us. Tell us what to do!"

"He can't," Shulig said with scorn. "He's just—"

The warrior-demon gliding along behind the *shedas* shot them a sharp look.

Anoc's heart thudded in his chest. He reached out and gripped Shulig's arm in warning.

The warrior-demon slowed, hovering just slightly above the ground as though it had no feet. It stared hard at them, and Anoc instinctively averted his gaze from those searching yellow eyes. He felt danger all around him, for the magic in this creature hummed with a power that made Anoc's skin crawl. Holding himself as still as a hare attempting to elude a predator, Anoc sensed something trying to finger his mind. Desperately he focused his thoughts on the sword he'd seen just before he was captured. It had been a beautiful, magnificent weapon, exactly what he'd always dreamed of owning, and the carvings on the hilt were extraordinary, beyond anything he'd ever imagined.

A hiss came from the demon, and it turned from him, following the others away.

The danger, momentarily, had passed. Lifting his gaze, Anoc dared breathe. But his relief was overshadowed by worry as he wondered if the demon had read the thoughts of the other boys and knew they meant to try something. *Stupid, stupid, stupid,* he castigated himself. He should have kept silent and found another way to gain their cooperation.

Only then did he notice that all the boys, even Shulig, were staring at him in amazement.

"What?" he asked.

"The demon looked at you and threw his power over you, but you withstood him," Parnak said, round-eyed.

"He commanded you to speak, but you did not," Holv said. "He even pointed at you, until you shimmered."

"I thought he meant to destroy you," Torjin piped up.

"But you did not obey him," Holv finished.

"It's true," Mald said in awe. "You *are* the Deliverer."

Shulig shook his head. "The power of the *shedas* protected Anoc. That's what you saw."

The sound of trumpets distracted Anoc from what they were saying. He saw the men stirring in the crowd, noticed the guards coming to attention. Everything around him seemed to sharpen, as though tremendous energy were converging on this moment of time. *I must not fail her,* he thought, aware that he still had much to do.

"Be quiet!" he said sharply to the other boys, cutting off their chatter. "Stand ready and watch."

"For what?" Shulig demanded.

"It is time," Anoc replied. He turned as the crowd parted to reveal the pale-eyes king coming on horseback. "Time for Faldain's reckoning, exactly as our *sheda* has planned it."

Chapter Nine

❧⟡❧

Dain stood impassively as the *shedas* were brought before him. Bound with spell-fire that blazed around their wrists and throats to keep them from casting magic, the women were filthy and disheveled, their eyes stabbing hatred. All three of Dain's battle *sorcerels* hovered close by, and the very air crawled with the conflicting forces of magic.

Omas edged closer to Dain's side, mumbling under his mustache, his drawn sword held ready. The rest of Dain's personal guard stood tense and alert nearby.

Vaunit came up, yellow eyes ablaze, mouth drawn to a thin line. The *sorcerel* smelled of smoke and magic. An aura of power shimmered upon his skin and sparked from the tips of his fingers and ears.

Warily Dain acknowledged him with a nod, suspecting that the *sorcerels* had not found it easy to capture the *shedas*, or to subdue them. Like all creatures of magic, *sorcerels* did not mix easily with humans, and when they had expended their powers for too long a time—as in today's battle—the risks associated with them increased. Magic built upon magic, one kind feeding the other, and whether used for good or ill, such potent forces could blend together if not properly controlled. Usually right after a battle, the *sorcerels* vanished in order to calm and settle themselves, and to avoid trouble with the men.

Perhaps, Dain thought, it would have been more prudent not to insist on confronting the *shedas* so soon. Except that he wanted everything finished.

The *sorcerel* swept his hand toward the bound and gagged *shedas* but spoke not.

Eight women stood before Dain, the *shedas* distinguished from their attendants by necklaces of tiny skulls and miniature bells of brass that tinkled and clacked with their movements. From their unwashed heads to their garish robes to the disfiguring mutilation scars on their bare arms, they were scrawny, weathered hags. By appearance alone, they barely looked to be any kind of threat at all. But Dain knew better. Standing there, even subdued by the power of the *sorcerels*, their magic wove together, combining into a force that hummed among them. It made his skin prickle.

"Vaunit," he said, "you have done well in bringing these women to me."

Vaunit inclined his head slightly; his yellow eyes were ablaze. "They are held," he said, "but still they attempt to work their spells. Let this end quickly."

The warning was clear. Casting the *sorcerel* a sharp look, Dain faced the assembly of his army, the priests, the prisoners, and this small cluster of *shedas* and *mamsas*. The air grew rife with anticipation, but he did not hurry as one by one he met the gaze of each *sheda*. The women looked furious.

Death/death/death/death . . . their chant of hatred flooded his thoughts before Vaunit lifted his hands and shielded Dain from the rest.

The air smelled burned and foul. Worried murmurs rose from the knights.

Dain gestured for silence. When he had it, he spoke in a loud, clear voice:

"As I have slain the body of this tribe, so let Vaunit, Tulmahrd, and Moboth destroy its heart. So let the powers of these *shedas* come to an end. So let their influence die."

Then he repeated the order in Gantese, next in Saelutian,

then in a Kladite dialect, then in Mandrian, then in the dwarf speak of Nold, and finally in harsh, guttural Grethori.

Several of the male prisoners jerked to their feet although it was the women and not the men who cried out protests. The younger *shedas* stared at Dain as though in shock, while the oldest among them, the ancient, withered crone who had brought him such harm, tipped back her head and rocked from side to side in silent laughter.

"Let the power of the *shedas* be broken to dust and ashes," Dain said, while Vaunit began to swirl a spell around the five. "Let the force of their magic be forever destroyed, theirs to command no longer. Let the mysteries of the Grethori Adauri fade from all knowledge forevermore. From the youngest to the oldest, let their magic die."

At the end of his pronouncement, a cheer rose from the knights, although several drew hasty signs of the Circle, and the priests clustered closer together, looking torn between disapproval at so pagan a rite and an eagerness to see it done.

For his part, Dain hid his distaste at what was to come and forced himself to watch impassively and without mercy, the sunshine gleaming on his armor, his stance assured and kingly. It was a sovereign's responsibility to dispense punishment and vengeance publicly, to remind his subjects of his authority and might. A man custom that his eld heritage deplored, but Dain had chosen to live as a man and king; therefore, he did not shirk what was required. He knew that for the rest of their miserable lives as slaves and laborers, this small group of prisoners would remember Faldain, their conqueror, and how he had smashed them, and would again if they tried to cause future trouble.

Vaunit and the other two *sorcerels* singled out a *sheda* and converged on her. One of the *mamsas* tried to throw herself between them, but green fire shot from Vaunit's fingers and knocked her sprawling.

Meanwhile, Tulmahrd and Moboth entwined sparking ropes of fire around the first victim until she was engulfed by their spell. She writhed and shuddered, her mouth stretching wide in a silent scream. Vaunit began chanting something awful, the words incomprehensible but discordant and disturbing.

The officers and guards around Dain moved restlessly, many of them frowning or averting their gaze.

When a black vapor streamed from the *sheda's* nostrils, Vaunit shouted something that made Dain's ears hurt, and the cloud exploded in a shower of foul-smelling ashes.

The other *sorcerels* spoke in triumph, and abruptly the spell-flames surrounding the *sheda* vanished. She swayed on her feet a moment, wide-eyed and ashen of face, before she crumpled to her knees and began to sob.

Wails of consternation rose from the Grethori women, but already the *sorcerels* were singling out the next *sheda*. It went as before, one at a time, with some of the *shedas* crying afterward, some stunned witless, and one screaming hysterically until she was struck unconscious. When Vaunit turned to the old crone, however, Dain held up his hand.

"Wait," he commanded. "The *mamsas* before her."

It was done as he wished, then she alone remained unbroken. The air stank of ashes, but whatever the *shedas* had been weaving was gone. The only remaining magic Dain could sense was that belonging to the *sorcerels*, and he relaxed slightly.

"Bring her forward," he said, ignoring the urgently whispered protests from his aides. "Vaunit, permit her to speak."

The *sorcerel* flicked his fingers in the old *sheda's* direction, and the binding flames around her throat faded away.

Leaning close to Dain's ear, Omas said, "Sire, take care! She could cast a curse on you."

Dain glanced at him impatiently. "I am well protected by my faith, yourself, and Vaunit. Why need I fear this woman?"

"Any creature is dangerous when cornered," Omas said. "I beg your majesty not to toy with her. Let it be ended, and quickly."

Frowning, Dain turned away from his protector. "Permit her to approach me."

Shoved forward, the *sheda* hobbled slowly on her crippled feet. She was stooped nearly double, her spine and shoulders so twisted with age they rendered her pathetic. Toothless and nearly blind, she sucked at her gums and mumbled to herself. But when she halted before him and lifted her seamed face, there was nothing senile about her gaze.

"Hail, Faldain, king of the wicked!" she called out in Grethori.

Omas raised his sword. "Thod smite her, but she dares already to curse your majesty!"

"Stop!" Dain ordered before the protector could attack. "'Tis impudence only. We have old scores to settle."

Omas's brown eyes pleaded with him. "Put an end to her magic, *then* talk to her."

But Dain wasn't sure this feeble old hag would survive the ordeal. Although he cared not whether she lived or died, he meant to have the last word with her.

Waving aside the nervous translator who came forth, Dain chose to speak to her directly in Grethori, for what he had to say to her was private and bitter.

"Look well, old woman. I swore I would put an end to your people, and I have."

"I have given them their beginning," she replied.

"Ah, more Grethori bravado, as empty as the wind," he said, forcing contempt into his tone. "No Deliverer saved your warriors or sister *shedas* today. Your prophecies are lies, old woman. In making me your enemy, you have led your people to their doom."

She smiled toothlessly. "If I am lies and no hope is left, then what is *this*?"

As she spoke, a vision filled his mind, one of a youth tall and straight, clad in Grethori war paint but swinging a sword of Netheran make and riding a warhorse instead of a stubby pony. Something about the young man looked familiar to Dain, but abruptly the vision vanished from his mind.

Jerking open his eyes, Dain saw Vaunit clutching the *sheda* by her white hair and shaking her hard enough to snap her frail old bones.

Orange fire shot from her misshapen hands, only to be burned up by Vaunit's green flames. She uttered a choked bleat of pain and subsided, her struggles spent. The air reeked anew of magic.

"Now I finish you," Vaunit growled.

"Wait!" Dain said sharply, and the *sorcerel* turned on him with such menace that Omas stepped between them.

"Desist," Dain commanded. "This vision, what . . ."

Her sly, cunning smile made him break off in realization that she was manipulating his curiosity, toying with him.

"Lies," he said harshly. "Your trickery avails nothing, for I do not believe what you've shown me."

"You believe," she retorted, still smiling. "But you depend too much on what is fragile. Which of your children can you trust?"

His anger roared up like hot oil thrown on flames. "Never again will you meddle with my family!"

"Are you so certain, great king?" she taunted softly. "My hand has been on your woman, on you, and on your children. All your great armies cannot change what is, what was, and what will be."

"You've paid my price," Dain said, gesturing at the battle-field and the slain. "Was the destruction of your people worth it? Was the life of my son worth the death of so many of yours?"

"Only one son fills your mind, Faldain. You are blind to all the rest. That makes you a fool."

"Perhaps," he replied. "But I am victor here."

She flicked him a contemptuous glance. "All that has been done here will come back to you tenfold, pale-eyes king, for you have sown the seeds of your people's destruction. All your coin, pride, armor, and horses will not save them. The Deliverer has seen all, and he will not forget. Your vengeance is feeble, but his will be great."

A ragged chorus of defiant yells rose from the prisoners.

Dain's brows knotted together. "The Deliverer is a myth, a lie."

"He is real! He will come!" she shouted.

"Why does he not stand with you now? Why does he hide?"

"You are blind and will never find him." Her gaze stabbed scorn at Vaunit. "And this demon you command cannot sift my thoughts and learn where he is. When he leads the upris-ing that is to come—"

"There will be no future uprising, old woman," Dain said with a shrug, tired of her lies. "And your prophecies are over."

"There is only one thing left between us, pale-eyes king,"

she replied, her face alight with madness. "One last act to seal what is to come. I am ready to die, Faldain. Are you?"

As she spoke, she suddenly pointed her gnarled finger at him. Something invisible struck his chest with enough force to rock him off-balance. Caught by surprise, he went staggering back, as though unhorsed by a jousting lance, and fell sprawling.

Shouts rose around him. Omas was already moving, roaring out a furious oath while he plunged his sword through the *sheda's* body.

She screeched a shrill, almost breathless cry, her rheumy eyes opening wide. Omas shoved her off his blade, and she fell in a small, crumpled heap on the ground.

Dain felt something black roar through his senses, buffeting him. It was as though he'd been caught up inside a twisting, malevolent wind that pummeled and deafened him. He struggled against it to no avail, faintly aware of commotion and shouting. He heard the boom of spell-fire cast too close, felt the singe of it scorch his face. The wind inside him vanished, and for an instant he sensed Vaunit next to him, calling out words he did not understand.

Even so, he was not free of whatever she'd flung at him. Unable to see or hear, he lay in darkness like a moth caught in a spider's web, and knew no more.

Anoc screamed as She Who Made Him fell. Her pain engulfed him. Her death was his death. For a moment he knew nothing, then he found himself swimming back to a place of sunlight and wind. He was sitting on the ground, shivering and dazed, as though his legs had buckled beneath him. The other boys stood clustered nearby in shocked silence before Parnak dared to grip his shoulder.

"They will kill us all," Parnak said in a soft moan, as wails from the broken *shedas* and other females filled the air. "We will all be slaughtered."

"No!" Shulig shouted. "This is our chance. Let us attack and fight our way free."

Anoc knew he should be shouting those words. He should be leading the boys forward and yelling the curse she'd taught him. She was to strike at the king, then he was to help their escape, but he could not move. He felt instead as though he'd floated far away and could barely hear the fierce arguments of the boys. All he could see was the face of She Who Made Him. She'd created him, raised him, fed him, and loved him. She'd given him everything; all that she was and did had been his world.

In all her preparations, she had never mentioned that she would die.

He'd had no warning, and now he sat in shock, unable to believe her gone. Was the death of the pale-eyes king worth hers? He did not think so. Unbearable, empty loneliness ached inside him.

Parnak knelt close by and began to rock back and forth, just like the females who were dropping to their knees and tearing their hair, lifting their voices in the grief chants.

"It's over for us," Parnak said, his voice shrill and ragged. "She has killed their king. They will slay us all."

As though to prove him right, the pale-eyes knights rushed at the prisoners, beating the females and shouting until they fell silent. The other *shedas* were shoved into the enclosure, while more knights gathered around the fallen king, and he was borne away in their arms, his dark head lolling.

Standing near the ropes, Shulig spat his contempt. One of the guards struck him so hard he fell sprawling and did not move. More guards crowded around, yelling and shaking their fists, a mob ready to draw weapons and slay all the prisoners.

Parnak yelled in shrill panic, and little Torjin began to cry. The hysteria was catching, spreading through Grethori and Netherans alike. Out on the battlefield, the piles of bodies were set on fire. Flames blazed high, billowing forth black smoke. Anoc watched, motionless and grim, while the bodies of the chieftains and She Who Made Him were carried out there and flung onto the flames. A small explosion went off when fire touched the *sheda's* body. But although the pale-eyes stumbled back, swearing and calling on their gods, her corpse did not arise as Anoc found himself hoping. She vanished in the fire, her frail body swiftly consumed.

He felt cold and sick and lost. This was not what he'd expected. He did not know what to do.

After a while, the officers came and restored order among the knights. A rumor circulated among the prisoners that the king was not dead, only stunned. But the mood of the pale-eyes remained ugly.

Anoc bowed his head in despair. That news was even worse, for it meant her death had been in vain, as everything today had been in vain. Surely the gods had turned their faces away from the people, to bring them so low.

Still, to the very last She Who Made Him had shown great courage, while he had taken no action at all. However futile, he should have tried to obey her instructions. Instead, he sat like a whipped dog and felt ashamed. This day was worse than *dralaig*, and he was no Deliverer, for nothing had he accomplished. Nothing.

"No more *shedas* to guide us," Parnak said hollowly. "She was the very last, Anoc."

The words echoed inside him: *the last, the last, the last.* "I know."

"What is to become of us? How can we keep the ways or the mysteries? We are lost. We might as well be dead, too."

Anoc had no answer for him. The death fires sent a horrible stench into the air, and he did not care. At sunset, food was flung at the prisoners, but Anoc did not eat. He hungered for a blood potion the way She Who Made Him prepared them. He hungered for *her.*

She had not yet weaned him from her blood although of late she'd been muttering that he must learn to feed himself. He always coaxed her with melting looks of entreaty and little smiles until she relented. Too late, he understood that her instincts had been wise. He should have been prepared for her death, and strong enough to survive on his own.

Instead, he felt helpless, like a blind pup abandoned by its she-wolf mother. Without the *sheda*, he knew he would die.

Feeling helpless and stricken, he shivered in the cool twilight air, remembering how she always talked to him as though he were her equal and could understand all that she said. She had hidden none of the mysteries from him, nor did she conceal her knowledge of magic when they were private together. And she had stirred many visions in his mind. Always, from the hour of his birth, had she believed in his destiny. Often had she expressed her pride in him, not to spoil him, but to make his spirit strong. Every night she'd fed him blood and sung him to sleep, her scarred fingers stroking his hair, her love for him a steadfast comfort.

Without her, I am nothing, he thought.

"Anoc," Parnak said softly in the gloom. "I have saved some of this grain for you. It is not meat, but food is food. Eat it."

Anoc said nothing. He did not look at his friend.

A hand curled around his fingers and squeezed them. "Anoc," Parnak said, "I heard that the king lives. That means we will be sold and not die."

"I thought he was Shartur-god," Anoc said dully. "I saw him in the battle. He saved my life, and I thought he was a god."

"The pale-eyes king is like no other man," Parnak said. "Who could blame you for such a mistake?"

"She made magic from him while he was her prisoner and from that was I born," Anoc said, unheeding. "But I saw what I wanted and heeded not what was foretold. I believed we would have victory. She said we would not, but I did not understand. And when the warrior-demon looked at me, he did not recognize me. Was she protecting me, even then, or is everything a falsehood?"

"He's rambling, gone from his wits," Parnak said worriedly. "What are we to do?"

"He's in shock," Shulig said. "Had she not weaned him?"

"I don't know."

The boys conferred, then there was a rustle of cloth, and someone pressed close against Anoc's shoulder.

"My blood is yours," Mald whispered. "I swear to serve the Deliverer with whatever is needed. Drink of me, and be strong again."

The smell of blood in the boy's wound roused Anoc from his stupor. He hesitated, before putting his tongue to Mald's shoulder. The blood tasted strange, ordinary. Disliking it, Anoc started to draw back, but a terrible hunger rose up in him, one too urgent to withstand.

And She Who Made Him whispered in his mind, *"Take what is given. Use what is offered. Survive! You are the beginning of Faldain's ending. Never forget that. Be brave, for I am with you still."*

The hatred of Netherans he'd known all his life hardened into something black, deep, vicious, and cold. His thoughts went to the pale-eyes king—a man so strong and powerful, a man so extraordinary that Anoc had mistaken him for a god—and the blackness inside Anoc coiled into determination.

"Saving my life was a mistake you will regret," he vowed.

His destiny had begun today, exactly as she'd foretold. Anoc understood now that it was not a gift or a right, but something fierce and terrible, something to be fought for, and fought for hard.

He felt as though he had left his childhood behind. Gone were his silly fancies of picking up a sword and leading the warriors to miraculous victory. He had changed, taken a step into the harsh realities of life, and there was no going back.

"I shall return to Nether and walk again the territory of my people," he swore silently. *"In her name, which is never to be spoken, I curse you, pale-eyes king, and all your get. I spit on you with the poison of a viper. I am your doom, and I shall learn your every weakness and stab it. I shall hunt you down as you have hunted us. No matter how far away you send my people, I shall lead them back. And I shall make you pay."*

Tears streamed down his cheeks, while in silence he pressed his mouth to Mald's wound and drank deep.

Chapter Ten

Dain ran for his life, arms and legs pumping, his breath sawing in his throat. A pack of hurlhounds pursued him silently.

They were gaining.

Although he tried to quicken his speed, he was nearly spent. He did not know how long he'd been running, or how he came to be there afoot and alone, but there wasn't time to remember. Fatigue burned his legs, making him stumble, which cost him more of the precious distance he had on his pursuers.

Glancing back, he saw they'd gained even more. They would catch him soon if he didn't double back or outwit them in some way. But there was no cover, no trees or undergrowth to hide in, no gullies or ditches, no streams to splash through to conceal his scent.

He ran through open country, his feet crunching over a thin crust of snow, before he slid across an icy patch and lost his footing. Although he avoided falling, he wrenched his knee hard enough to shoot pain up his leg. Gasping, he struggled on, the pain increasing with every step. With running impossible, he slowed to a hobble, moaning a little and swearing under his breath, before he was forced to stop.

Wincing, he shifted his weight off his throbbing leg and looked back again. The hurlhounds were still coming, black blurs coursing fast through the falling snow.

Catch/catch/catch/catch!

Kill/kill/kill!

The hot force of their minds nearly overpowered him. Gritting his teeth, he tried to run on but managed only two staggering steps before his injured knee gave under him.

Despair and fear clawed at him as he climbed back on his feet and turned at bay to face death. *Where is this place?* he wondered. *How came I here? Why am I to die alone?*

A howl rose on the air, and the pack slowed down just before it reached him.

Shivering with cold and squinting against the tiny spits of snow, Dain looked for the Believer directing these beasts, but saw no one. Gloomy twilight closed in; the falling snow reduced visibility even more.

He had no weapons to fight with, no salt in his pocket. There was not a stone to be found, not even a stick to serve as a feeble club. He lacked spurs or a cloak or gloves, items he could have used in defense. He knew not how he came to be there, without horse, men at arms, or armor.

When he counted perhaps a dozen of the huge, black-coated hounds, his heart sank at the odds. One or two he would have fought, but to be outnumbered by so many . . . morde, if only he had a weapon.

But suddenly he wasn't so certain they were hurlhounds, for they had yellow eyes instead of red, and black fur instead of oily scales. They were taller than hurlhounds and leaner, with upright ears and pointed muzzles.

"Thod's mercy," he whispered aloud in astonishment. "Wolves!" The largest he'd ever seen.

He sent his mind toward theirs, seeking enough control to dissuade them from attack.

But although a short time ago he'd felt their hot, primitive minds, now something kept him from touching them. As they slowed and surrounded him, he found no sense of them at all. Puzzled, he warily turned about. All beings, even the

Nonkind beasts, had a center of consciousness that could be touched. What was shielding them from him?

Were they shapeshifters? If so, he should still be able to sense them.

Were they illusion? he wondered.

They *looked* real as they paced around him, growling with hackles raised and fangs bared. He could not smell their scent, however.

Swearing softly to himself, he battled his confusion in an effort to stay calm. If a sight spell were being used on him, then they were illusion and could do him no harm. But dared he take the chance of not fighting them? If they were real, he might well be killed in a matter of moments.

Trying to decide, he looked for the pack leader, but none of the animals acted dominant over the others. Taking care to make no sudden movement that might provoke them, he grew heartened by their inaction. If they meant to attack him, he thought, wouldn't they have done so already?

"Illusion," he said firmly.

When he spoke, they all stopped circling him and stood frozen, staring intently at him with their intelligent yellow eyes.

It seemed to be an impasse, but Dain gathered his breath and sang of claws and teeth, of fur and hunting.

The wolves watched him as though fascinated. Heartened, he continued his song, weaving the simple illusion spell to make himself look wolfish, then limped forward, intending to pass through their circle.

As soon as he took a step, however, one of the wolves immediately crouched low, its belly almost dragging the ground, its muscles rippling beneath the heavy black fur. It sprang at him.

There was no time to regret his mistake. With a yell, Dain tried to dodge the attacking wolf, but it was too fast. The animal hit him hard, and knocked him backward to the ground with a jolt that snapped his teeth together. Pinning him, the heavy wolf went for his throat.

Desperately Dain tried to fend off the animal, and searing pain ripped through his forearm. He cried out, gripping handfuls of furred hide to hold back snapping jaws. The animal pawed him, ripping his clothing, and lunged so hard it nearly broke free of his hold. As its hot, fetid breath steamed against Dain's face, he felt his strength giving way.

A voice shouted nearby with deep authority.

Yelping, the wolf leaped off Dain and backed away.

Gasping for breath, Dain floundered a moment, his pale blood splattering the snow. As he struggled to sit up, he looked around for whoever had come to his aid, but saw no one save an enormous white wolf—its fur tipped with the faintest hue of gold—confronting the pack. The black wolves growled and snapped, showing their teeth, but the white wolf stood its ground.

When it howled, the sound hurt Dain's ears. The black wolves slunk away, vanishing into the gloomy snowfall like shadows.

Not sure what was happening, Dain glanced back at the white wolf, but it, too, had vanished.

Then his surroundings shimmered, and he found himself lying on his back in a gloomy place lit only by a single torch. Even moonlight would have been brighter than the dim and dreary illumination around him. Dain's eyes ached from the strain of trying to peer through the murk to see where he was. He smelled stone and rushes . . . a permanent dwelling.

If I'm dreaming, he thought, *'tis very odd.*

Even thinking left him feeling immensely weak and tired, drained to his very depths.

Soft chanting began, startling him.

Someone knelt beside him, brown head bowed as though in prayer. Other individuals stood in a ring around Dain. They were the ones chanting, he realized. Although the gloomy shadows concealed them, he thought he glimpsed the sleeve banding of a priestly robe. Sensing nothing harmful or menacing there, he relaxed, drifting away.

It seemed only a moment later that he awakened, but when he did he found more lamps lit. Fires were crackling merrily in several braziers, although he could not feel their heat.

Another illusion, like the wolves, he thought wearily.

He was so cold he could not shiver. His body seemed made of stone, immovable and dead. Dreams did not hurt this much, he thought. He supposed he must be injured and dying, but he could not remember why.

Vaunit flickered into sight beside him. The *sorcerel* reached his hands across Dain's body, never touching him, but making complex gestures in the air. And all the while his movements caused him to fade in and out, sometimes half-seen, other times completely invisible. He hummed in an odd tone that was discordant with the chanting.

Dain found himself wanting to hum along in unison, but the effort proved too great. Closing his eyes, he did not try.

"Faldain," Vaunit said, his voice faint and far away. "Faldain."

It was too much trouble to listen.

"Faldain!"

Dain came swimming up from so far away the dreadful cold did not matter. He came back angry, because he did not want to be aware of his misery again. He felt terribly tired. He wanted to be left alone.

"Faldain! Faldain!"

He opened his eyes. The priests stood nearby, while Vaunit bent over Dain. The *sorcerel's* elongated fingers were spread apart and pressing down hard on Dain's heart.

Blinking slowly, Dain focused his gaze on Vaunit's yellow eyes. "White wolf," he said weakly.

The *sorcerel* looked startled. "You saw?"

"Thank . . . you."

"Ah!" Vaunit said in a tone of great satisfaction, and took away his hand.

Released from the *sorcerel's* touch, Dain felt lighter, no longer made of stone. Relieved, he drew in a deep breath.

Vaunit looked around. "He is once more among us."

A confusing babble of voices rose up, and many people rushed at Dain from all sides, calling to him in an overlapping blur of noise that made his head ache. Their emotions overwhelmed him, and he tensed in alarm, for he was unable to protect himself.

Fortunately someone intervened, sending them away. They went unwillingly, their noises louder than ever.

After a moment, all grew quiet, and a single voice—trembling with suppressed emotion—whispered, "Sire?"

Sighing, Dain found himself looking up into Omas's haggard face. Dark circles under the protector's eyes told of sleepless nights and worry.

"Omas," Dain said in a feeble voice, and tried to smile.

The huge man choked out something inaudible and clutched Dain's hand, kissing it. When he looked up, his brown eyes held the sheen of tears. "Tomias be praised," he whispered. "We feared you lost to us forever."

Dain wanted to ask him what had happened, but it suddenly seemed like too much trouble.

Omas was moved aside then, and the priest Sovlin appeared in his place. A gray-haired man with a kindly face and calm eyes, Sovlin gave Dain a blessing, then pulled a small vial of silver from his sleeve.

"Will your majesty consent to take Chalice water?" he asked.

Dain was drifting again, tired and cold, but he managed a vestige of a nod. Omas gently lifted his shoulders, steadying his head, while Sovlin pressed the vial to his lips.

One tiny swallow was all Dain could manage. He sank into oblivion, barely aware of Omas's lowering him and asking the priest a question. Sovlin's voice, a soothing murmur without distinguishable words, was the last thing Dain heard.

Thereafter, he roused in a bed large enough to hold a village. Massive and black with age, the bed was piled with woolen blankets and fur robes to such an extent that Dain could barely move beneath them. A fire blazed on the hearth, warming the room, which was sparsely furnished, its unadorned walls constructed of simply hewn stone. Sunlight glinted around the edges of closed shutters.

Feeling hungry but disinclined to move, Dain listened to the sounds of drill commands being shouted outdoors and the steady tramp of feet. Lord Ivar walked quietly back and forth across the opposite end of the room, his head bowed in thought, but no one else was present.

"Ivar," Dain called softly.

With a start, the protector spun around and rushed to his side. "Your majesty!" he said gladly. "Let me call your attendants—"

"Stay a moment. This place. Where—"

"Nabov Hold. We brought your majesty back several days past. We thought—we feared—oh, sire, I am *glad* to see you so much better."

Dain found a smile for him, and said, "Food."

"Yes, of course. At once!"

After that, servants and aides filled the room until Dain regretted calling for them. He was given food and watched anxiously while he ate it. The physician came and went, a thin individual with a pointed beard and sly eyes. His long robes smelled too pungently of herbs. Reminded unpleasantly of Sulein, the physician at Thirst Hold who used to tutor him and try to pry into his secrets, Dain refused to swallow the potion prepared for him.

Rof, holding his writing box, perched on a stool and read portions of dispatches and reports until Chesil—wounded arm supported in a sling—made him leave so the king could rest.

By nightfall, Dain felt more himself, except for remaining chilled. Sitting next to the fire, attired in warm velvet and wrapped in fur, he permitted Sovlin a private audience.

The priest seated himself at the king's bidding and smiled in his gentle way. "It is good to see your majesty looking so improved."

"Thank you." Dain glanced at the door where Lord Ivar stood remote and impassive. "Let us not waste time with courtesies. I seek honest answers to my questions, not comforting."

"Your majesty wants to know what happened."

Dain frowned. "I remember the *sheda's* attack. They say I have lain unconscious for eight days."

"Yes, your majesty. We feared very much for your life."

"But Vaunit saved me?"

Sovlin hesitated, staring at his fingertips. "Yes, although I think our prayers helped as well."

Dain smiled politely. His dream about the wolves remained vivid in his mind. There had been magic done to draw him back to the land of the living, and he wanted to ask Vaunit more about it. "I am grateful to you and the other priests for your efforts."

Sovlin inclined his head.

"Has the old *sheda's* mischief done me lasting harm?" Dain asked.

"We fear so."

"Explain, please. She has thrown her magic at me before and availed not."

Sovlin frowned. "I understood your majesty escaped Grethori hands some years past with a serious fever—"

Dain gestured impatiently. "A small illness, nothing significant. Why is this different?"

Sovlin sighed with a little shrug. "It is, perhaps, a trifle premature to discuss this matter. The physicians attending your majesty feel it best to wait until we have returned to Grov before—"

"Don't evade me, Sovlin. 'Tis unworthy of you."

"Very well. The curse she used is a strange and peculiar one, drawn from very old magic, but not typical of the usual Grethori paganism."

"Adauri magic?" Dain asked. "Know you aught of such?"

"No, I am not trained in the primitive versions," the priest replied without apology. "But I would guess that it is not even that. Eld, perhaps?"

"Eld! But—"

"No explanation, sire. 'Tis only my theory. I do not understand it, nor do I know how it got past Vaunit's protections around you. All we can do at this point is watch you carefully, advise plenty of rest, and hope—"

A laugh suddenly broke from Dain. "Good priest, I have survived Nonkind venom, stabs from magicked blades, spells, poison, and countless wounds. If there's no more to this than—"

"Please, sire. This peril must not be dismissed." Sovlin pulled a silver vial from his sleeve. "Your majesty should partake of this daily until we reach Grov."

"Chalice water? But that's for—"

Sovlin placed his hand on Dain's arm. "Gently, your majesty. Do not become agitated."

"'Tis for those in extremis," Dain said in a hollow voice. "Those dying."

"I have every confidence that once we reach Grov, your

majesty's health will be completely restored. This"—Sovlin
held up the vial—"will keep your majesty alive until then."

Dain shifted restlessly. "Morde! My vengeance repaid.
How her ghost must be laughing."

"Vengeance has a way of going awry," Sovlin said gently.
"But let your majesty remember that the *sheda* is dead while
you are not."

Dain gave him a grim little smile.

"Take comfort in your faith, sire. In a few days if you continue to improve, we shall set forth to Grov in easy stages."

Dain started to speak, but Sovlin held up his hands. "Your
majesty has capable officers and staff. Allow them to take
charge of your army while you concentrate solely on recu-
peration. Back in Grov, once your majesty has consulted with
your eld healers, as is your wont, and drunk deeply from the
holy spring, you should be fully restored to health."

"Should," Dain said sharply. "Have you no stronger assurance?"

"Your majesty requested honesty."

Their eyes met, and Dain felt the breath leave his lungs. *No,*
he thought in disbelief, *I will not let the old crone destroy me.*

"I have tired your majesty. That was not my intention."

When Sovlin took his leave, Dain slumped in his chair,
staring blindly at the fire. His emotions were chaotic. Nothing seemed quite real. He remembered asking the *sheda* if the
price her people had paid was worthwhile. Now he looked at
his own reckoning, and found it steep indeed.

Dying . . . it did not seem possible. But he reminded himself that he was not dead yet, nor would he let the crone's
curse best him. Her evil, he vowed, would not prevail.

But he found himself shivering, and no matter how vigor-
ously the fire blazed, he felt none of its warmth.

PART II

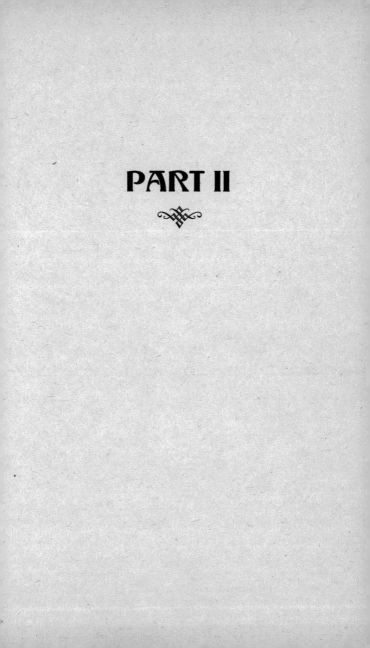

Chapter Eleven

To the somber beating of drums, the procession carrying the
bones of General Ilymir Volvn passed a slovenly village of
bewildered serfs, crossed a shallow stream, and ascended a
hill to the gates of Volvn Castle. There, steward, servants, and
knights awaited the return of the fortress's former lord and
master.

Riding a gray palfrey, Alexeika, queen of Nether, looked
discreetly about her, drinking in the sights of her birthplace,
a home she'd never truly known. *The younger ones do not
know or care,* she thought, watching the faces of the people.
But some of the older ones remember him.

Her gaze shifted to the forbidding stone walls towering
high atop the hill. Vines grew over their base in a choked
thicket that concealed the moat—long since allowed to go
dry. The massive gates, thick enough to withstand a battering
ram, stood wide open in welcome. Even so, it was a grim-
looking place, designed for war and defense.

Alexeika rode surrounded by her entourage of ladies-in-
waiting, advisers, aides, priests, and fifty of the Queen's
Guards wearing their distinctive cloaks of pale gray with her

coat of arms embroidered on their surcoats. Since last winter, when her claim of dispossession had finally been acknowledged and the deed of ownership granted officially to her husband, who privately put it into her hands, she had been planning this day.

With Faldain off to war, the children settled to their lessons, the arrival of Prince Guierre of Mandria as yet weeks away, Alexeika had set forth on her quest, returning to the battlefield where her father had died. Despite the span of years, the bones of the fallen lay little disturbed, moldering away in rusted heaps of armor overgrown with grass and vines.

Respectfully they gathered the general's remains, the priests blessing the pale, clean, weathered bones before they were placed inside a wooden coffer, and to Volvn Castle had they journeyed, bringing him home at last.

A command rang out from the castle ramparts, and the general's pennon was raised atop the tower, where it unfurled proudly in the warm spring sunshine.

"Volvn!" the knights cheered. "Volvn!"

Although she had not wept for him in years, her throat choked with emotion.

It did not matter just then that none of these hire-lances had ever served under her father. The shouts of respect would have pleased him.

She rode beneath the portcullis, through the narrow gateway, and into the bailey. Her first impression was of grim gray stone everywhere, forming the walls of the buildings, the steps leading into the keep, the paving stones of the yard. The shod hooves of the horses rang out and echoed off the walls. Although everything looked in order, and she could not fault the line of knights standing at crisp attention with swords raised, her keen eye noted cracks and crumbling, the sagging roofline of the north wing, and evidence of fire charring the stable windows. Tiny dried suckers dotted the surface of the chapel walls and door lintel, where vines had been pulled away. Wasps buzzed in drowsy counterpoint to the drone of flies, and the warm air smelled of freshly pulled weeds and the hog pen.

Among those standing gathered at the steps were Count

Chechnvy, governor of the treasury, several lords of the royal court with their lady wives, and Archduke Poultan Rvin, who had once been her father's closest friend. His appearance today, despite his obviously frail health, showed tremendous honor to her father, and Alexeika gave him a gracious nod.

The priest stood at the doorway of the chapel, waiting while his assistants stepped forward with swinging braziers of incense to surround the wagon containing the general's remains.

When Alexeika dismounted, her ladies hurried to straighten the folds of her gown and lightweight cloak. A straying end of her veil was tucked back beneath the heavy coil of her hair, to cover it as was proper, and a roll of Writ was placed in her hand.

She gave a nod, and her attendants parted to allow her to walk into the chapel. The knights carrying the coffer placed it before the altar, which was already alight with burning Element candles. As the priest took his place there, Alexeika was ushered into a wooden pew carved with the Volvn coat of arms. Her protector, Sir Pyron, positioned himself just outside the confines of the pew. Lady Nadilya placed a small velvet pillow atop the kneeling ledge for her use, while Lady Emila settled next to the queen with a small brass bowl of salt.

Smelling of mouse, the chapel was a small, gloomy place, fitted with the magnificent family pew and a double row of rustic benches for the use of servants and knights. The ceiling was perhaps rather fine, but its carving and strap work were obscured by years of grime. At any rate, Alexeika reminded herself that she was not there to gander at architecture but to show respect for her father.

Bowing her head as the service began, she tried to focus on what the priest was saying, but her mind kept straying to memories of her father and their life among the rebel forces. *That* had been the home she knew, that camp among the fjords up by the World's Rim. This castle, a place she'd yearned to see all her life, was awakening no memories. She felt no familiarity with it at all, except through what her father had described. Yet he'd never talked much about the place, perhaps because he was too pragmatic to dwell on what had been taken from him, or perhaps because it hurt too much.

The service ended. The salt was cast. A heavy slab of stone was shifted aside and the wooden coffer lowered into it. When the slab was replaced, and Alexeika went to stand beside it, she saw a dim, much-worn carving of some distant ancestor, his features indistinguishable. The Volvn coat of arms was carved beside him, and below that ran the family motto.

Crouching, she traced her fingers over the chiseled words, whispering them to herself. She had done right, she knew, in persisting with the quest to bring her father home.

"Lie in peace forever," she whispered, tracing the sign of the Circle.

Rising to her feet, she turned about and lifted her chin in satisfaction. It was done.

Outdoors, the sunshine seemed especially bright. Ignoring the approach of the steward, who was fended off by her attendants, Alexeika waited for the archduke to emerge from the chapel. Taking tiny, shuffling steps, Rvin tottered along with a manservant supporting him by one thin arm. The white-haired man walked close beside him.

When Rvin reached the queen, he executed a very shaky bow.

Alexeika gave him her hand, and the clasp of his fingers was dry and cool. He smiled at her, his dark blue eyes sharp with intelligence.

"Your presence honors my father," she said to him. "Thank you."

"Ilymir was my friend. We played together as boys. I stood next to him at his wedding. I attended the celebration feast when you were born."

Alexeika smiled. "My father spoke of you often, with great affection."

"Your majesty is a most beautiful and gracious queen, worthy of both your parents. I rejoice to see this castle once more under the Volvn flag."

She bowed her head. "It is good indeed."

"So many fine and noble men gone," Rvin said. "So many days of glory now in the past. By Thod's grace have I outlasted all the friends I knew, but Ilymir Volvn was the best of them all."

"I bid you to stay here as my guest," she said warmly, casting a glance at the man beside Rvin. "You and your attendants."

The archduke gestured vaguely. "My son, your majesty."

The white-haired man bowed to her with grave courtesy, making no attempt to speak.

Liking his quiet manner, she smiled at the archduke. "You are well served in your son. And both of you are welcome at Volvn Castle or the palace whenever you choose to visit."

"So would Ilymir have made me welcome. You are a true daughter to him, your majesty."

The son stepped forward. "If my father may have the queen's leave to retire? He grows weary."

"Of course."

She dispatched a servant to ensure they were treated with every courtesy, and crossed the hot courtyard with her courtiers around her. None chattered, as she feared they might; all seemed respectful of the occasion.

Inside the great hall, illuminated only by open windows, the emptiness of the space seemed acute. No tables stood there. No chairs. Empty hooks projected from the walls, but no banners, tapestries, or weapons hung from them.

A trifle daunted by such grim austerity, Alexeika halted in her tracks and gazed around. "It seems I have no hospitality to offer my guests. Not even a chair to sit in."

The steward hastened forward then, apologizing and seeking to explain. When he was cut off from making excuses, he bowed nervously and offered to see her conducted to her quarters.

"Rest?" Alexeika said blankly. "What need have I to rest?"

"Why, er, the occasion, majesty. The strain of the day. The emotions of your majesty's—uh—"

She gazed at him coolly, in no mood to be managed. "Prince Volvn has been dead these one-and-twenty years. My grief is not fresh."

"Of course, your majesty. I only thought—"

" 'Tis midday. Set up trestles and serve my guests and attendants food," she interrupted briskly. "Bring the benches from the chapel if there's naught else to sit on. After we dine, bid the master-at-arms to report to me."

"Yes, majesty," the steward said with a blink.

"I shall inspect the barracks, defense walls, and ramparts first. Then I shall want to see the storehouses and keep, including the written inventories. And tomorrow I shall ride the fields and orchards."

"But, your majesty!"

"Do you have some objection, steward?"

He gulped audibly. "No, of—of course not. It shall be done as you command."

Two days later, her inspections finished, she took refuge atop a lookout tower, high among the wheeling jackdaws and keebacks. Sir Pyron awaited her below, guarding the only steps leading to her vantage point. None of her other attendants were permitted to join her.

She desperately needed to be alone for a short time, to clear her thoughts and see her way.

It was no good wishing she could have brought her father's bones back to a clean and prosperous home, she told herself. He—forever a pragmatist—would not have expected it.

Royal life has made me soft and foolish, she thought. *If I'm not careful, I shall grow as fussy as my courtiers.*

For years she'd been so focused on regaining possession of her ancestral lands for her father's vindication that she'd seldom looked beyond that goal to the realities that would follow.

Morde, she thought, *what am I to do with it all?*

Resting her hands on the gritty crenellations, she stared across unruly meadows peppered with saplings and sprouts, the fallow fields stretching beyond the small patches cultivated by the serfs for their own use, the glistening rivulet so dammed upstream by the dens of water rats that it would be dry come high summer. Everywhere she turned, there were problems. Expensive ones.

The soft scrape of footsteps on the steps made her turn warily, although she knew Sir Pyron would not let an enemy up the steps.

Indeed, it was only Count Chechnvy. Always impeccably

groomed, his gray hair carefully combed beneath his brim-
less cap of green velvet, the governor of the treasury climbed
the last few steps of the tower and joined her with a bow.

Alexeika smiled. "So, Count Chechnvy, you have made
your own inspection of my castle. What think you?"

"That I was wise to see the place for myself," he replied
in his deep voice. "Its assets and inventories appear impres-
sive on parchment, but in reality the estate is nearly worthless. There can be no revenue from it without tremendous
investment and work. Even then, it will take years to turn a
profit. It will absorb at least half, if not more, of your
majesty's available funds."

His blunt answer made her eyes widen slightly. Chechnvy
was never a man to mince his words, but even so she found
herself taken aback by his criticism. He was unlikely to extend the loan she wanted.

"The land is good," she said.

"But fallow."

"That will have rested and improved the soil. There is
plenty of timber. The forests remain uncut."

"Until I am granted the liberty of riding a league in any direction, I cannot assure your majesty that they stand uncut.
What is visible from *here* looks untouched. The rest may be
gone."

She frowned in dismay.

"I recommend that my clerk ride across the entire property. Nothing should be assumed, given the circumstances."

"Very well."

"As for the rest." Chechnvy gestured with a sigh. "The
roof is falling in, the timbers have beetle rot, the storehouses
are empty, and all but one of the ovens have been dismantled.
It might interest your majesty to know I found oven bricks
forming steps to the scullery and more of them shoring up the
footbridge over the stream."

She stared, amazed as usual by his thoroughness.

"On this side, the castle looks intact, but the east ramparts
are crumbling, and a portion of the outer defense wall has
fallen." He pointed at the north wing. "Just to rebuild that
portion of the keep alone would cost—"

"What if it were not rebuilt?" she asked.

Now it was Chechnvy's turn to stare at her without speaking. His brows lifted.

"What if the walls and ramparts were mended, but the living quarters left as they are? That way, the majority of the investment could go toward purchasing flocks and seed for planting. The ovens and mill could be rebuilt, and the mill would be viable quickly, providing the stream could be cleared enough to let water flow properly. I should like to devote all the attention into the land and nurture it back to prosperity."

"Yes, it's possible," he said without enthusiasm. "But it would take time. Meanwhile, the buildings will fall to pieces."

She shrugged. "What of it? With good revenues, the keep could be rebuilt and redesigned, surely all to its good, and without incurring additional debt."

"I thought your majesty would have sentimental reasons for preserving the place as it is."

"Oh, Chechnvy, surely by now you know me better than that."

He bowed slightly. "Your majesty's grasp of business sense has always been remarkable."

For a woman. He did not say it, but she knew the thought must be going through his mind. Her brows drew together, but she remained quiet.

After a moment, his thin mouth twitched in what might have been a smile. "Such a plan will be costly. The debts will be heavy."

"But is it workable?"

"Yes, providing the timber is there. Judicious cutting of the forests could help offset the debt burden until crops and wool become viable." He sighed. "But it would require careful management. Your majesty would need years of patience and the right steward. Not the man currently holding the position."

"No," she agreed. "You will prepare figures for me?"

"I advise your majesty not to incur more debt at this time. The king's war against the Grethori has grown into a very costly burden. The royal treasury has sunk low, and 'tis only late spring. If his majesty's demands for equipment and supplies should prove heavy—"

"You will prepare figures for me?"

Chechnvy nodded. "Yes. But your majesty will not like them."

"No. I loathe debt. But this estate has value I don't want to waste."

Sounds of argument made them both look toward the steps. A moment later, a man in courier's livery came running up, with a red-faced Sir Pyron hot on his heels.

Sir Pyron grabbed the man by the back of his tabard before he could reach Alexeika. "The queen will receive ye when she's ready and not before!"

The courier twisted, but was unable to break free of Sir Pyron's grip. "Your majesty!" he gasped out urgently. "Give me leave to speak! Lord Thum bade me—"

Sir Pyron doubled his arm behind his back, and the man broke off with a yelp.

"Have done," Alexeika said sharply. "Release him at once."

Her protector shot her a look beneath his fierce brows, but obeyed. Wincing and clutching his arm, the courier shrugged off his dispatch pouch and handed over a single letter, much folded, and secured heavily with Lord Thum du Maltie's personal seals.

Alexeika broke these herself, turning partially away to gain a measure of privacy. The letter was written in Thum's distinctive hand, obviously not to be seen by clerks or intermediaries.

For a moment her breath came short. *Faldain,* she thought. Every time he set out on a fresh campaign she did not know if she would see him ride home again.

But there was no mention of the king in Thum's missive. Instead, he wrote that Tashalya had arrived in Grov and taken residence in the palace. And that Prince Guierre of Mandria had crossed the Netheran border six weeks ahead of schedule and was expected to arrive in Grov within the next few days.

"Morde," Alexeika muttered.

"Bad news, majesty?" Chechnvy asked.

She crumpled the letter in her hand and turned to face them, giving the courier a nod of dismissal.

"A difficulty has arisen," she said, keeping her voice as light as she could. "It is necessary for us to return to Grov at once."

"A difficulty . . . the children . . . some illness?" Chechnvy guessed.

She kept her expression untroubled, well aware that this astute man profited from gathering certain kinds of information from palace gossip and his access to the royal family. "Not at all," she replied coolly.

His brows rose in curiosity, but when she said nothing more, he bowed and left her as protocol demanded.

As soon as he was out of earshot, Sir Pyron scowled. "Bad trouble, majesty?"

Grateful that her protector was someone she could confide in honestly, Alexeika nodded. "Trouble enough. Those accursed Mandrians. Why couldn't they come when they're supposed to?"

Sir Pyron's jaw dropped. "Never say he's there already?"

"Aye, in Grov. Unsupervised in the palace, surrounded by Netheran courtiers who will be after him like a knot of snakes in a pit. And Tashalya is there, Thod alone knows why."

Sir Pyron blinked.

"We could be at war with Mandria if that poppet is offended," Alexeika continued. "You *know* what the Mandrians are like. Queen Pheresa is bad enough with her worries and ill humors, but the Gides . . . morde! I wish Faldain had never agreed to foster her brat in the first place. He'll be nothing but trouble. I know it."

"Now, yer majesty—"

She uttered a bitter laugh. "Ah, damne, he's already causing it. What possessed them to send him so early? This is the first time in years I've dared go anywhere without the children, and look what happens the instant I'm away. Come, Sir Pyron. We must be quick."

Chapter Twelve

The royal palace held many excellent hiding places, but one of the best, in Niklas's opinion, was atop the outer wall of the grounds where a gnarled old rowan tree grew so close it seemed almost to have rooted in the cracks between the stones. Lying on his stomach beneath the overhang of fragrant branches, Niklas could spend hours undiscovered, watching either the palace grounds or staring out at the spires of Grov.

He was there now, nearly invisible in his green tunic amidst the leaves, lying motionless as he watched members of the palace guard searching for him.

It wasn't fair, he thought resentfully, ignoring their calls. He'd dressed up in his best finery yesterday and greeted the Mandrian prince with full honors, even saying the horrid speech he'd been taught. He'd done his duty toward a guest, however unwanted, and that was enough. Niklas certainly didn't think he should have to spend his free time with Prince Guierre as well. After all, it wasn't as though they were going to be friends.

A hand closed around his ankle and squeezed, making

him jump so violently he bumped his skull on an overhead branch. Swearing under his breath and rubbing the top of his head, he twisted about to see who'd found him.

It wasn't Bouinyin, as he'd expected, but Syban, his little brother.

Niklas let out his breath angrily. "What do you think you're doing?"

"Found you, didn't I?" Syban chuckled softly with great satisfaction. "I know where lots of your hiding places are."

Niklas tried to push him away with his foot. "So what? Get out of here."

"Stop wiggling so much! You're making the tree shake, and they'll find us."

"They'll find *you* because you're leaving," Niklas said. "Go away."

"I don't want to," Syban said, and squirmed up alongside Niklas. The wall was almost wide enough for the two of them, and Syban propped himself up on his elbows just as Niklas was doing. He was sweaty and covered with dust. Bits of leaf and twig were caught in his light brown hair. "Look at them running!" he crowed, pointing. "Like ants when you pour water on their hill."

Niklas slapped his hand down and hissed at him. "Be quiet! You'll give us away."

Syban grinned. "This is your best spot. I can see why you like to come here. I'm glad I found it."

Niklas sighed to himself. Now that Syban *had* found it, the brat would never leave him alone. Niklas would have to find another refuge, but it wouldn't be the same.

"Oh, look!" Syban said. "One of the Mandrians has come out into the gardens. See how the guards have stopped searching for you? They don't want the Mandrians to know you're being bad, do they?"

Niklas squelched a momentary twinge of conscience and shrugged. "It's kind of an insult, I suppose."

"Can you cause a war with Mandria by insulting their prince?" Syban asked with glee. "If so, I'll—"

"Shut up. All you can think about is how to start a war."

"Well, I want to know. It might be useful someday."

"Only if you intend to commit treason against me."

Syban stuck his tongue out at Niklas and squirmed forward on his stomach. His shoulder bumped against Niklas, who had to grab a branch quickly to avoid losing his balance.

"Hey, rodent, watch out!" he whispered angrily. "You nearly knocked me off."

"So hang on," Syban said with indifference. He pushed some leaves apart and peered through them. "They're talking. Is that Mekov or Andreif? Which one's on duty today?"

"I don't know," Niklas said, filling his tone with extreme boredom in an attempt to discourage his little brother.

"I think it's Andreif," Syban said. "Mekov would have lost his temper by now. Wish I could see them well enough to tell. Care to lay a wager?"

"No," Niklas said repressively. "Mama told you not to gamble."

"She's not here. The guards let me wager with them."

"I know. And Mama told you not to go to the barracks."

Syban shrugged. At age nine, with huge green eyes, a pointed chin, and a shock of unruly brown hair always falling over his forehead, he was invariably curious, indifferent to rules, and as adept at getting himself out of trouble as a cat. "They like me at the guardhouse," he said, as though that justified anything. "I'm their unofficial mascot."

"Don't sound so proud of that," Niklas told him. "Before you came along, their mascot was an old cur with mange. They threw it meat to do tricks. They throw you coins."

Syban laughed, refusing to take offense. "Did you know Bouinyin's furious with you?"

Niklas frowned. He admired his protector and lived for Bouinyin's rare words of praise during their swordplay lessons. "I don't believe you."

"Well, I saw him talking to some guards by Mama's roses," Syban said. "He had that look he gets, all squinty-eyed and grim."

"He's just annoyed with the guards over something."

"Over *you,* because they can't find you." Syban twisted to look at Niklas, his green eyes serious. "What's so awful about the Mandrian? I haven't even seen him yet. The servants keep talking about how fabulous his clothes and dogs and horses are and how many attendants he brought. You met him yesterday. What's wrong with him?"

Niklas's disappointment came boiling up anew. Ferrin du Maltie, his best friend, had left to be fostered elsewhere. And all Niklas had instead was this Mandrian and a pesky little brother who still thought putting slimy grubs down the back of a maidservant's gown was great fun.

"Niklas misses Ferrin," Syban sang.

"Shut up!"

"You do!"

"What of it?"

Syban shrugged. "You said you wouldn't miss him. You said you were looking forward to having the Mandrian come. Liar, liar, tongue on fire."

"It's none of your affair. Why don't you go to the nursery and play with Dalena?"

"Stop pretending," Syban said shrewdly. "You're rotten at lying, and you can't bluff. After all that big talk about the things you and Guierre were going to do, you're out here hiding. Does he have two heads, an evil eye, warts?"

Niklas snorted, but refused to smile. "You always want to make a joke about things."

"Better than hiding like a coward."

"I'm *not* a coward."

"What then?"

"I hate him."

"Why? Sir Kourtsin says he brought his own bed, and it took five servants to carry it upstairs. And he has—"

"I don't care what he has!" Niklas burst out. "I don't care what he brought. He's worse than a girl! All blond ringlets and a little velvet cap to match his tunic, jewels hanging on him and a pomander on his belt instead of a dagger."

Looking disapproving, Syban whistled soft and low. "No dagger?"

"None. I wore mine," Niklas said. He'd been given the weapon for his birthday, and it was his most cherished possession. He took it everywhere and even slept with it beneath his pillow like a warrior should. Bouinyin was teaching him how to fight with it to defend himself. "The Mandrian is thirteen—"

"Older than you."

Niklas scowled. "He acts like a baby. He points for things to be handed to him, and can't even hold his own cup. A servant has to tip it while he drinks."

"Morde," Syban whispered.

"We ate together, after the speeches and things," Niklas went on, his disgust burning, "and there was a page to cut his meat for him and another to arrange his trencher for him and another to hold his cup for him. Thod's bones, but I'm amazed he did not have one to put the food in his mouth and another to move his jaws for him so he needn't chew."

"Is—is he a simpleton?" Syban asked.

"No. And one of the pages keeps a white square of cloth handy for him to wipe his fingers and his mouth."

"His mouth!" Syban echoed in astonishment. "What for?"

"To get the food smears cleaned away, the way you use the hem of your tunic."

"Oh."

"Only he's so dainty he doesn't get dirty. And I can't understand why Novtok forced me to study Mandrian when Guierre never spoke one word to me."

"Nothing?"

"Oh, he made some polite comment at the end of the meal before we parted, but he spoke through one of his attendants, like I was a peasant too far beneath him to be addressed directly."

"Maybe he's too stupid to learn Netheran," Syban said.

"Maybe."

Syban made a crude gagging sound and rolled onto his back, again nearly knocking Niklas off their perch. "I thought he would be fun. You said he would be."

"Well, I expected it," Niklas said defensively. "We're to study defense arts together, and go riding, and learn lance work. But how? Is he going to have someone hold his lance for him?"

Syban laughed so loudly that Niklas clamped a hand over his mouth.

"Quiet," Niklas muttered. "You'll give us away for—"

"I think, Prince Niklas," a deep voice said coldly, "that

you need no longer fear discovery. Come forth from there, if you please. Both of you."

Syban sat upright. "Bouinyin!" he whispered unnecessarily. "I told you he was angry."

Before Niklas could respond, Syban shot off the wall and slithered down the tree. "Well met, Count Bouinyin!" he cried out in a sunny voice. "And how are you today?"

Bouinyin made some terse reply, but Niklas didn't listen. Seething, he hugged his knees, knowing he couldn't descend and face his protector until he had his temper under control. *If Syban hadn't come and pestered me, chattering away nonstop and wiggling constantly, they would never have found me,* he thought, wanting to wring his little brother's neck. He knew Syban had done it on purpose, to give him away. Syban would consider it giving the guards a sporting chance. *But it's not a game,* Niklas thought angrily.

"Your highness knows that sulking is for peasants," Bouinyin said. "Please come down at once."

Heaving a sigh, Niklas obeyed, sliding to the ground with a small jolt. He tugged his rumpled tunic into place and faced his protector with a pretense of assurance he didn't feel.

Although a noble, Bouinyin was a warrior, not a courtier, a man of action like Niklas's father, Faldain. Of medium height, barrel-chested, and heavily muscled through the chest and shoulders, Bouinyin's air of dignity made him seem much larger and taller than he actually was. Entirely bald and sporting no beard, his chiseled face and tilted eyes showed a hint of Wandering Tribes blood. The estates of his family lay far to the northeast, and he'd grown up fighting Nonkind from his cradle. Courteous, quiet, and taciturn, he'd served as Niklas's protector for as long as Niklas could remember.

"You were to meet Prince Guierre at the stables today. Have you forgotten?"

"No," Niklas replied.

"So you have been rude intentionally?"

"I was polite to him yesterday. I don't have to be with him every moment, do I?"

"You were to meet him at the stables, show him your horse, and admire his. You were expected to offer him your horse for his use and refuse the offer of his. Those instructions were quite clear."

Niklas scowled. He hated how Bouinyin could make him feel wretched without saying anything in direct rebuke. "It's a stupid custom. He probably doesn't even know it. He probably would have kept my horse."

Bouinyin said nothing.

"Is it true he brought six horses with him?" Niklas asked. "*Six?* Didn't he think we'd have any if he wanted a change? And I doubt he can even ride."

"Of course he can ride."

"Oh, well, in a procession," Niklas said with scorn. "But not out in open country. Not galloping after game. Not to have fun."

Bouinyin sighed and stared across the grounds for a moment. "So your highness has decided to dislike him? There is no changing that decision?"

"I *wanted* him to come," Niklas said defensively. "You know that. But—ah, *morde*, he's terrible!"

"I hope your highness will not share that opinion with anyone," Bouinyin said coolly. "Rumors spread so quickly in the palace."

A tide of heat crept up from the neck of Niklas's tunic and warmed his face. He found himself unable to meet his protector's steady gaze.

"I see. Your brother, I suppose."

Niklas lifted his gaze and swiftly dropped it again. He nodded.

"Then it will be spread from guardhouse to servants to courtiers. The whole palace will know within the hour."

"I—I didn't mean harm," Niklas said. "You know what Syban's like."

"All the more reason to guard your tongue when in his company."

"He's just a child. No one will pay attention to him."

"Your highness knows better."

Niklas sighed. He did indeed. Syban loved to stir up trouble as much as he loved to gossip. He even accepted bribes from courtiers to share information and rumors. "All right,"

Niklas muttered. "I was a fool. I wasn't thinking. I just wanted to get away from everyone."

"Missing your friend is not grounds for slighting your guest."

"I just don't like him," Niklas said. "Why can't he stay in his own quarters and take his own lessons? Why do I have to entertain him?"

Bouinyin frowned. "Had the two of you been fostered together at another, more neutral, location, as was proposed—"

"Thod, no!" Niklas said in horror.

"—you could avoid him if you chose to throw away an excellent opportunity. But you're here, and your highness is host to Prince Guierre. In the absence of their majesties, you are obligated to make the entire Mandrian party feel welcome and comfortable among us. I thought you were old enough to understand your role and to perform it as a prince of the royal house should."

Feeling lower than a worm, Niklas hung his head. "I'm sorry," he whispered.

"'Tis useless to apologize to anyone other than the wounded party."

Niklas looked up, his mouth opening in dismay. "No," he whispered. "No, oh, no! You won't make me do that. He's—"

"What is he?" Bouinyin asked in a voice like iron. "A young man far from home, surrounded by strangers speaking a language that is not his own. Naturally he has his own customs and habits. Were you to journey south to Savroix, your highness would find yourself stared at, perhaps even ridiculed by the ignorant provincials of Mandria. Your clothing would be considered odd, your gestures misunderstood. People would say—"

"Yes, I understand," Niklas snapped. He hunched his shoulders. "All right! I'll apologize to him. I'll take him to see my one horse, and I'll even compliment all six of his. I'll escort him through Mama's garden and let him pick flowers if he wants to. I'll be polite and do my duty."

Bouinyin bowed. "Thank you, your highness. A wise decision."

Niklas glared at him. "But I won't like him, and I'll never make friends with him, no matter what!"

"Someday, when you are both sovereigns, you will wish you had."

"Why? He's stupid and silly. He'll make an awful king. It will be easy to take his kingdom away from him if I choose—"

Realizing what he was saying, Niklas broke off, his face on fire.

Bouinyin's eyes were chips of ice. "I think it's best if that remark is forgotten."

"Yes," Niklas said, in a very small voice.

Ashamed of himself, he didn't know why he was so angry, when as a rule he seldom lost his temper. He wished the adults would leave him alone, would stop trying to force him into what he didn't want to cope with right now. And he wished—with all his heart and soul—that Guierre had never come.

"If your highness is composed," Bouinyin said, not relenting a jot, "let us go and find your guest. After all, you have an apology to make."

Chapter Thirteen

Tashalya held her palms slightly above the surface of the basin of water, drawing forth the veils, then parting them. Before her spread the empty mist of the second world, cold and lonely as always.

"Solder!" she called. *"Solder, come forth to me!"*

He did not answer.

Calling with all her strength, she slipped into the second world, a place so cold and empty. She held the ways open as long as she could, until her body began to tremble from fatigue, and her head ached from the strain. But he did not come.

She was forced, at last, to come back across the threshold into the first world with a little jolt of disorientation. It was not wise to enter the second world so often. The aches in her body warned her that she was risking too much. Exhausted and disappointed, she blinked at the unfamiliar surroundings of her palace rooms. Gone were the things she remembered from her childhood. Gone, too, were the sun-colored walls and faded frieze of painted leaves along the edges of the ceiling. Someone had refurbished the suite of rooms since her last visit. The colors of the new hangings and pillows were hues of pale lavender, cream, and soft green. She loathed the serenity of it, felt irked by the soft sheen of the silks and the rich detailing of rugs and furnishings. Whoever had changed everything must have done so to insult her, to remind her forcibly of all she'd given up to become a *sorcerelle*.

In a fit of temper, she dashed the water basin onto the floor before jerking down the bed hangings, ripping and trampling the cloth. Then she started on everything else, smashing and overturning and tearing until she'd destroyed everything lovely.

A servant came knocking at her door. "Your highness?"

"Get out!" Tashalya screamed. "Get out!"

Whoever it was fled, and no one else bothered to inquire. Breathless from her tantrum, Tashalya kicked aside an embroidered footstool and surveyed the shambles with a satisfaction that quickly faded.

Why can't I summon him again? Why? Her thoughts buzzed endlessly in her head without an answer.

Kneeling beside a puddle on the floor, she sighed wearily and shoved back her uncombed hair. Although she felt driven to try to part the veils of seeing yet again, her mind felt hot and confused, unable to cope with yet another attempt. The harder she tried, the less success she seemed to have.

Solder, she thought. What a handsome man he'd been. So fine, so well muscled, so strong and manly. With eyes as keen and piercing as an eagle's. Only that one glimpse of him had she, and yet she could remember every detail.

She tapped her fingertip on the surface of the water to break apart her reflection. "I wish you would come to me," she whispered aloud.

The room grew icy cold, as though winter had replaced summer. Looking up, she saw a white mist forming across the floor, and there he stood, in her chamber, as large as life.

Astonished, Tashalya scrambled to her feet. As before, he wore his primitive wooden armor. Sunlight washed across him, and yet he did not fade. He looked solid, and she saw that his keen eyes were an intense dark blue, like a hot desert sky. When they met hers, she blushed.

"How come you here?" she whispered, half-afraid that if

she spoke he would vanish. "How have you reached all the way into the first world?"

"You called me, and I came," he replied. "Each time I am closer. Each time I can come more quickly."

As he spoke, she saw that his eyes were smiling right at her, smiling *to* her.

It gave her a warm feeling, as though she mattered to him. She found herself smiling back. "But I have been calling and calling you, for days. I'd almost given up."

"I came the instant you called *me.*"

"But—"

"I am not Solder, Tashalya of Nether. Solder will not come."

A part of her felt crashing disappointment, for she believed Solder held the answer to her question, but otherwise she barely cared. This man, this ghost, this *ciaglo* was smiling at her with blue eyes, and she liked it.

"What, then, is your name?" she asked.

His whole face lit up. "I am called Kaon."

"Kaon," she whispered. When she uttered his name, whispers and strange voices filled her mind for a moment before fading away. Liking it, she smiled. "Kaon."

He threw back his head and stretched wide his arms, inhaling deeply. "Ah, thank you for saying my name, good lady! Now the portals cannot close against me." He drew another deep breath, his chest expanding. "How good it is to see the light of day again, to see color and feel warmth. I'd almost forgotten the delight of it."

"Can you stay here?" she asked.

He laughed, turning himself about before holding up his palms to examine them. "For a short time, yes. Although the bridge between us is stronger after moonrise."

Something in the way he said that discomfited her. She fell silent.

He smiled at her. "Will you please say my name again?"

Don't, a tiny voice of instinct warned her. She frowned. "Kaon," she said firmly.

"Now you cannot lose me," he told her. "Whenever you summon me, night or day, I shall come to you."

Relief swept her. She gasped, pressing her fist against her

mouth to keep from crying out. "I thought my powers were failing. I didn't know—"

"You have been treated ill. These primitives do not understand you. They poison your will and confuse your mind with their lies."

"Are they lies?"

"They told you to fear me. They called me a *ciaglo*, a dangerous spirit, did they not?"

She nodded.

He stared deeply into her eyes, and she felt something loosening inside her, responding to his reassurance.

"Do you fear me, Tashalya?"

She shook her head.

"Do you trust me?"

"I—I do not know, as yet," she whispered.

He extended his hand to her, his movement slow and gentle as one might approach a skittish horse. "Will you come to me, Tashalya?"

"Why?"

He smiled. "You are very beautiful."

The compliment pleased her, even as Bona's warnings filled the back of her mind.

"Come to me, Tashalya."

She tossed her head, enjoying the flirtation. "I dare not."

"Why?"

"Because you want to kiss me."

"You're a beautiful girl. You were born to be kissed, and often."

She laughed. "No. I was born to be a *sorcerelle*. We do not—"

"But they've taken that away from you, remember?" he said softly, his voice serious now, his eyes soft with compassion.

Hurt filled her anew, cutting through her momentary pleasure and filling her eyes with hot tears.

"Ah, my poor princess," he whispered. "How hard you fight to be strong. Cruel have they been to you. Every person you trust, every person you let yourself care for, turns against you, do they not?"

She trembled, for his sympathy was cutting down her defenses. The tears spilled over, falling down her cheeks, and she could not stop them. How did he know? she wondered. How could he understand so much?

"Yes, good lady, I understand," he murmured, still holding out his hand to her. "I, too, have known rejection, the pain of being pushed aside for another. Of being ignored. Being misunderstood. Believe me, Tashalya; I know it well. You are different from any other maiden in the realm, but they are blind to how special and wonderful you are. Come here, and I will show you all that you can become."

She took a step toward him, her hand reaching out for his although she stopped short of touching him. The dangers associated with the ancients made her cautious.

"Who are you?" she whispered. "Come you truly from the past? Are you an ancient, or something else?"

"I am Kaon, as I have told you."

"A name is not enough," she said. "I must know more."

"Soon you will know much more than you ever imagined," he said, his lips curving slightly. She found herself staring at his mouth, fascinated by it, curious about how it would feel pressed to hers. Her heart began to thud. She felt as though she'd been caught by a force too strong to resist. It was strange, but exciting, too. She wanted to be careful, even as she wanted to surrender to it.

"Kaon," she said, and just saying his name warmed her despite the cold air around them. The more she said his name, the more she liked him, and the more she trusted him. "Please tell me. Are you an ancient?"

"I am."

"Are you—"

"I know where lies Truthseeker."

She caught her breath. Wide-eyed, she met his gaze, finding it fierce, compelling. She looked on him with sight, and saw impatience, lust, and courage swirl, yet also a glimmer of truth. He did indeed possess the knowledge she sought.

She trembled as the desire for the sword rose within her like a flood she could not control. Always she'd wanted it; as long as she could remember she'd held the longing for it in secret obsession. How did he know? she wondered.

"Yes, Truthseeker," he said softly, luring her with the

name. "The sword of god-steel that carried your father to victory over his enemies and gave him his throne. That's what you wanted to ask Solder, is it not?"

"Yes."

"Solder knows not. Truthseeker was never his sword."

"Was it yours?"

Kaon chuckled low, with a rich timbre to his voice that made her shiver. "Come to me," he said in a voice of command.

She obeyed him this time, her thoughts awash with conjecture, her heart racing. The moment she put her hand in his, however, his arm encircled her, catching her close.

His strength alarmed her, for she was not used to intimacy. Stiffening, she pushed against his chest, but his embrace only tightened. Laughing again, this time with triumph, he nuzzled her neck. When the touch of his lips came feather light beneath her ear, she caught her breath. The sudden tingling of her skin confused her. Her heart pounded so hard she felt dizzy, and the pull of temptation strengthened.

"This is forbidden to me," she whispered. "You know it is."

"No longer," he replied, kissing her throat. His fingers stroked her jawline, tipping back her head. His gaze held hers mesmerized.

"But I don't want to lose my powers," she whispered. "Not even—"

"Foolish one, what do you fear?" he asked. "Why cling to the small powers of *sorcerelles* when the glory and strength of the ancients can be yours?"

Confused and tempted, she tried again to speak, but his face drew closer to hers. She felt his breath, saw his lips parting. Her heart bolted inside her, like a hind leaping from cover in the forest.

"Kaon, no—"

His mouth silenced hers with a kiss that made the blood thunder in her ears. She could not breathe. She could not think. She felt . . . she felt . . .

Then abruptly the kiss was over. She found herself standing weak in his embrace, her breath in tangles, her body flushed hot.

"When you are ready, I shall teach you more," he murmured in her ear. "And remember, Truthseeker can be yours for the asking. If that's what you really want."

She blinked, nearly swooning, for he was no mortal, and his kiss had not been mere foolery. He'd taken something from her, some measure of her strength. Trying to pull her wits together, she struggled to make sense of him. "Kaon—"

But he was gone.

Chapter Fourteen

A thunderous knock on Tashalya's door startled her from her daze. "Enter," she called.

A page wearing the queen's livery looked inside, his mouth dropping open at the disarray of Tashalya's chamber. "Your highness, her majesty the queen requests your presence at once."

Confused, still caught by the emotions Kaon had aroused in her, Tashalya shoved back her hair. "She's returned? But I heard no—"

"The queen requests your presence immediately. Will you come with me, please?"

Tashalya frowned at the boy, regaining her natural hauteur. "I must change my attire. Send my servingwoman to me and await me outside."

But the page stepped back and beckoned to someone. Two of the queen's guards entered, booted feet loud on the bare floor, their hands on their sword hilts.

"Her majesty is not to be kept waiting," one of the men said.

Humiliation swept Tashalya. Was she to be dragged before her mother ill groomed and guarded, like someone in disgrace? But with humiliation came resentment, hot and bitter. Very well, she thought. If her mother would give her no time to prepare, let her mother be offended by uncombed hair and a crumpled gown.

With her head held high, Tashalya left her room. The guards fell into place behind her, gray cloaks swinging from their shoulders, their faces grim as though they escorted a prisoner. The page scurried ahead, as though Tashalya did not know the way through the long palace corridors and passageways to her own mother's chambers.

Courtiers loitered as usual in the gallery outside the queen's private domain. Fashionably attired, coiffed, and bejeweled, these idlers stared as Tashalya walked past them. She looked neither to the left nor the right, but walked past the stares and whispers, as a princess should.

At the queen's door, guards stood on duty, as did the queen's dour-faced protector Sir Pyron. Some of her majesty's ladies-in-waiting sat on low chairs. They stared at Tashalya with ill-concealed astonishment, while the page knocked for admittance.

Tashalya smiled to herself, rather enjoying the shock on their faces. She wished she'd returned as a completed *sorcerelle*, able to destroy them on the spot.

When the doors opened, and she entered, Sir Pyron followed her in silence. Clearly he did not trust her, and that pleased her, too.

Evidence of her mother's recent arrival filled the antechamber, for there were chests half-unpacked and servants bustling to and fro. The queen's small dog came frisking forth, wagging its plumy tail, only to stop at the sight of Tashalya. It bared its teeth in a growl, barking sharply.

Annoyed, she flicked *marzea* at it, making it yelp and run out of sight with its tail tucked between its legs.

Lady Nadilya emerged from the sitting room with a frown. "What is the—oh, your highness." She dropped into a curtsy. "I did not hear you announced."

Before Tashalya could respond to this rather ungracious greeting, Dalena came shoving past Lady Nadilya. Only six, the youngest of Tashalya's siblings had black hair and gray eyes like their father's. A thin, rather serious child, she glared at Tashalya and cried, "What did you do to Puppet?" before crawling on her knees under a chair to try and coax the little dog out.

"If you please, Princess Tashalya," Lady Nadilya said, avoiding her gaze, "come inside at once. The queen is impatient to see you."

Resentment boiled inside Tashalya. Was this the way she was to be welcomed by all who knew her? Was this the only homecoming she was to receive? Yes, she'd secluded herself for nearly a fortnight, but now that she'd made an appearance she expected more warmth and courtesy than this.

Then a qualm touched her. Suppose they knew about her disgrace? She'd discussed it with no one, but it was nearly impossible to keep secrets in the palace. Were they laughing at her, enjoying her failure?

"Come along, your highness," Lady Nadilya said impatiently. "Her majesty is waiting."

Feeling ill-used, Tashalya stepped forward.

But a glowering Sir Pyron blocked her path. "Whatever ye did to yon beast, try none of it against her majesty."

Tashalya gave him her iciest look and went on.

She found the queen standing by the window, reading a letter. Alexeika remained a beauty, still slender, with upright carriage and grace, her dark hair coiled into a heavy knot at the back of her head. She wore a gown of blue linen that enhanced the color of her eyes. A large sapphire ring graced one of her slim fingers, and a necklace of the same stones adorned her throat. Her complexion was lightly tanned from sunshine and travel, never the dead white hue so favored by most ladies at court. There were tiny lines radiating from the corners of her eyes from squinting into sun and wind, but somehow these imperfections made Alexeika seem vivid and alive, a woman who enjoyed life to the full, and did not let it pass her by.

She was the most remarkable woman Tashalya knew—for a mere mortal, that is—and one of the most attractive. In fact, each time Tashalya saw her mother, Alexeika's beauty seemed more pronounced rather than diminished. A part of Tashalya yearned to be like her, to emulate her intelligence, beauty, grace, and ruthless pragmatism. Even more did Tashalya want to be cherished by her, but as usual Tashalya held back behind a wall of defiance and anger, for she was never going to be like her mother, never going to please her mother. It was pointless to try.

"Your majesty sent for me?" she said in a sullen voice.

Alexeika looked up from the letter and smiled. "Tashalya!" she said with genuine gladness. She hurried forward, holding out her hands. "Come to me, child, and let me look at you! It has been too long."

Taking two unwilling steps forward, Tashalya found herself caught close in her mother's embrace. Here was the welcome she'd craved; only now she did not want it. Yet despite her confused emotions, she found herself inhaling Alexeika's faint perfume and remembering . . .

"Mama," called out a musical voice, "are you certain the aquamarines go with this gown?"

Mareitina skipped out of the queen's bedchamber, twisting about to unfasten a necklace. Stunned by her sister's transformation, Tashalya could not help but stare. The last time she'd seen Mareitina, her little sister was shy, gawky, and skinny, with a wealth of golden hair that overwhelmed her features. Now, she was all grown-up, a most comely maiden indeed. Her hair curled and tumbled down her back in soft, constant movement, caught back from her face with a silk ribbon. She wore a matching gown cut to enhance her womanly curves. Her face was one that men would sacrifice themselves for, sweet and gentle, yet radiant with a purity of spirit uncommonly found. Laughing, she whirled around, saw Tashalya, and came to a halt.

Her gentle, eldin eyes met Tashalya's stormy ones fearlessly. "Oh, hello, Tashie. Have you decided to stop being a hermit? All those messages I sent to you, didn't you care? Why wouldn't you receive me?"

Tashalya felt grubby and ugly beside this vision. In the citadel she'd been required to sacrifice her femininity in order to learn how to wield magic; she'd driven it deep in her efforts to master her lessons, but Mareitina—the reclusive, most eldin of them all—had obviously stopped playing with pebbles and twigs in the woods. Only two years lay between them, but Tashalya saw that the little sister she used to feel sorry for had eclipsed her.

"Mareitina," she said. Her throat closed, and she could find nothing else to say.

Dalena came storming back into the room, still glaring at Tashalya. "Mama, she *hurt* Puppet. He won't come out, and he growls when I try to touch him."

"That is because your eldest sister possesses a wicked temper she has not learned to govern," Alexeika said calmly, although her glance at Tashalya held reproach. "Why don't you and Mareitina take Puppet outside to the garden?"

Dalena grimaced. "The boys are out there. Syban said I'm too little to follow him around."

"The gardens are large enough to hold both of you. Go on, please. I wish to speak to Tashalya alone."

Mareitina cast Tashalya a swift look of concern, but hurried forward to take Dalena's hand. "Come along," she said cheerfully. "Let's go and pick some flowers, and Puppet can pretend he's hunting rabbits."

"He won't come out." Dalena stuck out her tongue at Tashalya. "She hurt him."

"I'll persuade him," Mareitina said, leading the child away.

Tashalya could hear her lilting voice cooing and coaxing the dog, and shortly afterward they all departed. Lady Nadilya curtsied to the queen and closed the doors to the sitting room, leaving Alexeika and Tashalya alone.

At that moment of complete privacy, Tashalya turned all her powers of concentration on her mother's thoughts. But her attempt to gaze on her mother with sight brought her nothing. Frowning, she gathered herself to try again, but a voice filled her mind:

"No," Samderaudin said.

Startled, Tashalya abandoned her attempt to govern the queen's mind. But it annoyed her to be thwarted, knocked aside the way one swatted a gnat. And it hurt unbearably to know that she would never attain the strength and mastery that Samderaudin possessed. *Unless Kaon's promise is true,* whispered her thoughts.

Smiling, Alexeika held up the letter. "I return home to

good news. Your father has defeated the Grethori. His war is over, praise Thod."

"His war?" Tashalya said in surprise. " 'Twas vengeance sworn to please *you*, Mama."

"The vengeance was for Ilymir," Alexeika corrected her. "And the king's triumph will benefit all of Nether."

"Yes, I've heard the official reasons," Tashalya said coldly.

Alexeika stared at her a moment with a slight crease between her brows. "Well, 'tis over," she said briskly, "and we need not trouble ourselves with those barbarians henceforth."

"How splendid never to be troubled with barbarians."

Despite the mockery in Tashalya's voice, Alexeika smiled, again refusing to be provoked. "Your father is on his way back and should be with us very soon. There will have to be a triumphal procession and much celebration planned for. Horse races and a joust, I think. He won't enjoy my commissioning a minstrel to compose a song about his exploits, so it will have to be Saelutian acrobats to entertain him at the banquet. Who else should perform? I hear that the Mandrians have brought new dances that they are teaching the court. If my ladies practice, perhaps they will be proficient by the time his majesty arrives. What think you?"

Tashalya folded her hands together and said nothing, letting the silence grow heavy between them.

"Well?" Alexeika asked her. "Have you nothing to suggest? Are we too frivolous for a *sorcerelle*? Would it harm you to smile a little, daughter? Or are you not pleased to learn of your father's success?"

"Naturally I rejoice in the news," Tashalya said.

Her flat tone brought disappointment—even hurt—to Alexeika's face. It pleased Tashalya to see it.

Putting away her letter, the queen seated herself gracefully and propped her feet atop a tiny stool. Tashalya started to take a nearby chair, but Alexeika said sharply, "How dare you sit in my presence without permission! You are here to explain yourself, Tashalya, not to make yourself comfortable."

Her sudden flare of temper scorched Tashalya, who jerked away from the chair and stood straight and stiff, her hands clenched at her sides, her face hot with resentment. *Were I completed,* Tashalya thought, *she would not dare speak to me this way.*

"Well?"

Tashalya lifted her chin. "There's nothing to explain. I am home."

"Usually your visits are planned weeks, even months, in advance so as not to interfere with your training. Why this sudden appearance?"

"Need I request an invitation?"

"No. But it is unusual behavior for you, not to mention inconvenient for us."

Tashalya frowned. "Oh, yes, I am always inconvenient, am I not? Always a problem for you."

"Don't be impertinent. You understand my meaning perfectly well. With the Mandrians here, your timing is less than ideal."

"I've kept to my quarters," Tashalya said before she could stop herself. "The Mandrian prince hasn't seen me."

Alexeika's gaze raked her up and down. "Which, in the circumstances, is just as well. I had meant to request that you join the rest of us in the garden this afternoon, but your attire is unsuitable."

"No one gave me a chance to make myself presentable. I—"

"These excuses waste time," Alexeika broke in impatiently. "A princess—indeed, any lady—should never look like a scullion. Now, Tashalya, no more evasions. Something has happened. You're not only unwashed and unkempt, but you're thin and haggard. Are you ill? Has something gone awry with your training? Did they hurt you in some way?"

The unexpectedness of her sympathy and concern caught Tashalya by surprise. Almost she was tempted to throw herself at her mother and sob out her troubles, but she knew the queen would not understand. Alexeika expected everyone to be as tough as herself. Her sympathy was always fleeting. Having survived a difficult childhood and adolescence, she believed her children were pampered and secure by comparison and expected them never to complain, never to express

any qualms or admit to difficulties. She never truly understood anything.

"Tashalya, I await an answer."

"I shan't be going back to the citadel. My training is—
over."

Even as Tashalya said it, her voice caught, and she had to
look away in order to master herself. Although she'd tried to
face it, the reality still seemed impossible to believe.

"Are you finished then?" Alexeika asked quietly. "Are you
truly a *sorcerelle*?"

"No! I'll never be one. I failed, and they've sent me away."

Alexeika's blue-gray eyes brightened, but she leaned forward, reaching out in concern. "Come to me."

Tashalya obeyed, giving her hand reluctantly to her
mother, then drawing it away almost as soon as it was
clasped. "You've no need to pretend. I know you're glad. You
never wanted me to join the sorcel-folk."

"No, I did not," Alexeika admitted. "I have prayed with all
my heart that you would be spared this life."

Tashalya snorted. "Then for once I've actually met your
majesty's expectations. I've pleased you. How astonishing."

"I know you can't help but feel bitter disappointment. You
wanted this very much and have worked hard—too hard, perhaps—for such a long time." Alexeika paused a moment. "It
can be cruel indeed to surrender a dream, especially when
we're forced to do so."

Unable to bear this false pity, Tashalya turned away. "You
know nothing about it. Don't try to pretend you do."

"Broken dreams and hard disappointments come to everyone, Tashalya. Don't imagine you're alone."

But I am, Tashalya thought. *She doesn't even know what a*
magecera *is. She has no inkling of my destiny—all that's been
stolen from me.*

"You're unhappy at the moment, but that will pass," Alexeika was saying. "The adjustment will be extremely hard, but
remember there are always other options."

"Such as what? Making a dynastic marriage for the good
of the realm?" Tashalya asked with scorn.

"Would that be so horrible?"

"Yes! I'm destined to be more than royal breeding stock."

"You're being deliberately vulgar."

"No, just honest. I can't sit in a corner, simpering and working embroidery, pretending that my lord and master is the center of my life."

"There's nothing dishonorable in marrying and having children."

"Of course you'd say that!" Tashalya said fiercely. "That's what you've dwindled into, a wife and mother. You—"

"Dwindled?" Alexeika glared at her. "How dare you! Did giving you birth abase me? There's nothing contemptible in such a miracle, and if you believe otherwise, you're a fool."

"You were a warrior once, or so you claim. You were brave and fierce and carried weapons into battle like a man. Now you just exist as an ornament."

"Tashalya, you will not insult me further."

"I'm not insulting you, just speaking the truth. You think you must support custom by folding your hands and following meekly in your husband's shadow, but I won't be forced into such a life."

"No one's coercing you. This hysteria is unnecessary."

Tashalya glared at her. "If I don't defend myself, who will? Say what you like, but I know you'll be planning my nuptials within the hour. I'm sure poor Mareitina is already betrothed, and I won't be—"

"Stop it at once!" Alexeika said sharply. "No one knows better than I what it is like to possess intelligence and abilities that our society will not honor because we are women. My father taught me how to plan battle strategy, how to lead men, how to marshal resources and outwit the enemy, but his followers wanted none of me."

"Yes," Tashalya said impatiently. "You were an outcast until Papa rescued you."

Alexeika looked affronted. "We joined forces and fought together to regain his throne."

"And then you stopped doing anything important."

Color tinged Alexeika's cheeks. Her eyes grew fierce. "That is quite enough. You're the firstborn of the king, yet Niklas will take the throne instead of you. Did you want to become a *sorcerelle* just to govern him?"

Tashalya's gaze snapped up in astonishment.

"No, I have not the ability to read minds, but neither am I a fool," Alexeika said. "Your ambitions have been obvious."

"What of it?" Tashalya retorted, flushing hot. "I could help him. I could!"

"Yes, had things gone as you planned, but life cannot be controlled."

Tashalya gestured impatiently. "That isn't—"

"No, you don't want to listen to me because you're so certain you know everything," Alexeika said, cutting her off ruthlessly. "Well, since childhood you've devoted yourself to the conviction that you were going to be a *sorcerelle*. And now that isn't going to happen. What, then, is your great destiny to be? Have you foretold it? Have you foreseen it?"

Her questions put Tashalya on the defensive. "I just know that I am meant to do something profound and important. Something that will change the world. I'm sure of it! I want—I want to—"

She broke off, frustrated that she could find no words to express the yearnings she felt.

"Yes, of course you do," Alexeika said gently. "So much desire, so much impatience to accomplish great things. That is the passion of the young and untried, Tashalya. Very natural at your age. But everything has changed drastically for you now. Give yourself a little time to adjust. And meanwhile, we shall—"

"Don't make plans for me. I've told you I am not interested."

Alexeika drew in a sharp breath. When she next spoke it was in a very altered tone. "Very well. When do you intend to depart?"

Tashalya turned to stare at her and found her mother looking cool and brisk.

A little disconcerted but also nettled by her mother's eagerness to see her gone, Tashalya tightened her mouth and did not answer.

"And where will you go?" the queen asked, as though chatting with a stranger. "Have you money? If I am not to make plans for you, I can only assume you have made plans for yourself."

Anger boiled up inside Tashalya. "You're mocking me."

"Am I? You come here, disrupt the household, frighten the servants with your fits and furies, destroy the chamber decorated for you with such care and love by your sister Mareitina as a gift, and insult me with a discourtesy I find appalling. You expect us all to indulge you while you sulk and rampage as much as you like. Well, it won't be tolerated. You're not a child anymore. You're nineteen, a woman grown, and you should behave accordingly."

"How could you possibly know how I *should* behave?" Tashalya retorted. "You know nothing about my life, about what I do or—or *am*! You cannot—"

"I know that living among *sorcerelles* has undone every lesson in simple courtesy you were taught as a child," Alexeika said. "You've grown into a rude, selfish, arrogant, perhaps even cruel young woman."

"Just because I won't be what you want me to be!"

"You're defensive and frightened—"

"Nothing frightens me!" Tashalya broke in furiously. "I'm no coward."

"I think you are," Alexeika said coolly. "You're using tantrums to hide it."

"I—"

"Living among people who lack magic at their fingertips is not a terrible thing. It will not harm you or mar your life. We've tried to give you everything you wanted, and now you must—"

"What? Rise above my troubles?" Tashalya broke in. "What is wrong with feeling disappointment and misery? Why should I pretend I do not care about this?"

"Humiliation and defeat are not overcome by wallowing in them."

"No, of course not. You can't possibly understand because you've never failed at anything."

Alexeika stared at her with exasperation. "You cannot be that naive. Why do you make foolish remarks you know to be untrue?"

Seething, feeling as though her mother had backed her into a corner, Tashalya said nothing.

"I suggest that you go to the mountain lodge for a few

weeks and calm yourself. Endeavor to think through your situation, and when we—"

"You mean I can return when Prince Guierre is no longer here," Tashalya said.

"Do not be absurd," Alexeika said in an icy voice. "You know the court will move there as soon as the weather grows too hot. Besides, if all goes well, his highness will stay with us for at least a year. So do stop trying to play the martyr. You're not being exiled, just getting the opportunity to think without your emotions clouding the issue."

Tashalya stared at her, seeing the cool lack of sympathy in her face, and suddenly felt overwhelmed. "Why do you always send me away?"

"Because you always want so desperately to go," Alexeika replied, looking surprised by her outburst. "As soon as you come home for a visit, you are busy scheming to leave again, or else you behave in such a vile manner that no one can abide your company. When you were little, you cried and cried until your father allowed you to leave us for training. You said that's what you wanted to do."

"Because no one wanted me here!"

"Nonsense. You're hysterical and overwrought, imagining things that simply aren't so."

"No, I think I am never welcome. You said my coming here now was ill timed. You're afraid my presence will cause trouble with the Mandrians."

"Their stance against magic is well-known. But since—"

"Oh, morde!" Tashalya said in exasperation. "Do you think I'll pounce on him in some corridor and work a spell on him? The Mandrians don't seem to be alarmed by Samderaudin's presence at court, so why—"

"Samderaudin is not here," Alexeika said.

"Yes, he is!"

Alexeika sighed and turned away. "I don't intend to continue arguing with you. My decision is made. You shall leave in the morning."

"No!" Tashalya took an involuntary step forward. "I want to stay here until Papa returns. At least grant me that long a reprieve before you send me away."

"I've told you this is no exile," Alexeika said. "Thod's

mercy, but you're making a drama that is unnecessary and very tiresome. You may have inherited my temper and my stubbornness, but I can't imagine—"

"Oh, yes, the gifts I have inherited," Tashalya muttered bitterly. "It seems I am in every way your majesty's daughter!"

Alexeika looked taken aback. "What mean you by such a remark?"

"Nothing! Nothing at all!"

"I suppose you think you can coax the king into whatever you please. You'll see him as soon as we go to the lodge."

"You said I should make the adjustment to a new life and accept what's happened. But now you want me to miss the festivities and celebrations. I am to be denied seeing Papa's triumph and all the processions." Tashalya scowled. "If that is not punishment—"

Alexeika came to her and cradled Tashalya's face between her hands. "Please, *please,* don't always make life so difficult for yourself. You could be so many things, so many wonderful—"

Tashalya jerked away from her. "What I want I can never have," she said bitterly. "Thanks to you!"

Alexeika's brows drew together. "I don't understand. What are you blaming me for?"

Pacing up and down, feeling as though she could no longer control the rage bottled inside her, Tashalya coiled her *marzea* until it was molten and lethal. How she wanted to lash out with it until this fine chamber was in ruins, and Alexeika was left shaking and terrified in the corner. She would like to see her mother humiliated that way, Tashalya thought. Oh, yes, she would like to see the proud Queen Alexeika stripped of her protection and arrogance, and brought to tears.

"Tashalya, answer me."

"There's no point! You'll never understand. And even if you did, you wouldn't care!"

"I am not here to be accused by the likes of you," Alexeika blazed. Suddenly at her most imperious, she glared at Tashalya with such ferocity that Tashalya's anger suffered a check. "Do not forget that I am your mother and your queen.

I will not be screamed at or blamed for your troubles. Whatever happened with your preceptress, I suspect that you brought it on yourself."

"So Samderaudin could not wait to run to you with tales—"

"Silence! I do not need to speak with him to understand my daughter." Alexeika tilted her dark head to one side. "I'm not a fool, despite your opinion. And although you despise anyone who does not wave magic about, you will treat me with respect."

"I—"

"Begin by modulating your tone and recalling your manners. You have been too long spoiled and indulged, but the privileges you've known as the princess royal are not yours by right of birth and can be taken away."

"Privileges!" Tashalya echoed with scorn. "I live an austere life, eat wretched food, endure the—"

"By your choice," Alexeika broke in. "So give me no complaints about the harsh conditions of your training. Your status and position, the deference paid to you by your father's courtiers, is provided by your father's command. Your privileges are grants only, whereas Niklas enjoys his by right. Do you see the difference?"

Astonished by her cold cruelty, Tashalya stared at her. "Of course I understand," she said in a voice of strangled fury. "From the moment Ilymir was born, and I saw how everyone fawned over him, I understood how things were. No sooner was he gone than you produced Niklas. Everyone adores him, not for himself, but for what he will be. Yes, I understand."

"Good," Alexeika said, not relenting. "Because it is your habit to ignore reality. Now, you must live as ordinary people do. I want you to understand absolutely that you have no power, no influence, no friends, and no means save what we give you. Think about that, Tashalya. This time your father will decide your future, not you."

"I don't—"

"This conversation has ended," Alexeika said, cutting her off. "You have made me lose my temper with you, which I was determined not to do. Go back to your quarters. No furniture or comforts will be brought to you since you've chosen to destroy what you had. And when you can behave yourself properly, you may join the rest of us. Not before."

"Am I to remain here, or will your guards remove me from the palace before nightfall?" Tashalya asked through her teeth.

"Leave me at once," Alexeika said.

The doors opened, and Sir Pyron stood there, looking grim. The servants and attendants clustered behind him, their faces avid with curiosity. Seething, her emotions raw, Tashalya had no doubt they'd overheard much of what had been said, for she could sense their glee and hostility.

At that moment she hated all of them, her mother most of all.

There was nothing she could do, however, other than to accept her dismissal. Red-faced and shaking, she hurried out, and heard someone's giggle and the gossiping whispers as the doors were shut behind her.

Chapter Fifteen

❦

Dain, with Lord Omas and Chesil beside him, stood on a knoll overlooking the meadow where his army had camped for the night. 'Twas a pleasant evening of early summer, the air soft and fragrant. Mountains stood as purple smudges on the horizon, and twilight pooled inky shadows beneath the trees rimming the meadow. They weren't far from a village; Dain could hear the distant lowing of kine and from time to time caught a whiff of woodsmoke.

A sentry moved among the trees, looking more like a man enjoying a stroll than one on alert for danger. But then, the whole camp was relaxed and easy, the men playing knuckle-bones by firelight or singing the bawdy song "A Maiden's Lace" at the top of their voices with much laughter and improvisation.

Halfway home, Dain thought, impatient with their slow progress. He wanted so desperately to gallop back to Grov, force-marching his men all the way, but he was finding the journey exhausting, the hours in the saddle harder to endure each day. To conceal his illness, they traveled at a leisured pace, and the men enjoyed their hero's welcome from the villages and towns, with cheering people lining the road.

Dain's staff was under strict orders not to relay the truth of his condition to the palace; not even the queen or his minister of state had been informed. To muzzle any spies, he bade Chesil personally check every message sent off in the dispatch cases, much to Rof's chagrin.

As for his illness, nothing helped. The physician's remedies were designed for men's stomachs and turned his. Each dawn he found it harder to drag himself from bed, harder to pretend he did not ache in every joint, harder to resist the lassitude that drained his vigor and left him as weak as a newborn kitten after the slightest exertion. He had scant appetite for whatever was served him and ate only to sustain his body. Sipping the Chalice water gave him temporary respite only, little more, and with a limited supply available, Sovlin stretched it out to be sure it would last until they reached Grov.

That particular evening, Dain felt peculiar, as though suspended in time and fading from this world, becoming someone not quite real, like Tobeszijian had been—a ghost caught between worlds.

From the corner of his vision flickered a shadow, not part of the gathering night but something taking cover within it. Alerted, Dain frowned in that direction, but there was nothing to see.

He pointed. "See you anything over there, Omas? Chesil?"

"No, sire," they answered.

Dain could not shake the uneasy sensation of being watched. The air felt suddenly cold, and he shivered, hunching his shoulders beneath his tunic.

"Perhaps we should head back," Omas suggested.

Dain found it a very long way to his tent, and his long legs were trembling from fatigue by the time he stumbled inside and sagged into a chair. His servant came to remove his boots and bring him a cup of wine he didn't want. At his request, a fire was kindled, but it could not dispel his chills.

Commander Adyul arrived to deliver the daily report, only to be intercepted by Chesil.

"You'll give the report to me, commander," he said, taking Adyul away. "His majesty is tired."

Rof brought in a fat dispatch pouch that had just arrived. Dain refused all the reports, accepting only Alexeika's letter.

But after he broke the seals and unfolded the heavy parchment, the lines of ink wavered before his eyes, and he could not focus on them enough to read.

The letter drifted from his hand to the rug, and he dozed, only vaguely aware of being undressed and put to bed by his worried attendants. The shadowy figure he'd glimpsed earlier came inside the tent and stood watching him.

Rousing, Dain called out. "Omas!"

"I'm here, sire," his protector said in reassurance.

A hand gripped Dain's. He fought to open his eyes and tell Omas about the intruder, but he was sinking too deep, too fast, and the warning was never given.

And if Omas watched while the king slept, so did the shadow.

In Grov that night, the bells finally stopped ringing in celebration, but people went on singing and dancing in the streets, while bonfires burned in the squares. Within the palace walls, the feasting and revelry ran very late, with much drunken laughter and cheers.

Tashalya lay curled upon the mattress brought to her by Callyn in defiance of the queen's order. It rested on the floor and was quite hard as a result. She'd thrown off her blanket, for the night air hung hot and sultry from an impending storm. In defiance of good sense, she'd left her window open to catch any stray breeze that might spring up; nor had she salted the windowsills.

If Nonkind crept in to seize her, she would welcome it, she thought bleakly.

She'd dozed fitfully for a while, but now lay restless and wide-awake, her thoughts swirling in the same, exhausted groove. She knew not what she was going to do. Her bid to stay until her father's return had sprung from defiance rather than an actual plan. She had no idea of what to ask him to do for her. All that she'd ever wanted had been closed to her.

There was nothing else, nowhere to turn, no idea to pursue, no alternative to accept.

Tears trickled hot from the corners of her eyes. There, in the secrecy of darkness, she could allow herself to cry.

Far away, she heard a rumble of thunder. Cool air poured into her chamber, and she sighed at the relief of it.

"Why tears, good lady?" murmured a voice.

Lightning flashed, illuminating the room, and she saw Kaon kneeling beside her makeshift bed, staring down at her. Startled, she jumped and grabbed her blanket to her chin.

"What are you doing here?" she whispered. "I did not summon you."

"Are we not bound to each other?" he replied in amusement. "Are you not in need of me?"

Lying there, she stared at him, very aware of Bona's warnings. No honorable man would be in her chamber like this. The very thought of it made her breath shorten. She knew she should scream for help, but she remained silent.

When he reached out, she flinched, but all he did was pick up her braid of hair.

"What are you doing?" she asked.

"Loosening the glory of your hair." He tugged the strands gently free. "You should never bind it."

She lifted her hand to stop him, but her fingers brushed his chest instead. He no longer wore his armor. His tunic was made of the thinnest silk, so fine and lightweight that her fingers felt the hard outline of his muscles. She curled her hand into a fist, unsure of what to do. All she knew was that she no longer controlled him, and she was afraid.

"That's better," he said, spreading her hair wide. His fingers touched her face ever so lightly, tracing the outline of her cheekbone, nose, and lips.

She shut her eyes a moment, enjoying his touch despite herself. "Why have you come to me?" she asked.

"Because you are sad. Because you need me."

The tender compassion in his voice made her cry anew. She shook her head. "No. Emotions do not matter. They interfere with—"

"Living? Why is it wrong to feel? You are beautiful, Tashalya. Let me teach you that."

"I summoned you only to answer my question. That is all."

"Why does your family not cherish you?" he murmured, caressing her jaw. "Why are you punished for what is not your fault?"

"Were you watching?" she asked.

"I sense your feelings now. I know your confusion, and your grief. I know you have been hurt, and that angers me. Let me right these wrongs, Tashalya."

Her emotions overwhelmed her. She did not know what to do or how to govern herself. He was too close, too tender, too enticing. He consumed her senses, and although she knew not how to resist him, she felt certain she must try.

"It's too late to help me," she said bitterly. "I am in exile. I shall end up a twisted, tormented thing like Callyn."

"Have you forgotten what I told you?" His fingertips rubbed gently along her lower lip, and obediently her mouth parted. "Lies, good lady, have they told you. All the power you shall ever need is yours. They fear you will become too strong for them."

"I believed that once. Now I'm not sure."

"Did I not promise you my secrets?" he murmured, and kissed her so very gently she almost imagined it.

Was he real tonight, she wondered, or merely a dream?

He chuckled as though reading her thoughts and let his fingers wander to her breast.

She sucked in a sharp breath, trying to sit up. His hands pressed her down, holding her effortlessly with a strength that was frightening.

"Kaon, I cannot do what you want," she said, trying to push him away. "You would rob me of the last—my gifts are all that's left. Please, Kaon, please! I—I can't—"

"Think not of lack, good lady, but of plenty. The *sorcerelles* are inferior to us."

Kaon untied the strings that closed the throat of her gown. She lifted her hands in a weak attempt to stop him, but she was too slow.

"Their methods are harsh," he continued. "So much pain and sacrifice in order to reach a fraction of what I know and can share." Leaning down, he kissed the little hollow at the base of her throat. "Will you trust me?"

Tears burned her eyes. She was trembling so much she hardly noticed what he was doing. "I can't, Kaon. I want to, but I can't."

"Bona lied to you," he whispered, caressing her. "You gave her your trust, didn't you? All those years of striving to learn her methods, to obey her rules, rewarded you with nothing but trickery. Your father lied to you, promising you training when in reality he forbade them to teach you true sorcery. Samderaudin lied to you, colluding with Bona. And today your mother lied to you. Pretending not to understand why you resent her. Was she not cruel when all you sought was comfort?"

"Yes," Tashalya said in a small, hurt voice. *A lifetime of betrayals,* she thought.

"You are special. You deserve better."

His kindness and praise were soothing. She gazed up at him. "Will you truly give me Truthseeker, Kaon? Will you?"

"Oh, yes," he said with a laugh, while thunder rumbled loud enough to shake the windows.

Rain blew in, but Tashalya didn't care. She gripped his wandering hands to hold them still, clinging hard to convince herself that he was real. His fingers tightened around hers, and it was flesh and bone she held, not wraith. When she sat up, this time he let her. Her loosened gown slipped off one shoulder, and a deft twitch of his fingers dropped the garment to her waist. Dreadfully shy, she would have pulled it up again, but he slid his palms across her skin in ways that made her forget modesty.

She thought of her mother's horror if this was discovered and suddenly smiled. The queen had ordered her locked in. Tashalya was unreachable to any mortal man, masked in darkness and storm.

Her mother would never know.

She liked Kaon very much, had done so since the first moment her eyes met his. Best of all, he was forbidden, and a surge of recklessness took hold of her, making her heart race. She'd tried so hard to do well, and it had gained her nothing but heartbreak. So she would do as she pleased, and Ashnod take the consequences.

"Kaon," she said, moaning his name in sudden need, and lifted her face to his.

This time his kiss was not gentle but so hard and masterful he swept her into a maelstrom of passion. Bewildered and needy, she clung to him, determined to surrender, yet ignorant of how to do so. She soon discovered that she had no need do anything. His mouth plundered hers until such heat filled her body she would have cried out had she the breath.

His tunic vanished, leaving his flesh solid and hot against hers, the contact of skin to skin making her tingle and tremble uncontrollably. His kisses took the breath from her and gave it back again, while her body grew ever more pliable, like clay warmed between the hands of a sculptor.

The storm outside rumbled and raged, flashing intermittent light into the room. She sank beneath him, defiant, eager, lost in sensation.

Her *marzea* gathered around her, lifting her in ways she'd never felt before, and vaguely she realized that he was doing something with it as well, commanding not just her flesh but also the very essence of her magic. And the pleasure of it ignited unquenchable fire. Never had she known that *marzea* could exist for any other purpose than to control the people and things around her. Never had she dreamed, in her innocence, that it could be melded with the force of another individual, enhanced, and magnified to this degree.

She arched back, flying through the magic. His mind took over her thoughts until she lost all coherence. He played her emotions as a musician might touch the strings of a zithren, and her heart sang for him. Gladly did she give, receiving the reward of what he gave in return, and only gradually did she become aware that pleasure and joy were being overtaken by something stronger. His grip tightened and grew urgent. She found herself driven by a heat and power so primitive, raw, and elemental that it engulfed her with dark fury. She felt a sudden instinctive need to resist, but it was too late, for she was possessed on every level of body, mind, and spirit.

And she saw visions of strange places and people who crossed leagues with every giant stride. She saw battles, with lightning flashing from the cloudless sky while the heavens ripped open and fire rained down. She heard the babble of a thousand voices speaking in languages she did not know. And she heard Kaon's voice, louder than all the others, commanding her with words she understood not at all, yet obeyed.

She knew then, in a tiny moment of clarity, what he'd done to possess her. She hadn't simply shared herself maid to man. No, she'd sold herself to him, and was no longer a mistress commanding a summoned *ciaglo*, but instead his slave and chattel, his possession. From that first moment on Bona's balcony when she'd touched him, she'd been running down a road to this moment, and there was no going back from it, no undoing anything.

When he called her name, the myriad forces possessing her spun her thoughts apart, shattered her *marzea*, and threatened to burst her heart. The glory he'd promised came up through her in a rush too powerful and strong.

Great Thod, she thought in desperation, crying out against his shoulder as she was swept too far, she was not made to bear this. He was an ancient, something more than a man, while she was only mortal . . .

It roared through her like an ocean tide, drowning her, tossing her about like flotsam. Worse than the pain, the force overtook her body first, then her thoughts and soul.

She could not even scream, for it consumed her, and she was lost.

Chapter Sixteen

The following day Alexeika was changing her gown in preparation for officially meeting Prince Guierre when Lady Nadilya came to her, wearing a troubled frown.

"Forgive me, your majesty, but Princess Tashalya's servant is here."

Alexeika held her breath while her laces were pulled tight. She was wearing a new gown of pale green silk. The skirt parted over an underskirt of cream, expertly tailored to hide pockets that held her salt purse and daggers. The long sleeves tapered to points over the backs of her hands, and the bodice was cut high. Last night's storm had cooled the air. The day held a refreshing sparkle, and she was humming to herself in happy contemplation of all the events she and the chamberlain had already planned for Faldain's homecoming.

But Lady Nadilya's announcement silenced her song. "Unless it is an apology, I have scant interest in anything Princess Tashalya has to say."

"Shall I then send the creature away, majesty? She seems agitated."

Alexeika kept herself from sighing. There was always the

chance that Tashalya had plunged into new, additional trouble. "Let the servant enter."

The woman crept into Alexeika's chamber, glancing about with one bright green eye. She looked as though she'd spent the night in the rainstorm and had not yet dried out. Her bright hair clung to her skull in a dank mat, and her pale, luminous skin, so heavily scarred, seemed to glow ever so slightly. Whatever she was, she had no place there. Alexeika's ladies-in-waiting drew back from her in aversion, and Sir Pyron's gaze never left her.

"You bring a message?" Alexeika asked crisply, hiding her revulsion. "What does her highness wish to say?"

"Not a message, your majesty," the servant said in a soft, pleasant voice. "The princess is ill, and I am concerned for her."

Worry filled Alexeika, but she stopped herself from showing much reaction. "I'm sure she must be wearied from her tantrums. She'll improve by and by."

"No, majesty. She is very ill with fever. She left her windows open last night, and the rain came in."

Consternation broke out among the ladies for a moment, while Alexeika struggled to control her exasperation. No doubt Tashalya had been hoping to invite Nonkind into the palace. It had been wicked indeed of her daughter to jeopardize so many lives. No one in the palace, from the king to the lowliest scullion, left any window or door open after nightfall. That was an ironclad rule of the household.

"She'll have to be punished," Alexeika said.

"But she's ill. She tosses and moans and will not awaken no matter what I try."

Alarm drenched Alexeika's anger. What if Tashalya were herself a Nonkind victim? Alexeika snapped her fingers at her attendants. "Finish these preparations, quickly. Lady Nadilya, send for a priest and a physician."

Nadilya curtsied and hastened away. Alexeika thought of something else and turned back to Tashalya's servant. "Is she delirious? Is she casting magic? Will there be danger to anyone who tends her?"

"I do not know, majesty. I have seen no use of the—no, I think there is no danger."

Alexeika considered this disjointed answer and decided not to send for Samderaudin as yet. Catching her veil from the slow fingers of her maidservant, Alexeika draped it over her hair and departed her quarters with Sir Pyron and Tashalya's minion at her heels.

She found Tashalya's chamber stripped bare save for a mattress lying on the floor. It disconcerted her to see her daughter in this empty space, and she found herself bitterly regretting confining Tashalya in such austerity.

Water stood puddled on the floor, leaving discolored streaks on the wood planks where it had dried. The air smelled of fire, although the tiled stove in the corner was closed for the summer.

Sir Pyron cast Alexeika a look of warning and advanced alone to where Tashalya lay, tossing and mumbling in a tangle of blanket. Impatiently, prey to every imaginable fear, Alexeika watched him crouch there, dagger in hand, and cautiously peer at the back of Tashalya's neck.

He lowered the girl gently and shook his head at Alexeika, who let out her breath with a little sob of relief as she hurried forward.

"Stay back, majesty!" he said in warning, and pulled back the blanket to examine every fold.

When he found nothing in the bedclothes, the servant crept forward to smooth the blanket back over her mistress's form. Tashalya looked flushed. Tendrils of her black hair clung to her damp temples, and she tossed back and forth, mumbling and whimpering.

Alexeika knelt beside her, heedless of crumpling her finery on the floor, and took her daughter's hand. It felt very hot. She pressed the backs of her fingers to Tashalya's cheek before smoothing the girl's hair from her brow.

"Tashie," she said now. "It's Mama. Can you hear me? Tashie, Mama is here."

Tashalya's eyes flickered open for a moment and looked at her. They were hazy with fever and something else. She began to cry.

Alexeika tightened her grip on Tashalya's hand and went on stroking her hair. "Hush, my love. Hush. It's going to be all right."

"Gone," Tashalya whimpered. "Gone!"

"Never mind. You'll feel better soon. I promise," Alexeika assured her.

Tashalya's eyes closed, and Alexeika looked around. "You," she said to the servant, "what are you called?"

"Callyn, your majesty."

"Summon the steward and have her bed and furniture returned. We must get her off the floor at once. Bring more blankets, a fresh bedgown, and cool water to bathe her brow. She needs to be drinking broth and water. Inform the kitchens to send a tray. Now get to it!"

Callyn obeyed.

Soon thereafter the physician arrived, a cautious sort in long robes who kept a prudent distance from the patient. The priest was braver. He examined Tashalya carefully and pronounced her free of Nonkind venom. After that, the physician was willing to peer into her eyes and listen to her chest.

Noticing the priest's troubled frown, Alexeika turned to him. "What is it?" she asked, keeping her voice low. "What ails her?"

"I would prefer, majesty, to consult with the physician before I venture a guess."

She felt that same little icy clutch at her heart once again, but she was forced to wait, consumed with impatience, while the two men went over to a corner and conferred in private. The priest, she noticed, kept asking the questions, and the physician kept shaking his head. When they finally turned to Alexeika, their faces were grave.

"She will need careful nursing during the next few days. Rest and absolute quiet. No visitors," the physician said. "The fever is from a slight inflammation, but provided she is kept warm and given fluids, she should recover speedily."

Relief rose in Alexeika, but she checked it, turning her gaze to the priest. "What else?"

"She seems to have suffered a violent shock of some kind. Her spirit is deeply troubled."

"Yes," Alexeika said, "she's had recent bad news and has taken the disappointment hard."

"Ah." The priest's expression cleared, and he tugged at his beard. "That explains it."

But Alexeika was not so sure. Tashalya had been dismissed from training weeks ago. Yesterday she'd been bitter and defiant, but far from collapse. *Could something else have happened?* Alexeika wondered. But with Tashalya locked in her chamber, Alexeika could not imagine what. *Perhaps,* she thought, *Tashalya attempted some feat of magic that hurt her.*

"The princess is highly strung," the physician announced, as though Alexeika were not fully aware of her daughter's temperament. "I advise an infusion of herbs and bitters, which should be ingested each hour today. Tomorrow she may have broth and sops."

Alexeika looked at the bed, where Tashalya now lay with Callyn hovering over her. "Should I sit with her for a time?"

"Not now," the physician said. "I've given her something to make her sleep. Perhaps your majesty might look in on her this evening."

Quietly, Alexeika walked over to Tashalya's bedside and gazed down at her daughter. Tear tracks were drying on Tashalya's flushed cheeks. She looked worn and exhausted, and very, very young.

I've been too hard on her, Alexeika thought in contrition. *She's not as strong as she pretends to be. I must remember this in the future.*

Bending down, she gently kissed Tashalya's hot brow and pressed her hand lovingly to the girl's face. Then she looked at Callyn.

"I would speak with you privately," she said.

The servant followed Alexeika over to the window. She stood quietly, keeping her gaze down in a submissive way that Alexeika found irksome.

"How long have you served my daughter? How well do you know her?"

"I have been her companion and handmaid for many years."

Alexeika hesitated, hating what she had to ask. "Tashalya and I quarreled yesterday. Afterward she was locked in this room. Could she have—did she try to harm herself in some way?"

Callyn's gaze flew up in astonishment. "No, your majesty! Oh, no!"

"Are you certain?" Alexeika persisted grimly. "She's been much distressed and unable to cope with her disappointment. Could her spirits have been so low that she would—would try something?"

"Never against herself," Callyn said, sounding shocked. Her gaze met Alexeika's frankly. "She is a fighter, majesty."

Alexeika frowned. "But if acting against herself meant harming someone else—striking at someone else, would she do that?"

Callyn looked down. "These are terrible questions, majesty," she whispered.

"Very well," Alexeika said. "Thank you."

Callyn made obeisance and limped back to Tashalya's bedside.

Watching her, Alexeika frowned. She was well aware that Callyn had not answered her last question. Despite her suspicions, she knew she must make no assumptions until she could talk to her difficult daughter, perhaps for once without accusations, quarreling, or recriminations.

"The princess is comfortable now, your majesty," the physician said. "Let us all depart that she may sleep."

Out in the passageway, Alexeika found a page hopping impatiently on one foot and then the other.

"Your majesty," he said in a shrill young voice, "with Lord Thum's compliments, I am to remind your grace that you are very late."

"Yes, I'm coming," she said, glancing back, but Tashalya's door had already closed.

On her way, she was soon joined by her attendants, who made her pause in the passageway for her skirts to be smoothed, her hair secured correctly beneath its veil, and a necklace of braided pearls fastened around her throat.

Shortly thereafter, she and her entourage walked into the Gallery of Glass to find most of the court assembled. A swift glance informed her that the Mandrians were even later than she. By all accounts the delegation with Prince Guierre was reportedly touchy, difficult to please, and inclined to complain about everything. *Now,* she thought, *if they could be induced to depart Grov, leaving Guierre behind, I would be very pleased indeed.*

Many people were seated at small tables, playing *torcata*, the new dice game that was all the rage. Musicians strummed zithrens softly in the background, and there was to be heard in general a happy babble, punctuated frequently by laughter.

It pleased her to see that the mood of celebration had not abated. A relaxed and happy court was less inclined to foment trouble and intrigue. Once Faldain returned, the court would be dismissed for the summer. The royal family would go to their mountain lodge to get away from the dismal heat, stinking river, and pestilence that always plagued Grov during the hottest months. They could live more informally, free of stifling duties and protocols. Faldain might even find time to teach the boys woodcraft and eldin lore.

Alexeika paused at the entrance and cast a quick glance back over her children standing like a row of ducklings behind her. Everyone looked reasonably well groomed and on good behavior. She smiled in approval and gave the chamberlain a nod.

He bowed low to her and turned about, announcing loudly: "Her majesty the queen! The crown prince! Their highnesses!"

At once conversations the length of the gallery broke off. People rose to their feet to make obeisance. Alexeika walked slowly along the length of the famous gallery, smiling and acknowledging those in her favor. Overhead, the globes of bard crystal swung gently from gilded chains, whispering harmonious melodies. The tall windows lining the outer wall stood open to catch the pleasant afternoon breeze, while the extravagant—and costly—mirrors opposite reflected colors and movement. Behind her came Niklas and Syban, then Mareitina and Dalena, followed by the queen's ladies-in-waiting, aides, and pages.

At the far end of the gallery stood the dais and Faldain's throne, embroidered with his coat of arms. Seeing it brought her a pang of loneliness. She missed him and could not wait for his return.

But no such feelings showed on her face as she seated herself on a low-backed chair next to the throne. Her ladies smoothed the complicated folds of her green-and-cream gown while the children separated to stand on either side of her chair. Mareitina's shyness had her blushing, and Alexeika noted how many of the men could not take their eyes from her. Niklas could also on occasion be shy. At the moment he looked very solemn and stiff, and Alexeika wished she'd had the opportunity to talk to him about Guierre before this formality.

If the boys did not take to each other—as she'd been informed they had not—then she could hardly blame Niklas. He and Ferrin du Maltie were closer than brothers, despite Niklas being a little older. Had things gone according to plan, Guierre's arrival should have come weeks after Ferrin's departure, instead of mere days. Niklas was not ready as yet to replace his good friend. And no matter how much Thum du Maltie wanted Niklas and Guierre to like each other, for the future of both realms, Alexeika had no intention of pressuring her son's affections.

However, she hoped that given the right circumstances, less adult supervision, and a little time, the boys might find common ground.

Niklas leaned over to her ear and whispered, "They're always late for every function."

Alexeika had already been warned of this behavior. Courtesy demanded that the Mandrians be there awaiting her arrival, but either they were unaware of that simple protocol or believed their prince to hold precedence over a queen consort.

Swallowing a sigh, she merely looked at Niklas, giving nothing away. He straightened with a slight frown, his gray eyes unhappy.

On the other hand, Syban and Dalena were preening with obvious enjoyment at being the center of attention. Several ladies of the court smiled and flirted with Syban, while he shamelessly accepted the sweetmeats and comfits slipped to him.

From the corner of her eye, Alexeika saw Mareitina quickly grip Dalena's arm to keep her from running somewhere. The child, Alexeika thought indulgently, was always on the fidget, full of energy, impossible to keep still for longer than a moment or two. Meanwhile, Alexeika had no intention of waiting for her young guest, however exalted his position. She caught the chamberlain's eye and signaled that she was ready to receive conversation.

Looking unnerved, the chamberlain sidled over to her. "Your majesty, the Mandrians—"

"—are not in attendance," she interjected smoothly, her voice serene. "Clearly there is to be no presentation today. Please notify the courtiers that they may mingle and converse freely."

With a bow, the chamberlain obeyed her. Murmurs of conversation buzzed immediately as people began to drift into groups. Partway across the room, she caught a glimpse of the minister of state. Although Lord Thum's auburn hair was untouched as yet by gray, his tall figure had thickened slightly over the years, and he'd acquired a slight stoop to his shoulders from long hours bent over reports and correspondence. He remained stalwart and loyal, a tireless, devoted friend to the king.

At the moment Lord Thum wore his most wooden expression, but Alexeika knew him well enough to sense the exasperation that must be seething beneath. He'd worked so hard to mend relations between Nether and Mandria. Bringing Guierre to be fostered was to have been something of a diplomatic triumph for Thum, but the Mandrians were certainly proving to be difficult and supercilious. Despite being weeks ahead of schedule, they were said to be deeply offended because neither the king nor queen had greeted their arrival.

As though we had nothing to do this spring save await the Heir of the Realm, Alexeika thought to herself. *Let them be offended. I have no patience for their little games.*

Thum was heading in Alexeika's direction. Meanwhile, the Countess Unshalin, a haughty woman with protuberant eyes and a receding chin, approached her with a magnificent curtsy.

"Your majesty," she began, "I—"

There was a stir at the other end of the gallery, and the chamberlain's voice rang out: "His royal highness, Prince Guierre. Count Horveul de Gide. Ambassador Toubeld. Cardinal Velain."

The crowd of courtiers parted, and the Mandrians walked in. Syban began to fidget despite Niklas's sharp jab with his elbow.

"Ow!" Syban complained, doubling over. "Mama—"

"Hush now," Alexeika said sternly, flicking him a glance that made him straighten immediately. "Not another sound from you."

Meanwhile, the prince was coming into sight. Alexeika resisted the temptation to lean forward, although she was eager to compare Pheresa's son with her own.

When Guierre reached her, she wanted to laugh. He looked ridiculous in a doublet with puffed sleeves and ruchings of silk at throat and wrists, especially when combined with leggings of a tapered, far-too-tight cut. His feathered cap was worn at a jaunty angle that ill suited his solemn expression. In fact, he looked as pale as a boy about to take examinations.

He was heavy through the jowls, double-chinned, and possessed of pale, soft hands adorned with rings. A pomander swung from his belt along with an elaborately beaded salt purse. He wore the heavy silver bracelet proclaiming his royal status, and also a thick chain with ruby studs hanging from it. Another ruby dangled from his ear. On a Saelutian sea captain such an affectation might have looked dashing, but on a thirteen-year-old boy who had not yet started to grow, change his voice, or sprout a beard, the effect was ludicrous.

Guierre bowed to her with quite a flourish. In turn, she rose to her feet and inclined her head.

"Your royal highness, welcome to Nether and welcome to my family," she said, infusing her voice with practiced warmth. She chose not to address him in Mandrian. " 'Tis my hope that you will find your year with us a happy and rewarding one."

He straightened, meeting her gaze with big eyes of melting brown, but did not return her smile. "I thank your majesty for her kind words of welcome," he replied, speaking Netheran with a thick accent. "But—" He hesitated, glancing at Gide, who was standing rather closer to the boy than was necessary. "But I will choose not to be remaining here. I will choose to be returning to Savroix as—as soon as your majesty gives me leave to go."

Chapter Seventeen

"Damne, I'll not stand for such nonsense!" Alexeika said, pacing back and forth in the council chamber.

Dusk was gathering outside the windows. She was anxious to return to Tashalya's bedside and see how the girl fared, but thus far—in the crisis provoked by Guierre's announcement—she'd not found the opportunity.

In the Hall of Kings, the court was gathering for a banquet feast. The confused roar of conversation, music, and robust laughter could be heard each time the door to the council chamber opened. It had been a long afternoon of audiences and meetings following Guierre's startling request to leave Nether. The terse little encounter in private with the Mandrian ambassador and Horveul de Gide, the prince not present, had not gone very well. The Mandrians had refused to discuss Guierre's decision or his reasons, insisting on permission to depart with the boy on the morrow.

Now, having summoned Lord Thum, Count Unshalin, and Archduke Vladno Krelinik, Alexeika found herself caught between the horrified realization of what would happen if Guierre went straight home to his mother and a strong desire to boot the boy and his officious advisers out of the palace tonight.

"What are they playing at?" she demanded, turning around and striding back across the room. "What do they really want?"

"Ah, the queen has put her finger on the crux of the situation," Vladno murmured. Lean, suave, and darkly handsome with a narrow, chinstrap beard and eyes dangerous to the equanimity of most ladies at court, the archduke leaned against the council table with his arms crossed. "Be assured, my lords, that this is nothing but a ploy for more negotiations."

"He was coached," Alexeika said. "That boy has no notion of why he was told to say what he did. Yet if they want more concessions, why didn't they say so this afternoon?"

"It's possible that the boy is truly homesick," Unshalin said in his pompous way, folding his hands across the top of his heavy stomach. "He looks to be a most cosseted youth. I've no doubt he was missing home within five leagues of Savroix."

"Most fosters find themselves unhappy as soon as they arrive," Alexeika said, dismissing this show of sympathy. She disliked Unshalin and thought him a fool, but he was a powerful member of both the Privy Council and the Kollegya, and had to be paid nominal respect. "'Tis part of the training, as each of you know."

The men nodded, no doubt recalling their own youthful experiences.

"Guierre stays," she said firmly. "I shall not grant him leave to go."

Thum cleared his throat, sending her an apologetic glance before saying, "In terms of strict legality, 'tis the king who must decide whether Guierre may break the agreement and depart."

Unshalin nodded. "Naturally."

Alexeika was not offended. She smiled at the three of them. "But that serves us very well. Until Faldain returns, Guierre must stay. Surely in the interval, we can work to change his mind."

"We must be very careful," Thum warned them. "Nothing

we do should suggest we are keeping Guierre against his
will. It could mean war."

"Is that what Gide's after?" Vladno asked while Unshalin
gaped in befuddlement.

"I don't know. I suspect he wants the boy to be fostered at
his estates."

"If Pheresa wanted that, she wouldn't have sent her son
here," Alexeika said.

Thum bowed to her. "Exactly. But still we must take care.
Gide wants influence over the boy, and if Guierre spends a
year with us, his uncle may never acquire it."

"Thod grant he never does," Alexeika muttered, resuming
her pacing. Her father had taught her to be a rapid and accu-
rate judge of a man's character, and in one glance she'd
known that she did not like or trust any of the three delegates
accompanying Guierre. The boy's situation wrung her heart.
She wanted to help him if she could.

Sighing, she sank into a chair, while Thum and the others
talked in low voices for a moment. Then Unshalin and
Vladno left, and Thum closed the door behind them.

In the circle of lamplight, with moths bumping clumsily
into the flames, Thum came over to the table and sat down
heavily across from her, pinching the bridge of his nose.

"You are tired," she said. "Your head must be aching. Why
don't you retire? I'll dismiss Amalina from her duties early."

"My wife would rather dance all night than watch me por-
ing over letters and documents," he said, waving away Alexeika's sympathy. "I'm well enough, thank you. This problem
did not catch me much by surprise."

"You anticipated it?" she asked, her brows rising.

He nodded. "When they came so early, and the delegates
did not immediately depart, I grew wary of the whole company. I suspect that Toubeld is nothing more than a spy. Gide
wants the boy for himself. And Velain, as sleek as a cat . . .
well, who can say what a churchman is up to?"

"Can they not be thwarted before Faldain comes home?"

Thum's hazel eyes warmed with compassion. Always a
friend to Faldain, he'd served his king well through the years,
settling here, in a land foreign to him, working long hours to
pull the kingdom into stability, guiding his king through the

treacherous ground of diplomacy and compromise, and watching over the network of spies and informants that kept him knowledgeable about affairs of state from Gant to Sae-lutia.

Alexeika knew very well that without Thum's hard work and absolute loyalty, Faldain would not have been free to leave his palace to wage so many wars, to take his occasional sojourns in the forest, to go on a king's progress across the realm so that the common folk could see their sovereign. Now, staring at this prosperous, astute, and powerful man, Alexeika could not help but remember a gawky youth with red hair and freckles kneeling astonished in the forest of Nold while Faldain knighted him. *Damne,* she thought, sud-denly wistful for their youthful adventures, *it seems a very long time ago.*

"I have an idea or two in mind," Thum admitted. "I am not sure they will work, and they could make more trouble if they fail."

She smiled in delight. "I knew you would have a solution! I'll ask for no details. If you did not want to confide in Vladno and Unshalin, you will not wish to trust me either."

" 'Tis not a matter of trust," Thum protested. "But it's best if you do not know."

"Can you blackmail Gide?" she asked.

He laughed. "Your majesty!"

"Very well. No more questions," she promised. "You have the patience to approach problems from the side. I always want to tackle them straight on. And Faldain—"

"—is too honest and forthright at times," Thum said, with a shrug. "But that is his way, and I'd not change him for the world."

A sense of longing for her husband swept over her. She looked away to keep her feelings private.

"It shan't be long now," Thum said quietly. "A matter of days."

"You've had another dispatch?"

He nodded. "No letters, just a duty report."

She didn't hide her disappointment. "I hoped for a letter, but I suppose he thinks he's too close to home to bother now. He does hate to write them."

"If your majesty would learn to read runes, he would write you daily."

The sally made her chuckle before she sobered and changed the subject. "What think you of Prince Guierre?"

"A comely lad, polished and affable. Exactly what I expected."

"Rather immature for his age?" she asked.

Thum shrugged. "He's been coddled, certainly. But then that is why he was sent here, to have some of the spoiling knocked off him."

"Niklas has very little to say about him." She frowned. "That is not a good sign, especially since Niklas is usually so ready to make new friends. I heard you had the chance to converse with Guierre alone a few days ago. Did you find him arrogant as well as spoiled?"

"Not arrogant, to my observation." Thum's expression puckered. "I confess that the first time I saw him he looked too much like Gavril."

"In coloring perhaps. But do you think—"

"No," Thum said hastily. "I doubt they are truly alike. It was just an old nightmare playing tricks with my mind." He sighed. "Gavril was vicious and petty. When we were fostered together at Thirst Hold, I found him unbearable. Yet the way he treated me was as nothing compared to his cruelty to Dain."

"This boy—"

"No. He has none of Gavril's fire and ambition. He's soft and gentle, perhaps too much so. Despite my first impression, he's not really handsome. Instead, he's—"

"Pretty?" she suggested.

Thum made a gesture of disgust. "Aye. I suppose that's it. He favors his mother."

"I thought you always considered her a great beauty."

"What's beautiful in a lady is less desirable in a man."

Alexeika's worries came back. "Am I foolish in seeking to keep him here? Could he not be the wrong influence on Niklas?"

"You need not fear for your son," Thum said with calm conviction. "Niklas is sound of character. Their association

can only do Guierre good. If they can be gotten past this un-
fortunate beginning."

"They need time," she said sharply. "Do not push Niklas,
for it will only make him more stubborn."

"Very well," Thum said mildly.

She gave him a stern look. "I mean what I say. Niklas will
not be maneuvered like a pawn on a game board."

"We all have our roles to play, majesty," Thum replied.

She did not like the way his eyes had grown remote and
ruthless. It frightened her that he was using Niklas in his po-
litical strategies, just as he sometimes used Faldain.

"Niklas is very young," she said, staring hard at Thum.
"Too young as yet."

"He's the crown prince, and old enough to be fostered
away."

"If this year with Guierre does not go well, or if Guierre
goes home now, you can be sure that Niklas will not be fostered next year in Mandria."

"Majesty!" Thum cried. " 'Tis all agreed. To back out after
all the—"

"I'll not put my son into Gide's hands, nor into the lord
consort's keeping."

"Please! Be not so hasty to undo months of negotiation.
You have no cause to complain against Lord Perrell. He is
considered to be a valiant man of honor."

"I see no good in these spiders spinning their webs around
Guierre," she said grimly. "And if you are going to spin webs
around Niklas as well, and subject him to the intrigues of
those blackguards, I'll have no part of it!"

Silence stretched between them while both glared in refusal to back down. Eventually Thum was the first to look
away.

"Your majesty's concern for Guierre does you great
credit," he said. "Whether he will ever realize it, he is blessed
indeed for having such a compassionate champion."

The praise softened her. "I just do not like to see something young and potentially fine ruined through mishandling.
Whether it's my son or another's, 'tis still wrong." Suddenly
her emotions overtook her, and she pressed her fingers to her

mouth. "As I've mishandled Tashalya. Oh, Thod's mercy, what am I to do with her?"

"I heard she is very ill," Thum said. "I am sorry."

Alexeika thought of her troubled, willful daughter and wished she dared confide her suspicions about Tashalya's illness. *Where did we fail?* she asked herself for the countless time. Despite all their efforts, Tashalya had never been the same after her abduction. Her imperious nature, her natural arrogance, her temper had all worsened after Faldain found her and brought her home. There had been nightmares and violence, wild tantrums, sobbing hysterics, icy bouts of silence. When at last—driven to their wits' end—they had sent the child away for training among the sorcel-folk, Alexeika's heart had broken anew at the prospect of her daughter spending her life in such a dark future. Still, she'd comforted herself during all these long years of separation by hoping Tashalya would gain contentment. She'd wanted Tashalya to be happy, to find a place where she belonged.

Now, that wasn't to be. And if Tashalya had indeed attempted to take her own life . . .

"It's time I checked on her," Alexeika said, rising to her feet. "I'm told she's improving, but I must see for myself."

He rose also. "Of course. It does seem strange for her to fall ill. I thought your children had enough eldin blood to avoid the usual maladies."

Alexeika felt heat suffuse her face. *He knows,* she thought wildly. *He suspects. Oh, he is too clever a man not to reason through this as I have.*

"She breaks my heart," Alexeika said. "Oh, Thum, I do not know how to help her."

"Perhaps she must learn how to help herself. I think your majesty has suffered enough for your children."

Startled, Alexeika could only stare at him.

He frowned. "Her troubles are *not* your fault. You should never blame yourself for what happened. That evil creature acted from the basest motives when he stole her from you. Nothing you did caused any of that to occur. And her choices since then are due to him and not to you."

Alexeika shook her head in bafflement. A part of her agreed with what he was saying, but it did not lessen the guilty anguish she lived with for somehow having failed her daughter.

"No more mistakes," she said fiercely. "None with my son, and none with Pheresa's. We must bring them up right and make good men of them. So much of the future depends on them and what they become." She held his gaze. "You must find a way to keep Guierre with us, Thum. Only you are clever enough to do it."

"I've told your majesty to leave all to me," he promised.

"Yes." She shuddered, rubbing her arms briskly. "But now that I've met Horveul de Gide, and the snakes he brought with him . . . now that I see how deep runs his influence on this boy, I wonder how many more of these vile creatures have surrounded Guierre all his life. Have they already destroyed him with their poisonous schemes, or is he still innocent and malleable, still worth saving?"

"You thought him worth saving the moment you met him."

"And perhaps I'm a fool."

"Your majesty is tired and worried about Princess Tashalya. Only yesterday did you return from that hard journey to attend your father's memorial. There has been all the excitement of the king's good news, and perhaps old memories stirred to life because of it." Thum gave her a kindly smile. "Too many emotional upheavals in too short a time. Do not borrow trouble before it comes, please."

But you hastened to foster your son away before Guierre arrived, she thought grimly. *What know you that you haven't shared with us?*

She could not bring herself to voice the question. She owed Thum almost as much as Faldain did and had no right to suspect him. A wave of weariness rolled over her, pressing down on her shoulders so that it took an effort to hold them erect.

"I'm sorry to have kept you so late," she said. "Thank you."

As she hastened out, gathering her protector and ladies as she headed to Tashalya's quarters, her thoughts turned again to Gavril. Before he went mad and had his soul taken—Thod help him—before he became a Nonkind fiend who nearly killed Faldain, he was said to be a handsome, well-favored young man, blond and blue-eyed, beautifully dressed, and surrounded by fawning, manipulative schemers who drove him to his ruin.

Guierre, older than Niklas, reared in a more sophisticated court, could well prove to be similar. Perhaps not as wicked or as arrogant, but certainly the wrong kind of influence.

As Thum had said, Niklas was sound of character, she reminded herself with pride. But he was only twelve, that special, in-between age of being neither child nor young man. He was vulnerable, although he would hate to know she thought so. While she did not believe he could be turned aside from what was good and moral, there was always the chance of him meeting harm and betrayal. No child, she had learned, was ever truly safe no matter how many precautions she used. But that did not stop her from trying to protect each of them.

She'd failed to guard Tashalya. She'd failed with Ilymir. And she'd failed with Gretchinka, the sweet baby girl born between Niklas and Syban, who'd died mysteriously in her crib.

Poor Guierre. He looked so ridiculous, so helpless among the wolves circling him. What was Pheresa thinking, Alexeika wondered with disgust, to raise such a stupid pudding of a son?

But as she neared Tashalya's door, where the guards stood on duty and a pair of servants dozed on stools, Alexeika's fierceness faded. She knew she had no business blaming Guierre for being such a little puppet. And if he stayed, then she must make the effort to help him as best she could. Not for Pheresa's sake, not even for Guierre's. But because one day he and Niklas would each be king of adjoining realms. It was as Thum kept saying . . . for the sake of Nether . . . for the sake of *Niklas* . . . she must improve Guierre and give him all the aid she could.

She sighed, feeling overwhelmed by it all, and hesitated in the passageway, while the guards snapped to attention, and the dozing servants scrambled to their feet.

The door swung open for her, and she steeled herself to go inside, where her daughter lay so still and wan in the dim light.

Tashalya seemed to sense her presence and opened her eyes. "Mama." She sighed, her voice so weak it frightened Alexeika anew.

Stripping the damp cloth from her brow, Alexeika checked her for fever and fancied that Tashalya was less hot than before. "I told you I would come again," she said softly.

Callyn emerged from the shadows, her skin glowing luminous and eerie. Alexeika's heart jumped, but she seated herself on the stool beside Tashalya with a calmness she did not feel, waving the creature back.

In silence Callyn retreated, but Alexeika could not feel easy with the servant there. She slid her free hand into her pocket, checking to make sure she had both salt and dagger.

"Mama," Tashalya moaned, twisting as though in pain. "Gone. *Gone!*"

"It doesn't matter now," Alexeika said, keeping her voice soothing. "Just lie still and try to sleep. I'm here with you."

"Stay," Tashalya said fretfully, clinging to her hand. "Stay with me!"

"Yes, of course I'll stay. Everything's going to be all right."

But tears spilled down Tashalya's cheeks. "No," she said, shivering. "It's all wrong, Mama. Everything is wrong now."

Callyn came forward, proffering a cup of brown liquid. "It is time for her to drink this, your majesty."

Taking the cup, Alexeika coaxed Tashalya into drinking the infusion. It smelled bitter, but Tashalya swallowed it, then shut her eyes while Alexeika turned her pillow and smoothed the blankets.

"Thank you, Mama," Tashalya whispered.

Alexeika bent and kissed her cheek. "Sleep now."

Tashalya's eyes drifted shut, and her breathing grew heavy and regular. Alexeika sat a long time on the uncomfortable stool, holding her daughter's hand that lay in hers with such quiet trust. She wished it could always be this way between them, and wondered again what had gone so wrong. And she grieved for all that she and Tashalya had lost along the way.

Chapter Eighteen

"No, your highness. Keep your elbow down and your wrist up. Try again. No!"

Frustrated, Niklas halted while Sir Talst came over to adjust his grip on the thinsword yet again. This was their first day of lessons with the weapon, but Niklas's initial burst of excitement had faded quickly when he realized that Guierre—despite not carrying a dagger—was far better at fighting than he.

It was a very hot day, with the sun broiling them on this small corner of practice ground reserved for their use. Nearby, knights were executing lance drills, thwacking the battered old quintains and striking through rings with their lances. On the opposite side of the field, cavalry practice raised an inordinate amount of dust, and from everywhere came distracting noise and activity. Niklas had discarded his tunic and stood bare-chested, breathing hard, determined to master this plague-riddled weapon if it was the last thing he did.

Under a shade tree, Guierre stood sipping cool water from his jeweled cup while a servant held his thinsword and another plied a fan to cool him. Only a sheen of perspiration on his face and his disheveled ringlets betrayed the fact that moments before he'd been demonstrating the correct footwork and form that earned Sir Talst's compliments.

By contrast, Niklas found himself tangle-footed and clumsy. The practice sword he held was a dull, battered thing with a peeling leather grip and a blunted end for safety.

"Please pay attention, Prince Niklas," Sir Talst said. "Hold your wrist at this exact angle. A firm grip, but do not throttle the hilt. Now, take the stance, please. Lower. Engage!"

It had looked so easy when he watched Guierre do it. Trying to show off, Niklas sprang at his teacher, sweeping his sword upward beneath Sir Talst's blade. It was a broadsword move he'd learned from Bouinyin during their practice bouts with wooden weapons, but it didn't work here. He found himself suddenly exposed to his teacher's weapon, glimpsed a look of horror on Sir Talst's face, and felt the lightest touch of steel slice across his shoulder.

The sting came fierce and hot, making Niklas flinch back. Sir Talst jumped to one side, throwing down his weapon and lifting his hands in surrender to Bouinyin, who came running up.

Ignoring the sword master, Bouinyin gripped Niklas and pressed a cloth to his wound.

Bald, suntanned, and muscular, his slanted eyes like flint, the protector glared at Sir Talst, who remained frozen in place.

"What in Thod's name were you doing?" Bouinyin shouted at him, while knights and servants gathered round anxiously.

"I'm all right," Niklas said, but no one was listening. The captain at arms and a duty officer hurried up, swiftly dispersing some of the crowd.

"Are you mad, Talst, giving these boys real weapons?" Bouinyin demanded.

"Prince Guierre brought his own, my lord."

"You have the sense of a gnat. They are weeks away from being proficient enough to handle steel."

"I saw no harm in letting them bout a little with me."

"No harm? You could have killed him."

"He didn't," Niklas said.

Sir Talst looked white about the mouth. "As Thod is my

witness, Lord Bouinyin, I had no idea he would do anything so stupid."

"What?" Bouinyin roared.

Sir Talst flicked Niklas an abashed look. "I—I mean, something so ill-advised. We were doing drills, to learn stance and footwork."

"Stance and footwork do not require a sword in hand," Bouinyin said, pressing harder on Niklas's shoulder.

Too hard. With a sharp intake of breath, Niklas winced and tried to pull away.

At once Bouinyin eased off. "I beg your highness's pardon," he said in a milder tone. "Come into the shade while I bind this."

"He's all right!" the captain at arms announced loudly to the spectators. "The bleeding has stopped. 'Tis only a scratch."

The men and idlers drifted away as Niklas found himself turned around and escorted over to the tree.

Guierre had been staring openmouthed. Now he stepped forward. "Are you being much hurt?" he asked, his accent thick. "My servant will give you water."

The jeweled cup was filled and handed over. Bouinyin took it for Niklas and peered at the contents.

Niklas expected him to pour it out, but instead the protector held it out. "Drink it," he said.

Niklas did not want Mandrian water, did not want Mandrian concern. He glared at Guierre resentfully, wondering how he could be so stupid and helpless about almost everything and yet so skilled with the thinsword. And he owned not just his own sword but also a *pair*. He was always showing off, and Niklas wished he'd gone back to Mandria the way he said he wanted to. *If I hadn't been so determined to show off, too,* Niklas thought glumly, *just to impress* him, *none of this would have happened.*

He lifted his gaze to Bouinyin. "I lost my temper, violated the first rule you taught me," he confessed miserably. "I just wanted to—"

"Not here," Bouinyin murmured in warning. "Drink the water."

Niklas took the heavy cup, its crust of jewels rough beneath his fingers, and forced himself to drink.

Meanwhile, Bouinyin had knotted a piece of cloth around Niklas's shoulder. "Barely a scratch. It will be healed by the morrow."

Guierre's servants relaxed visibly, murmuring to themselves, while Sir Thiely scowled at Bouinyin. The Mandrian prince looked at Niklas with envious admiration.

"First blood in combat," Guierre said. "You are ahead of me, there."

Some of Niklas's burning humiliation eased. He nodded curtly.

Watching them both, Bouinyin handed Niklas his tunic, and said repressively, "Hardly combat. Cuts and scratches during drills are expected. This is *not* first blood. And let neither of you compete over that."

Guierre sent Bouinyin a wide-eyed stare of innocence and bowed. Niklas said nothing. But as Bouinyin turned away, Guierre met Niklas's gaze and smiled slyly.

Amazed, Niklas stared back at him.

"Sir Talst," Bouinyin said, walking away for a moment, "the lesson is ended for today. Now, regarding your carelessness the moment I leave his highness unattended—"

Niklas heard nothing else he was saying, for Guierre was tugging at Niklas's sleeve.

"Whatever he says, your protector, it was combat for you. You jumped at Sir Talst in an effort to fight. And so it *is* first blood."

Niklas smiled. "Put like that, I suppose it is."

"I am admiring your courage," Guierre said. "But you are too determined and stiff with your lesson. May I, please?"

As he spoke, he reached out and took Niklas's hand. Niklas tried to jerk away, but Guierre held fast.

"Here and here," he said, forcing Niklas's fingers to flex. "You hold too tight. See?"

Niklas shook his head.

Guierre snapped his fingers at a servant, who brought his sword. The weapon was handed to Niklas hilt-first.

Hesitating, Niklas glanced at Bouinyin's back and slowly curled his fingers around the hilt. It was beautifully made, the grip wrapped in split leather that felt cushioned and comfortable in his hand. The balance, he realized with a spurt of excitement, was perfect—far different than the practice weapon he'd been using earlier.

"No," Guierre said quietly. "Is that how Sir Talst is teaching you to hold it? Wrong, all wrong. Here, like this. Light and firm."

Niklas adjusted his fingers, and this time Guierre nodded. "Better," he said.

Understanding flooded Niklas. He shifted his fingers slightly, flexing his wrist to move the sword up and down. It felt light and supple, almost an extension of his arm. He grinned in delight.

"Now you are seeing," Guierre said in approval.

Their eyes met in complete accord for the first time.

"Your highness," Bouinyin said, interrupting them. "That is quite enough for today."

Knowing better than to argue, Niklas reluctantly handed back the weapon with a polite bow. "Thank you," he said in Mandrian. "It was very kind of you to instruct me."

"'Twas my pleasure," Guierre replied.

Niklas decided that Guierre wasn't as bad as he'd first thought. "Would you like to come to the kennels with me?"

Guierre looked uncertain. "But the other lessons—"

"I need to rest," Niklas said firmly, and glanced at Bouinyin. "Please? May we be excused?"

A glimmer of a smile appeared on Bouinyin's face. "For a short time. Return at the noon bell."

"Come on," Niklas said to Guierre.

The boy glanced at his protector and spoke in swift Mandrian. Sir Thiely uttered a swift negative, but Bouinyin intervened.

"Quick," Niklas said, tugging at Guierre's sleeve, "while Bouinyin talks to him."

The boys dashed away, skirting the practice field before Niklas turned and headed behind the barracks. Guierre ran heavily at his heels as Niklas led him through the maze of alleys and passages surrounding the rear stable yard, guardhouse, and armory. He ducked beneath a mass of vines growing over the garden wall and pushed through a half-rotted gate, waiting impatiently on the other side for Guierre to gingerly eel his way through.

The boy looked hot and crumpled as he paused to pick twigs and leaves from his doublet.

"Come on!" Niklas headed deep into the thick, shady grove of tall sea hollies. A mat of low-growing herbs released fragrance beneath their feet.

Reaching an arbor covered by flowering vines filled with humming bees, Niklas flung himself down on a bench and contentedly wiped his brow with his forearm. "Morde, it's hot today," he said.

Guierre remained on the path, eyeing the arbor, the bees, and Niklas with doubt. "I am thinking we were going to the kennels."

"No. Here." Niklas grinned. "You don't think I was going to tell them where we'd really be, do you?"

Guierre gave him a queer little smile and looked down, kicking the ground with his toe.

"What's amiss with you? Haven't you escaped your leash before?"

Guierre's head snapped up. "Yes, of course. It cannot be for long, this escape, but it is good, the way things used to be with Bestin."

"Who's Bestin?"

"My friend and companion." Guierre looked sad. "We are exactly the same age. With him I could be informal, and he was permitted to visit me daily. When we were very young, we played idle games, and later we learned thinsword and wrestling together. Every day we went riding."

Hearing the misery in Guierre's voice, Niklas nodded. "It's hard to leave home, isn't it? Hard to leave your friends."

"Oh, Bestin was sent away from me last year." Guierre sighed. "Fostered with the Baron Edriel, as far from Savroix as it is possible to be going. I was expected to make new friends from boys of my level, not commoners like Bestin, but I was liking none of them. 'Tis not friendship when they flatter you in hopes of winning your favor."

"My friend has been fostered away, too," Niklas said.

"Ah, yes, Maltie, the son of your father's minister of state?"

"How did you know that?"

Guierre shrugged. "I had to learn everything about this kingdom Nether, how it is governed, the names of your father's Council, who the primary courtiers are, the manners and customs here."

Niklas blinked. It seemed a lot of unnecessary study. "I don't even know those things. Well, not all of them," he admitted.

"No, I am observing that you and your brother have no training yet in statecraft. It is being a puzzle, considering your position."

That mild needle of criticism made Niklas stiffen. "We don't do things the way Mandrians do."

"Obviously. Your court is most informal."

"And yours is so bound up in rules and protocol you can't even use the privy without asking someone's permission."

"True," Guierre agreed calmly. "Or belch."

"Or fart."

"Or vomit."

Suddenly they were laughing, and the little contest broke up.

"So much like having Bestin again," Guierre said happily. "Are you knowing how to swear coarsely? Like a knight?"

"Aye. What's the worst word you know?"

Guierre told him. Impressed, Niklas whistled. "Even Syban doesn't know that one."

"At home everyone is stifled," Guierre said. "That is why I am liking it here."

"You do?" Niklas asked, amazed. "But why ask to go home?"

"I was told to."

"And then you changed your mind, and decided to stay."

"I was told to."

Niklas found him strange. "Do you always do what you're told?"

"Yes, of course." Guierre gave him a sly look. "Officially. If I please them, sometimes I can be doing what I like."

"Aye, that's wise," Niklas agreed. "Bouinyin is awfully strict, but then he's good about letting me roam when I need to, like right now."

"My protector does not permit this roaming. He will be angry."

"Who cares? You're in Nether now. Do as you please."

"If I behave as I please, they will be sending me home. The queen will be embarrassed at my disgrace, and Lord Perrell will never—"

"You're hundreds of leagues from Savroix," Niklas said. "You have to learn our ways while you earn your knighthood. I don't think slipping away like this is going to disgrace you."

Guierre nodded. "You are giving me advice like Bestin would. Why do you bother, when you despise me so much?"

"I've never said so."

"But it's so obvious. From the first, your face has been saying everything you thought. The fat boy with the girlish curls, dressed in too much finery. You think me stupid and have been hating me."

Embarrassment spread through Niklas, and he felt ashamed of himself. "Sorry. I'm trying to be polite now."

"Ah, polite." Guierre nodded. "I hate this polite. Empty. Insincere."

Niklas stiffened. "I just wanted to know how you got so good with the thinsword. Maybe you'll give me more lessons?"

The heightened color in Guierre's face drained away, making his few freckles stand out against its pallor. "Do not be pitying me, flattering me like a lackey. How dare you!"

"I just—"

"You are having orders to be courteous to me. I loathe a liar!"

"I'm not—"

"Honesty when you don't like me, that I can be respecting. But to bring me here and insult me with this—"

"You're the one being insulting!" Niklas shouted. "You suspicious, stupid foreigner, don't you even understand when someone's trying to make friends with you? I meant my request, but if you don't want to give me help, just say so. There's no need to pick a fight about it."

Guierre opened his mouth, but said nothing. The fury faded from his face, and he turned aside. "I cannot do this," he muttered. "I cannot! I'm no good at it."

Completely bewildered by these sudden changes of mood, Niklas wondered if the boy were mad. Maybe that was why his attendants guarded him so closely.

"This isn't working," Niklas said at last. "I shouldn't have tried. You misunderstood everything today, so I'll just take you back."

Guierre rubbed his eyes with a sigh. "Still you are not angry?"

"No, just disappointed," Niklas admitted. "For a little while I thought you might become a friend. But now I don't think so."

"I am being sorry, too. You are kind, no matter what I am doing. I wish to be friends, but it is never to be possible."

"Why not?" A sudden suspicion touched Niklas. "Did they order you to quarrel with me?"

Guierre nodded.

"But your uncle left last week. You don't have to do what he and the ambassador told you."

"Don't I?" Guierre asked hopelessly.

"That's why you're here. To become part of our family and one of us. And when Papa gets home, you'll be—"

"No," Guierre said tonelessly. "I shall never be permitted to join your family's activities."

"Of course you will."

"No. I am having spies surround me everywhere."

"Who? Your servants? The cardinal?"

Guierre nodded. "And I'm expected to fail at my lessons."

"Morde, do you see conspiracies everywhere?" Niklas asked incredulously. "Why?"

"I knew you would not believe me." Looking annoyed, Guierre broke off a small branch and began stripping leaves from it. "I am being a fool in confiding in you."

"Are you mistreated?" Niklas asked.

Guierre froze, the branch dropping from his hand.

"Are you?"

"The Heir to the Realm is never punished," Guierre said, but his voice held a brittle, false quality that brought Niklas's brows together. "Not even for spending this morn with you unobserved."

"Yes, you are," Niklas said, suddenly angry on his behalf.

"Damne, that's infamous! I'll tell Bouinyin, and as soon as Papa comes home, he'll see that you have new servants and—"

"Please don't! If they know I am confiding in you, they will never let us talk again."

"Rubbish. You need some backbone—"

"What is this backbone?" Guierre asked warily.

When Niklas explained, Guierre shook his head. "Open defiance . . . I do not dare. Already they are busy to see me fail. So many delays with our lessons. The broken girth yesterday so we cannot go riding. The mishap today that cut you."

"That was just an accident."

"My servants bribed Sir Talst to be ending our lesson early."

Niklas drew a deep, shocked breath. "He cut me on purpose?"

"No! I do not know. No one intended you for getting hurt."

A hollow feeling spread through Niklas. "I have to tell Bouinyin."

"No! Already I am warning you to say nothing."

"Sir Talst can't be trusted."

"If you tell, we'll not be allowed to practice thinswords again. At least not with each other."

And if Sir Talst kills me one day, Niklas thought grimly, *our lessons will end just the same.*

"You see, I am to be kept indoors as much as possible," Guierre said. "No strenuous or difficult activities. Nothing to challenge me."

"This makes no sense. Why?"

Guierre shrugged. "If I never become much of a warrior, then I shall be easier to manage when I take the throne."

"How know you all this?"

"Safest to act stupid, but I listen and piece things together. Don't give me away, Niklas. I have been trusting you, and I ask for your help."

"My father—"

"He'll do nothing," Guierre said bitterly. "Fathers never do."

"Papa isn't like that," Niklas said in quick defense. "He's

very busy most of the time, but he does listen when I talk to
him."

Envy filled Guierre's brown eyes. "I wish mine—I would
like to be doing well here. I would like to be a renowned warrior, as valiant as my father . . . or yours. When I am going
home to Savroix, I would like to have done something heroic
to earn Lord Perrell's respect and perhaps his—I would like
his respect."

"You will," Niklas said. "We'll get better at our lessons as
soon as Sir Talst is dismissed. Bouinyin will teach us. And
Papa."

"Kings have no time to school green boys."

"Papa won his war. He'll have the rest of the summer to
spend with us. You'll like him, Guierre, and he'll help you. I
know he will."

"You have all the trusting belief of a child," Guierre said,
shaking his head. "But nothing is ever that simple."

"Prince Guierre!" called a Mandrian voice. "Your highness, come forth please!"

"Sir Thiely! I must go." Guierre gripped Niklas by his
tunic. "Promise me in Tomias's name that you'll be repeating
nothing of this."

"But—"

"Not to your protector. No one! Swear it."

Niklas pulled his tunic free of Guierre's hand. "Keep my
own attempted assassination a secret? I won't!"

Guierre drew a swift, angry breath.

"Prince Guierre!" Sir Thiely called again. "'Tis time for
mathematics. Your tutor awaits you."

"Is nothing I am saying of sense to you?" Guierre whispered in frustration. "Where is Netheran honor?"

"I have plenty of honor," Niklas said hotly. "But pretending and keeping secrets is not—"

"It is survival! Pretend we have quarreled. Do not act like
my friend. Then perhaps we can be talking like this again."

"That's silly." Niklas frowned. "If we get Bouinyin, he'll
see you're protected. You can even stay in my room until
your people are dismissed."

Guierre shook his head. "No, I am telling you, no! You

will only be making things worse for me. Please, Niklas! I need your help, but as I wish for it. My way, please!"

A stern-looking Sir Thiely came into sight. Niklas found himself sized up by a pair of eyes as cold as stone and dismissed before the man's gaze shifted to Guierre. *He looks at Guierre like a jailer, not a protector,* Niklas thought with a shiver.

"This is a long way from the kennels, your highness," Sir Thiely said in Mandrian.

Guierre's face assumed its usual vapid expression, and he waved languidly at the arbor. "We were going there, but see all the bees along this path? You know how I dislike to be stung."

Niklas had never heard a weaker excuse in his life, but the protector seemed to swallow it. He ushered his charge away as Guierre cast an imploring look over his shoulder.

The pungent aroma of herbs crushed underfoot warned Niklas of a silent presence behind him. He spun around, his heart thumping, only to find it was Bouinyin.

He exhaled in relief. "You!"

Bouinyin walked up, lithe and lean, very alert, almost smiling. "Your reaction time could be faster," he said critically. "But it was adequate. Why didn't you reach for your dagger?"

Heat flooded Niklas's face. He felt off guard, confused. "I thought you were a Mandrian. We're supposed to be hospitable."

"Always reach for your weapon when startled," Bouinyin instructed. "You need not draw it to be prepared."

Niklas nodded, paying scant attention. He wondered how long Bouinyin had been nearby and how much he might have overheard. Protectors were supposed to guard the secrets they witnessed, but did they?

"Did your highness have enough time?" Bouinyin asked.

"For what?"

Bouinyin's faint smile widened. His gaze was indulgent for once. "To make friends."

"Oh. He's odd. I can't decide whether I like him or not."

"'Tis a good start. Everyone will be pleased, especially Lord Thum. Come now," Bouinyin said briskly, moving him along the path. "Time to clean you up and take you to your lady mother."

Niklas hurried to keep up with Bouinyin's long strides. He'd never hesitated to talk to Bouinyin before, but suddenly he felt unsure. Guierre had made him look at adults in a new way, seeing double meanings in their words and actions.

But Bouinyin did leave me during the lesson, and I got hurt, he thought with newfound caution, feeling edgy and a little frightened. He was not supposed to know the full story of what had happened to Tashalya and Ilymir before he was born, but he'd heard that Ilymir's protector had been bribed to let Grethori assassins strike.

Would Bouinyin ever betray me? Niklas wondered, swallowing hard. *Or murder me for money? Am I being managed by Lord Thum and my protector the way Cardinal Velain and Sir Thiely manage Guierre?*

Disturbed, for all his life he'd trusted the people around him—especially Bouinyin—he wished more than ever that Guierre had never come here. But the Mandrian needed help, and Niklas was determined to do more than keep secrets. He made up his mind to tell his father everything as soon as possible. Papa, he was certain, would know what to do.

The broiling heat of the Gantese desert baked through Dain's skin, parching his lips and beating on his skull. The darsteed he was riding plodded across the sand, grumbling in its nostrils and lashing its barbed tail. The uneasy sensation of being watched kept Dain looking in all directions, but he saw nothing.

Half-dazed by the broiling sun and suffocating heat, burning with thirst, Dain knew he needed shelter soon. And he should be searching for . . . what? He could not remember. He had no weapons or supplies, not even a waterskin. And there should be someone with him.

"Thum," he said through cracked and peeling lips. "I have lost Thum."

"Dain, I'm over here!" called his friend's voice.

He saw Thum limping toward him. Coated with dust and emaciated, his hazel eyes bright with fever, Thum clutched his wounded leg as he shuffled through the sand in an effort to catch up.

Vague memories came to Dain of their captivity and escape, with Thum suffering the effects of Nonkind poison. Reining up, Dain started to dismount and run to his friend's aid.

"Stop, in the name of Thod!" Thum cried. "Don't get off that beast. You'll be trapped here forever if you do."

Already half out of the saddle, Dain frowned. "You need my help."

"Nay, Dain. If you love me, stay where you are! The past lies behind us. I'm only what you—"

Lightning crackled from a cloudless sky, and a huge bolt of white fire struck the ground near Thum. Nearly deafened by the bang of impact, Dain clung to the scaled neck of his rearing darsteed and struggled to regain control over the creature. By then, Thum was gone.

For a terrible moment Dain thought the lightning had struck his friend, but then he saw Thum's tracks heading away from the blackened slag.

"Thum!" he shouted. "Where are you? Thum!"

All he heard, however, was a rhythmic clanking noise that made no sense until a line of prisoners chained together came up over a low rise. They crossed the road in front of him, a long progression of men worn to skin and bone, their faces burned and peeling from the sun, their tattered clothing falling to pieces. They were herded by Believers riding black horses with cloven hooves.

Although Dain tensed at the sight of the Gantese, reaching for the sword he did not carry, the Believers ignored him as they rode past. And the condemned men kept coming. He could not begin to count them all.

He noticed that some of them carried their severed heads under their arms. Some walked with daggers still embedded in their sides, while others displayed gaping wounds turned black and septic. Dain realized that these prisoners must be newly rendered Nonkind marching into Gant to join the ranks of its undead armies.

Horrified, Dain tried to turn his mount away from the sight, but the darsteed planted its feet and would not budge.

When the final prisoner shuffled past him and vanished from sight, leaving only the dust to settle, a woman he didn't recognize stood on the road in front of him.

Young and comely enough in a feral way, she wore a sleeveless robe of green-and-yellow patterns. A mane of coarse black hair flowed unbound down her back to her waist, and her slender feet were unshod. She held a staff in one hand and a knife in the other.

"Faldain, pale-eyes king," she said.

Contempt rang through her voice. Although her body was slim and straight, something in the way she spoke made him think of the old *sheda*. He frowned at her, and when she met his gaze, he saw that this woman had the same malevolent, rheumy, ancient eyes as the old crone.

"You!" he said with loathing.

"Now you see me as I was," she said, arching her back and tossing her hair. "A great beauty in my day. Much coveted by the warriors who tried to win me."

Her vanity was as repulsive as the rest of her. "You're dead," Dain said. "Destroyed, and your magic broken."

"So are you dead."

"No!"

"Dying then. Why fight your destiny? Denials cannot change what is to come." She smiled, displaying teeth painted red and filed to points. "But I have always been attracted to fighters. They are real men, the only ones worth mating."

"You're a wraith," he said in disgust, "a figment of my dream. You exist no longer."

"I live inside you. My curse is a splinter in your heart, festering there, and you cannot escape it. My pale-eyes enemy, I have sworn your destruction, and from the grave will I have it."

"And to the grave will I fight you."

She grinned, casting aside her staff and lifting her knife. "Come down from your darsteed and fight me now. Let us finish this."

A dagger appeared in Dain's hand. He nearly flung it away, but she was taunting him now, crouching in a fighter's stance and calling out insults.

Temptation, hot and urgent, coiled inside him. Yes, he wanted to plunge his knife deep into her vitals. He wanted to repay her a thousandfold for all she'd done to him and his family. He wanted to see pain fill her eyes and hear death rattle in her throat.

His fingers tightened on the hilt.

"Afraid to kill a woman?" she called. "Afraid to pin me and feel me writhe beneath you? Afraid to feel the temptation of a true Grethori female? Let us mate and kill, kill and mate."

Although he was already halfway out of the saddle, her words stopped him cold, and he sensed the lies wrapped in her perverted suggestions. Remembering Thum's warning about not dismounting, he thought, *This place is full of trickery and traps.*

"Thum?" he called.

"No!" she snarled, grabbing his stirrup. "Heed not that fool! This is my—"

But Thum appeared on Dain's right, standing where he had before. "She tries to guide your dreams, my friend," he said. "But you are the master here."

"No!" the *sheda* said vehemently. "No! You want to kill me, pale-eyes king. You want to—"

"You are already dead," Dain said. "Begone."

Still snarling curses, she vanished. And so did the darsteed and the barren wasteland, leaving him in darkness.

Disoriented and confused, Dain turned about and bumped blindly into someone's chest.

"Easy, sire," Omas said in a soft rumble.

"Don't wake him," warned another voice, younger and not as deep. "Walk him back to his bed slowly."

"Thum," Dain said fretfully, worried about leaving his friend in that terrible place with the *sheda*. "Must find Thum."

"Does he want du Maltie?"

"Steady, Fordra," Omas said calmly. "He's only dreaming now. Pull the blankets over him."

Blinking awake, Dain found himself in his tent. A candle put forth feeble illumination in one corner, and he saw Omas's large bulk moving stealthily through the gloom.

"Help Thum," Dain said. "He warned me. Mustn't—"

Someone came up beside him and gripped his hand. "Thum is safe."

Hazily, Dain stared up into Thum's face bending over him. He smiled in relief, but those were yellow eyes he saw, not hazel ones.

"You," he said in sudden understanding. "Still on guard?"

"Still," Vaunit said, in reassurance.

"What did he mean by all that, Vaunit?" Omas asked. "What's troubling him so?"

But Dain's eyes drifted shut, and he slept before he heard the *sorcerel's* reply.

Chapter Nineteen

❧

Clouds dimmed the afternoon sun outside Tashalya's windows. She huddled listlessly in her chair, uninterested in Mareitina's chatter.

"He's from the northern forests beyond the World's Rim," Mareitina said happily. "I've seen him only twice during my last visit to our kinfolk, but I thought him very handsome. He's a healer of great renown, and I think Papa would approve of him."

Tashalya frowned, wondering if her sister understood how every word about this suitor ground the pain deeper. In silence Tashalya got to her feet and walked away.

Mareitina followed, her blue eyes contrite. "Do I weary you?"

"Yes."

"Would you rather I sang to you instead of talking?"

Tashalya saw only concern and affection in Mareitina's gentle face. How tempting to destroy Mareitina's contentment, to lash out with malice until her sister was driven away in tears.

But that impulse lasted only an instant before it died. With a burst of shame, Tashalya reminded herself of how timid Mareitina used to be, how fragile, before the eld folk healed her. Tashalya did not want to hurt her sister. Only it seemed unfair that Mareitina should have found her way through while Tashalya was still wandering in the dark.

"Tashie, please talk to me," Mareitina said softly. "I could help you so much if you would trust me." She tried to take Tashalya's hand, but Tashalya drew away.

"I don't want to discuss anything."

Mareitina began to sing low and sweetly in eldin. The melody sounded like rainfall, quiet and steady. Although Tashalya flinched and shut her eyes, the song soothed her heart a little. Like a parched flower, she turned toward the music, letting it bathe her wounded spirit in peace.

When the song ended, she sighed without knowing it. Silence stretched between them, then Mareitina took Tashalya's icy hand between her warm ones. "Oh," she said as though in surprise. "Oh, no! You have lost your magic."

Tashalya jerked her hand free and glared at her sister. "How dare you say that! You can't possibly know."

"But I do. Tashie, how dreadful."

"Stop it!" Tashalya turned away from her and crossed the room. "Go away, and leave me alone."

"What did you—" Mareitina's voice broke off, and she stared at Tashalya far too perceptively. "There's only one way you could lose your powers. Does Mama know?"

"No, and don't you tell her." Tashalya's face was burning now; it enraged her more. "Swear to me, Mareitina, that you'll say nothing. Nothing at all!"

"But why do you care if we know? If you have found love, a man who cares for you and who will make you happy, can we not share your good tidings? I know Mama has always wished for each of us to find the right person to spend our life with. She will be glad for you, as am I."

"Oh, yes, she cannot wait to see me wed," Tashalya said, circling restlessly. Her hands clutched at the air, then gripped her skirts, then brushed back an errant strand of hair. "But it's not—you don't know what you're talking about. It isn't like that. It's—"

She stopped, unwilling to shatter Mareitina's innocence.

"What is he like? Is he handsome? What is his name? Where did you meet him?"

Tashalya clapped her hands over her ears. "Stop! I can't bear this!"

"I'm sorry," Mareitina said, her eyes awash with sympathy. "You miss him terribly, don't you? Is your heart breaking at being parted from him? Is that why you pine so?"

"You're a romantic fool."

"Tashie—"

"Well, I'm not. It's a waste of time, of—of *everything*."

"Oh," Mareitina said with a blink, looking astonished. "Was it not a mutual union, then? Were you—oh, Tashie!"

"Stop saying 'Oh, Tashie' like you have any idea of what you mean. And don't cry. I need no questions, no suspicions."

"But how cruel this is!" Mareitina said, tears spilling down her cheeks. "How did it happen? Why didn't you tell Mama at once?"

"I'm not telling her anything, and neither are you."

"But you need help. Without your magic, you're vulnerable to all kinds of—"

"I tell you I'm fine!" Tashalya said fiercely.

"No, you're not. You need a healer to sing you well again."

"I don't want a healer. I don't want your silly tears. And I don't want you here. Go away! And don't you dare tell anyone what you imagine, because you're wrong about everything."

Mareitina blinked. "I do not carry tales," she said, with dignity.

"You used to."

"Oh, Tashie. We were children then. Now we are grown."

But Tashalya didn't feel like an adult. She felt like the greatest idiot born, one of those stupid females who let passion and a man's sweet pleadings sweep her past prudence. Her world lay in ashes at her feet, and there was no mending it.

"Please go," she said wearily. "I'm so very tired."

"I'll come back later." Mareitina kissed Tashalya's cheek, pretending not to notice her flinch. "I promise I'll find a way to help you."

"Don't." Tashalya met her troubled gaze. "I mean it, Mareitina. Don't do anything. And don't talk about it."

Mareitina crossed the room and opened the door, only to step back quickly. "Samderaudin," she said in a quiet, cautious voice. Her hair writhed in agitation on her shoulders, and, giving him a wary nod, she slipped away like quicksilver.

Tashalya watched her go with a jaundiced eye. *Coward,* she thought in scorn. *So much for helping me. You could not wait to run away.*

Samderaudin glided into the room, levitating ever so slightly above the floor. He lifted one long talon, and the door closed as though pushed by an invisible hand. The potent force of his *marzea* glowed around him, still visible to her eyes although she supposed she would lose that ability, too. Just its presence was enough to unsettle her.

Feeling cornered and wary, Tashalya faced him with false calm. "What are you doing here?" she asked, not bothering with courtesy.

"You sent for me."

"I needed you a long time ago," she said with resentment. "Now there's nothing you can do."

His yellow, heavy-lidded eyes regarded her coldly. "A fool bent on a course of self-destruction requires no help."

Her gaze snapped up. She drew in her breath. "You know? Is there nothing private in my life?"

"You are plucked," he said with harsh indifference. "Forbidden. Forbidden. All laws, rules, and prudence have you disobeyed."

"What does it matter now? My training was over from the day I left the citadel."

"Not true."

"What do you mean?"

He spread his fingers to sketch a gesture, leaving a tiny trail of fire burning momentarily in the air.

She read the symbol with a frown and a dawning sense of disquiet. "Test? What kind of test?"

"The final one. The one designed to prove your true character and worth before you were to be given the Cup of Nostaul."

"No," she breathed. Her ears were roaring. "No! That isn't true! Bona said I was finished, that I'd failed. She said my talents were fading and that I would never be a *sorcerelle*. That's why she dismissed me and sent me home."

"It is called the Final Lie, Tashalya," he said. "It addresses what an apprentice most fears and forces her to face it."

Horrified, she felt dizzy and sick. Mutely she shook her head.

"Your greatest fear is failure," he said. "Your ambitions to become a *magecera*, the most powerful of our females, were high indeed. Your zeal and obsession to succeed drove you to work very hard at your studies, although when you came among us you were already gifted far beyond what some will ever achieve. Fear drove you. Fear of failure. Fear of rejection. Fear of being less than your dreams."

Her heart burned, and far away, deep inside her, hysteria, even madness, screamed. *Why? Why?* she cried silently.

"Bona told you the lie," he said in his cold, unemotional way, his yellow eyes holding no sympathy. "And I brought you here to observe how you would proceed."

"That's why you wouldn't come when I tried to consult you," she said, her lips so stiff she could barely speak. "Why you wouldn't help me."

"Where is your *marzea* now, Tashalya? Where are your ambitions to become as great and powerful as Bona?"

"Don't taunt me! You know it's gone, all of it. Gone as though I never had it! You're saying that I threw it away when all the time I—I—"

She broke off, squeezing her fists against her chest, feeling as though she would die.

"The laws we abide by keep magic in order, Tashalya. We are potent beings, commanding mysteries that put us far beyond the reach of mortals. We must govern ourselves, for no one else can do so. You climbed almost to our level, but for a short experience of pleasure you relinquished everything you stood to gain. Was the exchange worthwhile?"

"Stop," she gasped, feeling as though every word was an arrow, striking deep. "Please stop."

He peered at her without compassion. "Few women survive intimacy with a *ciaglo*, which indicates how gifted you were."

Wracked with humiliation, she said nothing. Samderaudin had been kind to her in his remote way when she was younger; at least she'd thought him kind. No doubt that emotion was as foreign to him as any other. For his heart was as cold as stone, and his voice held nothing at all but finality.

"I just wanted to be loved," she whispered. "Is that so wrong?"

When he did not reply, the silence grew heavy.

Finally, the last shards of her pride crumbling, she drew an unsteady breath. "Am I with child?"

His brows drew together, and for an instant his eyes blazed fire. His whole body seemed to transfigure into a ball of flames, and the room shook with the energy of his rage.

Tashalya did not cringe away. She stood there unmoved, unafraid of his magic, not caring whether he burned her to cinders or not.

After a moment the flames died away, and he hovered before her in his physical form, levitating effortlessly, although sparks still flew from fingertip to fingertip.

"Can a ghost sire corporeal children?" he asked her.

She flushed then, but held her ground. "Kaon is an ancient, not a ghost. He haunts not the night alone, but has appeared to me twice by day. His flesh is solid to my touch. He—he is real, even if he has returned from the past. Am I with child? If I am, what is to become of me?"

Samderaudin muttered something that made the walls of her chamber shake. "You have chosen the path of a woman. You will discover the answer in a woman's way."

Her eyes burned. For a moment she thought wildly, *If I am pregnant I shall kill myself.*

Samderaudin snorted as though reading her thoughts. "You never look past your immediate concerns. Love you want, but you love nothing. Trust you cannot. Believe you will not. Without faith, Tashalya, you are more crippled than Callyn. Until you learn that lesson and the true merit of sacrifice, you are to be pitied."

He left her too stunned and broken to weep. She sank into

a chair. How long she remained knotted in despair she did not know.

After a while there came an imperious rapping on the door, and before she could order her visitor away, her mother came in, beautifully gowned for riding, her gloves and whip still in one hand, daggers strapped to her waist.

Alexeika's blue-gray eyes were blazing. "You may go," she said to Callyn, who hesitated, then crept out and quietly shut the door.

"You do not look well at all," Alexeika said. "I was led to believe you much improved."

Tashalya sat straighter. "Forgive me for disappointing your majesty."

"Stop that!" Alexeika snapped. "What happened between you and your sister?"

"Nothing."

"Mareitina was to keep your company, to cheer you. I just came upon her in tears, quite unable to tell me what is the matter. What have you done to her?"

Her mother's unfairness rekindled Tashalya's spirits. She scowled. "Nothing happened. We didn't quarrel. 'Tis her tender heart that makes her cry over my rejection from the citadel. That's all."

Alexeika nodded, but her eyes remained stormy and unconvinced.

"Why do you always think the worst of me?" Tashalya cried. "She could be crying over a mouse killed by the cat, for all you know. But immediately you assume that I'm at fault."

"True." Alexeika drew a deep breath and rubbed her eyes. "I beg your pardon. When I worry about you both, it makes me sharp-tongued."

Surprised by Alexeika's apology, Tashalya wished it were a more heartfelt one than these token words.

"You do understand why I worry?" Alexeika went on. "She's not very strong, Tashalya, not like you. Her spirit has always been too gentle for our life here, and the least trouble can upset her."

"I know that," Tashalya said impatiently. "She talked about her friends and sang to me. I can't keep things from her. I didn't tell her about the citadel, if that's what you're thinking."

"You're troubled as well," Alexeika said quietly. "Do you want to discuss it with me? I would help you if I could."

Despite the urge to pour out her heartbreak, Tashalya fought the temptation. She knew that Alexeika would not help her. She would only say what a fool Tashalya had been. She would blame Tashalya for letting the seduction happen and pay no heed to the vicious deception practiced by Bona and Samderaudin.

Their trickery is not fair, Tashalya thought. *It is as though they wanted me to fail.*

"Keep your secrets, then," Alexeika said. "I cannot help you if you will not be helped. And if I find that you've deceived me and deliberately did anything to Mareitina—"

"What punishment could you administer that would be worse than what I now face?" Tashalya muttered.

The queen gasped, but said nothing more. Tashalya kept her face averted and heard rather than saw her mother leave the room.

As soon as the door slammed, she allowed tears to trickle down her cheeks. She wished her mother had stayed, had at least tried to comfort her torment. *If she really loved me, nothing I did or said could drive her away,* Tashalya told herself, and felt lonelier than ever.

She ate nothing brought to her that evening, and when it was time to retire she sent a worried Callyn away.

Restlessly she paced up and down but could find no comfort for wondering if her father—perhaps both parents—had given orders to Samderaudin never to let Tashalya become completed.

It would explain why Alexeika had shown so little sympathy when Tashalya came home from the citadel. If her suspicions were true, Tashalya told herself, she would never forgive her mother and father. Never.

She pushed open a window, ignoring the salt sprinkled liberally across her windowsills, and gazed out at an indigo sky where a pale crescent of new moon was rising. Far in the distance she heard the faint songs of boatmen on the river. Insects sang in the shrubbery, and a sentry on the wall called out the watch and was answered.

"Oh, Kaon," she sighed. "What have I sacrificed for you?"

"Ignorance for knowledge," he replied. "Paltry magic for divine. Old beliefs for new ones."

Startled, she spun about. There he stood in the shadows, more silhouette than substance.

She felt light-headed with joy at seeing him, but took no step forward.

He held out his hand. "Afraid?" he asked softly.

"No." Recklessly she put her hand in his.

And felt at once a tingling shock of contact between his flesh and hers. Her body contracted with a rush of ice and heat, and desire pulsed within her.

He lifted her hand to his lips with such gentleness she felt dizzy. Although she wanted to rush into his arms, she still held back.

"This is not my fearless lady," he murmured. "Why so cold to me this night? Have I stayed away from you so long you've forgotten me already?"

"I've forgotten nothing."

He laughed, and she blushed at the way he mistook her answer.

"I've been ill," she said, nettled. "When I regained my senses, I knew not where you were, nor when you might return."

"But is not that the way between maid and man?" he asked, lightly tracing the outline of her jaw with his knuckle. "To give and wait? To take and leave?"

"It's no way I care for."

Moving away from her, Kaon sniffed the air. "The old fiend's been here. And told you things to make you unhappy. Did he speak of me? Did he tell you the legends of my life? My history?"

"No. Samderaudin said that their sending me here was part of the final test before I was to be completed." Her emotions welled up beyond her control, making her tremble and want comfort. "I have lost everything, Kaon. My—my *marzea* is gone. I cannot part the veils of seeing. I cannot

gaze with sight on others. I am lost and blind. All that I was
has been taken from me."

"Ah, so that is why you have not called me until now."

Her eyes burned. "I told you how it would be, and you
didn't listen. I tried to make you understand, and you didn't
care. And now it's too late."

Kaon pulled her into his arms, holding her close while she
wept against him. "Did I not promise you greater powers than
those of a *sorcerelle*?" he murmured, kissing her ear lightly.
"Ah, my sweet mortal maid, if you knew who I truly am, you
would not doubt my promise. I have not forgotten you."

She lifted her face to his and let him kiss her. He was gentle with her, brushing his lips over hers so lightly she longed
for more.

"You asked me for Truthseeker, and you shall have it," he
said. "But I must have something in return."

"What can I give to you?" she asked, bemused as he nib-
bled at her mouth. "I have nothing now—"

"Never say that. Don't believe them, for they want to
destroy you."

"My parents? Yes, but I don't know why," she said sadly.

"You are good and sweet and brave," he said fiercely.
"You brought me back from the mists of eternity. You have
given me the bonding of your heart, spirit, mind, and body.
Forever are you mine."

Gripping her hard, he kissed her until she was robbed of
breath and sense. Her heart hammered out of control, and she
felt suddenly so weak her legs would not support her. She
sagged, but he caught her, lifting her easily in his arms.

She clung to his neck. "Kaon," she cried softly, wanting
him and yet frightened anew. "I cannot do this. You are too
strong, and I'm too frail—"

He laughed, a deep satisfied sound of male triumph. "But
don't you understand, good lady? I give you a little of my
strength each time; a little of my power goes to you. Did you
not see visions before?"

"Yes, but—"

"And so will you learn other wonders. New gifts will I bestow on you, like this." He pushed his hand inside her bodice,
and fire seemed to flow from his fingers through her body,

making her burn and ache until she trembled, uttering soft little cries. Then the fire faded, leaving her gasping and limp against his chest, barely conscious while he carried her to the bed.

"Look at me," he commanded.

She opened her eyes, and saw no longer her dark-shrouded chamber but instead rooms within rooms, furnished in different styles according to the fashions of history, filled with people who spoke and moved about yet no longer existed.

And Kaon leaned over her, handsome and youthful and vital. He was garbed in silk, yet wore armor, yet was clad in a robe fashioned of metal and flame. So rapidly did his appearance change back and forth that he almost seemed to flicker.

Bewildered, she lifted a hand as though to catch hold of him and stop this shifting vision. "What is happening?" she asked.

"I've given you true sight," he said. He touched her eyelids, closing them momentarily. "Now look again."

When she opened her eyes, the room had ceased to shift and transform itself. Yet it did not look quite as it had before. Something was different about it, something she could not quite identify. She noticed that the door to her chamber was glowing, as were the windows. Protections, she realized, and wanted to laugh at the idea of entertaining him beneath the very noses of the servants, who could not enter. Perhaps they could not hear either, for none had tried as yet to see to whom she was talking.

He chuckled, loosening her hair and spreading its wealth across the pillows. "You'll have ample time to learn how to use this talent later," he told her. "While I prepare you, let us talk about Truthseeker. And the Chalice."

She sat bolt upright. "The Chalice!"

"That is what you will give me in exchange for the sword you've sought so long."

"But I can't."

"Yes, indeed you can," he said. "But *will* you?"

"What do you want with it?"

"My dear good lady, have you never considered where the Chalice came from?"

"The gods gave it to Solder. Along with the Ring for its protection."

"A Ring, which your father can no longer use."

"Would you have me take that as well?"

"No. Only the Chalice."

"But, Kaon, it's sacred," she said, still shocked. "Nether's people depend on it for protection."

"Do you not think it is equally important to us?" His hands gripped her shoulders lightly. "Think, Tashalya. Do you really suppose the gods would bestow something so powerful on frail, foolish mortals? Did it never occur to you that perhaps Solder stole it from where it truly belongs?"

"Stole the Chalice?" she echoed, blinking in astonishment. "But that isn't what the history scrolls say."

"But perhaps it is the truth. Suppose Truthseeker was stolen as well."

"But, Kaon—"

"Was Truthseeker not hidden away, concealed from the use of men, until your father took it for his use?"

"It was given to him."

"By whom? A man with as little right to it as a sparrow. Ordinary mortals cannot resist such relics as these and yearn to possess them, yet they should not be in any man's keeping. They are too strong for mortal control and belong not in your world."

She was much struck by what he said. "Then you're saying that our religion, the very foundation of our kingdom, is based on simple thievery? Can this be true?"

"Why not? Legends grow and entwine until men think they have been in place forever, but antiquity shrouds the truth, obscuring it."

"But even the eldin worship the Chalice, and they would not accept deceit."

"Have you seen it?"

"Yes, of course."

"Is it not beautiful?"

"The most beautiful thing I've ever seen."

"Then why should the eldin not worship it, as men do?"
he asked.

"But, Kaon—"

With a swift tug, he pulled her laces open, baring her to
the waist. She shivered with a wave of desire, forgetting her
question.

Terror and splendor, she thought. Ecstasy and annihila-
tion. The chance of death excited her even more than knowing how dangerous and forbidden Kaon was. For she had
truly burned her bridges, and the tests and deceptions were
over now. What else had she, save Kaon?

Caught in the spell woven by his caresses, she no longer
cared what he did, as long as he continued. Her head fell back
and she sighed.

"Will you do it?" he asked between kisses.

"Take the Chalice?" she murmured.

"Yes."

She hesitated. "Those who try to steal it for evil purposes
die. Is that what I am to do, dearest one? Die for you?"

"No, you are to live. With me and because of me. You
have wanted to hold history like a plaything in your hand. To
build and destroy kingdoms for your amusement. And so you
shall, good lady. Now be not afraid. Cease to think like a
mortal, or even a *sorcerelle*. You are destined to be neither of
those things. That, I swear to you."

"What is my destiny, Kaon?" she whispered. "What am I
to be?"

"Mine," he said fiercely. "Now agree."

She stared at his mouth instead, her breathing tangled and
rapid, and lifted her arms to him in invitation.

"Agree," he said, his touch making her shudder and gasp.

She gripped his arm. "Kaon, please!"

"You must say it, to seal our bargain."

"I agree," she said, on fire with impatience. "I swear to
our bargain."

"You will steal the Chalice."

"I will steal the Chalice, though I know not how."

"Oh, you are clever, good lady. You will think of a way.
And you will do it soon, very soon."

"Whenever you say," she promised recklessly to make him hurry. "And you will give me Truthseeker?"

"I shall guide you to it," he promised. "And give you magic stronger than any *sorcerelle* possesses."

She laughed, ignoring the little voice of warning at the back of her thoughts. She would show them, she thought as Kaon gathered her close with a mastery that set her blood afire and turned her heart to thunder.

PART III

Chapter Twenty

❧

The trade fair was a bewildering place to Anoc. Shackled at wrists and ankles, with a collar around his throat and a gag in his mouth to keep him from biting, Anoc stood in a small forest clearing atop a stump. The trader selling him was a pale-eyes Netheran, greasy-haired and pocked of face, with cold ruthless eyes and innumerable pockets sewn into the lining of his clothes to hoard his money.

Anoc was the last of the boys in his tribe to be sold. The others had already gone, led away in separate directions. Only Parnak had looked back, with eyes haunted by uncertainty, but not even he had voiced a farewell. It was not the Grethori way.

The dwarves looking to buy swarmed Anoc, jabbing him from all sides with stubby forefingers, muttering and arguing in their queer tongue. He understood nothing they said, but he knew what the looks of assessment meant. Was he strong enough to work? Would he be expensive to feed? Could he be trained, or was he too witless or too feral to use? He stood there, trying not to react when they poked or pinched him. He did not care where he was taken or what he was set to do.

Slave's work, he thought, was better than being killed. Thus far, he'd survived despite nearly starving on the journey from Nether. Mald he had bled dry, and the boy died. Thereafter, with no fresh blood to sustain him, Anoc had walked on wobbly legs with his stomach cramping and nauseated until he adjusted to the daily ration of lentil porridge served by their captors. Now, he ate whatever he could find: grubs, berries, roots, sometimes an unwary rodent he managed to pounce on and eat raw while the creature's blood and marrow were still warm.

Clad only in a pair of tattered, filthy leggings held up by a length of rope, and worn-out footgear, he stood on the stump, disdaining the dwarf who counted his ribs and fingers, or the one who jabbered endless questions at him, or the one who tried to look at his teeth despite the gag and had to be shooed back by the trader.

Anoc had no intention of biting anyone, at least not until it could serve more purpose than venting his temper. He hoped that if he cooperated and acted docile, a sympathetic dullard might purchase him. Sympathy could lead to trust, and trust to carelessness. Anoc intended to escape as soon as possible and make his way northward, back to the territory of his clan. Each of the boys had agreed to do the same.

There were five trading rings, five auction stumps altogether, and the ones dealing females did the briskest trade. Since none of them were Grethori, Anoc paid them no attention. In addition to slaves, horses, kine, and dogs were being sold along with a smattering of livestock probably stolen from prosperous farmsteads. The weapons makers were also doing a brisk trade, and people of all descriptions wandered about, examining merchandise or haggling sharply.

An old dwarf with matted hair and eyes the color of tree moss kept circling Anoc and scowling at him. Aware from his observations that few dwarves bought slaves, Anoc ignored him as just an idler whose gold would remain in his pockets.

A pale-eyes man in a long tunic and matching cloak looked like someone more likely to buy. Anoc watched him without appearing to do so, taking note of the man's soft hands and pale, unlined features. This mild, indecisive-looking man was the master Anoc wanted. He would be generous with food and probably would not administer beatings. And when the time came, he would be easy to escape.

Seeing the man fingering his purse as though counting his coins, Anoc smiled to himself and tried to look as docile and meek a boy as someone of Grethori blood and training could.

But once the bidding started, it was the old dwarf who won. Afterward, when Anoc was pulled off the stump, his heavy iron shackles struck off, and a rope noosed around his neck instead, he stared at the pale-eyes in disappointment. Only a sharp tug of the rope suddenly tightening on his throat caught his attention.

The dwarf who had bought him grunted something incomprehensible, then pointed and jerked the rope again.

Anoc followed him into the crowd, not liking it when the dwarf shortened the length of rope and twisted the noose until it was tight against his throat. Holding Anoc expertly, the dwarf walked him through the press of people, some of whom turned to look or pointed.

At the edge of the fair, they came to a female with bulbous, wide-set eyes and frowsy gray hair sitting beneath a tree and guarding a collection of packs and bundles. Armed with a stave heavily carved with the faces of what Anoc supposed were demons and spirits, she wore a cowled tunic unbelted over a pair of men's leggings. Short leather boots covered her feet.

She stared at Anoc with a frown and shook her head at the dwarf, who grunted something in reply. After that she said nothing else, but simply loaded Anoc with as many of the heavy bundles as she could lash to his back, handed one pack to the old one, and carried the rest herself. The two dwarves set out along a trail that wound into the forest, with Anoc trudging along behind.

They walked until sunset, when gloomy shadows began to gather among the trees and even Anoc's keen vision could no longer be sure of the trail. Footsore and weary, he was glad to halt. The bundles seemed to weigh more than ever, and his shoulder muscles burned from fatigue.

The old one cast about, fingering bark and sniffing the air, until he found a faint set of marks carved into a tree. Then he turned off the trail. The female and Anoc followed, winding through the dense undergrowth to a tree of enormous girth. Kneeling, the old one dug into the ground with his hands, scooping aside leaf mold until he suddenly plunged headfirst into the ground and was swallowed whole.

Astonished, Anoc stared, wondering what kind of magic existed in this forest, where the ground itself ate people.

The female tugged at his rope, pointing where the old one had gone. Bracing his feet, Anoc refused to budge.

She shouted at him and probably swore, but he did not move. When she shook her stave at him, he retreated as far as the sudden slack in the rope would let him and reached for the noose.

No sooner did his hands close on the rope, however, than he was yanked off his feet and found himself flat on the ground, with the wind half-knocked from him. The female planted her foot on him firmly, bundles and all, and laughed.

Angered, he struggled, but remained pinned until she finally let him up. As soon as he was on his hands and knees, she kicked him sprawling over to where the ground had eaten the old one.

She spoke sharply, pointing, but Anoc was already scrambling back.

This time she hit him with the stave, making his head ring and the trees dance crazily around him.

The old one's head popped out of the ground, startling Anoc so much he almost yelped. Snorting leaves and dirt from his nostrils, the old one gripped Anoc by the noose and yanked him headfirst into the hole, with the female pushing him from behind.

Terrified, Anoc found himself plummeting into a darkness that smelled of animal and dirt. He nearly landed on his head and flipped onto his knees, his heart thudding, his eyes unable to pierce the dark. The old one tugged at him, forcing him to crawl forward, while the female came slithering down into the tunnel after him.

They fetched up inside the hollow trunk of the gigantic tree. Tiny orbs of light illuminated the space. Anoc found himself looking at niches carved into the wood that held crudely whittled cups and bark spoons. The old one shrugged off his belts and leather jerkin, hanging them on pegs.

The female unlashed Anoc's load, stacking the bundles neatly to one side. Relieved to be free of his burden, he saw her pointing and meekly took his place, crouching on the ground and watching them with wary, ashamed eyes.

His display of cowardice had embarrassed him. It was not good for the enemy to see weakness or fear. But he curbed his feelings, telling himself that perhaps it would make them confident with him.

Rummaging in a pack, the female brought out packets of food wrapped in cloth. Smelling meat, Anoc felt his stomach rumbling and wanted to grab a portion from her slow hands and cram it into his mouth. But mindful of her stave, he waited to see if she would feed him at all.

She served the old one first, handing him a waterskin and seeing him settled cross-legged on the ground. Sitting beside him, she arranged her food the way she wanted it, pouring water into one of the wooden cups. Finally, she tossed a packet at Anoc, the way one would a dog.

He began gnawing on it without bothering to unwrap the cloth.

Her stave thudded across his shoulder, making him flinch and drop the packet. Grumbling at him, she took the food, unwrapped it, and dumped it on the ground in front of him, before folding the cloth and putting it away. Still grumbling, she spoke to the old one, who simply laughed and shrugged.

Ignored by them, Anoc debated whether to refuse the food altogether, but he was too hungry for pride. The dried strips of meat tasted strongly of salt, smoke, and mold, but he ate all he was given. When she filled a cup with water and set it on the ground before him, he was careful to use it properly, swallowing the contents in three huge gulps before putting the cup down in the same place.

She smiled at him in approval, and he knew a moment's satisfaction before he ruthlessly stamped the feeling to dust.

That night he slept poorly inside the tree. He was tired enough to take rest wherever he found it, but the confined space disturbed him, and the air grew stuffy and damp. Listening to the dwarves snoring, he yearned to be in the open, under a wide night sky glittering with stars.

The next day was much the same. They trudged on

through a forest that grew ever thicker and denser until Anoc rarely glimpsed the sky and the gloom was like twilight all day long. Feeling hemmed in and uneasy, he tried to keep his bearings, but it was difficult. Having grown up in the barren, empty plains, where game was scarce and water even harder to find, he struggled to sort through myriad scents of game overlaid with trees, brush, vines, and the springy, half-rotted leaf mold underfoot.

There might be plentiful hunting, but already he loathed his surroundings. Not only was it impossible to see more than a few steps in any direction, or to watch the sky, but also he was constantly raking through branches, snagging on brambles, being tripped by vines and roots. Tiny speckled insects stuck to his skin, sucking blood until he learned how to pick them off, and their bites left sores that festered if he scratched them.

By the time they reached a small settlement at a cross-roads, Anoc was so weary and befuddled that he did not care where they were as long as the journey ended. His feet had blisters, and his bare back was rubbed raw from pack sores. His welts and bites itched mercilessly, and he was ravenous despite the diet of dried meat and water, supplemented by the sour little berries he managed to pick on the way.

But it seemed the settlement was their destination. Dwarves spilled forth to greet them, calling "Barath!" to the old one and "Shelon!" to the female.

Crouching on his haunches, thankful to rest, Anoc watched the dwarves chatter, exchanging news with the re-turned travelers. One of the packs was opened for its contents to be shared with the others. The heavy bundles, however, were stowed away in a lean-to built adjoining a massive tree. Anoc did this under Shelon's direction. When she was satis-fied and had locked up, she marched him to a creek nearby and prodded him with her stave until he stood knee deep and shivering in the icy water. She pantomimed washing, and al-though he understood her meaning, he pretended not to.

All his defiance earned was a beating, delivered expertly. Then she pointed and repeated her command until he obeyed her, resentfully shedding his ragged leggings and immersing himself in the swift-moving water. Buffeted and shivering, he came floundering out when she finally gestured permission and stood naked, shriveled, and wretched on the bank. She herded him back through the settlement in his bare hide for anyone to see.

It was customary for Anoc's people to strip captives to shame them. He had not been raised to be modest, but he understood what Shelon was trying to do to him. By the time they reached Barath's burrow, he was almost dry and no longer shivering. She did not urge him to crawl inside, however, but instead took him around to a place behind the lean-to where the mossy ground had been trampled to bare, hard dirt. He saw a bench, a blackened fire ring of stones, and a small shelf tacked onto the rear wall of the lean-to. He also saw an iron ring driven into the trunk of the huge tree, with a length of chain attached to it.

Anoc's heart grew small and knotted inside his chest. He took a step backward, but her stave whacked his spine and drove him onto his knees. For a moment all he felt was agony from the expert blow, as though she'd broken his back, and he could not quite catch his breath.

Vaguely he grew aware of something stiff being fastened around his throat. In alarm he struggled to his feet, staggering a little, but he was too late. The heavy leather collar was in place and secured in such a way that his frantic fingers could not gain the trick of undoing it. Chained like a dog, with not even a stitch of clothing to wear, and no shelter from the rain that began to fall, he turned about to glare at her through his tangle of damp black hair.

Shelon smiled at him, her bulbous eyes alight with satisfaction, and laughed as she walked away.

The drizzle swiftly turned into a downpour, and although summer rain was no hardship, Anoc sank down close to the lean-to wall in a futile effort to gain a little shelter.

The rain came and went intermittently for hours. When night fell, no one fed him, although he smelled aromatic fragrances from cook pots. His ravenous stomach gnawed and rumbled. Holding out his tongue, he managed to lick a few drops of water to soothe his thirst, but the night grew long and cool and miserable. He curled up, halfway under the bench, and slept in the mud, while the dwarves laughed, sang songs to the sprightly tunes of their piper, and made merry.

Chapter Twenty-one

Tashalya, holding up her skirts to keep from dragging them in the heavy, early-morning dew, made her way along a secluded garden path in search of Prince Guierre. The chapel bell was ringing, calling those in the palace to worship. In the distance, other bells were ringing across the city, but all the usual bustle of mass day did not reach the deserted gardens.

"Now, where are you," she muttered impatiently beneath her breath.

By the latest courier, her father was no more than a day's ride distant from Grov, moving his army slowly homeward, creating quite a stir of celebration among his happy, cheering subjects along the way. No one could talk of anything save the procession of triumph, the tournament, and the banquet feasts to come. Already the palace was festooned with garlands of flowers and bright ribbons over all the primary doorways. New banners hung from the balconies and bright pennons flew from the towers. The servants wore their best livery, and the courtiers were much occupied with tailors, dressmakers, and jewelers, requiring those worthies to work far into the night to make new finery in time for the festivities.

Tashalya had devised a daring plan, but much of it depended on the Mandrian prince. At first she'd thought of getting Niklas to help her, but he was not easily deceived. By all accounts Prince Guierre was as innocent and gullible as a newborn. If so, he would be perfect for her purposes, but as yet, she'd not found a chance even to meet him, much less trick him into helping her. And time was running out.

But today's dawn had brought a message from the prince's servants whom Callyn had bribed. It was said that the prince had argued with his tutors and spiritual adviser, had stormed out of his chambers on the official pretext of going riding, and had instead given his protector the slip. It was believed he had concealed himself somewhere in the palace grounds. A discreet search was being conducted, and Tashalya took care to avoid the guards and servants roaming the gardens.

The first three hiding places she went to proved to be empty. Frustrated, longing to be able to extend her senses and find him immediately, Tashalya tried to think of where a sulky boy might go.

Shortly thereafter, she pushed through a hedge of blooming shrubbery swarming with pollen-drunk bees and delicate, multicolored flinits moving from flower to flower. Behind the grove planted by Tashalya's eldin grandmother lay a small clearing between the sea hollies and the garden wall. An old circle of stones had been placed there, surrounding a rough slab of rock that looked like a bench but was in fact an extremely ancient outdoor altar. Someone had put a bowl of salt on it, along with a bouquet of freshly picked flowers and a small wand of peeled ash.

And on the opposite side of the altar, Guierre was crouched on his haunches, idly picking up pebbles and tossing them at the wall. Sunlight poured over him, gilding his bright head and striking fire from the diamonds sewn to his ornate doublet.

Tashalya paused, taking a moment just to stare at him. The sight Kaon had given her wasn't proving to be useful. Forcing patience, she shut her eyes a moment and focused in the

old eldin ways. Just being quiet and seeking empathy . . .
paying heed to the emotions pouring from this boy.

He was bitterly unhappy, resentful, upset. He was lonely,
too.

Opening her eyes, Tashalya curled her lips in a small,
cold, satisfied smile. Yes, she thought, she could put him to
excellent use. But it would require a delicate approach.

Carefully she tucked back a wayward strand of hair, adjusted her veil, and smoothed out her skirts. She was wearing
a very pretty gown of blue-gray chosen to enhance her eyes
and coloring. The gown belonged to the queen, loaned to
Tashalya to wear for her father's homecoming. Although
Tashalya would have preferred to wear rags rather than her
mother's clothing, she had to admit to herself that she felt
rather attractive and feminine today. She wished Kaon were
here to see her, then hurriedly squelched the thought. It was
important that she concentrate on what she'd come to do.

Stepping onto the path, she walked briskly up to the old
circle of stones, ignoring Guierre's start of surprise. He
jumped to his feet, looking at her like a fawn discovered in
the woods.

She smiled at him and gave him a small curtsy before
going forward to dip her fingers in the salt bowl. She sprinkled salt carefully around the altar, mouthing the words she'd
been taught as a child and no longer believed, made the sign
of the Circle, and stepped back.

With another dazzling smile at the boy, she said, "Forgive
me for having disturbed you."

Turning to leave, she took several steps before he came
after her.

"Wait, please," he said, sounding nervous and shy. "Please."

She stopped and faced him. "Yes?"

"What you just did . . . would you be explaining it to me?"

"It's an old eldin rite. Nothing a Mandrian would be interested in."

His chubby face flushed. He was perspiring a little in the
heat, and his brow had grown dewy beneath his ringlets.
After a moment of hesitation, he lifted soft brown eyes to
hers.

"You made the sign of the Circle, so you're not pagan," he said. "Please, won't you explain? I'd really like to know."

So she walked back to the small altar with him, keeping her voice kind and lighthearted as she explained what the placement of the stones meant, what the salt was for, and why ash was favored by the gods.

"Someone has placed these things here to honor Thod, Riva, and the lesser members of the pantheon," she said. "The flowers have no significance in the ritual, but are simply a gift of beauty that's been offered."

"But Thod is given highest respect?" he asked a bit anxiously.

"Yes, of course Thod is honored above all others," she replied. "The Circle encompasses the beliefs of both eldin and human. There is no schism between them . . . save what has come about in recent history."

"The Reformation," he said, nodding. "I am knowing all about that."

"Well, you're Mandrian, aren't you?" She smiled to take any sting from her remark, and added, "If you're so curious, why do you not attend service this day? Your presence would be welcomed."

His expression darkened. "I'm not being allowed to go."

"Why not?"

"It's complicated."

"Is it not because you are Prince Guierre and too prominent of estate and influence to attend a pre-Reform service?" she asked.

His eyes flashed to hers. "Why—how did you know?"

" 'Tis not hard to guess," she said. "Since I know who you are."

"Everyone is knowing who I am," he muttered, kicking his toe on the gravel. "I was just interested in seeing—well, I'm having curiosity about things. You Netherans follow Writ and believe in the Circle and Thod, so what would have been the harm?"

"None at all."

"Just one service. I wasn't going to be converting my faith, or turning away from Tomias," he said sulkily.

"No one would expect you to."

He sighed. "I am wishing Velain understood that. He is forbidding me to go. He has not that right. He—"

Abruptly Guierre broke off and scowled.

"I'm sorry," Tashalya said, trying to talk to him as her sister might. "It's never easy to be told what to do all the time, is it?"

He didn't answer. She wasn't sure he was listening.

"I'm not allowed to attend the service either," she said.

He looked up, blinking a bit. "Why not?"

"Haven't you guessed who I am?"

He shook his head. "Forgive me. I—"

"Yes, I know," she broke in with a laugh. "We should have officials, and an appointed meeting in a public venue, and all the pomp, but let's be informal this morning. I am Tashalya, the princess royal of Nether." She curtsied. "And honored to meet the Heir of the Realm of Mandria."

He goggled at her, hissing in a breath. The color drained from his face, and for a moment she thought he was going to flee. But he stood his ground—rather to his credit, she thought. Although he gulped a couple of times, his eyes shifting rapidly in all directions, he managed to bow.

"P-princess Tashalya, the honor is m-mine," he stammered.

She laughed again. "I rather doubt that. Haven't you been warned about me?"

"I—I—" He stopped and drew a deep breath, staring at the ground. "I have been told that you are a—oh, morde!"

"Are you wishing now you hadn't given your protector the slip?" she asked, making him blush bright red. "Don't be afraid. I don't have any magic, good or bad, although for a time it was thought I did."

"You don't?"

"No."

His gaze flashed to hers, then darted away again. "Why didn't I meet you with the rest of the family?"

"Because I've been ill."

"Oh, I'm sorry. You are being better now?"

"Yes, quite well," she said, using Mareitina's lilting tone. "It's very warm here in the sunlight. May we stroll into the shade while we talk?"

"Of course," he said, politely offering his arm.

She rested her fingertips on it, feeling his tension. The boy was most polished in address and manners, she thought, and although he was still frightened, his Mandrian courtesy had not failed him. She'd relied on that. Now she had to charm her way into his trust.

"It's good to be home," she said. Pretending to take no notice of his unease, she plucked a cluster of white berries from one of the hollies and twirled it between her fingers. "I've been away for such a long time."

"My advisers were having assurance you would not be here."

"Oh, no one expected me to be sent home," she said, allowing bitterness to creep into her voice. "As long as it was thought I was going to manifest special powers, I lived in exile. But I have been thoroughly tested by the most terrifying creatures. Have you ever seen a *sorcerel*?"

Pursing his mouth small and tight, he shook his head.

"Well, I hope you never do." She shuddered. "Dreadful. The whole ordeal will give me nightmares for the rest of my life. And yet in no fashion could they induce me to perform magic. I was so frightened, but I have survived the testing and returned."

He said nothing.

"Did you know that the whole time I was away, I could not attend service or even read Writ?"

"That's terrible!"

"Yes, I know. You cannot imagine how lonely I was, or how frightened. If only I could convince the priests to let me reenter the Circle and take sacrament, but that will come in time, I suppose."

He was quiet for several moments, although he no longer seemed to be as tense. "You are being treated most unfairly."

"Not so much. I was not subjected to cruelty. Just kept in exile and so very lonely. That's not so dreadful."

"But it is!" he said in outrage. "To be judged and condemned before anything was being proven . . . 'tis monstrously unjust."

"If only more were as kind as you." She smiled at him. "I did not know Mandrians could be so compassionate. I

thought someone like you would condemn me the moment
you knew who I was. Of course, were I in Mandria, I would
be stoned."

"No, no, we are not being that harsh," he assured her. "Cardinal Velain is with me. I could take you to meet him, and I'm
sure he would be counseling you in any spiritual matters."

"Thank you," she said, trying not to shy away in horror at
the idea. "How kind, but I am not supposed to speak to anyone at present. Not officially. I'm not supposed to be talking
to you at all."

"Why not?"

"Because I might offend you."

"Never," he said manfully. "I find you most agreeable
and—and pretty, too. And I wish to be lodging a protest about
how you're treated."

"Please do not," she said, sending him an imploring look.
"Please, please say nothing. They would know I've confided
in you, and I would be in the most awful trouble." She
stopped, casting her gaze down, and bit her lip as though in
agitation. "I suffered enough, and I'm not very brave anymore."

"I think you courageous for a girl," he said.

She dazzled him with a smile. "Truly? How kind of you to
say so. I can almost believe you."

"You must! Don't be having fear of Velain. I'm sure he is
wanting to help you."

"I'm frightened of priests now. They've condemned me
so."

"He wouldn't—well, he might appear a bit harsh,"
Guierre said thoughtfully. "Not that he's cruel, but he is strict
about matters of Writ. But if you've been proven clear of
your affliction, then I'm sure he would be accepting you and
praying for you."

Gritting her teeth, Tashalya inclined her head respectfully.
"I should be thankful for prayers on my behalf."

"You know, many in my mother's realm are wishing to
come on a pilgrimage here to see the Chalice. Your father is
not permitting them."

"That seems unfair."

"Oh, I am not speaking ill of his majesty the king,"

Guierre said hastily, "but that's really why I am wanting to attend palace chapel today. I would love to be seeing the Chalice. It saved my mother's life, you know."

"Yes."

"Mandrians revere its holy worth, and my mother is called the Lady of the Chalice because she alone of us has seen it, and been touched by its purity. I wish your father would be allowing her to journey here someday to see it again."

"Has Queen Pheresa expressed a wish to do this?"

"No. I just thought it would be pleasing her."

Tashalya sent him a sly glance. "Wouldn't it be wonderful if you could take the Chalice to her?"

His face lit up, and for a moment he looked lost in a dream. "Yes," he whispered. "That would be a noble deed, a great and brave deed."

"Very noble," Tashalya murmured. She longed for her *marzea*, even a tiny thread of it, to influence his mind. "How brave and wonderful everyone would think you for bringing it to her."

"No one in all Mandria has ever been doing anything like it," he said. "No knight—however brave and valiant—could be surpassing such action."

"The ultimate quest, taking the Chalice to Savroix," Tashalya whispered.

He sighed, then laughed a bit self-consciously, tumbling out of his fantasies. "Alas, it is not to be."

"Would you like to see the Chalice?"

He brightened, forgetting to evade her gaze. "Very much!" Then his eagerness died. "But already I am in quarrel with Velain, and shall have to be doing penance this afternoon for losing my temper."

"We could look at it in its place of safekeeping sometime. The guards are kind and would let us into the—"

"Your highness!" called a testy voice. "Come forth from hiding."

Guierre jumped like a guilty cat. "I must go," he said in a rush.

"Wait!" she called softly. "Don't you want to—"

"I must go!"

And he ran down the path out of sight.

Chapter Twenty-two

Niklas came out of bed like a catapulted stone and raced to the window. But it was barely dawn and only a faint rosy glow lit the morning sky. It was too early to implement his plan. Still, he felt excited, too full of anticipation to go back to sleep. He might as well get ready.

Turning around, he found Syban sitting up in bed staring at him. Niklas froze in his tracks. The last thing he wanted was his little brother tagging along.

"What is it?" Syban whispered. "Has the procession started?"

"No."

"Then what are you doing up so early?"

"I thought I heard a noise. It's nothing."

Syban's brown hair was sticking up. He yawned and knuckled his eyes. "Are you going back to sleep?"

"Just lie back down."

"I will if you will."

Niklas frowned. Why, he wondered, did Syban possess this unerring instinct for sensing when he was trying to do something important or secret? Reluctantly, he went back to

bed and lay down, worried that he'd fall asleep and miss his
opportunity to sneak out of the palace. There wasn't much
time. At midmorning, he and his siblings were to present
themselves to the queen in the courtyard, ready to ride into
the city. They were to wait for the king in front of the cathedral, where his majesty would participate in a ceremony of
public thanksgiving. The troops would be dismissed, to
march back out of Grov and camp in the meadows west of
the city's walls. The king, his family, and officers, along
with the Queen's Guard and the Palace Guard, would then
ride back to the palace. There would be an outdoor feast afterward, with horse races to follow and the opening rounds
of the jousting.

The latter interested Niklas. For the past several days,
contestants had been arriving. And of course many of the
knights on duty at the palace would be competing as well.
Niklas wanted to watch them practicing, but Bouinyin had
refused to let him skip his lessons to do so.

So Niklas had formed a plan to sneak out of the palace
this morning and explore the camp of visiting knights, their
squires and minions. He would see the preparations first-
hand, meet some of the men, see what kind of oil their lackeys used on their chain mail and weapons, watch them being
strapped into padded undertunics for extra protection, and
maybe get to handle a lance or a sword belonging to a champion.

It had taken much persuasion to get Guierre to agree to
go with him. But the invitation for Guierre to ride in the procession with the royal family was an honor that the Mandrians could not refuse, and the prospect of it had so heartened
Guierre that he'd consented to sneak out early with Niklas.
Although Niklas wasn't certain that Guierre had the guts to
do it, this little adventure was a kind of test. If Guierre
turned up, Niklas told himself, then he would show Guierre
his best hiding places on the grounds and how to use the servants' passageways through the palace. And Niklas was determined to talk to his father about Guierre *today*.

Meanwhile, there was Syban to escape first.

When at last Syban's breathing grew heavy and regular,

Niklas eased out of bed and stood in the gloom, watching his brother sleep.

His heart was thumping with excitement. As quietly as he could, he pulled on leggings and tucked his shoes and dagger into the waist, leaving his long sleeping robe on to conceal everything. He tiptoed out of the chamber he shared with Syban and went softly through the nursery past Dalena's cot. The cupboards bulged with her playthings and Syban's collections and Niklas's cherished sets of carved wooden knights, enough for two armies including several Nonkind monsters. There was a table where they ate their meals and did their lessons, and another cupboard of scrolls and discarded toys that none of them used anymore.

Their old nurse Niesha, as wide as she was tall, gaptoothed, perpetually red in the face, and as kindhearted as she was stout, snored on her bed in the corner. Niklas eased past her and met the gaze of the protector on duty.

Sir Kourtsin started to rise from his chair, but Niklas darted inside the privy closet, shut the door, and flung himself breathlessly against the wall with a sense of relief.

Stripping off his robe, he pulled on his shoes and tightened his belt. In the summer, most of the stableboys, gardeners, and lackeys went about their work bare-chested, clad in leggings and little else. Dressed the same, Niklas was certain that he would pass unnoticed among the workers. He would see everything he wanted, then hurry back in time to join his mother.

A soft knock on the outer nursery door caught his attention. Niklas eased open the privy door just enough to peer out. He saw Sir Ayavar coming on duty, relieving Sir Kourtsin. The two men stepped out into the corridor to chat softly for a moment, and Niklas bolted from the privy, careful to leave the door ajar. He whisked himself silently across the room and through the servants' door into the narrow, dusty passage beyond.

No one called after him, and he grinned to himself in satisfaction at having executed his plan perfectly. The protectors would see the privy door standing open and assume he'd gone back to bed. They'd never know he'd given them the slip until it was too late to stop him.

After that, it was easy. He threaded his way through the maze of passages and back staircases, pressing himself against the wall occasionally to get out of the way of yawning chambermaids carrying pails of water, laundry bundles, or trays of food upstairs.

The palace was stirring to life, its army of servants hurrying to and fro. The great kitchens looked like an anthill, boiling with activity. Niklas decided against begging for a pastry. Instead, he hurried across the scullery yard, its flagstones wet and slippery from spilled slops and soapy water dumped out of the huge kettles.

No one paid him any heed, other than the woman who shouted at him to bring more firewood. Hurrying to the place at the rear of the stables where he was supposed to meet Guierre, Niklas gazed about with deep satisfaction.

It was going to be the best day of his life. He knew it already.

In the barracks a trumpet sounded, rousing the men. They came stumbling outdoors, blinking and yawning, abristle with beards, their hair on end, their eyes bloodshot. Moaning and grumbling, they filed into the sluice house, and Niklas grinned at the sounds of good-natured teasing, loud swearing, and general roughhousing that went on in there.

Meanwhile, the sun had risen. A cock crowed from atop a pile of horse fodder, and Niklas grew restless. It was a waste of precious time waiting for Guierre, he decided. He might as well go on.

"Hie!" called a voice.

Jumping, Niklas whirled about and found himself facing Guierre. The Mandrian boy's curls were uncombed, and his face still showed creases from sleep, but he was there, dressed in one of his fancy doublets and those ridiculous leggings, clutching his salt purse in one hand and a disreputable old dagger in the other.

"Look what I am finding!" he said in excitement, holding up the weapon. The hilt looked half–burned away and the rusty blade was nicked along its edge. "It was just lying on the ground. Is it being thrown away?"

"Aye, no doubt." Niklas grabbed Guierre's arm and hustled him into the shadows beneath the wall. "What took you so long?"

"Am I late?" Guierre asked, his brown eyes glowing with excitement and defiance. "I was getting lost several times, but the prettiest girl kindly showed me the way, and after that I am having no trouble."

"Morde," Niklas muttered. "You were supposed to get here unseen. Not ask directions."

"I am risking much displeasure and trouble to have this adventure. I am being brave in joining you."

After that, Niklas lacked the heart to call him a dunce for leaving a trail any lackwit could follow. Instead, he tugged at Guierre's doublet. "You must lose this."

"What is lose? I have it now. It is not being lost."

"Take it off. Quickly!"

"Why?"

"Because you look like a prince, and we'll be noticed."

"But why are we to go incognito?" Guierre asked. "Are you thinking it will avoid punishment?"

"Never mind!" Niklas yanked at Guierre's laces. "Get it off. We'll stash it somewhere and collect it when we come back."

"But am I to be walking half-naked like you? Publicly?" Guierre looked horrified. "I could not be doing something so immodest."

"We'll be stopped and turned back if we're recognized."

"But my—"

Niklas pulled the doublet over his head with ruthless efficiency before Guierre could stop him, wadded it up, and jumped atop a water barrel to tuck the garment onto a high windowsill. "There," he said, jumping down and gripping Guierre by his arm. "Come on. We'll have to hurry now if we're to see anything."

"I am not liking to run," Guierre moaned, but Niklas dragged him along anyway.

Guierre's plumpness jiggled when he trotted along, and his skin was so white and dainty he might have been a court lady. His narrow, very tight leggings were immodest indeed when worn alone, and whistles and catcalls from the sluice house told Niklas they were attracting too much notice. With

his ears burning Niklas yanked Guierre out of sight behind a
shed and pushed him to the ground.

Guierre tried to get up, but Niklas shoved him down
again and knelt on him, smearing dirt across his chest and
shoulders.

"You're getting me filthy," Guierre protested, struggling.
"Stop it at once. How dare you!"

"Idiot," Niklas said breathlessly, jumping up to grab a
servant's tabard from a nearby basket. "Here, wear this."

Guierre frowned at the tabard Niklas pulled from the
shed. "Servants' attire? I will not—"

"Wear it or stay behind," Niklas said so fiercely that
Guierre put on the garment.

"Your father must do all for me that you are promising,
or I shall be in disgrace forever," he muttered.

After that, they had no difficulty tagging along behind a
cluster of squires and boot boys streaming across the practice field. Listening to the chatter, mostly the squires sizing
up contestants with shrewd comments, Niklas felt at least
three years older and part of the proceedings. He and
Guierre exchanged surreptitious grins, and Niklas decided
that he would cheer on Sir Oleg from Myriot because the
man was said to fight with Gantese cunning and the heart of
a beyar.

Among the tents, everything was milling chaos. Suits of
mail were being polished with oil and fierce amounts of
elbow grease. A collection of swords and daggers stood
buried hilt deep in buckets of sand. The farrier was already at
work beside a fire roaring in an iron tub, his hammer tapping
expertly as he shaped a horseshoe on his anvil. Heralds in
vivid livery scurried from one tent to another, unrolling
parchment to inform the contestants of their order of combat.

The knights themselves generally lounged about, scratching their beards and gossiping with each other. A few kept to
themselves, intently stretching their muscles and pacing
about restlessly, while others knelt inside their tents, clutching their Circles as they prayed for victory.

Niklas watched everything with delight. It was much better than he'd imagined it would be, and he wished he could
stay all morning.

"Bestin would love to be seeing this," Guierre said, grinning. Just in time he dodged out of the way of a boy leading three massive warhorses. "I wish I could be a squire, do not you?"

"Aye," Niklas said happily. "But we'd better head back now."

"Oh, no. Not just yet," Guierre protested. "I want to see yon wrestling match."

Before Niklas could argue with him, he darted over to a cleared space behind the tents, where some burly youths were grappling while a small crowd of onlookers cheered them on. Guierre shouted encouragement, and soon Niklas was cheering and yelling, too.

A hand clamped hard on his shoulder without warning, sending his heart into his throat. Grabbing his dagger, he whirled around, but before he could defend himself his feet were swept out from beneath him. He sat down hard enough to jolt his teeth together, and dropped his dagger. Eyes watering, gasping for breath, he was jerked ruthlessly to his feet.

Bouinyin picked up his dagger and handed it over hilt first. "Good morning, your highness," his protector said, slanted eyes flinty. "I trust you've been enjoying yourself?"

Relieved, Niklas sheathed his dagger and glanced at Guierre with a shrug. "Aye, I have."

Sir Thiely, looking thunderous, joined them then. He said something soft and angry that sobered Guierre at once.

"What is it?" Niklas demanded. "What's he saying to you?"

"I am not to be riding in the procession," Guierre said miserably. "I am to be going to my quarters forever. I told you how it would be."

Furious, Niklas glared at Sir Thiely before turning to Bouinyin. "That's not fair! This was my idea. I persuaded him to come here. He shouldn't be punished."

Count Bouinyin, immaculately groomed, his tanned, bald head adorned by a feathered cap, bowed. "Prince Guierre has accepted his invitation to attend and participate in today's activities. His presence is expected by both their majesties. What say you, Sir Thiely? There's been no harm done despite their foolish prank."

The Mandrian protector did not look appeased. Scowling, he tugged at the tabard Guierre was wearing and muttered something that reddened his charge's face.

"Guierre has to come with us," Niklas said worriedly, feeling guilty. "He has to."

"We'll see," Bouinyin said. "Now hurry. You've little time."

Niklas and Guierre were marched rapidly back to the palace, where they parted. Trotting up the heavily carved staircase to the nursery wing, Niklas was lectured on the evils of wandering about without his protector and the pitfalls of loitering among ruffians, including joust competitors. Bouinyin went on about the dangers of running into spies, pickpockets, and flesh traders who abducted young boys and hauled them downriver to slaver auctions. Worried about Guierre, Niklas barely listened.

As soon as he and Bouinyin entered the nursery Niklas found general pandemonium. Niesha and two assistants were struggling to dress Dalena.

"I want to dress like the boys!" she shouted, biting one of the servants trying to comb her long, tangled curls. "I don't want to be a girl today. I want to be like Papa's soldiers!"

Syban, his brown hair slicked to his skull, sat at the table. Instead of eating his breakfast, he was trying to balance a pastry on his nose. It wobbled and fell off, adorning his new tunic with a trail of sugar dust.

Niesha squawked in horror and rushed to clean him, but Syban eluded her and came running over to Niklas. "Sneak! You slipped off without me! You went to see the knights, didn't you?"

"Naturally." Niklas wished he had his own room like Guierre, away from the brats. "I wasn't taking you anywhere."

Syban swung a furious fist at Niklas's eye that Niklas dodged. He shoved Syban back hard enough to make the younger boy stagger.

Howling, Syban rushed him again, but Bouinyin intervened, holding Syban by the back of his tunic so that the boy flailed and kicked to no avail.

"That's enough, both of you," Bouinyin said. "Keep behaving like barbarians, and neither of you will see the triumph or ride in the procession."

Niklas stared at Bouinyin in horror. "Syban started it."

"And you're old enough to stop it."

Niklas silenced his protests, contenting himself with glaring at Syban, who stuck out his tongue in response.

"You'll never sneak off from me again," Syban promised him. "You're always getting to do things that I want to do, too."

"Enough." Bouinyin's icy gaze swept them both. "One more squabble, and you'll be confined to your room for the day."

Just like poor Guierre, Niklas thought, with a flood of disappointment.

"You can't do that to us," Syban told Bouinyin arrogantly. "Our presence is expected."

Bouinyin looked unmoved. "Her majesty will understand if your highness is unable to attend the celebrations."

Syban opened his mouth, but Niklas jabbed him with an elbow. "Just shut up. He means what he says."

Not waiting for Syban's reaction, Niklas strode into the bedchamber, kicking off his shoes as he went, and washed himself before donning the finery laid out neatly on his bed.

Syban followed him in there and watched, much to his annoyance.

Niklas's new blue tunic itched, chafing him at the throat where it was cut a bit too tight. Belting on his dagger, he crammed a salt purse into his pocket and picked up a small pile of coins provided by his mother for spending later at the fair.

It wasn't the usual amount of money Niklas expected, however. Frowning, he glared at his little brother and held out his hand.

"What?" Syban asked, wide-eyed and far too innocent.

"Hand over what you took."

"I didn't—"

"Hand it over," Niklas interrupted, keeping his voice

quiet so Bouinyin wouldn't overhear. "Or I swear I'll take you behind the stables and thrash you to a pulp."

Scowling, Syban dug into his pocket and pulled out a handful of skannen that he tossed on the floor. Coins rolled everywhere. Niklas curled his fists, wanting to make the brat pick them up, but instead crossed the room back and forth, angrily gathering the money.

"What do you want with it?" Syban muttered. "You never spend any. I've a sure tip on the best man at lance, and I could put it to excellent use."

"You're not supposed to gamble."

"I'm not supposed to dice with the men in the barracks," Syban corrected him. "This is different."

"Gambling is gambling, no matter where you do it."

Syban stuck out his tongue, making a grotesque face that Niklas hoped would freeze in place forever. Then the brat wouldn't be able to eat; he would starve to death; and Niklas would be rid of him.

"Someday I'll be rich," Syban bragged. "I've quite a hoard already."

"I know," Niklas said coolly. "It's hidden under that loose board by your bed."

Syban's gleeful expression faded to one perplexed and furious.

Niklas smirked at him. "Didn't think I knew where it was, did you? Now you can worry for the rest of the day whether I've been in it, or whether I'll tell Dalena about it, or whether—"

"Stop it! Don't you dare!"

Niklas clapped his hand over Syban's mouth, holding him when the younger boy struggled.

"Shut up, idiot," he whispered in Syban's ear. "You're going to get us trapped here for the day if you don't behave."

Syban stopped struggling, but as soon as Niklas released him, he wrenched himself over to the opposite side of the room. "I can get out of this room if I have to," he boasted.

Before Niklas could answer, Bouinyin opened the door and cast a suspicious glance at both of them. "Ready?" he asked.

Walking out, Niklas saw that Niesha and her assistants

had prevailed over Dalena. The little girl was beautifully gowned, her dark hair combed and shining. Only the mutinous set of her face and her snapping eyes announced that she had no intentions of behaving as prettily as she looked.

While Bouinyin conferred with Sir Ayavar, Niklas picked up his circlet of eldin silver and fitted it on his brow, then handed Syban his.

"You'll be sorry," Syban whispered angrily. "I was going to tell you something important about Guierre, but now I won't."

"What are you talking about?"

But Syban clamped his lips together and sailed out of the nursery without another word. Sir Ayavar hastened after him, leaving Niesha to walk out with Dalena held firmly by one hand. By the time Niklas followed with Bouinyin at his heels, Mareitina was coming down the passageway to join them. Her golden tresses were waving and curling in constant motion on her shoulders, and she wore a pale pink gown adorned with silk roses and braided pearls.

The sight of her made everyone smile. Forgetting about Syban and his stupid secrets, Niklas politely offered his arm to her. "Are you ready to see Papa?" he asked.

Her long lashes swept down for a moment. "Yes, but I do not like to be in such large crowds," she said softly. "All those warriors coming among us with their weapons, still tainted by battle."

It would be glorious, Niklas thought, but he suddenly felt protective of her. She was his favorite sister, so pretty and gentle. He loved her very much, and he wanted to guard her from anything that might distress her.

"Don't worry," he promised. "It's been weeks since the men fought. The priests will have cleansed them, Papa especially. You'll hardly notice."

Her expression lightened. "Thank you, dear brother. You are kind to reassure me."

They all headed along the passageway. Syban marched in front, with Dalena tugging at her nurse's hand in an effort to keep up with him.

"Niklas," Mareitina asked, sounding puzzled, "why is Syban so angry with you?"

"'Tis nothing," Niklas said, unconcerned. "I reminded him not to gamble, and he's taken offense."

But Mareitina looked worried, and for a moment her hand tightened on his arm. "It seems more than that. Be careful, Niklas."

"Of the rodent? Why?"

"I don't know," she said. "Just be careful."

Chapter Twenty-three

❧

As soon as she saw her children, Alexeika sensed that all was not well with them, but that was to be expected with such a lively brood. For the moment they looked clean and presentable. Even Tashalya, coming along with no entourage other than her crippled servant, could not be faulted today. The girl was gowned in lavender, a hue most becoming to her complexion, and her dark hair was coiled at the base of her neck in a style that made her look womanly indeed.

She seemed serene, even happy. A bit surprised, Alexeika had no time to question the change but instead accepted her eldest daughter's good mood with relief and smiled at them all.

"Well met, children," she said, as they made obeisance to her. "This is a happy day indeed when we can finally welcome your father home."

Before she could say more, there was a little stir among the courtiers. Prince Guierre—rather sulky-looking—appeared with his retinue.

Clad in cloth of gold and arrayed with jewels, Guierre fairly glittered. His doublet was longer than usual, Alexeika was glad to see, but cut far too stylishly, with padded shoulders and an exaggerated narrowing of the waist. His leggings were once again narrow and tight, banded with sewn-on strips of cloth of silver so that when he walked his legs shimmered. He wore far too many diamonds; indeed, in Alexeika's estimation he was not dressed appropriately for his age at all. She wondered who permitted the boy to make such dreadful choices. Was he never guided by his attendants?

By contrast, her own sons looked plain, almost somber, with Niklas in blue and Syban in brown. Alexeika had hoped that Guierre would abandon some of his fashionable excesses in light of her sons' example, but it seemed the Mandrian prince wanted to look his most outlandish in honor of Faldain's return. Alexeika already knew what her husband—a king renowned for his simple tastes—would think of such a little peacock.

Alexeika swept everyone outside, descending the wide stone steps to the equipages awaiting them.

Niklas and Guierre rode with her, as was their right of rank. Tashalya and Mareitina went in the next carriage with the younger children. Mareitina and Dalena were laughing together, but Tashalya looked annoyed.

It couldn't be helped. Settling herself, Alexeika gestured a command. The drivers whipped up the beribboned horses, and they rolled forward through the tall gates and onto the road.

Crowds of people were gathered along the entire route between the palace and town, cheering and waving. The protectors and guards rode in close formation, alert for trouble, but nothing marred the joyous occasion.

The morning sun shone hot from a cloudless sky. Erect and smiling, Alexeika waved to the crowd. Her heart was light, buoyant with anticipation at seeing Faldain. As she chatted with the boys, she found Guierre very adept at adult conversation, even witty. When she laughed at some of his remarks she saw him visibly relaxing. His charm was undeniable, even if much of it was a façade.

Again her heart was wrung with pity for this neglected, obviously lonely boy who thought he must be a courtier in order to earn her attention. *Pheresa is a fool to raise him so formally,* Alexeika thought. *Were he mine I would cherish him and teach him how to have confidence in himself.*

Asking him questions about his interests away from his studies, she discovered that his days were too structured, as she'd suspected. He lacked spontaneity and impulsiveness because he was managed so closely. And she promised herself to change some of that, just as soon as these festivities were at an end, she and Faldain had a little time to themselves, and she could think again.

They reached the cathedral square and alighted, climbing the steps of the massive structure still under construction. Scaffolding covered one side of it, and piles of stone stood in heaps ready for the masons to resume work. Ignoring this, for what part of Grov or the palace was never not under repair, Alexeika led her family to the shady side porch.

Reformation churchmen in vestments of blinding white silk, their yellow sashes folded precisely, their jeweled Circles hanging around their necks, bowed to her in reserved welcome. Alexeika returned the acknowledgment coolly. There remained a religious schism in Nether, for the Reformed Church would not relinquish its toehold gained under King Muncel's reign of terror, and did not hesitate to criticize Faldain for having brought back the older ways of worship. Still, there were times—such as this one—when priests of both persuasions had to join forces to offer a united service.

Lord Thum bowed to her, his gaze sweeping over the children with a smile. He looked longest at Guierre, but the boy's startling appearance did not even provoke a flicker in Thum's hazel eyes.

You have grown too adept a diplomat, she thought.

The drums began to beat in the distance. Alexeika's heart caught. Eagerly, she looked in the direction that Faldain would be coming.

Dalena tugged at her skirt. "Mama, I hear the drums!"

"Yes, darling," she whispered. "Be quiet now."

"Papa's nearly here," Syban said, springing up on his toes as though to see.

Dalena jumped up and down. "He's coming! He's coming!"

Niklas looked aglow with anticipation, his narrow,

sometimes-too-serious face alight beneath his unruly shock of black hair. Mareitina was blushing and wide-eyed, trembling a little. And Tashalya stood apart from the others, lovely and remote, her smile too brittle, her eyes suspiciously bright. Alexeika hoped she would be able to control her uncertain emotions. There must be no upsets today, nothing to mar the king's homecoming.

"Look!" Niklas said, as though he could not contain himself.

And there, coming into sight around the end of a row of buildings, rode the pennon bearers in perfect formation, the flags of king and realm flying in the breeze. The drummers followed them, pounding a steady cadence. Then came trumpeters. They blared out a fanfare that made Alexeika's spirits leap, and the crowd behind the barricades roared and surged forward with such enthusiasm the mounted guards could barely hold them in check.

The king rode into sight.

How splendid he looked, Alexeika thought. He was mounted astride an enormous black stallion magnificently caparisoned. Prancing and tossing its fine head, the animal champed at the bit and pawed the ground, but Faldain controlled it effortlessly. The king wore burgundy and gold, his long black hair flowing loose upon his shoulders rather than braided back warrior style. He had left off his armor, indicating that the war had ended, and Alexeika could not help but admire the erect grace of his carriage in the saddle, the slight tilt of his head as he spoke to one of his aides, the calm way he held out his hand in acknowledgment to the cheering crowd.

She had loved him at first sight, and each time he returned to her, she fell in love with him all over again. Giddily, she smiled, drinking in the sight of his dear face and form, and it was all she could do not to rush down the steps to meet him.

He drew rein in the center of the square and dismounted wearily. She watched him turn and say something to Chesil Matkevskiet, who stood in close attendance. Then the priests began descending the steps. Chanting rose up in sweet unison, quieting the crowd.

The little mass began, and Mareitina helped Alexeika

hush Dalena and Syban, urging them to stand in quiet respect
as the prayers of thanksgiving were said.

The priest's voice was cold and ritualized. Alexeika supposed that he disapproved of Faldain's insistence that this be
done outside in the open air. *Like pagans,* Alexeika thought
with a smile. But it enabled the common people to see their
king blessed by the Circle, enabled them to bow their heads
and worship, too. Had this service been conducted inside the
cathedral, they would not have been permitted to enter or participate.

He always thinks of his people, Alexeika thought proudly.
Her eyes grew misty and stung a little. She loved him so
much, and respected him for all the sacrifice and hardship
he'd put himself through, year after year, to bring this victory
about. At last his realm could know peace. Her heart felt calm
and satisfied, content to know that little Ilymir was finally
avenged.

Involuntarily her gaze shifted to Niklas, then Syban, and
she gave thanks to Thod for these two healthy boys. *We are
blessed indeed in our children,* she thought.

When the service ended, Alexeika left the porch alone to
greet her husband. She curtsied low to him, her head bowed,
her heart thudding wildly in her breast.

"Alexeika," he said, raising her hand to his lips.

The exhaustion in his dear face shocked her. He looked
like a man worn to the limits of his endurance. Lines were
carved in his face, and he had dark smudges beneath his eyes.
Their usual keen gaze looked a little blurred, and his hand
felt hot to hers, as though he suffered fever.

Concerned, she wanted to hurry him indoors and order
drink and a chair brought to him at once. *He should not be
standing in this heat,* she thought worriedly. *He needs cool
shade and a place to rest.*

Yet even as she opened her mouth to issue orders, she noticed how close and watchful Chesil and Lord Omas were.
The worry in their eyes told her something was dreadfully
wrong, so wrong it must not be mentioned publicly. He must
be terribly wounded, she thought frantically. Was he hiding
his injury through sheer force of will? And suddenly it made
sense why his journey home had been so slow. *Oh, dear*

Thod, have mercy, she prayed. *Let him recover from this hurt. Let him be all right.*

Her fingers tightened on his.

"Alexeika, my beloved," Faldain said. His voice dragged a little, but he managed to give her a smile so tender she could not help but smile back.

"Faldain," she whispered, mindful of everyone watching. "How glad I am to see you come home to me."

"Home," he said with a sigh. His attention seemed to wander for a moment, but then he pulled himself together. "Are the children here?"

"Oh, yes. All of them."

She beckoned, and they came spilling down the steps with noisy delight. Even Tashalya came, following at the rear with Mareitina, who was casting uneasy glances at the crowd. But the younger ones, including Niklas, had no hesitation in swarming around their father.

"Papa! Papa!" they shouted.

While the courtiers laughed and applauded, Faldain bent to kiss little Dalena. He tousled Syban's hair and clapped Niklas on the shoulder, then held out his hand to Mareitina, who rushed to him and flung her arms around his neck.

Only Tashalya held back, looking stiff and uncertain. But when Faldain smiled at her she went to him, much to Alexeika's relief. Curtsying low, she gripped his hand and kissed it.

As the crowd renewed its cheering, Alexeika saw young Guierre standing on the steps beside Lord Thum. The boy looked so wistful she impulsively beckoned to him.

He hesitated, but Thum spoke to him with a smile of encouragement. The boy came forward, his face red and unsure.

"Faldain," Alexeika said, breaking in on the children's excited chatter to their father, "may I present to you Prince Guierre of Mandria."

Guierre bowed in his lavish way. Faldain watched him, indulgently allowing Dalena to cling to his leg and Syban to nestle close to his side. The king's gray eyes slid sideways to meet Alexeika's, and for a moment their gaze met in complete accord, sharing an amusement they dared not show.

"Your majesty," Guierre said, his accent thicker than ever.

"I am being honored beyond all expression. I wish to be offering my joy at your success and to thank you for granting me a place at your court."

Faldain's dark brows lifted as he gave the boy a little nod. "Welcome, Prince Guierre," he said in fluent Mandrian. "Are you feeling at home among us? Adjusting to our customs?"

"Oh, yes, your majesty."

"Papa," Niklas said urgently, "I want to ask—"

But Faldain's broad shoulders seemed to sag a little. Alexeika touched her son's shoulder. "Not now, darling," she murmured, and saw Niklas compress his mouth in frustration.

"Let us proceed," Faldain said.

Alexeika looked at Chesil for guidance, and the Agya gave her a tiny shake of his head, his expression rather grim. The king's horse was brought forward. Lord Omas bent to murmur something in Faldain's ear, but the king shrugged him off and climbed into the saddle.

To Alexeika, watching him worriedly, the effort he expended was visible, but no one else seemed to notice.

As the noisy cheering grew deafening, she turned to Lord Thum, who had joined them, looking somewhat taken aback by Faldain's failure to acknowledge him.

"Thum, he's ill, or injured," she murmured softly. "Something's very wrong."

At once Thum's hazel eyes narrowed with concern. "Then the sooner the procession takes him to the palace, the better. I'll speak to Chesil and see if I can discover what's amiss."

Horses meanwhile were being brought up for Niklas, Syban, and Guierre. Alexeika gathered her daughters back into the open carriage, although Tashalya stared at her father as though she yearned to ride beside him the way she used to when she was little.

Alexeika touched her shoulder gently. "Come," she said.

Tashalya's face turned stony, and the hostility returned to her icy blue eyes as she climbed in next to Mareitina. Alexeika sighed, but she could not be bothered with her daughter's moods now.

All Alexeika wanted to do was rush back to the palace and see what ailed her husband, but of course that was impossible. Under the broiling sun, they wound slowly along. The people lining the road cheered themselves hoarse, waving and running alongside whenever the guards did not press them back.

Alexeika forced herself to smile and wave back although she could not stop her gaze from straying to Faldain's back, wondering how long he could keep up this pretense. Yet not once did he falter, although his movements were slow. Syban, far too excited, whooped like a Grethori and spurred his startled horse, causing it to buck a little. The boy only laughed, however, and spurred it again as though trying to force it to bolt with him.

Faldain called Syban close and spoke to him, resting his hand on the boy's small shoulder for a moment while Syban grinned up at him with such admiration it warmed Alexeika's heart. Whatever he said to the child had the desired effect, for Syban behaved himself thereafter, much to Alexeika's relief.

Niklas was riding on his father's opposite side, waving a bit shyly to the crowd but displaying his excellent horsemanship. Guierre, riding stirrup to stirrup with him, seemed unsure of the enthusiastic crowd at first.

Faldain turned his head to speak to the two boys, and Guierre began to smile.

It pleased Alexeika to see him blossoming under the king's attention. She never ceased to marvel at how patient and good Faldain was with the children. When he played with them, he was almost like a young boy himself, racing about the grounds or wrestling with them in the grass. Alexeika could not wait to see him fling Guierre down and tussle with him. 'Twould do the boy a world of good.

Then at long, long last they were passing through the ornate palace gates, making their way through the park and grounds. As soon as her carriage rolled to a halt in the courtyard, Alexeika was climbing down without waiting for assistance. She headed for Faldain, who dismounted, seemed to trip, and caught himself against the saddle. Alarmed, she almost called out, but Faldain straightened immediately with a smile, making a joke of his clumsiness.

Halfway up the steps, he paused and turned around as though looking for her. A trifle out of breath from hurrying, she caught up with him and saw the apology in his gray eyes.

"Forgive me," he said. "I am most absentminded today."

"Faldain," she said worriedly, "what—"

But the courtiers were crowding close, wishing him their congratulations, each trying to attract his attention. She dared say nothing else in so public an arena, but walked beside him, smiling until her face felt it might break, her worry intensifying with every passing moment.

And all the while she was berating herself for having planned so elaborate a celebration, for the entire day was crammed with one event after another. They had not the slightest chance of speaking privately, nor could he retire to rest without attracting notice and disappointment.

While they were taking their seats in the Hall for the midday banquet, she kept a tight hold on his hand while he dropped rather heavily into his chair. She noticed how adeptly Chesil intercepted the cup poured for his majesty and replaced it with another. Faldain drank deeply and handed off the drained cup, sinking back in his chair with a sigh.

"Was that the last?" he asked.

"Yes, majesty," Chesil replied quietly, his dark eyes intent on Faldain's face. "I'll go at once to fetch the—"

"No, stay here with me. I'll do for now."

"Beloved," Alexeika asked softly. "I can see how ill you are. Shall I cancel the—"

"No," he said, giving her a smile. His eyes had brightened, and he looked almost hale. "Let's not disappoint these people. I'm sure they've been anticipating today's festivities."

"But—"

He tightened his grip on her hand in warning. "It's all right, now that I'm home. Don't worry. Just smile beside me and look beautiful. I'll explain the whole business anon."

And so she did as he asked her, sitting poised and gracious while the king smiled at the courtiers parading past him, laughingly applauded the antics of the acrobats, behaved in fine fettle all around . . . and ate not a single morsel of the lavish feast set before him.

Chapter Twenty-four

The bundle of cloaks, hauberks, and a pack of supplies seemed too heavy for Callyn to carry. She limped slower and slower along the passageway until Tashalya turned on her with exasperation.

"Will you hurry!" she whispered.

Callyn's pallid face glistened with perspiration. Her blind eye stared at nothing, while her green one implored her mistress.

Tashalya ignored her disapproval. There would never be a more perfect opportunity to steal the Chalice, while everyone's attention was on the king and the festivities.

"Hurry," Tashalya said again and shoved open a door. Darkness yawned before them.

"Your highness—"

"Silence! I'll listen to none of your moaning. Be sure no one sees you. I'll join you as soon as I can."

"But—"

"Go." Giving her a shove across the threshold, Tashalya slammed the door and bolted it. She spared no worry for

Callyn, left alone in the dark; the servant could see well enough to find her way.

Brushing off her hands, Tashalya hurried off to accomplish the next phase of her plan.

The court had adjourned outdoors. By the distant sound of the cheering crowd, the horse races had already commenced. Tashalya walked outside at a demure pace, with a pair of pages as escort.

Reaching the stands, she found the crowds jammed so tightly it was nearly impossible to get through. The royal box where sat the king and queen, the minister of state, and all their attendants and favorites, was shaded by an awning. Servants kept the occupants plied with cool drink, fruit, and sugared comfits. Tashalya saw her father leaning over the edge to hand a prize to the winner of the race.

She couldn't help pausing a moment to watch him. He looked handsome and at his ease, smiling as he spoke to the victor, his power and authority a mantle on his shoulders. The Ring of Solder gleamed milky pale on his tanned finger, and there was no other man or eld to match him. The victor said something that made her father laugh, shaking back his long hair, and he seated himself with the powerful grace of a natural athlete. Unlike most of his courtiers, there was nothing soft or corpulent about the king. He seemed ageless and splendid, sitting there in the shade beside his lady queen, who had eyes for no one but him.

Still smiling, Faldain took Alexeika's hand and kissed it lightly, sending her a look of affection.

A pang of longing went through Tashalya. How she wished to know such love as her parents shared. How she wished to feel as content and settled, to know that her accomplishments rang with glory and renown, and that everything she did would be approved and lauded. How she hoped that when she grew to be as old as her parents she would still have Kaon's love. Because when he wasn't with her, she didn't feel sure.

Tashalya steeled herself against soft emotions, sweeping them aside. The royal children sat apart from their parents in a different section of the stands. Tashalya made her way through the crush of people to where Mareitina was surrounded by the others. Guierre was with them, much to Tashalya's relief. A cluster of servants, along with Count Bouinyin, Sir Ayavar, and Guierre's protector, Sir Thiely, stood at the rear of the box, letting the children shout and make as much noise as they pleased.

Mareitina looked pink from too much sun and wearied by all the commotion. She greeted Tashalya with relief, but Dalena immediately climbed into Mareitina's lap and gave Tashalya a grumpy shove.

"I don't want her here!" she said. "She's mean."

"Hush," Mareitina chastised her gently. "You shouldn't say that about our sister."

"It's true! It's true! I want her to go away!"

Mareitina cast a look of apology at Tashalya. "She needs a nap, poor sweetling. She's very tired and getting cranky."

"She needs a lesson in manners," Tashalya retorted.

Dalena stuck out her tongue at her eldest sister, then buried her face against Mareitina and began to cry.

The nurse came forward and tried to take Dalena from her, but Dalena clung tighter, and all of Mareitina's petting and soothing murmurs only made her cry harder.

Syban reached over and tweaked a lock of Dalena's black hair. "The next horse race is starting. You're missing it."

"Don't want to see a horse race!" Dalena howled.

"She should be taken to the nursery," Tashalya said, trying not to sound too eager. "Why don't you go with her, Mareitina? The heat doesn't agree with you."

"Too many people," Mareitina agreed with a sigh. She hesitated, glancing over toward the royal box. "But Mama asked me to watch—"

"I'll stay with the boys," Tashalya said, sitting down on the bench next to Niklas and giving him a perfunctory smile. He squeezed over to make room for her and turned his attention back to the race.

Hoping that Mareitina was sufficiently distracted to sense nothing of what she was up to, Tashalya flapped her hand at her sister. "Go, Mareitina," she said. "It's all right."

"If you're sure."

Tashalya nodded, and Mareitina rose to her feet, holding

Dalena in her arms. "And you," Tashalya said to Syban, "aren't you ready to go indoors, too?"

He was jumping and shouting at the riders, urging on his favorite at the top of his lungs. She had to yank on the hem of his tunic to get his attention.

When she repeated her question, he scowled and pulled free. "Don't be stupid. I'm not a baby, and I don't need a nap."

Gritting her teeth, Tashalya managed to keep her temper. Dalena, Mareitina, and the nurse Niesha left, with Sir Ayavar pushing a way through the crowd for them.

Quietly, well aware of the two remaining protectors watching her like hawks, Tashalya sat through the next two races with every pretense of interest. Syban whooped and screeched over the outcome of the final one.

"Won money, didn't I!" he crowed to Niklas, who frowned and tried to ignore him. He whirled around. "Tashie, guess what? I won my wager."

"When are you going to collect it?" she asked.

A look of cunning crossed his small face. "Later, at the barracks, I suppose. I'm getting rich, you know. I win more than I lose." He cast Niklas a scornful glance. "Just wait, Niklas, until I have five times the money you do to spend at the fair."

"And what," Tashalya asked Syban, "are you going to spend your money on? Sweets?"

"Nah! A dagger."

Niklas sat up straight at that announcement, and even Guierre looked impressed.

"This wager you have won," Guierre said. "Will it be bringing you such a large sum of money?"

"Sure. And I'll buy a lot better weapon than that rubbish you found."

Niklas punched his arm. "Hush! Don't be rude."

Guierre managed a little smile and shrug. "Oh, it is true what he says. My dagger isn't much, and the smith says it cannot be repaired. I am thinking to throw it away and buy one at this fair, too."

"Well, the one I get will be better than the one Niklas is so proud of," Syban boasted. "I'm going to buy a dwarf-forged one."

"Mine is dwarf-forged," Niklas said.

"Then one eldin-made."

"You can't afford it."

"Can't I? You just wait!"

"I don't have to wait. Mine was a gift from Papa. And that's something you can't buy."

Syban's face puckered, but Tashalya had listened to enough small-boy squabbles. She gripped her youngest brother's arm, and said, "Why don't you go and collect your money now?"

"Aye, why don't you just *go?*" Niklas chimed in.

Syban shook his head. "I can wait."

"Better not," Tashalya whispered to him. "If it's the barracks' pool, everyone will be grabbing their winnings to bet on the jousting. There may not be any left for you if you don't hurry to claim it."

Syban's eyes widened. He darted toward the crowd, but Count Bouinyin intercepted him.

"Better stay where you are, Prince Syban."

Syban began at once to argue loudly, and while Bouinyin was distracted, Tashalya moved along the bench to settle next to Guierre.

The Mandrian boy gave her one of his sweet smiles. "These races have been excellent," he said, looking excited. "I don't know when I've had such fun."

"I thought perhaps you might want to see what we've been talking about," Tashalya whispered.

Guierre stared at her so blankly she had to fight back exasperation.

"Remember?" she said, giving him a look that caused him to blink and jerk in his breath.

"Oh, yes, the—"

"Yes," she said, to keep him from blurting it out. "You said you wanted to see it."

"Of course, but—"

"This is a perfect time, while everyone is watching the tournament. I know a way to get you inside."

"Now?" Guierre glanced at the arena. The sand was being raked and the jousting lane set into place.

Bouinyin came back to their bench, gripping a wriggling Syban by his shoulder. "Your highness," he said to Niklas, "have I your leave to escort Prince Syban on his errand?"

"Yes, of course," Niklas said. "Anything to be rid of the rodent."

"I'm coming right back, worm breath," Syban said.

Bouinyin cleared his throat in warning, and both boys fell silent.

Tashalya gave the protector a smile of approval. "Yes, I think it a splendid idea if these two are parted for a while."

Bouinyin flicked her a glance that did not meet her eyes. "My duty is with Prince Niklas," he said stiffly. "I have tried to persuade this young man to wait for Sir Ayavar's return, but he will not."

"It's fine," Niklas said. "You have my permission to leave me."

Bouinyin's expression looked icy with disapproval. He glanced at Tashalya once more, and she could sense the hostile suspicion pouring from him. "'Tis not a question of permission, your highness," he said repressively to Niklas. "Sir Thiely remains here on duty. Your highness must assure me that you will not leave this box while I'm gone."

"No, I'm staying," Niklas said. "The joust is about to start. If you two don't hurry, you'll miss the best part."

"I'll keep an eye on my brother, Count Bouinyin," Tashalya said gaily, but the protector's expression remained cold.

He bowed to her without a word, leaving her feeling rebuffed and rather annoyed, and with a swift word to Sir Thiely, who shrugged, marched young Syban away.

Tashalya let out her breath. She'd expected trouble from Bouinyin, but fortunately Syban had helped her greatly. Now all she had to do was deal with Sir Thiely. Although thus far her plan was working perfectly, she did not know enough about the Mandrian protector to manipulate him easily.

Out in the arena, competition with the lance was starting. Keyed up, trying to gauge the right moment, Tashalya paid little heed to the heralds bawling out the names of the first pair of contestants. The knights, arrayed in armor and hel-

mets, their shields painted in bright colors and their lances
fluttering with the ribbons of their ladies' favors, galloped
around the arena, drew rein to bow before the king and
queen, and parted to ride to their opposite starting positions.

The signal was given. They galloped toward each other,
lances aimed and deadly, and met with a resounding crash of
splintering wood. One of the contestants went tumbling over
the rump of his horse and hit the ground hard enough to
bounce.

A cheer rose from the crowd, and Niklas jumped to his
feet in excitement. Guierre looked equally absorbed. They
started arguing over some point of technique that Tashalya
suspected neither really understood.

Bored, she fanned herself and edged closer to Guierre.
"Let's go," she said, tugging his sleeve to gain his attention.
"Tell your protector that I feel faint from the heat and wish to
be escorted indoors."

Looking torn, Guierre frowned at her. Fresh cheering
made his head whip around to watch the new contestants riding out. "Why don't we wait until the interval?"

"It's now or not at all," she said quietly. "I begin to doubt
that you're truly interested."

He moaned a little in disappointment. "All right."

"What are you whispering about?" Niklas asked. "What
are you doing?"

"I'm overheated in this sun," Tashalya said. "I'm going
indoors, and I need an escort."

"You had none when you came to join us."

She glared at her little brother, wanting to box his ears and
burn his tongue. The meddler needed to be taught a lesson.

"Oh, but, Niklas, no lady should be without an escort,"
Guierre said. "Not when she is requesting one."

He rose to his feet, holding out his arm to Tashalya. Smiling, she placed her fingertips correctly on his sleeve.

Sir Thiely came forward, asking a sharp question in Mandrian. Guierre answered him swiftly in the same language.

Tashalya stared down at Niklas. "You'd better come with
us," she said. "We can't leave you here alone."

He scowled. "I'm not missing the joust."

"Niklas, must I argue with you in public, before our guests?"

He rose to his feet then, but looked sulky. "I promised Bouinyin I would stay here."

"Yes, but I am unwell. We cannot leave you here alone."

"You could wait until the interval."

"Don't be churlish. If I stay in this heat any longer, I shall faint."

He shrugged, scowling.

"You're not going to be missing anything," Guierre assured him. "It will be well worth your while to come with us. You will be seeing why shortly."

"What?"

"Come," Tashalya broke in hastily, afraid Guierre's clumsy hints would give too much away. "Let's hurry so you two can come back as quickly as possible."

So their little party forced its way through the crowd that parted for them reluctantly. Tashalya saw her mother look their way, noting their departure. But they were clustered properly together and escorted by two of Guierre's servants and his burly protector.

Niklas waved in his parents' direction, and they waved back.

At that moment, Tashalya could have hugged him for doing exactly the right thing to allay any possible suspicions. She smiled to herself with smug satisfaction all the way back to the palace.

Once inside, however, and standing just outside the double doors that led into the Hall of Kings, Niklas balked. "You're going to do *what*?"

"Hush," Tashalya cautioned him, wishing Guierre hadn't blurted out their secret quite so hastily. The guards who were supposed to be stationed at these doors were absent, just as Kaon had promised they would be. The guards on duty inside the Hall were supposed to be gone as well. The plan was to position Guierre, Niklas, and the protector *inside* the Hall before anything was said.

If Sir Thiely grew too suspicious, the plan would likely fail on the spot, for she did not see how she could force an armed man inside the Hall without her *marzea*.

"Niklas, don't be so discourteous," she said. "Prince Guierre wants to see the Chalice, and I told him this would be the perfect time to look at it, while everyone is busy."

Scowling at them both, Niklas planted his fists on his hips. "Are you mad? You can't go in the Chapel."

"Prince Guierre can. And so can you. Escort him to the Holy Circle while I wait in the Hall with Sir Thiely."

"Well, how silly," Niklas said. "We can do this anytime. How could you ask us to miss half the jousting for something like this?"

"Yes, that is being a shame," Guierre agreed. "But she said this was the best moment. It will not take long. Just a peek and then we'll go back."

"No! Besides, I've seen it before—"

"But I have not."

The two boys glared at each other, but Niklas only shook his head and shot Tashalya a disgusted look.

"Niklas, please," she said.

"No. I'm going back right now."

She tried to catch his arm, but he shook her off and marched away. Sir Thiely watched him go, looking quizzical, and didn't try to stop him.

"He mustn't go by himself," Tashalya said urgently to Guierre.

The Mandrian prince pointed at his protector. "Bring him back."

But Sir Thiely shook his head with a curt negative.

Guierre sent Tashalya an embarrassed look of apology. "He says he cannot leave me."

Barely containing her exasperation, she watched her brother escape the net, taking part of her revenge with him. Short of chasing him, however, she could not bring him back. She hoped he wouldn't tell anyone what they were doing.

"I'm sorry," she said quietly to Guierre, absolutely determined that he would not get away as well. "My brothers have the manners of barbarians."

The boy looked a little hurt by Niklas's defection, but shrugged. "'Tis nothing."

"Let's hurry," she said.

Guierre walked docilely into the Hall, pausing only while Sir Thiely looked around for possible danger.

Guierre's servants followed, closing the doors behind them. It was very quiet and gloomy inside the large chamber. The guards who should have been standing near the trapdoor leading to the Chalice were absent. Tashalya drew a deep breath of relief, trying to stay calm.

Tapestries depicting various accounts of Netheran history hung from the walls. Swords and ancient weapons were arranged in decorative patterns above the enormous hearth. The remains of the midday feast had been cleared away, but the long tables had been left in place for tonight's banquet.

"Why are we being in here?" Guierre asked. "I thought we were going to be seeing the Chalice."

"This is the oldest part of the palace," she replied. "It is built over the ancient Chapel and the First Circle."

"The First Circle," he breathed, looking awed. "Oh, I see."

At the far end of the Hall, Tashalya went to a small table supporting a paneatha with icons of the gods hanging from its branches. Reaching behind it, she fumbled a moment on the wall before she found the catch. There came a click, and a section of the floor dropped open.

Guierre craned his neck. "How dark it looks down there," he whispered.

Sir Thiely spoke, obviously adjuring him to wait. The protector pushed past them, gesturing adamantly for them to stay where they were.

Kaon, she thought, *hurry!*

And as though her lover heard her thoughts, a white mist came swirling from within the cold fireplace, skirting the yawning hole, and gathering before a clearly startled Sir Thiely.

The protector shouted at it, plunging his sword through the mist to no avail. Guierre yelled something, but Tashalya clamped her hand over his mouth under the pretext of holding him close.

"Be quiet," she whispered, as startled by this manifestation as the Mandrians. "In Thod's name, be quiet."

Guierre obeyed her, his breath hot and moist against her palm, his body trembling in her arms.

Sir Thiely slashed again at the mist, but it engulfed him, buffeting him on all sides until he suddenly uttered a short, shrill scream and tumbled down the steps, vanishing from sight.

"Sir Thiely!" Guierre tore from Tashalya's hands and ran forward.

She caught him from behind and pulled him back. "No," she said. "Get back from it."

"But it's killed him."

"Be still," she whispered, holding him fast while the mist poured past them, flowing now toward Guierre's servants. Screaming, they flung open the doors, but the mist overtook them before they crossed the threshold, dragging them down and leaving them limp on the floor.

"Tomias, save us," Guierre was praying. "What are we to do?"

As though it heard his voice, the mist rose from its victims and came straight at Guierre and Tashalya this time. The boy was shaking with fear.

She had no idea whether Kaon's familiar had killed the men, and she didn't care. What mattered now was playing her part.

"Give me your Circle," she whispered.

Guierre was fumbling in his pocket and drew out his salt purse.

"No!" she said sharply. "This isn't Nonkind. Your Circle!"

He produced it from beneath his doublet, and she yanked its chain over his head so roughly she dislodged his cap. Holding up the Circle, she spoke words of repudiation, being careful to use only conventional sayings of Writ that Guierre would recognize.

The mist halted and gathered before them, and Tashalya spoke again. This time the mist spread out until it was very thin, and vanished from sight.

Guierre loosed a little sob. "Oh, merciful Thod. What was it?"

"I don't know." She tossed his Circle at him and ran to close the heavy doors before she knelt by the fallen servants.

"Sir Thiely," Guierre cried, and raced down the dark steps. Afraid the little fool would stumble and break his neck in

the gloom, Tashalya sprang after him. By the time she
reached the bottom of the worn, crumbling steps, she found
Guierre on his knees beside his protector.

The air there was cool. A soft, unworldly light lit the
gloom, casting barely enough illumination to see by.

"Is he much hurt?" she asked. "Perhaps he is only knocked
unconscious."

But Guierre was crying. Tashalya rolled Sir Thiely onto
his back with her toe. The man had fallen on his sword. His
hauberk was gashed open with a fearsome wound. Blood had
pooled beneath him, staining his clothing, and his sightless
eyes stared at nothing.

Shocked, Tashalya drew back. She had not meant for
something like that to happen. And for the first time, as she
gazed at Guierre's horrified, grieving face, she was glad that
Niklas had not stayed with them to see it.

"Oh, Kaon," she breathed.

"He's dead," Guierre said, sobbing. "Sir Thiely is dead!"

She hesitated before resting her hand on his shoulder. The
servants struck down in the Hall were dead as well, but not
like this. "I'm sorry, Guierre," she said softly, and meant it.

"What was that awful thing? Why did it come forth from
the Chapel and attack us?"

Belatedly she gathered her wits and remembered the role
she still had to play. "We can't stay here. Quick, boy. With
me."

But Guierre flinched back. "Where? Why is this happening?"

"Let us hurry. We've little time."

"For what? I have no understanding."

"There's no time to explain. Come!"

When she reached for him, Guierre drew his dagger and
scrambled back from her, wild-eyed and shaking. "If this is
an abduction, I shall be fighting you, maiden or no!"

"I'm your friend, you fool," she said impatiently. "Or have
you forgotten that I just saved your life?"

Looking ashamed, he lowered his weapon. "But what is
this being about?"

"The Chalice," she said. "It has to be. You notice there are
no guards on duty. And no priests are down here. The place

is deserted, everything left unguarded. We haven't much time
if we're to foil the plot."

"What plot?" he asked, scrambling after her like an un-
gainly puppy. "I don't understand! Who is trying to steal the
Chalice?"

"I know not as yet, but I mean to stop this foul deed." She
glanced at him. "And I need you to help me."

"Yes, of course," he said breathlessly, as she paused to
pick up a torch and strikebox lying on a nearby bench. She lit
the torch, and yellow flames drove the gloom back. "But how
come you to be knowing about this?"

"There's no time to explain everything."

Tashalya saw the altar ahead, illuminated by the pale radiant glow from the Chalice standing atop its pillar. The air
smelled damp from the sacred spring, and fragrant vines
wreathed green and lush about the altar although no sunlight
reached there. Fear touched her heart, and she felt suddenly
short of breath. *I cannot do this,* she thought. *I am lying to
this boy in the presence of the Chalice. I cannot risk my soul
this way.*

Something feather light brushed the back of her neck,
making her shiver, and Kaon's voice whispered in her mind:
You can.

She shut her eyes, drawing strength from his encouragement and telling herself she had to do her part, no matter how
much her courage quailed. Kaon had explained to her that he
could not enter the Chapel, and if they succeeded in taking
the Chalice, he could not join her until they reached their
place of rendezvous. Truthseeker, he had told her, was hidden
in a special, very rare place where the first and second worlds
coexisted and the Chalice had no power. There, he could take
it, and there would he give her Truthseeker in return.

Very much aware of the impurity of her heart, Tashalya
was not sure how close the Chalice would allow her to approach.

"Tashalya, please," Guierre said, his voice on the brink of
hysteria. "I am not understanding anything."

"I know. I'm very sorry. They're bound to be coming for
the Chalice at any moment. There's been a rumor about a
possible plot. No one's paid much attention because the

Chalice is always so well guarded, but it's up to us to take action."

"There's no one but us," he said in a very small voice.

"Whoever conjured up that mist will soon be coming to take the Chalice."

"We should be warning the king."

"There's no time."

"But surely if we call the guards—"

"Guierre," she broke in ruthlessly, "either you will help me here and now, or you won't. If you're afraid, then run away and save yourself."

His chin went up, his eyes flashing with anger. "How dare you say I'm being afraid! I'm a Gide and the son of the queen. I'll help!"

"Then go take down the Chalice."

He gulped, his face turning white in the unsteady torchlight. "You mean t-touch it?"

"Yes, and hurry!" She tore off the veil covering her hair. "Swathe it in this and take care you do not drop it."

Still shocked, he took the cloth and walked over to the pillar, where he stared up at the Chalice. Its light shone over him, gleaming on his curls, and he reverently made the sign of the Circle before reaching up to clasp the holy vessel.

Tashalya held her breath. But no flash of fire came. Guierre did not scream in agony or go reeling back. He was not burned to cinders.

Yes, my innocent, Tashalya thought in delight. *Oh, yes!*

He lifted it down carefully, wrapping it in the cloth as he muttered, "Revered Tomias, prophet most high, preserve me in this task and give me the strength by which to serve."

He didn't wrap it very well. The Chalice still glowed from between the folds in the cloth. But Tashalya smiled in satisfaction.

When Guierre started back the way they'd come, she blocked his path. "No. We dare not go back into the palace."

"But—"

"Until we know who's involved in this plot, whom can we trust?"

His face looked chalky in the torchlight as he cradled the Chalice in his arms. "Is there being another way?"

She led him past the sacred spring along a narrow, rough-hewn passageway where the walls glistened with moisture. When they emerged into a shallow cave open to the afternoon light, Tashalya extinguished her torch and tossed it down.

He suddenly gasped. "Merciful Tomias!"

Tashalya whirled around, but it was only Callyn who had appeared. Still holding the bundle of cloaks and supplies, Callyn stared hard at Guierre with her single sighted eye, making him blanch.

Hastily, Tashalya stepped between them. "Callyn, Thod be thanked that it's only you."

Guierre's eyes widened. "You know this—uh, you know her?"

"She is my servant. Please don't stare at her too much. The poor creature was tortured by Kladites and much maimed before she came into my service."

"Oh," he breathed, swallowing the ridiculous story like a river carp snapping bait. "They are horrid barbarians. But why is she here? How did she know to come?"

"I had planned a little surprise for you and Niklas," Tashalya replied, ignoring Callyn's frown. "These are cloaks and hauberks belonging to the palace guard. Old ones they'll never miss. I thought you two might enjoy disguising yourselves as my armed escorts for the rest of the afternoon, even going out to see the army after the jousting."

"Oh, yes," he said eagerly, his voice filled with suppressed excitement. "That does sound like it is being the greatest fun." Then all the pleasure died from his brown eyes. "Only now—"

"Now there can be no games," she said quietly, sounding sympathetic and gentle. "Except perhaps you can still disguise yourself? It might help us get away. Callyn, see if one of those hauberks will fit his highness."

"But where are we going?" Guierre asked in bewilderment. "Surely we must be taking the Chalice straight to the king. Or at least seeking out the duty captain of the guard and reporting that—that *creature*. And the priests must be clearing the Hall of magic. Then we—"

"Guierre, you were nearly killed," she said. "I must keep you safe as well as the Chalice. Whom can I trust at present to give us aid? Until I know, I dare not take risks with your safety."

"But Cardinal Velain—"

"Yes, of course, but let us first leave the palace grounds and hide the Chalice. Then we'll send Callyn to his eminence, asking him to get word to my father. Does that sound like a good plan to you?"

Guierre nodded, although he cast a dubious glance at Callyn.

"Good," Tashalya said, flinging a cloak around his shoulders. "Ah, this will do. Make sure you stand straight and tall. Walk with a swagger if you can."

"But, Tashalya—"

"Now, no more questions, Guierre, please. We must hurry!"

Chapter Twenty-five

When he left Tashalya and Guierre at the Hall of Kings, Niklas got only as far as the courtyard before he slowed, frowning, and stopped.

Something was wrong. He did not know what Tashalya was up to, but his sister had a look in her pale blue eyes that worried him. He knew very well that she wasn't permitted near the Chalice of Eternal Life, and what she'd said about him showing it to Guierre was nonsense.

Besides, where were the guards? he thought. There should have been men on duty at the entrance to the Hall of Kings. Not even for a jousting tournament would they have been excused from duty.

A cold finger of worry slid up his spine. He reversed his direction and headed back inside the palace.

The place felt deserted and empty as he hurried along. He found his heart thumping a bit harder as he cautiously pushed open one of the tall heavy doors.

It bumped against something. Peering inside, Niklas found himself staring at a body sprawled on the floor.

With a hiss of breath, he drew his dagger and opened his mouth to shout for help.

But some instinct held him silent. He crouched, feeling for life, and found none. Both men—Guierre's servants— were dead. Niklas's ears buzzed, and he could not seem to think clearly. He wanted Bouinyin and grew angry because his protector had deserted him to go off with Syban.

The smart thing to do, he knew, would be to run for help. The brave thing to do would be to go after Tashalya and Guierre, and help them.

Although he ached to be brave, he'd been trained by Bouinyin to be prudent. Making no sound, he retreated from the bodies and got to his feet.

That's when he heard a muffled shout. It sounded like Guierre's voice, and Niklas ran inside the Hall with his dagger in his fist. The daylight coming in from the high, narrow windows failed to illuminate the vast room very well. Bent double, Niklas scuttled down the length of the room between two rows of tables, using them for cover in case the assassin lingered there.

And all the while a voice in his head was saying, *This is stupid. This is stupid.* But he could not abandon Guierre, especially since no other help was close at hand.

The damned joust, he thought angrily. Every servant and courtier was attending it. And what a perfect distraction for abductors and assassins to do their work. If Tashalya had sold Guierre to cutthroats, then he would . . . he would . . .

Near the table used by the king and queen during banquet feasts, Niklas paused a moment and saw the yawning trapdoor leading into the ancient Holy Chapel.

Scared, he glanced over his shoulder at the doors so far away, wishing rescue would come through them. But since it didn't, he ventured warily into the open and made for the trapdoor.

At that moment, a white vaporous mist boiled from the huge hearth and headed straight for him. Niklas froze in his tracks, his heart in his throat, his eyes staring wide with disbelief.

It moved incredibly fast, and although it did not stink like Nonkind, he felt instinctive fear flood his entire body. He ducked low as the mist sailed by. It tried to descend over him like a smothering blanket, and Niklas tucked himself into a ball and somersaulted away from it, scrambling for the steps into the Chapel.

He felt the mist coming after him, swooping low this time, and with a fierce cry he dived headfirst, scooting down the steps on his belly. Landing with a jolt at the bottom, he looked up dazedly and saw the mist retreating from the hole.

"Morde," he breathed, winded and bruised.

He sat up, realizing he'd dropped his dagger somewhere, and found himself next to another body. Startled, he drew up his legs to avoid it.

It was dark down there, too dark.

A terrible feeling came over Niklas. He knew not what he'd stumbled into, but he remembered how angry Tashalya had seemed when he left her and Guierre. Was he supposed to be abducted, too? Both crown princes, both worth enormous ransom . . . Niklas's mouth went dry.

Fumbling about in the dark, he located a torch and the strikebox. It took his shaking hands several attempts before he managed to light the pitch. A flare of torchlight pushed back the darkness, and he stared at the blood-soaked body of Sir Thiely.

Horrified, he barely choked back his nausea and turned away, picking up his dagger and stumbling toward the First Circle. He could hear the tiny spring bubbling in its pool where it came from a fissure in the rock, but the Chalice of Eternal Life was gone.

Holding the torch as high as he could, Niklas stared and stared at the pillar, but disbelief and shock could not change facts. His sister, he realized, had taken both Guierre and the Chalice.

He'd heard all the rumors about her, heard the gossip and malicious remarks dropped by courtiers when they thought he couldn't overhear. He knew that she was in training to be a *sorcerelle* someday, and that Mama wasn't happy about it. And he knew that there was trouble of some sort behind her current visit home.

Until now, he'd paid little attention, but this made him

ashamed of her. She'd dishonored his family, and the Chalice would probably kill her.

Niklas knew he needed help, but the idea of going back the way he'd come and facing that horrible mist was beyond his courage. He decided to follow his sister, seeing where she was going and who she was in league with. *Then,* he assured himself, he would tell Bouinyin and Papa, and set the guards in pursuit of her.

Deep in the Dark Forest, Anoc was slowly adapting to the ways of the dwarves. Cruelty and indifference were not unknown to him, but the horrible food, the tight confinement inside the burrows and tunnels underground, and the demeaning work wore on his spirit.

Shelon had given him clothes that didn't fit. She'd cut off his long dark hair, although he'd struggled so ferociously against it that she'd finally trussed him with ropes to do the job. Thoroughly ashamed, for the loss of his hair was the greatest humiliation he'd known, Anoc knew he could never present himself as a Grethori warrior or even as the Deliverer until it grew back. And how many years would that take? How was he to braid the finger bones of his slain enemies in his locks of war if he went shorn?

From that point forward he hated and resented Shelon with all his heart. She seemed not to mind his sullenness and bursts of temper. She beat and starved him into submission, and once she learned how much he craved fresh-killed raw meat, she fed him grain porridges and lentils until his strength leaked out of his limbs and his mind blurred. Once in a great while she would toss him a live mouse or a freshly killed rabbit, watching while he tore it to pieces and devoured it, bones, bits of fur, and all. On these occasions, he found himself feeling almost grateful to her for such generosity, but he recognized her trickery in training him to submit.

He tried refusing to touch the next mouse she gave him, letting it run away and escape into the bushes. But she merely shrugged, feeding him nothing for days until he shivered in need for blood and flesh, and knew not how he could survive.

After that, he ate the meat she gave him and defied her no more. The training could go both ways, he decided. If she thought she'd broken him, then she would begin to rely on him. And that, he vowed, was when he would snap her neck and suck the marrow from her bones.

Barath, his master, proved to be a trader of metal goods, mostly cups and bowls that he then sold to travelers on the river.

Daily Barath went to the landing near the settlement, with Anoc carrying his goods for sale, items that would be displayed on a wooden shelf beneath a tree. Barath loved to talk to his customers, laughing and slapping his knee, haggling long for a mutual price.

Shelon, his daughter, was a trapper and hunter. She roamed the forest, coming home just before darkfall with the game she'd taken from her snares. She would set Anoc to work with the hides she skinned, having him scrape off the hair and tan them to suppleness. He considered this the work of females, but he did it with sufficient skill to earn her satisfaction.

Some days she would sit next to Barath on the riverbank, smoking a wooden pipe that stank noxiously, offering her leather goods for sale. She sewed footgear, quivers for arrows, belts, and money and salt purses, all utilitarian objects that were plain and functional, no more. When Anoc began to make the items for her, cutting intricate patterns into the leather, her goods drew sharp interest and higher prices. She rewarded him with kinder treatment, feeding him better. She also taught him words of the dwarf tongue, although it demeaned his mouth to say them. She drew symbols on the ground that she called runes, and insisted that he cut the designs into the leather.

Anoc, his fingers caressing the hilt of the knife he used for such work, bided his time and watched her grow happy with the money she hoarded. Greedily, she increased his workload, and when he took scraps of leather and fashioned them into a fitted pouch to roll the leather-working tools in, she smiled and thumped him on the back, allowing him to keep it among his few possessions behind the shed. He owned a bowl, a tiny disk of stone with a hole in the center that Shelon called a button, a small container made of woven straw in which he concealed strands of her hair and some of her dried dung, a spare cowled tunic too wide and short for him, a jerkin of leather scraps that he'd sewn for himself, and a blanket with a hole chewed in one end. He also kept concealed a collection of fist-sized stones worn smooth by the river, and a leather sling made in secret. He had a straight, smooth stick, supple but very strong, with one end sharpened and hardened in the fire to form a primitive spear. He had a short stick whittled into a stabbing weapon, and now he had leatherworking tools of awl, gut sewing thread, three steel needles, and a cutting knife with a curved, extremely sharp blade.

Barath insisted that he learn the care and maintenance of metal. Gradually Anoc came to appreciate an excellently made piece of steel or silver or iron. He learned how keeping it cleaned and oiled prevented deterioration.

"Sword blade does not dull if kept clean?" Anoc asked one day.

"It must be sharpened properly, with skill, and all rust kept off it. Rust weakens the metal."

"And so sword breaks in battle fight."

Barath stared at him. "Rust also eats holes in bowls so they can no longer hold water."

"Blood on sword blade is rust?"

"It causes the blade to rust, aye."

"Then blood is cleaned and sword stays good," Anoc said.

"That's right. That's how them Netherans whipped you folks. Grethori never understood how to take care of weapons. Steal the best and let 'em rust and get nicked, then howl when they shatter in a fight." Smoking his pipe, Barath tapped Anoc's shoulder with its stem and pointed at Shelon, busy fitting new steel tips to her arrows. "She ain't no fighter, but she keeps to the same good sense in caring for her weapons. Arrow tips always clean and sharp. Skinning knife kept to a fine edge. No rust, ever. And them things she uses will last her all her life."

"You make swords?"

"Never did," Barath replied, sucking on his pipe. "Apprenticed to a silversmith, learned how to make cups and spoons, fancy things for trade to Mandria and Nether."

"Pale-eyes."

Barath uttered a croupy laugh, hawked, and spat. He admired the distance his spittle traveled, then said, "The only pale-eyes I know are them eld folk. Don't see many about these days. Now they can forge some fine blades, if I do have to say it."

"Quit talking to him about swords and weapons, Pap," Shelon said with a frown. "Just get him all stirred up again and thinking about things that be of no use to him now."

"Too young to fight. His teeth ain't filed yet."

"Don't matter." She kicked Anoc out of her way and crouched down beside Barath to refill her pipe and light it. Soon both of them were wreathed in clouds of stink.

Anoc edged as far away from them as his chain would let him.

"Fighting's born in them," Shelon said, puffing away. "Like a baby viper in a snake nest. No longer than my finger, but it'll strike. That's in it. Same with him. Can't be trusted, and can't be taught much neither. Too stupid, these Grethori." She laughed, displaying square yellow teeth. "But he ain't bad with the leather."

"Pretty good, I'd say," Barath replied.

Her gaze went to Anoc, who was trying to stare back with flat indifference despite his anger. He understood almost everything she said now; perhaps she didn't realize that. Or perhaps she didn't care.

"I think he's gentled enough to be sold to Karth," she said to her father.

"So soon?"

"He's even picked up a bit of our clan speak. I'll have him draw some runes for Karth. It'll make him look smart, see?"

Barath grinned around his pipe and gave her a thump of approval. "Smart, you are. He can speak and write and work leather. Don't cause trouble. Don't soil the burrow. Aye, he'll fetch a high price."

"Then I can buy two new ones at the next auction and train 'em good, too," she said with satisfaction. "Getting me a good hoard of gold, Pap."

Anoc bowed his head, forcing his hands to keep busy with the hide he was supposed to be scraping, while his insides churned. Who was Karth? How far away would he be taken?

What would Karth do with him? How soon would she sell him?

"Karth'll be coming on the river any day, I'm thinking," Barath said.

"Aye. Rushing it a bit, but this one's ready." She eyed Anoc with open speculation. "Just to be safe, I won't give him any more meat until he's sold. Don't want him too feisty."

"Don't want him weak and stupid, neither," Barath said. "Feed him up and keep him strong. And I seen you letting him keep those leather tools between chores. Best not trust him too far." Barath tapped his temple with the stem of his pipe. "Him's still thinking about swords and fighting."

"Stirred up," she said, nodding.

"Aye."

Anoc went on working, keeping his head down as though he couldn't understand them. His heart burned at their cunning. Without the tools it would be harder, but he could still escape. It would have to be the stabbing stick to her heart, he decided, and not the leather knife across her fat throat.

Chapter Twenty-six

Niklas had a stitch in his side from running, but he grimly kept going, tracking his sister, Guierre, and a third person through the wooded parkland surrounding the palace. They had a long start on him and were keeping to cover, which made it difficult for him to follow. Each time he lost their tracks, he felt an increasing sense of panic, certain that Tashalya had just vanished in a blaze of green fire the way Samderaudin sometimes did, but he always picked up the trail again.

He couldn't help but think that on any other day guards on patrol would have crossed his path several times already. But when he most urgently needed them, they failed to turn up. *No doubt watching the joust,* he thought bitterly.

He couldn't understand where Tashalya was going. The fact that she was heading away from the main gates reassured him slightly, but at the same time her direction made so little sense that he feared more trickery.

She had to be mad to steal the Chalice. Or, he wondered, was Guierre taking it to Mandria?

Immediately he told himself not to be stupid. Guierre

wouldn't have slain Sir Thiely, and he certainly hadn't conjured up that evil mist.

Hoping Tashalya was just going to hide the Chalice somewhere on the grounds, although he couldn't imagine why, Niklas fantasized about bringing it back to his father and earning lavish praise for his brave deed. But he knew it would not be that simple.

Meanwhile, surely Bouinyin had discovered him missing by now. Niklas felt sorry for all the times he'd given his protector the slip, for he wanted Bouinyin to find him, and soon. And why, he wondered, catching a distant glimpse of Guierre's golden head, didn't the Mandrian break away from Tashalya? From what Niklas could tell, Guierre wasn't trying to help himself at all. Had he no spirit, or had she enspelled him?

Each time Niklas felt tempted to leave Guierre to his fate, he thought about Sir Thiely and felt sick again, determined to do all he could. If any harm befell Guierre, Nether and Mandria would go to war, and Niklas did not want his father to have to fight again so soon.

The path grew steeper, for Tashalya's party was still heading uphill toward the bluff. Stopping beside one of the rowan trees growing next to the outer wall, Niklas gulped for breath and sank down on his heels. His legs were trembling with fatigue, and sweat had stuck his tunic to his back. The heat was like an oven, and he was thirsty.

Why had she chosen the bluff? he wondered. It overlooked the river, but below the wall's base, a sheer cliff face dropped to the water. It was impossible to descend.

Just as he stood up to continue, he heard a furtive rustle from atop the wall, and something dropped on his shoulders, knocking him flat.

He would have screamed had not all the air been driven from his lungs. Wheezing in agony, he writhed and choked for breath, and when he could finally sit up he found Syban crouched on the ground in front of him, grinning evilly.

"Told you I'd make you sorry," Syban said.

Niklas gasped in another breath, trying to slow his racing heartbeat. At that moment he could have strangled the brat, but although his fingers clenched and unclenched, he couldn't pull himself together enough to attack.

"You're as white as milk," Syban informed him. "Bet you thought I was a shapeshifter, ready to bite venom in your neck." He sprang at Niklas. "Grrr!"

Niklas rolled with him and pinned him flat. Before Syban could yell, Niklas clamped a hand over his mouth.

"Shut up!" he whispered furiously. "Little fool, you'll give us away."

Panting, Syban stopped squirming, but Niklas did not trust him as yet. "There's trouble," he said softly in his brother's ear. "Bad trouble. Guierre's been abducted, and his protector is slain. I've tracked them this far, but I'm afraid they've found some means of getting him over the wall. I'm going to keep following them, but you must run back to the guards. Find the duty captain, or Bouinyin—anyone who'll listen to you—and bring help. Will you do that?"

Syban nodded, and Niklas let him up.

Springing out of reach, Syban whirled around and stuck out his tongue. "Can't you think of a better game than that?" he taunted.

"This is no game," Niklas said grimly. "Tashalya has lost her reason. She's stealing Guierre away."

"So? Let her. He's not much fun."

"You barbarian," Niklas said fiercely. "There could be war from this, or worse. And Papa will have to fight it."

"Good!"

"No, it's not good. The Mandrians are our allies, and Guierre's decent enough. I'm not playing, Syban. You must run and fetch help."

"While you follow them?"

"Aye. Hurry. Please!"

Syban stared at him. Dirt was smudged across the younger boy's face, and the knees of his leggings were torn. His green eyes assessed Niklas before he shook his head. "I'm not missing anything."

Fury swept Niklas with such force that he was momentarily helpless, unable to move or even speak. All he knew was an overwhelming urge to smack Syban, to shake him until every tooth rattled in his stupid head.

Instead, he pushed past his brother. "Get out of my way."

But Syban hopped after him. "Are you serious about this? A real abduction? Doesn't Bouinyin know?"

Niklas whirled around and shoved him so hard against a tree that Syban's eyes watered.

"Why don't you jump higher and shake all the bushes," Niklas said in a low, furious voice. "Why don't you scream and shout for attention? Maybe we'll end up abducted, too, along with Guierre. Or assassinated."

"What's that mean?"

"Killed, you *idiot*. Like our brother Ilymir."

Syban grew pale. He didn't speak, and Niklas released him, running in an effort to make up the time he'd lost. He was still furious with the rodent, and he had to wonder why the gods had let Syban, instead of Bouinyin, find him.

The trees thinned out and stopped, opening to grassland the rest of the way to the hilltop. The outer wall shortened to less than half its usual height where it ran along the bluff, and it was too narrow on top for sentries to patrol. But what need? No one could breach the walls from that direction.

So what, Niklas wondered in frustration, was Tashalya going to do? Fly away with the Chalice?

At the edge of the trees, he paused, reluctant to go into the open. He could see Tashalya clearly for she was no longer attempting to hide. She halted her little party next to the old lean-to and went to peer over the top of the wall. Guierre knelt on the ground, cradling something in his arms.

The Chalice, Niklas thought, feeling queer in the pit of his stomach.

The third person looked like Tashalya's strange servant. She set down what looked like a heavy bundle, then she and Tashalya broke the latch with a stone and pulled open the door of the tiny lean-to.

That puzzled Niklas, for he could not imagine what they wanted in there. He had peered through the cracks between the rotting wall boards once, seeing nothing but a scythe and a pair of wooden rakes standing propped in one corner. Such mundane contents did not entice him inside, and the space was too tiny to commandeer into a play fortress. As a structure, it was so old and decayed it looked as though it might fall in at any moment. Vines with crimson flowers grew across the rickety roof, providing a nesting place for birds. The gardeners didn't even hide flasks of mead in it, the way they did in another lean-to closer to the gardens.

Tashalya's servant did not reappear, but Tashalya beckoned to Guierre, who went inside.

Niklas frowned, feeling suddenly hollow. "Trapdoor," he whispered. "A secret passage!"

"What?" Syban asked, bouncing up beside him and making him jump. "What secret passage? Where?"

Niklas swallowed his heart back where it belonged and glared at the pest. "I told you to get help."

"And I said I wouldn't." Syban looked past him. "I don't see anyone. This game is stupid."

"Then why don't you leave?"

"Because you want me to."

Loathing him, Niklas tried to think. It was too late to go for help now. Help lay at the opposite end of the vast grounds. He could never run all that way and fetch anyone back in time before Tashalya reached the river. No doubt she had a boat waiting for her. If she was going to be stopped, it had to be immediately, and he was the only one to do it.

He broke from cover, racing across the grass to the lean-to. Syban shouted after him, but Niklas did not glance back.

Reaching the lean-to, he shouldered his way past the door and found the trapdoor standing open. Niklas stared down into a hole apparently bored through solid rock. Iron rungs were bolted to one side of the shaft. Niklas hesitated, not liking the feel of cool, dank air rising against his face, but then he gathered his courage. *If Guierre the pudding can do it, so can I,* he thought, and climbed in. Bits of rust flaked off the rungs, scratching his hands. He wondered if the metal was strong enough to support his weight. If he fell, how far would he drop to his death?

Syban flung himself at Niklas, gripping his sleeve. "No!" he whispered, looking scared. All the mischief had faded from his eyes. "It's a trap, full of 'sassins. Don't go down there."

"I have to," Niklas said with cold anger, "because you wouldn't get help while we still had a chance."

Dismay crumpled Syban's face, but Niklas couldn't forgive him. He gave Syban a one-handed shove that sent him sprawling on his backside.

"In Thod's name, go and get Bouinyin," Niklas said. "Tashalya is taking Guierre and the Chalice away. Tell Bouinyin that, and hurry!"

During the long interval between jousting events, it was customary for nobles to stroll through the maze of tents serving as the competitors' camp. Knights, bruised and winded, were sitting on stools under awnings, wincing while their squires patched up their hurts and pounded on stiffening muscles to loosen them. Other lackeys hurried back and forth, seeking lost spurs, fetching favors and love notes from ladies in the stands, mending broken straps, racking lances, carrying swords to the grinding wheel to have a fresh edge put on. And the lords and ladies of the court wandered freely through the confusion. The lords wished to chat with their favorites, encouraging the knights whom they sponsored or wagered on. The ladies eyed the masculinity on display, seeking glimpses of bared, muscular chests and bulging arms as knights washed to cool off, changed undertunics, and adjusted their hauberks.

Alexeika, strolling through the melee beside her husband, had little patience for the giggles and whispered comments of her ladies-in-waiting. The busy knights, preoccupied with the contest, often ignored many of the foppish courtiers, but the appearance of King Faldain sent them to their feet, grinning at the honor he paid them. Many were battered veterans, scarred, broken-nosed, missing ears and teeth. His majesty chatted with the men, examining swords and admiring gear and horses. It was the kind of common touch that Faldain did so well, Alexeika thought with admiration.

But she remained worried. Although he seemed in better form now than this morning, he'd grown quite pale again. She wished he had chosen to rest during the interval instead of exerting himself.

When a trumpet sounded the end of the interval, the crowd of spectators headed back to the stands. Several knights cheered the king. Smiling, Faldain turned around in acknowledgment. Then he winced, lifting one hand to his temple, and collapsed in midstep.

He went down so suddenly, with so little warning, that even as Omas and Chesil rushed forward, Alexeika was still staring. By the time she reached him, the men were lifting Faldain from the ground. His head lolled, and he did not rouse from his swoon.

"Gently!" Alexeika cried, gripping his hand. It felt icy cold, and she berated herself for not having insisted he take to his bed. What did a silly joust matter when he was so ill? "Omas, go carefully with him."

If the protector heard her, he gave no indication, but nothing could have been more solicitous than the way he laid his king upon the board stretcher brought from the physician's pen at a run, or the way he walked next to Faldain, his large hand resting upon his master's chest as the king was carried to the palace.

Alexeika hurried along on the other side of the stretcher, watching her husband's unconscious face so anxiously she had no memory of the walk. Suddenly she found herself indoors. People milled around, babbling their distress and confusion.

Chesil took charge, issuing orders for the king to be taken to his chambers at once. An aide came—one of Omas's sons—and escorted her through the crowd.

Halfway up the stairs, she found her way blocked by Count Bouinyin, stone-faced and fuming. "Has your majesty seen Prince Niklas?" he asked.

"Not now, my lord," the aide said brusquely, brushing him aside, but Alexeika turned back with a fresh stab of anxiety.

"Are you saying he's missing?" she asked.

Bouinyin's gaze flicked ever so slightly to meet the aide's before returning to hers. *They are managing me,* she thought with annoyance, but put it aside to be dealt with later.

"Is he missing?" she asked again.

"No, your majesty. Be not alarmed. He is with Prince Guierre."

"Yet you are not!" she said sharply. "And you know not where the boys have gone?"

Bouinyin looked irked by having to admit it. "Sir Thiely is with them, but I—"

"And who is this knight?"

"Prince Guierre's protector, so they're well enough, but I dislike leaving Prince Niklas on such a day with so many visitors on the grounds."

Behind her, Sir Pyron muttered something beneath his breath. Alexeika glared at Bouinyin, whom until that moment she'd considered to be excellent at his job. "I wonder how you saw fit to leave his highness at all," she said. "If you cannot do your duty, and find him speedily, seek out someone who can."

Bouinyin bowed to her, his face grim indeed, and she headed on up the stairs. But in the passageway leading to the king's chamber of state, she encountered Captain Mekov of her personal guard, striding along in his gray cloak. She stopped him.

"Captain, please see if you can assist Count Bouinyin. Their highnesses are—"

"—hiding from him again?" Mekov said with a grin. His ruddy face sobered almost at once, however. "Not the day for it."

She hurried on, telling herself that the boys would naturally be found at the arena, agog over the weapons, armor, and horses. Why Bouinyin was searching for them here inside the palace, she did not understand. But there was no time to think about that now.

The doors to Faldain's chamber stood wide open. The guards on duty were useless at the moment, for courtiers, members of the council and Kollegya, several physicians, and busy servants were streaming in and out.

Alexeika swept into the confusion, seeing in a glance that Faldain had been placed on his bed, with a pair of physicians bending over him. She turned on everyone else.

"How dare you make this noise?" she said fiercely. "How dare you gawk as though you watch a mummery? His majesty needs peace and quiet. All of you will go immediately."

The idle curious were driven out, but Count Unshalin, Archduke Krelinik, and Lord Pertok remained, standing in one corner of the vast room, murmuring to each other while their gaze remained on the unconscious king. Alexeika stood at Faldain's bedside while the physicians examined him.

"What is it?" she kept asking. "What ails him?"

The door opened to admit a group of three non-Reformed priests, looking wide-eyed and flustered. One was carrying a wooden box carved with interlocking Circles. The sight of it made Alexeika's vision shrink to a very small portion. She felt icy cold and light-headed, but she gritted her teeth and held on, telling herself this was no time to faint.

Chesil hastened to the priests. "*Aychi!* Hurry. Hurry! He has left this too late, I fear. Be quick!"

The priest holding the box was already raising the lid, while another drew forth a small, stoppered vial of Chalice water.

Chesil swore a fearsome oath. "What is this?" he demanded, his dark eyes ablaze. "The Chalice was to be fetched, *neya?* The Chalice! This is not strong enough."

Someone in the room gasped, and several people made the sign of the Circle. Alexeika felt as though her breath had frozen in her lungs.

The priest with the vial walked over to the bed, and while a physician lifted Faldain's head, he administered the water, murmuring a prayer.

Trembling, Alexeika reached for Faldain's hand, but Omas eased her back. "Let them tend him, your majesty."

With difficulty she pried her gaze away from Faldain's pale, haggard face and lifted it to meet Omas's worried eyes. "Is he dying?" she whispered.

"All he needs is the Chalice," Omas replied, but he was frowning at the priests.

She turned to stare at them, too, wondering why they hadn't brought it. One of the priests was speaking softly to Chesil, and the aide's swarthy face suddenly turned a queer, ashen hue.

"Chesil?" she said. "What's amiss here? Why do they not attend his majesty as is required?"

The priest holding the little vial lifted stricken eyes to look at her, but he said nothing as Faldain was laid gently back upon his pillows and the covers pulled up to his chin.

Chesil reached out blindly and gripped one of the massive, carved bedposts. He bowed his head.

"Chesil!" she said sharply. "Answer me! What is wrong?"

When the Agya raised his head and faced her, the anguish contorting his features made her gasp. Again she heard that roaring in her ears.

"It's gone," he said.

"What?"

"It's gone. The Chalice." He stared at her, shaking his head hopelessly at the unconscious Faldain. "*Aychi a meht sala.* Someone has stolen the Chalice. It cannot be found, and without it our king will surely die."

Chapter Twenty-seven

Niklas climbed down the metal rungs until his hands and shoulders were aching from the strain. Daylight reaching into the shaft grew dimmer until darkness surrounded him. He listened to his frightened breathing and tried hard not to panic. But if this shaft went much deeper, he did not think he could make it.

Just then his foot, in reaching for the next rung, bumped against solid ground. He lost his handhold and stumbled backward. For a terrified instant he thought he was falling, and flailed his arms wildly, but then his back hit a wall, and he realized that he was standing upright and safe.

Drenched with perspiration, trembling all over, he tried to recover his wits. He heard the low murmur of voices coming from somewhere to his right. Blindly he groped his way in that direction, bumped into another wall, and ran his hands over damp stone and soil until he felt emptiness and knew he'd found a passageway.

Still, the hardest thing he'd ever done was to force himself to enter it. Bravery and noble deeds were one thing when there were torches to see by; but in the dark it was much harder to hang on to his courage.

He heard Tashalya's voice—cool, rather imperious, self-assured. It infuriated him that she had no remorse about what she was doing.

Angrily he found his nerve and groped along the passageway, trying not to imagine what might await him.

Then ahead of him flickered a light. Suddenly he could see the shadowy walls of the passage, which opened out into a small cavern of sorts. Torches burned in sconces on the walls, casting unsteady light. A natural jut of rock formed a small landing lapped by water. A boat bobbed lightly on its moorings there. Tashalya and Guierre stood watching the servant loading the boat with two bundles and a wooden box wrapped in what looked like an old cloak.

Clutching his dagger, Niklas rushed from the passageway. "Hold there!" he cried, his voice echoing through the cavern. "Stop! I won't let you get away with this!"

Guierre spun around with such a start he nearly toppled into the water. But Tashalya smiled at Niklas, her icy blue eyes triumphant.

"At last," she said calmly. "I thought you would dawdle forever. Put that dagger away and come along."

Her matter-of-fact reaction punctured Niklas's bravado. He stared at her, feeling rather foolish.

Guierre frowned at him. "Do you come accusing us of something?"

"Aye, stealing the Chalice!"

Guierre's mouth dropped open, then he turned red. "That's a lie! You will be unsaying it."

"I won't! You thieved it from the Chapel, the pair of you, and left Sir Thiely dead." Niklas glared at his sister. "Whatever you're up to, Tashie, it's gone far enough. Take the Chalice back now before it's missed and maybe you—"

"Is that your best offer?" she asked with amusement.

Niklas frowned, unsure of what to say. She wasn't ashamed. She didn't act guilty. She didn't seem to be afraid despite the weapon he held.

"Niklas, no, no," Guierre said, his accent thicker than ever, "you are being misunderstood about everything. We are *saving* the Chalice. There is a plot afoot, and a horrible apparition is having slain Sir Thiely."

"Aye, I saw the mist," Niklas said grimly. "But it could not enter the Chapel. If you got past it that far, you were safe enough. Why run? Why steal the Chalice?"

"We are not stealing it. Someone else intends that," Guierre said earnestly. "We are protecting it."

"Why not call the guards? Or take it to the king?" Niklas asked.

Guierre shot a frustrated look over his shoulder at Tashalya. "He is not believing us."

"Where are you going with it?" Niklas demanded of her. "All the way to Mandria?"

She only smiled smugly, but Guierre's clenched fists came up.

"How dare you be saying such a thing to me!" he sputtered. "You dare insult me with the basest—"

A thump and a sharp cry came from the passageway behind Niklas. He turned around, but heard only ominous silence.

"Have you brought the guards?" Tashalya asked.

Niklas didn't answer. A terrible, nameless fear had gripped him. Taking one of the torches, he plunged back through the passageway and found Syban lying crumpled—white and very still—at the bottom of the ladder. One of his arms was twisted beneath him at a wrong angle. Just seeing it made Niklas feel ill.

Horrified, and not quite certain what to do, he dropped to his knees beside his little brother. "Oh, Syban," he whispered. "Syban!"

He forced himself to touch the child's throat and felt life there, beating strongly. Niklas began to cry in relief.

"What is it?" Tashalya asked sharply, coming up from behind him. "Is he dead?"

Niklas shook his head, unable to speak.

Her hand touched his shoulder. "Move out of the way."

Niklas obeyed, and she lifted Syban gently. "Hold his arm while I carry him," she said. "We're going to hurt him a little moving him like this, but it can't be helped."

"Tashalya—"

"Do as I say!"

Niklas held Syban's arm as supportively as he could, but the shifting of the broken bones in his clumsy hands made him feel clammy and light-headed. Gritting his teeth, he sidled along through the passage beside Tashalya, trying his best not to hurt Syban, who looked so little and white.

"Morde a day!" Guierre cried when they emerged onto the landing. "What's happened?"

The servant with the brass-colored hair had been gouging the ground with a stick, but she came hobbling over and took Syban from Tashalya.

"What will she do?" Niklas cried. "I don't want her tending him."

"Don't be a fool," Tashalya said sharply. "Callyn knows what's best for him." She took Syban's broken arm and folded it gently across his stomach, steadying it while Callyn laid him in the boat.

"It will need splinting," the servant said. "And he has hit his head very hard. He needs—"

"Later," Tashalya said. "Niklas, get in the boat with Guierre."

Guierre moved to obey her, but Niklas hung back suspiciously.

"We mustn't go anywhere," he said. "Syban's hurt. We have to get help for him."

"Stop being stupid." Her tone was razor-sharp. "We can't climb out the way we came, not with an injured child. We'll have to float out on the river, then make our way back to the palace."

"But couldn't we—"

"Niklas!"

The ferocity in her blue eyes silenced him. He climbed into the boat and sat down next to Syban, who moaned a little. The child was sweating now, and Niklas awkwardly pushed his untidy brown hair off his brow. An ugly lump was swelling on his temple.

I won't leave you, Niklas promised his little brother silently.

Guierre untied the ropes and sat down next to Tashalya, who smiled at him. When Callyn pushed them away from the landing with an oar, the current swung the boat's prow around. Guierre's air of suppressed excitement made Niklas frown.

He didn't need rescuing, Niklas thought resentfully. *He's a willing part of this. I was a fool to go after them, trying to be so brave. And now what are we to do?*

The boat glided forward, away from the torchlight, drawn by the current into a dark tunnel. The sound of the river rushing along was very loud there.

"Keep your heads low," Tashalya warned them.

Niklas ducked just in time as they went swooping out beneath a low overhang to emerge at the base of the cliff into a little swirl of white, foaming rapids. Niklas clutched at the side of the boat, hanging on for dear life, as they shot downstream. Guierre whooped loudly, his golden curls soaked by the spray, and Tashalya was leaning forward just as eagerly, shouting, "Faster, Callyn! Faster! Steer us to the center!"

The servant woman seemed to be an expert on the water. She guided the craft out to the middle of the river, where it ran the deepest and the fastest. They seemed to shoot past the palace in the span of a heartbeat, rushing past the walls of the city, its spires silhouetted against the late afternoon sun. Squinting at the walls, Niklas could not see any sentries because of the sun's angle. It made his eyes water, and he turned his gaze elsewhere, blinking until the purple spots stopped dancing across his vision.

Boat traffic was heavy and congested along the slower edges of the river. Long cargo barges moved the slowest of all. Craft coming upriver were being drawn along by long teams of yoked kine on the bank, the drivers cracking whips and shouting. Other barges were already moored by the merchant warehouses, where men worked to unload the cargo. Niklas had never been on the river before. The water was murky brown by the wharves and warehouses, and it stank with dead fish and floating garbage. He found himself staring at all the sights around him, fascinated despite the ever-growing worry in the pit of his stomach.

"We could stop over there and get help," he said, pointing at one of the wharves. Suddenly he reached up and waved his arms over his head. "Hie!" he shouted. "Hie!"

The men unloading cargo ignored him. Only a boat captain, clad in a dingy green tunic and wearing a cap with a long top hanging down to his shoulder, waved back at him.

Disappointed, Niklas subsided. The last of the wharves fell behind them, and Callyn guided them past a larger, slower-moving craft, wallowing low in the water as though heavily loaded. Its busy crew paid them no heed, and Niklas did not try to attract their attention. Ahead, the river curved in a wide bend toward the forest. When he looked back, the palace stood high on its hill above the city, gilded by the slanting rays of the sun.

He glanced at his sister's face, seeing her laughing and leaning forward as though to urge the little boat even faster. And he knew she had no intention of taking any of them back.

Night draped the windows of the king's privy chamber, commandeered by Lord Thum as a central base of operations. Alexeika paced up and down the wooden floor, weary but unable to sit down, hugging herself with an ever-growing sense of foreboding.

In the next room, Faldain lay surrounded by priests and attendants while an eldin healer worked to save him. Down the passageway in the Council chamber, his majesty's other advisers and ministers had gathered, waiting for whatever might happen. The crown prince, summoned most urgently to appear, had been reported missing, along with his brother and Prince Guierre. Men in Guierre's service—including his protector—had been discovered lying dead in the Hall and Chapel of the Chalice, and Cardinal Velain was in an uproar, demanding action while accusing everyone in the palace of complicity.

The guards assigned to duty at the Chapel entrance were also dead, killed by magical means. The *sorcerel* Tulmahrd was said to be examining the Hall of Kings, hunting the source of magic that had been used there. Although Samderaudin had been summoned to the privy chamber, he had not yet appeared.

A frantic count of the remaining royal children had been made, and all were accounted for, except Princess Tashalya.

Count Bouinyin, standing at rigid attention, reported why he came to leave Prince Niklas under the protection of Sir Thiely. He also explained how Prince Syban had deliberately tricked him, telling him Niklas intended to lure Guierre to the stables to see if they could ride some of the horses that had raced. Bouinyin had escorted Syban to Sir Ayavar inside the nursery, then headed immediately back to the jousting stands. When he found everyone in the children's box gone, he'd searched the stables, the tents, and finally the palace, to no avail. He had, however, found tracks in the Chapel and traced them to the outside entrance, then across the grounds to a secret passage leading to the river. From there, he said, his voice stiff and clipped, the trail was lost.

"Abducted to the river," Alexeika whispered. "Oh, Thod."

"Your majesty—"

She turned away from him. "No, Bouinyin."

"That will be all at present, count," Lord Thum said coldly. "Ask Sir Ayavar to come in."

This protector, younger and less in command of himself than Bouinyin, began apologizing until Thum cut him off and asked a number of pointed questions. Unable to bear explanations of how Syban regularly gave his attendants the slip, Alexeika returned to Faldain's chamber.

His eyes were open, but hazy and unfocused. She took his hand in hers, sending the healer a silent question.

The eld, a slender man with silver hair that curled and shifted in constant motion, looked exhausted by his efforts. Shaking his head, he made a gesture of futility.

Tears pricked her eyes. She looked down at Faldain, smoothing back his hair, murmuring comfort to him until she was sent for.

Reluctantly she left him and returned to the privy chamber. Samderaudin had arrived, his yellow eyes fierce, the burned smell of magic strong upon his robes. Little sparks were dancing off his fingertips, and those present gave him ample room. With Vaunit standing beside him, the potent hum of their power overwhelmed the crowded space. Then the healer came in, along with a priest, two of the physicians, and Chesil.

Thum insisted that Alexeika take a chair. "Chesil will now explain what happened to his majesty."

When the Agya finished describing the battle, the service of thanksgiving, and the final confrontation with the *sheda* who had cursed the king with her dying breath, Alexeika shot to her feet. "That—"

"Er, yes," Thum broke in, "an enemy of long standing."

"*Enemy* is too kind a word for her," Alexeika raged. "What has she done to him? How could she hurt him?" Without waiting for an answer, she turned on Vaunit. "You were supposed to protect him. How could she strike at him when you were there?"

Vaunit said nothing.

It was the eld healer who stepped forward, clearing his throat. "Reactive magic is very old, very primitive. It takes whatever powers or elements of magic are natural to the victim and turns them against him. Thus, it takes eld poison to sicken an eld. It takes eld magic to strike through protections."

"She was Grethori, not eld," Alexeika said. "I don't understand."

"She would have had to draw on some element of eld. Blood is the strongest element, although how she would have obtained it, I cannot guess." The healer glanced at the two *sorcerels*, who looked impassive. "Such a spell as the *sheda* used is a mark of desperation and great cunning. It is extremely powerful, for the maker of such a spell must die in its casting. All the strength of that sacrifice goes into it, making it nearly—"

"You're saying he's going to die," Alexeika said in a voice she did not recognize. "You cannot heal him."

The eld sighed. "My efforts can only worsen his condition. That is the evil of this magic. The Chalice is his only hope."

"This we knew," Chesil muttered.

"Who has taken it?" Alexeika asked. "Who could do so evil a deed, and live?"

"Tashalya," Samderaudin said.

Alexeika felt as though an arrow had hit her. In pain, she stumbled back and sat down, bowing her head.

Chesil went to her. "Your majesty—"

She gripped his thin, hard hand, fighting to regain her composure, well aware that she must not weaken now. In their concern, they might try to send her away, and she could not stand that. She must stay to the end.

"From the moment we learned Tashalya was missing, I feared her involvement." Again she looked at Samderaudin. "Could she possibly have known about her father? Could she have deliberately done this to prevent him from—"

"No," he said, cutting off such painful questions. "None of this does she know. No longer can she part the veils of seeing. She is as blind as any mortal, perhaps more so, and acts from other reasons."

"But still she's taken it, *neya*?" Chesil asked fiercely. He saluted Alexeika. "I will go after her. I will search until—"

"Thank you, Sir Chesil," Thum said, his voice cool in contrast to the Agya's passion, "but there isn't time for a search. Every moment counts."

"We cannot undo the spell, but we can slow its effects," Sovlin said. "There is a special remedy, requiring several priests—"

"Pheresa," Alexeika whispered.

He frowned. "I beg your majesty's pardon?"

"Yes," Thum said, snapping his fingers. "Pheresa!" He came over to Alexeika, his face lit with hope. "She was protected by some kind of Mandrian shield of prayer. It slowed the poison's progression through her body and preserved her until we could get help."

Alexeika looked at the priest. "Is that what you mean?"

"Er, similar, your majesty. We can weave our life force with the king's, using our strength to hold him alive, but—"

She was on her feet. "How long? How long?"

"A few days."

"A dozen or so priests sustained the spell around Pheresa," Thum said eagerly. "They were able to keep her alive for many weeks. If you used more priests—"

"Whatever the Mandrians did, our method is different. It is not the number of men, but the—"

"Can you give his majesty more than a few days?" Alexeika asked.

Sovlin frowned uncertainly. "Perhaps a week, but—"

"Tashalya has a small start on us," Alexeika said, thinking aloud. "With the royal barge—it's fast at full oar—we can surely overtake her."

"No," Samderaudin said. "You will not find her on the river."

"Where then?" Alexeika demanded. "She could be heading in any direction. Oh, morde! What is she doing?"

Thum scowled, his face red beneath his freckles. "I think, majesty, with the heirs to both Nether and Mandria in her possession, as well as the Chalice of Eternal Life, she must imagine she rules the world just now. And perhaps she does."

Alexeika resumed her furious pacing. "There's no time to bargain our way through ransoms, or whatever she will demand." She stopped. "Samderaudin, if the veils are parted, can she be found?"

"Her path is concealed by what guides her now."

"Who is her ally?" Alexeika demanded. "A Gantese agent?"

Someone in the room swore.

"There are other forces of darkness besides Gantese," Samderaudin replied. "Tashalya's ally has killed for her in this world and is growing stronger. If you hope to prevail against it, you must hurry."

"But how?" Alexeika demanded in frustration. "Where am I to search? How am I to find my children and the Chalice?"

"Faldain knows."

Taken aback, she pressed her hand to her brow in despair. Of what use to her were riddles and mysteries when her beloved lay dying and her children were in danger?

A tap on the door preceded Count Bouinyin, who was holding a scrap of parchment in his fingers.

Wild, nameless hope filled her. "What is that?"

"One of the guards found strange marks scratched in the mud near the boat landing where they set forth. He tried to copy the marks on this paper, but he thinks they might be gibberish."

"But you do not."

Grimly Bouinyin handed over the parchment. As soon as

she saw the marks, she felt the blood drain too fast from her head. "Runes," she said to Thum. "Can you read them?"

He shook his head. "Dain could."

Not even for a moment did she consider rousing her beloved to ask him to translate. She turned to Samderaudin and held out the paper.

"Ancient runes," he said. "Not dwarf runes. The language of sorcel-folk. Not for mortals to see."

As he spoke, he pointed at the parchment, and it crumbled to ash in Alexeika's fingers. Startled, she flinched back, but not even the faintest touch of fire had she felt, and she was not burned.

Sir Pyron and Bouinyin reached for their weapons while Chesil stepped between the queen and the *sorcerel*.

"Halt, all of you!" Alexeika ordered. "I am unharmed."

Samderaudin swept his hand through the air. Symbols burned in the air, spelling out *Truthseeker.*

She drew in a sharp breath and glanced at Thum. He nodded.

"Truthseeker?" Chesil said in puzzlement, then hissed. "*Aychi,* of course! The great sword of god-steel carried long ago by the king. He dueled my father with it. Yes, I remember this weapon."

Alexeika was remembering, too. Faldain, when he was a boy of eighteen, broad-shouldered but still leggy and growing, his tunic sleeves forever too short. Faldain, courageous enough to ride into Nether without an army to face his many foes. Already becoming a legend, the boy had carried Truthseeker into the center of Gant and fought the Chief Believer with it. And when he entered Grov on that fateful day, just before the great battle against Muncel, he rode a darsteed and carried the sword of god-steel that no common man dared touch.

"He went after the Chalice," she said aloud. "He'd been wounded. Oh, Thod, he was so terribly hurt."

"But he got on that damned darsteed," Thum said, nodding, "and vanished into thin air."

"And when he came back to the battle, he had the Chalice but wielded a different sword."

"Aye, his father's."

"Tobeszijian's," Chesil whispered in awe. "The great sword Mirengard."

"He's never discussed that exchange, never said where he hid Truthseeker." Alexeika smiled involuntarily. "Tashalya used to tease him about it, asking him so many questions . . ."

Her voice trailed off in horror, and she glanced at Samderaudin. "All these years . . . has she been after it since she was kidnapped?"

The *sorcerel* nodded. "Tulvak Sahm's revenge is still at work."

"But why?" Thum asked in bewilderment. "What could she possibly do with it?"

"God-steel is not for mortal hands," Samderaudin said. "That is why Faldain surrendered it. But it was hard for him, very hard. Tashalya is not as strong as her father."

"Do you think she intends to ransom the Chalice for Truthseeker?" Thum asked, frowning. "But how could she possibly imagine such an exchange would profit her?"

"We can speculate about her motives later," Alexeika said. "If she's going after the sword, she must have somehow learned its location. That's where we must go, with all haste."

"Yes, but how?" Thum asked.

She waved this detail aside. "Chesil, I shall need you and Count Bouinyin with me. Assemble a detail of men and order the barge prepared."

Bowing, both hurried out.

Thum was staring at her in consternation. "Your majesty isn't going."

"What in Thod's name am I to do here, save helplessly watch my husband die?"

"That is a wife's duty."

"And what is a mother's duty?" she asked furiously. "My children are out there. And it's my daughter who has done this infamous deed. Who would you send instead of me, lord minister?"

"You're needed here. The other children . . . the danger—"

Her temper came close to snapping. " 'Tis not the children in the palace who need me now. For my husband's sake, for his life, I am going."

"Then I am, too," Thum said.

Surprised, she stared at him.

"He's my friend," Thum said gruffly.

"Yes, and thank you. But who will hold the Council in check? Who will keep those ambitious fools in the Kollegya from seizing power?"

"I can't stay here and watch him die any more than you can." Thum's hazel eyes met hers with equal determination. "And I've not grown so soft that I can't ride or fight."

She disagreed, but knew not how to say so without wounding him.

Samderaudin interrupted by saying, "The priests begin the spell. If you intend to question Faldain, hurry."

Heedless of Thum's attempt to stop her, she rushed back to Faldain's side. Filing in, the priests were already humming in unison, without words or melody. One priest was holding a large wooden bowl of salt, and each of the others took a handful.

Faldain lay pale and still; she could hardly see his chest rising and falling. When she curled her hand around his, there seemed to be barely any life left in it. Her fierce determination faltered. Thum was right, she thought. She dared not rouse her beloved now. He was far too weak.

Mutely, she bent over and kissed his hand, afraid even to lift it from his side. The Ring of Solder was glowing on his finger in a muted way as though its magical strength was ebbing with his life.

She caught her breath in a silent sob, and suddenly Samderaudin was at her side.

"Ask him," he said.

"He's too weak. He could die."

Samderaudin extended his hand across Faldain's chest, and with a faint exhalation the king's eyes dragged open.

"Ask him."

"Beloved," she whispered, bending low so Faldain could hear her, "where is Truthseeker? You must tell me. It's very important."

His eyelids drooped as though they would close, then opened again. "No," he rasped out.

"Tashalya has taken—" She caught herself just in time.

"Tashalya has taken the boys into danger. I must get to Truth-seeker before she does."

"Not safe," Faldain whispered, his gaze wandering to meet hers. "Can't tell."

"You can," Samderaudin said in a voice that throbbed with power. He brushed his palm lightly across Faldain's brow. "Well have you guarded the secret, but Tashalya has learned where to find it. She goes there now."

"Harm . . ."

"Yes, she can do great harm," Alexeika said. "I have to stop her."

Alarm filled Faldain's face. He struggled to lift his head. "To Nold . . . to . . ."

His head dropped back on the pillow, and he did not rouse again. Silently Samderaudin glided away.

Staring at her husband, Alexeika paid little heed to the tears running down her cheeks. Someone was gently drawing her back, forcing her to relinquish his hand. The Ring of Solder slid off his finger, and she took it for Niklas, in case the worst happened.

I must preserve his succession, she thought fiercely, biting her lip to hold her emotions in check. Desperately she ached to touch Faldain once more, but the priests were surrounding his bed, each man extending his right hand toward the king. She had the awful feeling that she might never again hear Faldain's voice, or feel the hard strength of his muscles and frame, or see the tiny quirk of the special smile he reserved for her alone.

"We must begin our work, your majesty," Sovlin said. "Please, we must be alone with him now. You do understand there can be no disturbances, nothing to upset the balance of the spell once it is woven."

She nodded, swiping tears from her face, and pulled herself together as a queen and general's daughter should.

Turning to Lord Omas, she said, "I rely on you to guard the king well. There are fools in this court who want only to gawk, and others base enough to seek to capture the dying breath of a king for the special curative powers it's supposed to have."

"There'll be none of that," Omas said fiercely.

She gazed up at the man, so large and strong, so deeply loyal. He looked drawn with grief, nearly exhausted, and she worried about whether he could stand fast, no matter what the cost.

"The Kollegya will want to keep vigil on his majesty, to name the moment of his dying so they can proclaim a successor. You will not let them in."

"I swear my obedience," Omas promised. "No one, not even a servant, will enter unless I lie slain."

"Thod forbid," she whispered. "Take care, and see that the men who relieve your vigil are equally to be trusted."

He nodded. "Rely on me."

She gripped his sleeve in gratitude.

"Well?" Thum demanded impatiently. "Did the king say anything about where to find it?"

The hopelessness of her task overwhelmed her for a moment. "He understood, and he tried. But he was too weak."

She began to cry again, and angrily rubbed her eyes. "I don't care. I'll search for them somehow. I can't let her do this to him. I won't!"

Samderaudin came through the passageway door. "Will you come?" he asked. "Time is short."

"What are we to do?" she asked bleakly. "He said Nold, but we could spend years in the Dark Forest and never find—"

"What he could not say, he thought," Samderaudin said. "I will guide you."

Chapter Twenty-eight

The dwarf settlement was making merry. A band of visitors carrying short, wide-bladed swords, bows, and quivers of arrows had arrived at dusk, to be greeted with loud and joyous welcome. Now, although it was past moonrise, supper fires still burned, and Barath and Shelon sat with the others, drinking hard, smoking their pipes, exchanging news with their guests.

Chained out behind the lean-to, Anoc sat in the darkness, slapping at hungry insects as he tried to listen to what was being said. They often talked too fast for his limited vocabulary, but he learned the band was on its way downriver to raid settlements of a different clan.

There was much joking about this, with lively bursts of laughter and more rounds of fermented drink that made all the dwarves silly and thick-tongued. Then he heard Shelon's voice saying words like "slave" and "good price" that warned him she was selling him here and now.

He wanted to go upriver, not the direction these raiders were headed. He wanted to be no one's property again. So he slid his fingers between his throat and the stout leather collar, taking care not to rattle the chain. Some days past, before she took the leather-working tools away from him, he had made cuts inside the collar, not deep enough to be noticeable, but he hoped enough to weaken it.

He pulled with all his strength, gritting his teeth with the effort, but the leather did not break. He knew every link in the chain, and there was no flaw to be found. The bolt holding it to the tree was sunk deep and could not be budged. Only the collar offered him any chance of escape, and it was thick, stiff, and heavy, its buckle an intricate puzzle he could not solve.

But the leather . . . He strained again, twisting and worrying it until sweat ran down his back and chest, and his fingers grew sore.

The leather gave, just a little, and he renewed his efforts until it parted, and suddenly he was free.

He tumbled onto his side and lay there a moment, feeling slightly stunned by his success. But he knew better than to waste time rejoicing. Swiftly scrambling to his feet, he hurriedly gathered his possessions and weapons, tying them in the scrap of blanket. It was tempting to enter the burrow and steal food and the hoard of gold, but he did neither. He could hunt what he needed to eat and had no use for the gold, save to torment Shelon. Since he planned to kill her soon, it was not important.

Slinging his bundle across his shoulder with a leather string, Anoc moved silently into the forest. Aware that dwarves were excellent trackers, he laid a false trail to the river landing, where he slid waist deep into the water. It was shockingly cold, and the swiftness of the current surprised him. He was careful to hang on to the weeds growing along the edge of the bank to keep himself from being swept away, for he could not swim, but he took care also not to crush the stems as he moved downstream well past the curve in the river. Finding a tree branch hanging low over the water, he grabbed it and pulled himself out, climbing into the tree without setting foot on the ground.

Water streamed from his clothing as he perched there to rest. Later, he moved into an adjoining tree, using the thick vines entwined through their canopies. He found a tree with a hollow trunk, and an opening big enough to wedge himself inside. It was very cramped, and smelled of animal and rotten nuts, but he felt safe. At dawn, he was awakened by Shelon's screaming. She swore and yelled, rousing the settlement, and then she went tracking, but she found him not.

He lived in the hollow tree for three days, venturing from hiding only to drink from the river, waiting patiently while she roamed and searched to no avail. The raiders went on their way, and the forest grew quiet and still once more.

Shelon gave up hunting him and went back to trapping game. Anoc settled himself near one of her snares and waited until she came to check on it. His sling and stone were ready, and the stabbing stick lay on the ground before him. Hidden in the brush, he watched her as she kicked at her empty trap, then knelt with a grunt to check the string he'd broken.

Her back was to him. He whirled the sling once and released it before she could notice the sound. The stone thudded into the back of her skull, stunning her enough to tip her forward onto her hands and knees.

Springing from cover, Anoc tackled her before she could straighten. Despite being groggy and caught by surprise, she was strong enough to rear back. But he snaked his left arm around her heavy throat while he stabbed her with a hard, upward thrust.

She gurgled and choked, trying to speak, then she sagged in his hold. He sprang back from her warily, not certain she was dead, but although she twitched a little she soon lay still. Picking up a branch, he used it to roll her over. She sprawled on her back, his weapon jutting from her midsection, her bulbous eyes staring sightlessly.

Joy filled him. He threw back his head and danced, but uttered no cry. Instead, he took her dagger and cut his first trophies. It was not high honor to kill a female, but she was a vanquished enemy. He took her weapons, traps, footgear, then he broke her finger bones and sucked the warm marrow from them. And he felt strong afterward, a warrior.

Brushing out his tracks, he climbed back into a tree and made his way north, staying close to the river without venturing into the open along the bank. He walked and hunted, eating as much as he pleased, enjoying his freedom, oblivious to the solitude.

Before he had been sold in the slaver's auction, he had set his hand briefly on the shoulders of the other boys, even Shulig. In this way had he marked each one. And from that marking, he now possessed a general sense of where to find them. The distances were great. It would take him maybe more than a season to gather them, but he did not mind. For his purpose was clear, and his patience long.

Besides, he'd discovered something else since escaping. For the first time in his life he was eating all the meat he wanted, raw and bloody, and his clothes gapped where his tunic was too short. His leggings were too short as well, and getting tight around the waist. And the tunic that had been too wide for him now fit across the shoulders.

When he stripped off to dry himself after a rain, he could see muscles starting to bulge and ripple in his arms and stomach. At last, after many years of frustration, he was *growing*.

No longer did he grieve for She Who Made Him, for the diet of blood and magic she'd fed him all his life had kept him small and undersized. In a way, he'd been as much her slave and possession as Shelon's, but never again would he belong to another. From now on, any who joined him would be *his*, following not the Grethori way but *his* way.

So had it been foretold.

It was very late at night when Syban came to. He whimpered, trying to sit up, then cried out in pain.

Awakened, Niklas sat up in the dark, not sure at first where he was. Then everything came back to him in a rush, and he bent over his brother, pushing him down. "Lie still," he whispered.

"It hurts. It hurts!"

"Hush. I know." Niklas glanced around and saw Guierre curled beneath a blanket up near the prow of their boat, now tied to the bank. A thin moon hung in the sky above them. He thought it might be an opportunity to escape, but he had no idea where they were.

Syban was writhing, crying now. "I want to go home!"

"Well, we can't," Niklas said, trying to keep his voice

matter-of-fact so Syban wouldn't panic more. "Hush and try to lie still. You're only making it worse."

"But it hurts. My arm hurts bad!"

"It's broken."

"Is my head broken, too?"

Niklas smiled a little in the dark. "No. But you hit it pretty hard when you fell."

"I want Mama. I want Niesha."

"I know. I'm sorry."

A movement from behind him made him jump. He twisted about and saw a hunched, crooked shadow creeping up beside him. Callyn's skin was emitting a soft, pale glow. Niklas's heart bounced against his ribs, and his breath grew short. Reaching for his dagger, he found it gone.

"The little boy is in pain. I can help," Callyn said.

Her soft voice held compassion and sympathy, but Niklas didn't trust her. Whatever she was, since she belonged to Tashalya she might be capable of doing almost anything to them.

"Go away," he said in a fierce whisper, tightening his grip on Syban's shoulder. "Leave us alone."

"I can help."

"We don't want your help."

She stared at him, the scars on her throat and cheek dark against the soft luminosity of her skin. "You should not fear me," she said. "I am not the one who will harm you."

Niklas's mouth went dry. "You mean T-Tashalya?"

"Let me help the little boy."

"No. Leave him be."

"I will set the bone, so it will heal straight and true. I will ease his pain, and he can go back to sleep."

Syban moaned, his fingers twisting Niklas's sleeve. "It hurts! I want Mama! I want to go home!"

"Syban, stop it. We can't right now," Niklas said, worried and desperate.

"Let me help him," Callyn said, "before her highness returns."

"Where's she gone?"

Callyn reached past him for Syban, murmuring soothingly to him, so that the child quieted for a moment. "Change

places with me, please," she said to Niklas. "If you will hold
his shoulders while I set the bone?"

Feeling a little sick, Niklas nodded in the dark. "All right."

"What's she going to do?" Syban fretted. "Niklas!"

"Hush. I'm right here. It will hurt, but then you'll be better. You can be a warrior about it, can't you?" Niklas asked
him bracingly.

"I—I guess so," Syban said, in a woebegone little voice.

"Give him this," Guierre said, sitting up. He fumbled
about and pressed what felt like a strap of leather into
Niklas's hand. "Let him bite it."

Niklas pushed it into Syban's mouth. "You bite on this
hard, understand? Hard, Syban. Don't scream. Just try to bite
it in two."

"Now," Callyn said.

Niklas pushed down on Syban's small shoulders, while
Guierre held the child's legs. Callyn set the arm, working
swiftly to pull it into place and splint it. Syban screamed
against the strap, then it was over. The child collapsed, silent
now, his frame shuddering. Niklas found himself crying, too.

He rubbed his sleeve across his face, hoping no one noticed, and took the leather strap from between his brother's
jaws. "Pretty brave of you," he said hoarsely.

Still trembling, Syban said nothing. Callyn gave him
something to drink and covered him up.

"He will sleep now," she said. "Poor child. He has no
place in this."

"Do any of us?" Niklas asked bitterly. "Where *is* Tashalya?"

Callyn hesitated. "She'll be back very soon."

"But where is she? What is she doing?"

"Meeting with that which has no place among us."

Niklas thought of the deadly white mist that had tried to
kill him in the Hall. "What is it?" he asked. "Where has it
come from?"

"I cannot tell you. Ask me no more about it."

"It killed Guierre's servants," Niklas persisted. He
glanced at Guierre, who did not seem to hear. "What has she
summoned?"

"A ghost," Callyn whispered. "Worse than a ghost."

"Do you want to see it?" Guierre asked. "The Chalice?"

Niklas frowned at him. "Are you mad? Why do you ask?"

"It's secured in a box now, strapped up tight so that she no longer is needing me to carry it for her," Guierre replied bitterly. "I was a fool. I was believing everything said. She told me big lies and used me, and now she'll use me as a hostage. You as well."

"No, she won't," Niklas said grimly. He reached for the mooring rope, but Callyn's hand closed around his wrist.

Such heat came from her fingers that he cried out in surprise and dropped the rope.

"What in Thod's name are you?" he asked.

"You will not attempt to escape when she is gone to meet with—when she is gone," Callyn said.

"But she's wrong, Callyn," Niklas said, trying to win the servant over to their side. "You know what she's doing is evil. Help us."

"No."

"But why? Why not let us get away?"

"No."

He frowned. "If you fear her, come with us."

"No."

In desperation he turned to Guierre. "Where's the Chalice?"

"Why? Do you want to be seeing it now?"

"No. I'm going to throw it in the river and make her—"

"You'll not!" Guierre exclaimed. "That—that is being sacrilege!"

"Better it's lost forever than defiled by what my sister plans for it."

Guierre gripped the front of Niklas's tunic and shook him. "You will not be doing this!"

Niklas tried to shove him back, and for a moment they grappled while the boat rocked dangerously.

Tashalya's laughter rang out, freezing both of them in place. She appeared on the bank, a shadow in long skirts. "Do you have any idea of how clearly voices carry on the water?" she asked. "Niklas, how diverting you are. Such big ideas of being the brave hero and saving the day. Only no one will help you. Such a pity."

Her mockery stung his pride. Guierre's grip had loosened,

and Niklas brushed the other boy's hands away, losing his balance as the boat rocked and sitting down rather faster than he intended. He felt tired, scared, and humiliated. Her mockery seemed worse than anything else.

Humming happily to herself, Tashalya stepped aboard the boat and sat down, pushing Guierre back to the prow before fussing with her hair.

There was something peculiar about her, Niklas thought. She smelled burned, like magic. He drew as far back from her as he could get and kept his hand protectively on the sleeping Syban's shoulder.

"We'll spend another day on the river, Callyn," Tashalya said. "There should be no difficulties until we reach where the waters merge into the Charva. I understand that can be a challenge for a craft as small as ours. I want to be past that point before dark."

"Yes, your highness."

"And then we'll hire horses the rest of the way." Tashalya laughed and clapped her hands together like a little girl. "It's not far, not far at all. I cannot wait!"

"Tashalya," Niklas asked, "where are you taking us?"

"Somewhere special," she replied. "A place where the first and second worlds coexist, layered in the same place, and it is as easy to be in one as the other."

"I don't understand."

"Why should you? But I have waited for this a very long time."

"Then why—"

"Oh, shut up!" she said, suddenly angry. "Learn to hold that silly tongue of yours, you stupid brat!"

"I won't. You've no right to talk to me like—"

Tashalya gripped him by his tunic front and bent him backward over the side of the boat until his head touched the water. Wood dug into his spine. Fearing his back might break while she drowned him, Niklas flailed wildly but could not get free. She pushed his head lower.

"Now, listen to me," she said in a voice so cold and cruel he stopped struggling. "You will obey me without question. I shall think for you, and I shall decide for you. I shall put the words in your mouth and the thoughts in your head. I shall make your policies and rule the kingdom with you as my puppet. Forget having any ideas of your own, or privileges, or rights. You will be forever mine to command, and I shall talk to you as I please."

Gasping for breath, fighting not to scream at the agony in his back, Niklas grabbed her wrists in an effort to break her hold.

She plunged his head underwater so fast he didn't have time to hold his breath. Water surged up his nose, choking him before she pulled him up and shoved him roughly to the bottom of the boat.

Choking and coughing, spitting up the small amount of water he'd swallowed, he huddled there with his hair dripping into his eyes.

Tashalya grabbed his hair and yanked his head back to force him to look at her. "Have I made myself clear?" she asked him very softly. "This is your future I'm foretelling. Do you understand it? Answer me!"

He wanted to hit her. He wanted to butt her in the face with the top of his head and bloody her nose. He wanted to hold her under the water until she struggled and choked. He wanted to make her cry, the way he was fighting back his tears right now.

"I have many ways of punishing you, Niklas," she warned him. "This is but the first."

"Yes, Tashalya," he forced himself to say. "Everything you've said is very clear."

"Liar," she said. "You're puffed up with defiance, but I'll train you exactly the way I want you. And you, Guierre, you are already trained to be a puppet for the Gides when you take your throne. Only you will be *my* puppet instead."

"Merciful Tomias," he whispered, sounding horrified.

She laughed. "Tomias has nothing to do with this."

She's mad, Niklas thought, shoving back his wet hair as he huddled beneath the cloak Callyn gave him for a blanket. *I've got to stop her, but how?*

Opening his eyes, Dain found himself lying spread-eagled on the ground, surrounded by a grove of saplings. A stormy wind blew, whipping their slender trunks. Their rustling leaves seemed to whisper, *Stay safe. Stay safe.* When a few drops of rain splattered his face, he scrambled quickly to his feet. Thunder rumbled ominously in the sky, but as yet the storm held off.

Another dream, he thought wearily, wondering what enemy he would face this time. The air felt charged, smelling tangy and hot, yet he was as cold as ice, shivering, holding his arms tight against his body to conserve warmth. Wind lashed his face, blowing back his hair. He wanted to leave the grove and find better shelter, but the saplings grew so close together they were like fence palings, an impenetrable barrier on three sides.

Behind him, a sheer precipice dropped into a gorge choked with brush and jagged rock. He peered over, realizing he could not go that way.

Lightning flashed very close, the bolt banging into the hillside and splitting a tree. Flames shot up through the canopy, and the tree fell over slowly, its roots snapping out of the soil. With a horrendous groan it toppled into the gorge, carrying lesser uprooted bushes and small trees with it. Thunder boomed overhead, sending Dain to his knees with his hands clapped to his ears.

Rain pelted down, hammering his skull and shoulders, drenching him immediately. Despite a gust of wind that nearly toppled him, he staggered upright. The saplings were being whipped back and forth. When one of them snapped off, he thought he heard a scream.

More lightning clawed its way across the sky, lighting up some of the clouds from within, ripping others apart while the thunder made the very ground rattle. Up here on the mountaintop Dain was practically in the belly of the storm, much too close, too exposed. The rain blew this way and that as the wind shifted. Another sapling snapped and fell, then another.

He realized he could escape the grove now. Climbing free, he hurried into the nearby forest, slithering downhill a ways until he reached the shelter of a large tree. Thankful for the respite, he slung back his dripping hair and gulped in deep breaths.

"Faldain of Nether," said a voice, "beware what comes."

Warily he turned around, bracing one hand against the trunk of the tree. It trembled slightly beneath his touch, and he jerked back.

"Beware the danger," the voice said again. It was rough and primitive, very old. Realizing the tree was speaking to him, Dain retreated.

The tree shook its limbs, showering him with droplets of water. "Root yourself deep against this storm."

Just then, Dain saw lights glimmering downhill. Flickering here and there through the trees and undergrowth, the lights came closer, moving fast in his direction.

Warily, Dain picked up a stout stick from the ground.

Beyars were coming, he saw, padding on all fours through the woods with eldin riders on their backs. They carried spears, and fairlight flickered from their fingertips to light their way through the rain-lashed gloom.

Relieved, for he did not fear the eld folk, Dain lowered the club. They might, he thought, be kinsmen.

But when at last they halted before him, he recognized none of them. Their leader was slim and fair, his hair tied back severely. Pointed of ear and chin, with hostile eyes a pale, silver-green hue, he wore a torque of silver with unfamiliar symbols hammered into its surface.

"Faldain of Nether. Son of Nereisse."

"I am Faldain."

"We are the spirit bearers. We've come to escort you to the third world with the honor that is your right."

Dain glanced involuntarily at the grove of saplings behind him.

"The guardians of your life cannot help you now," the eld said. "Their Circle was not strong enough to sustain you."

A sense of shock spread through Dain, making him slow to respond. "I'm not dead yet," he protested in disbelief.

"So say all newly deceased."

"I'm not dead!"

The eld's silvery green eyes did not waver. "There's little time to escort you, for the enemies of all spirits gather." He pointed at the stormy skies overhead. "Come with us now, Faldain, and let us guard you on your journey. Otherwise, you will be doomed to wander forever, your spirit lost in torment."

"This is a dream of my illness, a product of the curse that fevers my mind," Dain said. "I am not dead."

"The chains binding you to the first world are strong. Our task is to break them for you—"

"No!" Suspiciously Dain retreated, his hand tightening on his club. "I don't think you're what you claim."

"We are spirit bearers for the eldin. We will take you—"

"You're taking me nowhere. Begone!"

The eldin pointed with their spears in the direction they wanted Dain to go. He glanced uphill, confused, but determined not to cooperate.

"You must come," the leader told him.

"No."

Without warning, a spear jabbed at him and only Dain's quick sidestep kept its sharp tip from slicing his arm. When he knocked the spear aside with his club, the rider holding that weapon vanished into thin air, along with the beyar.

Illusions, Dain thought, remembering the tree's warning. *But in these dreams illusions conceal traps. Take care.*

Another rider rushed him. Brandishing his club like a broadsword, Dain swung at him, but missed. A spear tip jabbed his side, skidding across his ribs on a fiery trail of pain.

Yelling, he jumped aside. It was not a fatal wound, but, morde, it hurt. He saw no blood, but the pain distracted him so that he barely had time to reset his feet before another rider came at him.

This time when he swung, the blow connected, and he knocked the rider off his beyar. The rider vanished like the first, but the beyar swiped Dain with a mighty paw, knocking him backward and sending him tumbling downhill. Flailing in an effort to halt his fall, he hit a boulder so hard it jolted the breath from him and left him stunned.

Hearing the remaining spirit bearers coming for him, Dain struggled to lift his head. *Must get up,* he thought groggily. *Must fight.*

But his vision blurred, and he could not seem to command his body. Then the world went black.

Chapter Twenty-nine

❧

The royal barge was a long, spacious craft, its jutting prow a vibrant red, with sinuous, scaled river dragons painted on its tall sides. Fifty long oars—twenty-five a side—flashed in and out of the water in perfect unison, kept on time by a man pounding the rhythm belowdecks. They were flying downriver. Archers stood watch on all sides for trouble from Nonkind or pirates that sometimes attacked craft from the banks. Alexeika had twenty knights on board, along with horses, Sir Pyron, her most trusted maidservant, Samderaudin, and Count Bouinyin. Lord Thum had brought his protector and a manservant, and Chesil Matkevskiet had brought his squire.

A small force, she thought, pacing worriedly along the deck. Too small, perhaps, against the unknown. Samderaudin in private had explained to her about the *ciaglo*, a creature who was more than a ghost, more than a demon, more than a haunting spirit—something no longer mortal if it ever had been, and capable of such cunning deception that it could possess the heart and soul of its victim and manipulate her however it desired.

"Why did she call it to her?" Alexeika asked, appalled. "Surely she knew the risk!"

"She did not care. She is reckless."

"And defiant, and rebellious," Alexeika added sadly. A wealth of regrets filled her for all the things that had gone wrong for Tashalya, things Alexeika couldn't undo. "Will it turn against her? Will it harm her?"

"Only if she ceases to serve it."

"Is that likely to happen?"

Samderaudin was drawing aimless little trails of fire through the air and did not answer.

"Why didn't you warn me about this when it began?" Alexeika asked.

"You could not stop what she had begun. Only she can stop it."

"But will she? How can we bring her to her senses? Tulvak Sahm's been dead for thirteen years. Are we never to be free of him?"

Samderaudin remained silent.

"This *ciaglo*," Alexeika said, sighing. "What did you mean when you said it gets stronger?"

"It comes into the first world by invitation. Although it may take a physical form, usually it manifests itself as vapor. It comes to the first world violent and hungry, and if the summoner is careless or untrained, often the *ciaglo* destroys her in the first or second meeting before fading back whence it came."

Alexeika drew in a sharp breath, wide-eyed as she recalled Tashalya's mysterious illness. *It was happening then,* she thought, *and I never suspected the truth.* A bubble of panic rose inside her.

"The creature may preserve its summoner from harm, appearing to be fond of her, while it kills others instead. It draws their life to strengthen itself. When it no longer depends on the summoner to enter the first world, but can come and go of its own volition, then it is dangerous indeed."

"How are we to fight it?" she asked.

"Deny what it wants. Keep it from killing. Its summoner must send it back whence it came."

"Tashalya?"

"All depends on her."

"Will she do it? Can she be made to see reason?"

Samderaudin did not answer.

"I can't talk to her these days without quarrelling," Alexeika said wearily. "She's so angry at me, and I don't know why. For years I tried to excuse her behavior, thinking it best to give her time to recover from what that madman did to her, but—but she's had time, hasn't she? She isn't going to get better."

"Tashalya must make her choices," the *sorcerel* said.

"I want so desperately to help her."

"You want to save Faldain's life. Which matters more?"

Shocked, Alexeika could not answer, and that had been the end of their conversation. Now, pacing along the deck while the men tried to stay out of her way, Alexeika continued to worry. How was she to choose between daughter and husband? And how dare Tashalya put her in this position by taking such stupid risks?

Breathless with anger, she paused by the railing and stared at the dense, nearly impenetrable forest growing down to the water's edge. Nold was a gloomy, mysterious land, a place where bandits and wanted men took refuge, where half the trails seemed to lead to dead ends, and almost anything could be hidden.

Now her children had ventured into this dangerous, untamed land. The Chalice's presence would surely keep them safe from Nonkind attack, but could it protect them from the ghostly predator that Tashalya had set loose? Or from the thieves, ruffians, and warmongering dwarf clans?

And what about Mareitina and Dalena left behind in the palace? Alexeika thought of the night she departed Grov to embark on this desperate journey. She'd donned her hauberk and cloak, strapping on her twin daggers and pulling her father's sword Severgard from its wrappings. Then she'd slipped into the nursery where little Dalena slept, her cheeks rosy against the pillow, her dark hair a tangled cloud around her head. Mareitina had been sitting there, watching her little sister sleep.

She shrank back a little from the sight of Alexeika and her weapons, but Alexeika had gathered the girl close, hugging her tightly, loving her so desperately, before she kissed her cheek and let her go.

"Bid me Thod speed, sweetling," Alexeika whispered. "I go to bring Niklas and Syban home."

"And Tashie?" Mareitina asked softly, her blue eyes sad.

"I'll try."

"Oh, Mama!"

Mareitina had wept then, while Alexeika held her. "I'm sorry," she said against Mareitina's pale hair. "I don't understand why she's done this, but I'll do what I can for her. Watch over your little sister and pray for your father's recovery."

"I will," Mareitina said, gripping Alexeika's hands and kissing them. "Thod speed, Mama. Bring them all safely home."

Now, standing at the railing with the smell of river and forest in her nostrils, Alexeika did not know how she was to succeed.

Niklas shifted restlessly in the boat, bored and cramped from sitting. It was dark, and the insects were singing in the reeds that grew along the bank. Others were biting. Niklas slapped his neck and moved again, wishing Syban wouldn't curl up so close against him. There wasn't enough room, and he longed to get out and stretch his legs.

It was their last night on the river, for Tashalya said come morning they would take horses the rest of the way. They were moored for the night in a narrow cut off the main channel, hiding well in among the bushes and staying quiet. They weren't far from a settlement, and now and then if the breeze shifted just right, Niklas could hear bursts of raucous laughter and carousing song. It sounded far worse than the barracks on the nights when the sentries were given strong drink instead of ale.

He wondered where in the woods Tashalya had gone. Callyn said it was none of their business, but Niklas disagreed.

He thought now would be a good time for them to jump onto the bank and make a run for it to the settlement. But when he eased up to the prow and whispered to Guierre that they try it, Guierre shook his head.

"We dare not go there," Guierre whispered very softly. "Bestin and I have heard the knights talk about inns that welcome road travelers in for a night's shelter, then the people are being robbed, their throats cut, and bodies thrown into the Charva. I do not think the ruffians who are giving these places custom would be helping us."

"I have a few skannen, and my circlet would pay them well," Niklas said stubbornly.

"Perhaps, and they might take your payment and be vanishing, too." Guierre sighed. "Morde, Niklas, but I find adventure most uncomfortable."

Niklas gave up trying to persuade him and moved back to the middle of the boat. It was hard to respect such a pudding heart, he thought in disappointment. Guierre was far too prudent ever to be a hero.

Syban, his arm tied in a makeshift sling, was feeling better. At the moment, protesting that he was hungry, not sleepy, he was trying to cajole Callyn into giving him food.

"You've supped," she said. "That is enough."

"But I'm still hungry."

"The rations must last us all a long time. You've had your portion."

"So give me some of tomorrow's," he wheedled. "Please?"

A burst of shouting and cheers rose through the forest. Niklas stared in that direction, and when the noise subsided, he said, "She shouldn't be wandering around by herself. Why doesn't the guide travel with us? Why all the mystery? We know she's a traitor. She needn't hide it."

"Be glad it does not come here," Callyn muttered, pulling Syban's sly little paw off the rations bag. "No, your highness. Not another morsel tonight."

"Aw, Callyn, you're too strict about everything," he complained.

"You'll be glad I'm strict when breakfast comes."

While she was distracted, Niklas jumped onto the bank, ignoring her call to come back. As he headed into the woods, he hoped Guierre would follow him, but Guierre did not. Other than Syban's startled shout—hastily muffled—there was no other sound.

Niklas shrugged. He was going to see what Tashalya was up to, and scout around the settlement.

He glanced overhead, studying the angle of the skimpy moon. Stars twinkled against the inky sky, but once he went into the forest he wouldn't be able to use them. Hesitating only a moment, he reached out and broke a small twig on a hackberry bush. Its pungent, distinctive smell filled his nostrils, and he continued to break twigs at regular intervals. Such a trail of scent wouldn't last long, but the breeze was scant and the air warm. He thought it would serve to guide his return.

Trying to make little noise, he angled in the direction of the settlement. Tashalya had moored them so close to it because she intended to hire horses on the morrow, or so she claimed. *If nothing else,* Niklas thought, *we can break away from her once we're mounted and ride for home.* Meanwhile, he wanted to see the mercenaries for himself.

He did not get far, however, before he became aware of a strange panting noise ahead of him. Freezing in his tracks, Niklas listened. He thought at first it might be an animal of some kind, but then he heard a throaty chuckle, the way servant girls sometimes laughed behind the stables.

Wrinkling his nose in distaste, he started to turn away, but when he heard a soft breathy sound, for some reason he thought, *Tashalya.* The idea that she might be in danger persuaded him to creep forward.

Carefully, making no sound at all, he crawled through the thick undergrowth until he came to a small clearing, where the faintest moonlight trickled down.

Tashalya was lying on the ground with her eyes closed. At first she was so still and silent he thought her dead. But then she moved, writhing a little as she lifted her arms. She made that strange, muffled little sound before she laughed.

Puzzled, Niklas did not understand what she could possibly be doing. He'd long given up trying to comprehend his eldest sister, but curiosity drew him forward.

"Tashalya!" he whispered.

She breathed deep and hard, her eyes closed, unaware of his presence.

Was she spell hit? he wondered. Or had she lost her wits?

Whatever afflicted her, it wasn't safe for her to be out there like this.

But when he tugged cautiously at her sleeve, she did not wake. Her mouth opened, letting out a deep sigh, and she smiled, stretching her arms over her head and arching her back.

Niklas had seen a man fall down in the street once and twitch and jerk all over. He'd foamed at the mouth, and people had run away from him, claiming he was possessed.

Although he wanted to run away, Niklas stayed.

"Tashalya!" he said, pressing his hand to her cheek. Her skin felt cool and normal. But it was madness to lie there, dreaming in the forest without even salt sprinkled around for protection against Nonkind. He shook her harder. "Wake up, Tashalya. Wake up!"

But she shifted languidly, rubbing her cheek against his fingers, and grew very quiet, as though falling into deep slumber.

A little repelled, although he wasn't sure why, Niklas backed away from her. He supposed he could try to carry her back to the boat, but he didn't think he could lift her. Then a cold, uneasy feeling lifted the hair on the back of his neck. He looked around sharply, but saw nothing unusual among the shadows.

Still, he had the sudden conviction that he shouldn't be there, that Tashalya would be very angry with him if she woke up and caught him spying on her.

He felt like a coward for retreating. No valiant knight worth his spurs would abandon a lady in the forest like this, he told himself, but he scuttled out of the clearing just the same and dived into the bushes.

At that moment Tashalya sat up and looked around, yawning and stretching. She lifted her mass of hair with both hands, cooling her neck, then dropped her tresses and shook them with a satisfied little chuckle. She murmured to someone who wasn't there, reaching out to caress the air.

Niklas's heart pounded as though he'd been running. There was something dark and dangerous about her just then. He remembered her threats and cruelty and told himself she deserved no chivalry. Using all his woods lore, he sneaked

away as fast as he could, retracing his way along the scent
trail he'd created.

When he parted the weeds on the bank and slid back into
the boat, Guierre jumped violently. Callyn was sitting upright, with a sleeping Syban gathered against her. Niklas
could feel her disapproval, but he didn't care.

"Come on," he said to Guierre. "Help me gather up our
things and cast off our moorings. We're leaving."

"What?" Guierre said, blinking in the moonlight. "But—"

"No questions. Hurry. I want to be gone before Tashalya
returns."

Callyn eased away from Syban, laying him flat in the bottom of the boat. "You will not take this craft," she said.

"Fine," Niklas said shortly, and picked up the cloak he
used as a blanket. "Then we'll walk to the settlement. But
we're going. Guierre, get the Chalice while I wake up Syban."

"Have you gone mad?" Guierre asked. "The settlement is
dangerous. We are being robbed there, the Chalice taken
from us."

"No, we're smarter than that," Niklas said impatiently, remembering to keep his voice low. "I thought you wanted to
get away from her. This is our chance."

"But in the dark?" Guierre said. "With you giving me orders as though I am being your lackey? This is not agreeable
to me."

Niklas couldn't believe Guierre would just sit there, refusing to escape. "Too bad," he said tersely. "Register your
complaints with the chamberlain later, but just come on!"

"I have been thinking it better to wait until morning with
light we are seeing by," Guierre said. "When we get horses,
we can be galloping quickly away. Maybe then have a chance
to—"

"No," Niklas said, on the verge of losing his temper. "No!
We have to go now."

He bent and tugged at the box where it was wedged between two ribs of the boat. But Guierre leaned over and
gripped his wrist.

"Gently," he said. "You must be having proper respect."

Niklas shook him off. "And why don't you try to find
some courage, you fat coward?"

Guierre jumped to his feet, making the boat rock. "I am having courage aplenty!"

"Both of you, sit down and be quiet," Callyn said. "Her highness will be furious if she hears you making so much noise."

"I don't care," Niklas said. "She can fall on the ground and have a fit like a mad dog. She's supposed to be a *sorcerelle*, isn't she? But she's yet to do one bit of magic that I've seen."

"That does not mean she will not, young prince," Callyn said sternly. "Do not provoke her."

"So this afternoon when we got rained on, why didn't she cast a spell to keep us dry?" he retorted.

Big-eyed in the moonlight, Guierre was making the sign of the Circle, but that only angered Niklas more.

"She's nothing but a liar, a thief, and a kidnapper," he said. "She's cruel and rotten, and I think she's gone mad. There's no guide, no one!"

"You saw her?" Callyn asked. "You spied?"

"She's made everything up," Niklas said.

"You have insulted me," Guierre said haughtily. "You are being stupid and foolish, wanting to take stupid chances. You are offensive."

"And cowardice offends me. I know what a knight—what any man of honor—would do." Niklas bent down and grabbed the box.

Guierre gripped the other side of it. "No! Careful. You are being—"

Niklas yanked it out of his hands, but their struggle tipped over the boat. Niklas went flying into the river and sank immediately, swallowing enough water to choke himself. Panicked, he kicked hard and shot to the surface. Coughing and floundering, he nearly went under again.

Guierre bobbed up beside him, grabbing him around the shoulders. "Can you be swimming?" he asked.

Niklas was coughing too hard to answer. Guierre swam expertly, tugging him along to the bank, where he hoisted him partially onto land. Syban was crying somewhere, and Niklas raised his head in sudden concern. But then he felt sick and levered himself up just in time to spew out a foul

mess of river water. After that, he crawled over to where
Syban was sitting in the muddy weeds, holding his arm and
sobbing.

Niklas tried to gather him close, but Syban pushed at him.
"It hurts! It hurts!"

Callyn and Guierre were still in the water, struggling to
right the boat. Niklas knew he should help them, but his
lungs and stomach hurt and he still felt queasy. He saw a
cloak floating on the water, and suddenly shot to his feet in
horror.

"Oh, morde!" he said.

By then Guierre was climbing onto the bank, sopping wet,
and slinging water everywhere. "What?" Then he sucked in
an audible breath, and the boys stared at each other.

"The Chalice," they said together.

Guierre began to mutter in Mandrian, while Niklas
plopped down on the bank in despair. He felt as though he
wanted to be sick again. It was gone into the river, lost forever by now, and what were they to do?

"Oh, Thod," he whispered, feeling unable to breathe. "Oh,
Thod. Oh, Thod!"

Callyn stared at them both without a word, then dived
back into the river.

Guierre crouched by the water's edge, peering into the
darkness anxiously. "Do you think she can find it?"

Niklas gripped his wet hair with both hands. "It's gone,"
he said hopelessly, unable to get past the disaster. He'd been
a fool, losing his temper and showing off, trying to be heroic
and grown up. Trying to take charge. Look where that had
landed him. He wanted to cry, but he wouldn't let himself be
unmanned before Guierre, who was taking this so calmly
Niklas wanted to hit him.

"She does not come up. How long can she be holding her
breath, I wonder?" Guierre said.

Fury boiled in Niklas, and he flung himself at Guierre,
tackling him from the side and driving a fist under his ribs.

Guierre grunted, then squirmed out from under him, hit-
ting back with more force than Niklas expected. It hurt, and
Niklas fought him, giving as many blows as he received, tus-
sling and rolling over and over in the mud until they both half

fell in the water. Niklas's face went under, and he panicked, flailing and sputtering in an effort to breathe.

Guierre let him go, and Niklas retreated up the bank on his hands and knees, feeling humiliated and sore. As Guierre slung back his dripping hair and shook out his wet clothes, Niklas scowled at him in grudging respect.

"I didn't know you could hit like that," he said.

"Oh, yes, Bestin and I used to fight often. I am good, I think."

"Aye." Niklas touched his rib cage and winced a little. "Pretty good. Better than me."

"That is because I am weighing more than you and can hit harder. When you are growing muscles, you will be good, too."

Pleased by the compliment, Niklas sat up straighter. "Really?"

"Yes."

"I'm sorry I picked the fight. I was wrong to call you names. You are no coward, and—and not fat." Niklas held out his hand.

Without hesitation, Guierre clasped it hard. "Thank you. I am accepting this apology. We are being friends, now?"

"Aye, friends."

They grinned at each other a moment, then sobered. When Guierre stared out at the river and sighed, Niklas sighed, too. It looked to him as though Callyn had drowned herself.

"What is done now?" Guierre asked finally.

Niklas didn't answer. He tugged off his tunic and wrung it out, glancing over at where Syban was sitting. The little boy had at least stopped crying, but still cradled his arm in obvious pain. Niklas felt sorry for him but didn't know how to comfort him just now when he desperately needed reassurance himself.

"Niklas?" Guierre persisted.

"I don't know. We can't row upriver with just one steering oar. Now we have no food, and no—" He broke off, unwilling to say it. He wondered how they were going to explain any of this to Tashalya when she came back.

Then there came a ripple in the water, and Callyn surfaced, blowing out her breath and shaking back her hair.

Niklas scrambled up, peering through the gloom in an effort to see her.

"She is holding something," Guierre whispered, gripping his arm. "Morde, I think—I think—"

"She has it!" Niklas went running into the water, stumbling awkwardly and half falling in with a splash. He paddled to meet her, but she would not let him take the box she was pushing in front of her as she swam.

Guierre waited on the bank, crouching to lift the box when she reached him. He handled it carefully. Niklas flopped out on his belly unaided while Guierre gave Callyn assistance.

She sank down on one elbow, breathing hard while they gathered around her. Her skin was glowing brighter than ever.

"I didn't know you could swim that long underwater," Niklas said in amazement. "I can't believe you found it."

"Difficult," she said, still trying to catch her breath. "The current was pushing it along the bottom."

Relief swept over Niklas in a wave. He shut his eyes while Callyn stowed the Chalice back in the boat, grateful beyond all comprehension at its recovery.

Squelching back up the bank to the boys, Callyn stopped in front of Niklas and slapped him hard enough to make him stagger. "You fool!" she said in a low, furious voice, glaring at him through the shadows. "You nearly cost us everything."

Shocked, Niklas refused to touch his stinging cheek. His eyes were watering from the blow, and he couldn't believe what had just happened. No one had ever struck him like that, least of all a servant. But there was no Bouinyin to run to and complain. No captain of the guard to flog her. He opened his mouth, but realized how vulnerable he was—they all three were—and dared say nothing.

"Get in the boat, all of you," she said. "And cause no more trouble."

Guierre cast Niklas a troubled look. "Callyn—"

"Silence! Do as I say. Princess Tashalya is not the only one who can hurt you. Remember that, all of you."

Chapter Thirty

At dawn, when Tashalya returned to the boat feeling magnificently, splendidly ravished, she did not need the gift of sight
to perceive at once that something had happened. The boys
were subdued and damp, and the food was gone. Callyn, her
white robe mud-stained and bedraggled, explained that the
boat had tipped, dumping them all in the river, but Tashalya
suspected the boys had been either roughhousing or trying to
escape; she cared little which.

"I nearly drowned," Syban announced. "And I hurt my
arm again."

Tashalya ignored him. "The Chalice?"

Niklas and Guierre exchanged guilty looks, but Callyn
said, "It is here and well, your highness."

Tashalya pointed at the forest. "Go into the woods and
stay there out of sight until I come back. I'm going to trade
for some horses."

The boys stood rooted in place, rebellion in their faces.

"You haven't any magic, have you?" Niklas said. "You're
going to lose us in the forest because you don't really know

where you're going. And you're afraid of the Chalice, afraid it will burn you to ashes."

Tashalya's gaze narrowed as she advanced on Niklas, but he stood his ground, his clear gray eyes assessing her with disdain.

"I'm not afraid of you," he said, "and we're not going to do what you tell us. We're going home, and taking the Chalice back."

She glared at him, anger gathering inside her like a force.

"Your highness, no," Callyn said in supplication. "He's just a boy."

"A rebellious boy with a mouth that should be silenced," Tashalya said. "A boy who needs another lesson in obedience."

Niklas lifted his chin. "I do not obey you," he replied in a cool little voice that reminded Tashalya of their father. "I will never serve you, never."

Drawing the dagger she'd taken from him, she slashed his arm so swiftly he never had a chance to dodge. Openmouthed with astonishment, he stared down at his ripped sleeve.

"Morde!" Guierre cried. "You are bleeding. You are hurt!"

Tashalya saw the pain well up in Niklas's eyes, driving out his defiance. His face quivered, his mouth twisting as he fought not to make a sound. He gripped his wound, blood welling between his fingers, and sat down abruptly as though his knees would not support him.

She held up the dagger to display its bloody point. "A prince bleeds like anyone else. If you cannot be useful to me, then I'll not hesitate to leave you behind. 'Tis a long, difficult walk back to Grov alone. I think you'll be carrion within a day or two, the vultures picking your bones."

All the boys were staring transfixed at the dagger. She wondered if in their shock they were listening at all. Impatiently she put the dagger away and plucked the circlets from her brothers' brows.

"Hide yourself just out of sight in the trees. Callyn, guard them and hold the Chalice at all times. Do not set it down."

"His highness needs tending."

"He can bind the cut himself," Tashalya said harshly.

"He's only scratched a little." She snapped her fingers. "Syban, come with me."

The child, as dirty as an urchin, gazed up at her with doubtful green eyes.

His hesitation annoyed her. "That was an order, not a request!"

"Go with her," Niklas said quietly.

"But she hurt you," Syban said. "She really hurt you."

"I'm all right. Go on. She won't do anything to you."

"That's stupid!" Syban said gruffly. "She's too mean to trust."

"Come!" Tashalya called. "Hurry up!"

"Go," Niklas said. "Don't make her angry at you, too."

Annoyed that the child obeyed his brother rather than her, Tashalya watched Syban join her with his pointed little chin jutted out, his eyes flinty and suspicious. He was angrier than scared, she saw, suddenly admiring his courage. She believed him tougher than either Niklas or Guierre, no matter how much older they were.

And so she gave him a little smile. "Let's go and deal with some cutthroats. You can watch my back as my knight protector while I bargain. Wouldn't you like that?"

He marched beside her, his arm in its filthy sling, as prickly as a ditch thistle. Amused, she didn't even mind when she heard Guierre saying in an appalled voice, "Your sister. Your own sister. By the name of Tomias, truly she is a terrible creature."

Truly, Tashalya thought with pride, *I am.*

The trade took longer than she expected. In her view it was a simple transaction, exchanging silver for horses, but the dwarf had to examine the workmanship of the circlets with much muttering and head shaking. Finally, when she was ready to scream with vexation, they came to terms.

She got three spavined, swaybacked horses that looked ready to be slaughtered for dog meat. Putting Syban up on the back of one, she led the other two, hampered by her long skirts and wishing for a groom to do the service for her. She could feel curious eyes boring into her back as she left the settlement, but she pretended to take no notice.

The raw dismay on the boys' faces when they saw the

horses told her they'd been intending to break away from her as soon as they were mounted. Really, she thought, Niklas was trying so hard to manly and brave, and failing at every turn. She decided to break his spirit as soon as Kaon gave her the magic he'd promised.

"Callyn, you will take charge of the box," she commanded. "Syban will ride with me. Niklas, you and Guierre will share a horse."

Niklas was sulking, and it was Guierre who protested this time.

"No," he said firmly, shaking his ringlets. "This is not being possible, that I share a horse while the servant rides alone." He crossed his arms, his chin jutting stubbornly. "I shall not agree."

"Then stay behind," she said coolly, handing one set of reins to Niklas and another to Callyn. Syban tried to slip away, but she caught him by his earlobe and tugged until he yelped. "I'm sure the men in yon settlement will be very interested in how best to ransom you."

Guierre gulped, glancing past her as though expecting to see cutthroats coming down the trail. He didn't know, of course, that last night's carousers were still snoring, which was exactly why Tashalya had chosen to do her bargaining in the settlement so early. She had no intention of becoming a bandit's next victim and seeing the Chalice dragged off as swag.

"Get on," she said.

Red-faced, Guierre obeyed her, then leaned down to give Niklas a helping hand. Niklas' arm was bandaged with a strip cut from the hem of his tunic. No blood was showing through the bindings, which satisfied Tashalya that he wasn't seriously hurt. At least he'd learned to hold his tongue, and that pleased her.

Smiling to herself, Tashalya lifted Syban onto her horse and climbed into the disreputable old saddle behind him. He tried to wriggle off, but she clamped an arm firmly around him, inadvertently putting pressure on his broken arm.

"Ow!" he shouted, whipping his head around to glare up at her with teary green eyes. "You're mean and hateful, Tashie. Dalena was right."

She frowned but knew it was too late to apologize. Perhaps, she thought, it was better if he feared her, too. "Then behave," she said coldly.

"Give him to me," Niklas said. "I'll take care of him now."

"Oh, Syban and I have a perfect understanding," Tashalya replied. "Besides, you and Guierre won't be going far without him, will you?"

The defeated look on Niklas's face was enough to make her laugh. Humming, she kicked her horse forward, leading her little party deep into the forest. She headed west a long way, then doubled back and angled southwest.

"We are lost," Guierre announced. "It is of a certainty."

Niklas rolled his eyes. "Do you have any idea of where you're going, Tashalya? Why doesn't your guide help you?"

"Be silent," she snapped. "If we don't obscure our trail, we might as well invite the bandits back there to track us."

After that, Niklas had little to say.

They rode until well after midday, pausing only to rest the horses before pressing on. Syban grew fretful, begging her to stop, wanting food and water, complaining that his arm hurt. His whining scraped Tashalya's nerves until she could barely pay heed to Kaon's whisper-light guidance in her mind. Although her little brother had amused her at first, she was now ready to abandon him in the forest.

Tashalya ached from the long, unaccustomed hours in the saddle. Her shoulders hurt from the effort of holding Syban still, and her cheek was smarting from being whipped by a branch she didn't duck in time. It began to rain, a steady downpour that soaked their clothing and plastered their hair to their heads. Tashalya's horse lowered its scrawny neck and trudged along at a flat walk, refusing to perk up no matter how hard she kicked it.

"I want to stop. I want to stop. I want to stop," Syban whined.

At that moment, her horse headed down a little slope and splashed through a stream to a small clearing at the base of a steep hill.

"*Here,*" said Kaon's voice in her mind.

Reining up, she blinked against the rain streaming down

her face and gazed about. Where was the cave? She didn't
see it.

Syban wiggled down, and she let him go.

Niklas jumped off his horse and set his hand protectively
on his brother's small shoulder.

"This is the place," Tashalya said, still searching, but the
undergrowth was so thick along the edges of the clearing that
she found nothing.

Niklas gave her a sharp look. "What are you seeking?"

"A cave." She let her gaze move along the hill's natural in-
cline, finding a narrow, rocky trail of sorts. She pointed
halfway up. "Where those bushes are!"

Niklas headed in that direction.

Guierre scrambled off the horse, but didn't follow. Instead
he came and stood by Tashalya's stirrup. "Are we hiding the
Chalice in a cave? Is that being our quest?"

"Of course," she said lightly, watching Niklas climb the
steep trail. "I told you we would keep it safely hidden."

"Or is the party you've sold it to awaiting us there? Is it
being a trap you send Niklas into?"

She shot Guierre a sharp look, a tide of heat filling her
face. That made her even more angry, especially when he
nodded.

"I see."

"No, you *don't* see!" she said furiously. "You understand
nothing! I am going to—"

Abruptly she broke off, refusing to defend her actions to
this boy.

Guierre looked at her with contempt. "Treason is a hard
business, I am thinking. That is why you are being so harsh
with us. Because you are in your heart a little sorry for what
you do."

"How dare you!" She pulled her foot from its stirrup to
kick him in the face, but he dodged, gripping her foot with
unexpected strength and holding it until she yanked free.

"I am sorry, princess," he said, his solemn face looking
unexpectedly mature. "Sorry that I was believing you and
wanting at first to help you. We could have been having a
noble quest indeed, if you had not lied to us."

His moralizing shamed her, but impatiently she quelled

the feeling and looked up where Niklas was tugging at the bushes obscuring the mouth of the cave. She had nothing else to say to Guierre, certainly no explanations and no excuses.

She suddenly feared her brother would find Truthseeker first. Jealous, determined that no hand save hers would touch it, she jumped off her horse. "Niklas, wait!" she called.

Niklas yelled as he lost his footing in the mud and went skidding down the trail. He landed awkwardly and lay as though stunned.

Realizing she was standing frozen, holding her breath, Tashalya gathered her skirts and went running up the trail, finding it treacherous and slippery in the rain. She stumbled partway up, swore, and reached Niklas, who was slowly righting himself, holding his weight off one foot and clutching his wounded arm. Pale, his gray eyes enormous, he stared at her without a word.

"What happened?" she asked.

"Someone's in there."

"I smell trolk," Callyn announced.

At the base of the little hill, Guierre backed up, making the sign of the Circle. "Morde a day!" he swore. "We're having no weapons or protectors to take on such a beast."

"It's just a spell to guard the cave from prowlers," Tashalya said impatiently. "No trolk is in there."

"Something is," Niklas insisted. He took a step and winced. "Just as I started inside the cave, it looked out at me."

She laughed in happy anticipation and pushed past him. "Kaon!" she called. "Kaon, I'm coming!"

"No, Tashalya!" Niklas said. "It's dangerous."

She laughed again. "Not to me. Kaon!"

Her lover did not return her hail, but she was too busy hurrying up the precarious trail to notice.

"Callyn, bring the Chalice quickly," she said.

When she reached the mouth of the cave and peered into its shadowy interior, she saw no sign of Kaon. Still, she did not doubt he was close by.

Glancing over her shoulder, she saw Callyn making slow progress indeed, hobbling awkwardly on the trail. Impatiently Tashalya longed for a competent servant instead of this cripple.

"Stop!" she shouted. "Give the box to Niklas and let him bring the Chalice the rest of the way."

Callyn held out the box to Niklas. Looking sulky and reluctant, he refused to take it.

"Hurry!" Tashalya called, but he crossed his arms over his chest.

Although she wanted to scream at him, she forced down her ire and sweetened her voice. "Oh, do come," she said. "There's nothing to fear in this cave."

"Don't do it!" Guierre shouted. "She's going to be selling it."

Tashalya gestured at the empty forest around them. "To whom? I swear to you it's not going to any harm."

Niklas looked bewildered and weary. "Why not the truth for once? Tell us the real reason why you've brought it—and us—here."

She smiled. "Don't you remember those stories we used to listen to when we were little?"

"What stories?" he asked suspiciously.

"Of how the Chalice used to be lost from Nether, hidden far away to keep it out of the clutches of the tyrant Muncel, and how Papa was the only one who knew where to find it? Papa came here, Niklas, to this cave. And this is where he found the Chalice and carried it back to Nether in triumph on the day he became king."

Syban, his face rapt as he listened to the story, walked forward until he stood below her at the base of the hill. "Truly?" he asked, his green eyes shining. "Did Papa really do all those brave things?"

She smiled at the child. "Yes."

Niklas stubbornly shook his head. "I've heard all about the Battle of Grov. No one has ever mentioned a cave. Papa hasn't."

Annoyance filled her anew. Now that she did tell them the truth, Niklas refused to believe her. She wanted to shake him. "It's one of Papa's secrets," she said. "And I know all about it."

"Why would he tell you and not the rest of us?"

"Because I'm the eldest. I've known since before you were born."

"But why bring the Chalice back here?" Niklas persisted. "Why take it from Nether in the first place?"

"Because it belongs with the—"

"Tashalya, hurry," called Kaon's voice.

She whirled around eagerly, her heart thudding with the anticipation of pleasing him. "Yes, yes!" she called, then frowned at her brother. "Niklas, no more questions. Just bring it at once."

As soon as she saw Niklas taking the wooden box from Callyn, Tashalya ducked into the cave.

Gloomy daylight filtered into the shallow cave, which held plenty of shadows. The rear wall had a niche of sorts carved into the stone, and she wondered if the Chalice had stood there during the years it was presumed lost. She felt buoyant at having done the impossible and looked forward to Kaon's praise and kisses.

But still she did not see him. "Kaon?" she called. "Where are you?"

When he did not answer, she searched hurriedly for Truthseeker. It should have been propped up against the wall or laid reverently atop a stack of stones, but, when she finally found it, the fabled weapon lay on the ground near the wall as though tossed away.

Intense excitement rushed through her, making her momentarily dizzy. The scabbard was coated with dust, the hilt spun over with cobwebs, but even in this begrimed state, the magnificence of the sword was obvious.

"Truthseeker," she whispered.

She bent down, but before she even touched the hilt, she heard Callyn urgently calling. Rushing outside, Tashalya saw Niklas limping down the trail with the box, while Guierre was boosting Syban onto a horse.

Their audacity filled her with rage. These stupid little boys, she thought furiously. Would they never stop trying to be heroic?

"Stop where you are!" Tashalya shouted. "I warned you not to try your tricks again."

Niklas glanced over his shoulder but did not stop. "Hurry," he told the others. "Don't listen to her."

"No!" she screamed. "Niklas, I forbid you! Bring the Chalice to me now, or face the consequences!"

He stopped and faced her, holding the box under his uninjured arm, his face set with stubborn determination. "You're a traitor and a thief. Lie all you want, but you have no right to whatever you're doing, and we're going to stop you."

"You can't run away from me!" she shouted at him. "You fools, you'll die in the forest."

"If we do get lost and perish, 'twill be with honor," Niklas said staunchly.

"Honor!"

"Aye, something you don't have." Niklas grimaced. "I'm ashamed to call you sister."

She didn't hesitate or think. Drawing the dagger, she shouted, "Then die!" and flung it at him with all her might.

When his head thumped painfully over something hard and knobby, Dain came to abruptly. It was twilight, shadows pooling beneath the trees, and he could hear distant thunder still rumbling in the sky. He smelled forest, stone, and fire, but nothing made sense. The false eldin and their beyars in his previous dream had all disappeared, except for the leader, who was dragging Dain along by his heels.

Snagging a bush, Dain held on tight, but the bush crumbled in his hands and disappeared.

When the eld glanced back to snarl something at him, Dain saw that his face was the *sheda's*.

Surprised, Dain kicked with all his strength and twisted free. She tried to tackle him, but he ducked her, using her impetus to send her flying past him. Without waiting to see her hit the ground, Dain ran.

The hill was steep, the ground slippery. Rain was still falling, although not as hard as before. Dain ran toward the little grove of saplings, hearing the *sheda* panting curses as she came after him.

Just as he reached the saplings, however, something hard struck him in the back, driving him to his knees.

The *sheda* clung to his back, hissing and snarling in his ear as she pressed her knife to his throat. He twisted in her hold, grabbing a handful of hair and yanking it so hard she howled. At the same time he rammed his elbow deep into her stomach. With a grunt she sagged away, and he vaulted through the broken section back inside the little grove of saplings, where he thought he'd be safe.

But she came scrambling after him, and his heart sank in the realization that this was no longer a refuge. Crouching, she swung her knife from side to side, advancing steadily as she drove him, step by step, toward the precipice.

All the while she was laughing with gleeful triumph. "Now!" she shouted. "You die, pale-eyes king, and no demon magic will save you this time. My curse is too strong!"

Although she feinted, pretending to spring at him, he refused to retreat farther. A swift glance told him he was less than a stride from the edge. He watched her closely in anticipation of her real attack. His heart was pounding; his warrior-honed senses stayed attuned to her, although he did not attempt to enter her thoughts. Had he a weapon at hand, he could have dispatched her with no trouble, but even without one he was far from helpless. If she thought she had him trapped, she was wrong.

Screaming, she launched herself at him. He grabbed her by the wrists, dropping to his back with the intent of sending her flying over the edge, but she writhed and squirmed in his grasp, incredibly strong, and did not go over.

Instead, they rolled across the ground, him feeling the edge of the cliff beneath his shoulders, both of them struggling for the knife. He was her superior in weight and strength, yet she fought like a wild canar, using her fingernails and teeth as much as her fists.

As they strained against each other, the *sheda's* expression grew sly with cunning. "Do you know your witch-girl daughter has betrayed you? Blood and kinship mean nothing to her. She is consort to a demon, and has stolen the Chalice you wait for."

He blinked, not believing her, and with a snarl the *sheda* reared up, trying to drive the knife into his throat.

Dain twisted her wrist hard to deflect the blow, and, as she

grunted in pain, he knocked her arm to the side. The knife
went sailing into thin air, gone. The *sheda* swore ferociously
until Dain's forearm struck her across the throat.

Gagging and coughing, she sagged onto her side, and he
got on top, pinning her. His hands tightened around her neck
until she flailed and thrashed, her face growing purple.

She spat things at him that he didn't comprehend. Not caring, he applied relentless pressure. Already her voice and
struggles were weakening. The madness in her gaze grew
dim, and her eyes rolled in their sockets.

"Tashalya," she whispered. "Deliverer."

"What?" Dain asked.

The *sheda* gasped and shuddered, and although he dis-
trusted her, Dain eased his throttling grip just enough to give
her air.

Wheezing for breath, she opened her eyes. "Witch-girl."

"My daughter is no witch."

"Demon . . . kill you . . . she—"

"The only one about to die is you."

"How can the dead die?" the *sheda* whispered hoarsely.
"Witch-girl daughter, her betrayal . . . already seals . . . your
doom."

"Liar! There's no betrayal. She—"

"Heroes know nothing. You look but never . . . see truth.
Such passion in her . . . worthy of Grethori . . . order your
demons to bring me back to life . . . let me see the Deliverer
meet his destiny . . . with Tashalya."

"Never!" Dain said grimly. "You're finished. Dead in the
first world. Dead here as well. Once the Chalice is brought to
me, no more will you haunt me or strike at my children."

The *sheda* tried to laugh and choked instead. "Never are
you free," she whispered. "The Deliverer will hunt . . . children . . . Faldain's children."

Terrible fear sank through Dain. He shook her. "Who is
this Deliverer? Who?"

But she lay quiet in his hands, the rain falling on her sightless eyes. Dain stared at her in consternation, his emotions
tangled and frantic as he tried to sort through her twisted
malevolence, picking truth from all the lies and threats.

Angrily he shoved her body over the precipice. "Damn

you!" he shouted. His voice echoed through the chasm
below. "Damn you!"

Unexpected pain pierced his body, the agony so intense it
locked up his joints and stole his breath. Shuddering, he collapsed, flinging out his arm in an effort to save himself, and
landed with his head and arm hanging over the precipice.

Must go back, he thought dimly. *Must warn them . . .
keep . . . Tashalya . . . all children . . . safe.*

But the fight with the *sheda* had robbed him of the last of
his strength.

The last thing he heard was the drumming rain. His last
emotion was despair because he would not see his daughters
again, or his sons. He would never be able to tell Alexeika
how much he . . .

Chapter Thirty-one

◆

Tashalya was too angry to aim true. Instead of plunging into Niklas's throat, the dagger smacked him clumsily in the head and knocked him off the ledge. He landed on the ground below so hard he bounced, rolled over once, and lay limp and still.

The box holding the Chalice fell with him, and smashed to pieces when it landed, rolling the Chalice out into the mud.

"Niklas!" Syban cried. "Oh, Niklas!"

Guierre gripped the child's small shoulder, watching big-eyed and solemn while Callyn knelt beside Niklas. Gently she touched his shoulder, his face, his throat. He did not move, but lay there, a small crumpled figure soaked by the falling rain.

Watching, Tashalya felt as though she'd become two persons, the one horrified and the one still angry enough to hope him dead.

"The little fool deserved it!" she said, but her voice sounded oddly breathless and strange. "I warned him not to defy me. Leave him, Callyn, and bring me that Chalice."

Callyn bowed her head, her brass-colored hair hanging in

wet strings in the pouring rain. Obediently, she moved over
to the Chalice and tried to use pieces of wood to lift it without touching it.

Dismounting, Guierre ran to the servant. "In the name of
Tomias, do not obey her," he said. "You know this is wrong."

"Callyn!" Tashalya shouted, fearful that Guierre might in-
cite her servant to rebellion. She wanted to race down the
trail and grab the Chalice, but dared not. "Hurry! Ignore him,
and bring it to me quickly!"

Clutching the Chalice in a fold of her robe, Callyn headed
up the trail, but Guierre blocked her path.

"No! No!" he said urgently, his brown eyes pleading with
her. "You will be damning yourself if you help her. Put aside
her authority and do not be joining in her evil deeds."

"Evil!" Tashalya shouted. "What right have you to judge
me? Get out of her way, and leave her be! Callyn, come to me
now!"

Guierre gripped Callyn's sleeve. "Please, do not! If you
are not caring for your soul, then let me be paying you to go
no farther."

Callyn hesitated, and for a terrible moment Tashalya
thought she might actually listen to the boy. But then Callyn
gently extracted herself from his grasp, shaking her head at
the coins he offered her, and started up the trail.

"Halt in the king's name!" shouted a voice.

Tashalya's sense of triumph was dashed as though a
bucket of cold water had been flung over her.

Disbelieving, she looked eastward as a group of riders
galloped out of the woods and across the stream. Knights and
archers, they rode under no flag, but Tashalya saw that their
leader was Queen Alexeika.

Garbed like a man in a hauberk, leggings, and mud-
splashed boots, armed with daggers and sword, riding
astride, Alexeika reined up her horse so hard it reared. She
handled the animal effortlessly, gesturing and shouting at the
men to fan out. With her hair entirely concealed inside a mail
coif, her oval face looked set and resolute, with blue-gray
eyes that flashed with authority. Samderaudin hovered near
her, entirely dry despite the downpour soaking everyone else,

his long, dark talons emitting a stream of *marzea* that to untrained eyes would appear to be little sparks of green fire.

Astonished, Tashalya stood frozen where she was. She had been careful to cover her trail, and Kaon had promised to obscure their thoughts to prevent court *sorcerels* from finding them. How, then, had the queen found her so quickly? Was there *nothing* her mother could not do?

"Hold where you are!" Alexeika commanded, her voice ringing out. She pointed her whip at Callyn, and two archers immediately aimed their bows at the servant. "You, put down the Chalice and back away from it."

Callyn flicked a glance at Samderaudin and obeyed the order.

"No," Tashalya breathed. Without Callyn's help she knew she could not give Kaon the Chalice. To come so close, only to be thwarted . . . but there was still Truthseeker. Determined to get the sword, Tashalya kept a wary eye on the archers and held herself ready, waiting for her chance.

"Mama!" Syban shouted tearfully, scrambling off his horse to run to Alexeika's stirrup. "Mama, I got hurt, and she's killed Niklas!"

The queen jumped down, hugging Syban briefly and cupping his narrow chin in her hand while Count Bouinyin ran to Niklas. When the queen joined him, kneeling in the mud, Tashalya scrambled back up the trail.

Someone shouted, and an arrow whizzed past her head, but she plunged inside the cave, tripping in her haste and landing hard on her hands and knees. Breathless, cursing her hampering skirts, she scrambled forward and grabbed Truthseeker's hilt.

The sword came to life in her hands. She felt a shocking jolt of magic run up her wrists and arms, the power of it so strong it nearly stopped her heart. Grimly, she fought the urge to drop it and regained her feet. From outside, pursuit was coming. She had only moments.

The sword hummed audibly, and she tightened her grip. It was heavier than she expected, and resisting her ownership, but hers. Holding it, she squared her shoulders, feeling invincible.

"Kaon, come forth," she called.

"Tashalya," he answered.

She turned, panting from her efforts to hold the sword, and saw him standing beneath a shimmering arc of silver fire. A passageway opened behind him, paved with glowing tiles of glass. Kaon had never looked more handsome and appealing. He beckoned to her, smiling a little, his eyes . . . his beautiful eyes drawing her forward.

"Tashalya, my beauty, my love," he said, his voice like stars and music together. "Enter my world and join with me as we have pledged. Bring your offering of the Chalice of Eternal Life."

"I—I can't give you the Chalice," Tashalya said. "But I shall come to you gladly. Oh, let me enter your world, Kaon, before they get here."

His smile vanished, replaced by fury. "The Chalice! You swore to bring it."

"Yes, yes, I brought it," she said hastily. "It's here, outside this cave."

"Of what use is that? You know I can but reach a short distance into the first world. Bring it, Tashalya. Now."

"But I daren't touch it, and my servant has been captured by the queen and her men." Tashalya smiled at him, trying to appease the fury darkening his face. "Give me the powers you have promised, my love, and I'll vanquish my mother. Come forth and help me, and together we'll—"

"No!" he shouted. "You know I cannot touch it in the first world. You must bring it to me within mine."

"An impasse, Tashalya?" asked the queen's voice coolly.

Startled, Tashalya turned, seeing her mother standing just inside the cave's mouth. Raindrops were beading silver on her majesty's chain mail. Slim and tall, elegant even in her warrior's garb, Alexeika held a shining sword in her fist.

Severgard, Tashalya thought with a jolt of recognition. She noted how the queen held that magicked weapon in one hand as though it weighed nothing. And despite her resentment and fury, despite her dismay over displeasing Kaon, Tashalya felt grudging admiration for this woman, who must really have done the legendary deeds attributed to her.

"I see you have your sword at last," Alexeika went on,

talking only to Tashalya as though Kaon wasn't there. "Does this satisfy you?"

"No!" Tashalya shouted, sweeping Truthseeker around clumsily.

The queen immediately set her feet with Severgard at the ready. "Are we to come to blows, daughter?" she asked coolly. "I'm trained in the arts of war. You're not. Put down your weapon and end this absurdity."

"Truthseeker is mine now," Tashalya declared. She glanced over her shoulder where Kaon still stood under the arc of fire. "Kaon, let me come to you now."

"The Chalice," he replied coldly. "Or nothing."

Frantically, Tashalya turned on her mother. "Stand aside! Let me pass."

"To do what? Give the Chalice to your demon?" Alexeika's chin lifted. "Never!"

With a wordless cry, Tashalya appealed to Kaon. "You see how she stands against me. Please give me refuge now. Please, Kaon!"

His handsome face remained implacable. "The Chalice, good lady. You've come this close. Do not fail me now."

"But I—"

"I shall wait here until you come back." He smiled at her, warm and charming again, his eyes drawing her forward. She walked toward him, unable to resist the love they shared. She would do anything to please him, she thought, even if it meant risking her life.

"Tashalya, in Thod's name, go no farther!" Alexeika said sharply.

Tashalya glanced back at her with scorn. "Where do you think I'm going, Mother? What do you think is going to become of me?"

"Do not give yourself to that monster!"

Tashalya frowned. "Kaon is beautiful! Can't you see him?"

"He's filth and pestilence, trickery and deceit. Look at what he really is, Tashalya. A *ciaglo*." She grimaced in abhorrence. "Look on his truth before you choose disaster."

"I have given myself to him, woman to man," Tashalya

said proudly. "We are bonded and pledged, and you cannot part us."

The shock on Alexeika's face delighted Tashalya so much she laughed. "I choose his world, his love. You'll be forever rid of me."

"No! Tashalya, no!"

"But first I am going past you to get the Chalice. Stand aside."

The queen's head came up, her nostrils flaring with anger, her mouth set. She held Severgard in readiness. "The Chalice you shall not have."

"It doesn't belong to you!"

"Your father—"

"It doesn't belong to Papa either. How dare you keep it like a prize in your treasury! You don't even know what it really is. You just—"

"Do *you* know what it is?" Alexeika broke in. "Do you? Or are you just repeating the *ciaglo's* lies?"

"You'll never understand anything."

"I don't have to. The Chalice is going back with us. Your foolishness has cost—"

"I don't care! I don't care!" Tashalya shouted, refusing to listen. She hated her mother. "Kaon, help me!"

Samderaudin entered the cave, and Tashalya heard Kaon hiss behind her with rage. Samderaudin hurled green fire at Kaon, and in fear for him Tashalya screamed, "No!"

But the fire passed harmlessly through Kaon and scorched the wall. Relieved, Tashalya gulped in a breath and tried to run to his side, but found herself unable to move.

"Release me!" she said angrily, but the *sorcerel* ignored her.

As Kaon straightened and turned to face them, Tashalya saw that his face and body were changing appearance. No longer was his countenance a man's. Instead, it contorted, elongating into something almost bestial. His jaws gaped open, revealing long, jagged fangs, and his eyes—his lovely mesmerizing eyes—had become flaming orbs of hatred and fury. He hissed and spat, trying to step through the doorway he held open between their worlds, but Samderaudin shouted something that pushed him back.

Alexeika rushed forward and grabbed Tashalya, dragging her out of the way just as Kaon dissolved into white mist and rushed at them. Samderaudin blocked his path, however, using the concentrated force of his *marzea* to form a shield the mist could not pass through. Then he pushed the mist back.

"Hurry! Hurry!" Panting, Alexeika hustled Tashalya out of there and shoved her down the trail so fast that Tashalya nearly dropped Truthseeker in an effort to keep from stumbling.

When they reached the bottom and stood safely on level ground, Tashalya whirled around in a rage.

"How dare you interfere!" she shouted. "How dare you come between me and Kaon!"

"Is that demon what you want?" Alexeika replied with equal heat. Her gaze raked Tashalya with contempt. "Is that the best you can do?"

"He loves me, and he is no demon! Whatever Samderaudin did to render him ugly is—"

"Samderaudin showed you his true form. This creature has mesmerized and deceived you from the moment you summoned him. Or don't you understand what a *ciaglo* is, daughter, what it does, and how it gathers its victims?"

Taken aback for a moment, Tashalya frowned in an effort to rally. "He isn't a ghost. He's an ancient who's come from the past. He—"

"Listen to your own ravings," Alexeika broke in harshly. "Your training has taught you this is untrue."

"Training was a lie! Everything was a lie!" Tashalya's resentment spilled out. "Samderaudin and Bona tricked me into failing. They told me I couldn't become a *sorcerelle* because my powers were dwindling, because I'd inherited your instability with magic."

Alexeika's expression changed, and her eyes softened. "Oh, Tashalya."

But pity was the last thing Tashalya wanted. She took a step back. "You don't care. You've never cared. All you wanted was a normal daughter, but I can't be normal. I can't be what you want of me. I never could. And now I've killed my brother and stolen the Chalice, and given up my *marzea* for the man I love, and you're taking that away, too. Samderaudin will kill him, then what will I have? What will I have?"

She began to cry, huge ugly sobs breaking from her with such force she dropped to her knees in the mud with Truthseeker cradled against her.

Alexeika gently touched her wet hair. "Tashalya—"

"No!" she moaned, sobbing harder. "Leave me alone. I want Kaon!"

The white mist came boiling out of the cave in response to her call. The knights yelled in alarm, and Alexeika whirled around with a gasp.

Looking up through her tears, Tashalya saw the mist rushing toward her. In wonder, she rose to her feet, realizing then that Kaon must have prevailed over Samderaudin after all. As joy and relief filled her, she lifted her arms to the mist.

"Kaon!" she called out.

"Tashalya, no!" Alexeika screamed. "Chesil!"

Strong arms grabbed Tashalya from behind, yanking her out of the mist's path just in time. It sailed past her while she struggled furiously. "Let me go. Let me go!"

But she could not break free of the Agya who held her clamped against his side, his weapon in his other hand. And Tashalya saw the mist turn and come for her again. She lifted her face, yearning for Kaon, and saw some hint of his features deep within the swirling center of the mist as it came closer. She saw his eyes, his beautiful eyes . . . only they weren't lovely anymore, but fearsome and horrible still.

Fear and doubt struck her, but it was too late. Chesil was shouting in her ear as the cold mist touched them. Tashalya screamed, and Alexeika plunged Severgard deep into the mist's center.

It exploded with a force that knocked Chesil and Tashalya backward. He released her when they fell, and Tashalya scrambled away from him, regaining her feet quickly. She looked around, but did not see Kaon anywhere. Her mother lay sprawled in the mud like a rag doll dropped at the end of play. Tashalya drew in a sharp breath, staring transfixed with a queer, unnameable sensation in the pit of her stomach.

"Mama," she whispered.

Samderaudin flew from the cave, *marzea* still glowing on

his hands. But there was nothing left to fight, and he dropped abruptly from his levitation to kneel on the ground, panting hard.

Crying, Tashalya headed for her mother, but it was Lord Thum, suddenly running, who reached her majesty even before Sir Pyron. The men lifted Alexeika, propping her against her protector's knee, and pushed back her coif so that her long dark hair spilled free. Her bloody face was ashen.

Guierre stood out of the way, gripping Syban to keep him back. Niklas was sitting up dazedly, propping his head in his hands while Bouinyin supported him.

Seeing her brother still alive, Tashalya felt something bleak and terrible lift from her heart, only to clamp tight again as she looked back at her mother.

She forced herself to walk toward the queen, although her body seemed made from lead. More knights gathered around her majesty, their faces knotted with grief and worry. Someone elbowed Tashalya aside.

"We must get her out of this rain," Lord Thum was saying. "Chesil, can you carry her?"

"Nay, I'll do it," Sir Pyron said grimly.

As they lifted her gently into his arms, the queen stirred and moaned, turning her head.

Tashalya sobbed in relief, clapping one hand over her mouth.

"Give her to drink of the Chalice," Lord Thum said. "Quickly!"

He turned about as he spoke, his gaze sliding past Tashalya as though she did not exist. Chesil ran downhill to a horse and lifted the Chalice from a saddlebag, filling the vessel from the stream.

Gently Lord Thum put the Chalice to Alexeika's lips while someone spoke a prayer aloud.

Alexeika drank a little, choked, then roused and drank deeply. Thum, holding the Chalice reverently, stepped back while a wobbly Niklas limped up and pressed his palm tenderly to his mother's cheek.

"Mama," he whispered, "please, in Thod's name, be all right."

Alexeika sighed and opened her eyes fully. She smiled at her son.

Watching, Tashalya had never felt such relief. Yet it was mixed with envy. She, always the outsider, found her eyes filling with tears, and she began to tremble. Gratitude or shock, she no longer knew what she felt.

"I'll do now," Alexeika said. "Put me on my feet, Sir Pyron."

The protector obeyed, his craggy face puckered with emotion. Alexeika looked around her a little vaguely, focused on Niklas and smiled at him again before enfolding him in her arms.

"Praise Thod that you boys are all safe."

Syban came running up to her. "Mama, you're the bravest girl I know. You look like a knight, and you fought that demon and beat it."

"Well, perhaps," Alexeika said, glancing at Samderaudin uncertainly.

"And, Mama, did you know my arm is black with bruises where it's broke inside?"

"Is it?" she said with a shaky laugh, putting her hand to her brow and wiping away blood. "Were you brave when someone set it for you?"

"Callyn pulled it. I heard the bones grind together."

"Aye, he was awfully brave and stalwart," Niklas said, putting his arm around Syban's shoulders.

Syban bounced up and down. "And I've got teeth marks in this leather strap from when I didn't yell. Want to see?"

Some of the knights started laughing. Much encouraged, Syban pulled the strap from his pocket and ran about, showing it off like a trophy.

"Guierre," Alexeika said, to the bedraggled prince. When he came to her shyly, she touched his curls with kindness and a smile. He bowed low over her hand, kissing it as though he'd witnessed a miracle.

Watching her mother charm and reward everyone, Tashalya found her amazement growing. *They've destroyed Kaon,* she thought bleakly, *and do not care.*

Samderaudin, apparently recovered, glided over to Tashalya as though he'd read her thoughts.

Tashalya lifted her chin with her last tatters of defiance. "What befalls me, now that I'm ruined, disgraced, and dishonored? Am I to be abandoned out here, to starve in the forest? Am I to be marched back to Grov in chains?"

He turned away in silence, leaving her frowning fiercely, on the verge of tears.

Alexeika, finished with seeing the Chalice secured once more in a saddlebag, apparently heard Tashalya's remarks. Striding over to her daughter, Alexeika slapped her hard across the face.

Her cheek on fire, caught entirely by surprise, Tashalya staggered back, dropping Truthseeker in the mud.

Alexeika glared at her. "You sniveling, ungrateful little— you still can't think about anyone except yourself. How dare you! How dare you!"

Shocked by this outburst, Tashalya could only stare at her in bewilderment, but Lord Thum interceded at that point, saying, "Your majesty, she doesn't know. Please remember that she doesn't know."

"Then it's time she did, time she understood exactly what she's done to her father."

"Tell her quickly, please, but be calm," he advised. "Remember what your majesty wishes to ask."

Alexeika shut her eyes a moment as though she could not bear what he was saying. "Aye," she said in resignation. "Any price, for that."

Lord Thum backed away with an unreadable glance at Tashalya.

"Count Bouinyin," Alexeika said without taking her fiery gaze from her daughter, "please escort the boys into the woods for a short while if you think it will not pain Niklas to walk."

"Mama?" Niklas said in confusion. The lump on his temple was red and swollen. "What's wrong?"

Alexeika barely glanced at him. "Your sister and I must talk privately."

"She's no sister of mine! She—"

"Come, Prince Niklas," Bouinyin said, intervening. "Let us go into the woods while you three give me your report."

"Oh, yes," Niklas said, shooting Tashalya a look of withering contempt. "You will want to know about the traitor."

Sighing, Tashalya bent and picked up Truthseeker, wiping mud from its scabbard. They were trying to frighten her, but she assured herself that such tactics weren't going to work. With Kaon gone, nothing else mattered.

Sir Pyron stepped between her and the queen. "I'll relieve ye of that weapon now."

"No!" Tashalya said sharply, clutching it to her. " 'Tis mine. You can't take it from me!"

"Aye, I can and will. Now give it over, or I'll—"

"Sir Pyron, don't waste time arguing with her," Alexeika broke in. "I want to settle this quickly."

"She ain't to be trusted."

Alexeika gave him a wan smile. "Leave it for now."

Grumbling, he backed away. Meanwhile, Bouinyin had already marshaled the boys out of earshot, and a very grim Lord Thum and Sir Chesil retreated to the horses. Tashalya steeled herself against the lecture that was coming. Fiery scolding about dishonor and treason that she didn't want to hear.

But instead Alexeika said, "Your father is dying, Tashalya."

Shocked anew, her defiance crumbling, Tashalya stared. "What?"

Disappointment filled Alexeika's eyes. "I hoped you might care. I see that you don't. Still, I wanted you to be told. You are old enough to understand that actions have consequences, and yours are so dire I know not how you will live with yourself once you know the whole of it."

"Yes, Mama," Tashalya said impatiently. "You—"

Alexeika lifted her hand. "Remain silent while I have my say. There's little time, and I don't intend to waste much of it dealing with you. Faldain is dying, and we must get the Chalice back to him without delay."

Tashalya felt as though she were dreaming. Only a short time ago she thought her mother had been killed, and now Alexeika was standing there, as fierce and hard as ever, her voice cold and clipped as she spoke.

"Your father came home ill, very ill, and he collapsed the

afternoon of the joust while you were busy stealing the Chalice."

"Are you blaming me for that?"

Exasperation pinched Alexeika's face. "For Thod's sake, you selfish—*no*, I am not blaming you for his illness. But if he dies, you'll be responsible for it."

"How?"

"He could have been cured at once, had the Chalice been there. As it is, he may already have—" Breaking off, she stood with raw, naked grief in her face, her eyes brimming with tears.

"Papa can't fall ill," Tashalya said. "He's eldin. Are you saying he took a mortal blow in battle?"

Alexeika shook her head. "The Grethori *sheda* cursed him with her dying breath. We know not how her magic pierced his protections, but it is killing him the same way as eld poison. The how and why of it does not matter at present. Saving him does."

"But—"

"The men have told me how much he suffered on the long journey back to Grov, how bravely he endured." Tears spilled down Alexeika's cheeks. "You see, he thought he had only to come home to be cured. He had no inkling that his daughter, his favorite child, had been suborned into removing the only means available to save his life. Oh, Tashalya, how could you do this? When he risked his life to save you from Ashnod and nearly died from a soultaker?"

Abruptly burying her face in her hands, Alexeika wept.

Tashalya understood now why her mother was so angry with her, so frantic. She saw that she'd been tricked and manipulated by Kaon, who'd used her like a cheap drab and then tried to kill her. The shameful humiliation of it burned so much that she kenw not what to say.

"You see," Alexeika went on, sniffing hard. "I had to come racing after you, to get the Chalice."

"Yes, of course," Tashalya murmured, unable to stop herself. "'Tis a good thing Niklas and Syban cannot hear you confess that you value the Chalice over them."

Alexeika drew back, staring at Tashalya in disbelief.

"With all that's happened, with your father's life at stake, can you not put off your defiance for even a moment?"

Tashalya flushed, and Alexeika went on, "The Chalice is your father's only hope, but there's so little time. I love him so terribly, so desperately . . . I cannot bear to lose him."

"The way I loved Kaon," Tashalya said softly, resenting how he'd tricked her. What a fool she'd been, a stupid, gullible fool. "I thought he—"

"How dare you!" Alexeika gasped. "That you could compare your father—his decency and goodness, all that he stands for—to that vile filth of a demon—"

"No, I didn't mean—"

"Enough!" Alexeika's face twisted with repugnance. "I'll never forgive you for this. Never!"

Seeing the condemnation—even hatred—blazing in her mother's eyes, Tashalya was unprepared for how much it hurt. "But I didn't—"

Alexeika turned on her heel and strode away, leaving Tashalya alone in the rain. The queen rapped out orders for the men to mount up. As they complied, Lord Thum spoke to her majesty, who shook her head, glaring at Tashalya all the while.

Tashalya turned her back on all of them. What was to happen to her now? she wondered. If her father died and Niklas became king, he would probably order her execution.

The sound of approaching footsteps made her glance up, bracing herself for arrest.

But it was Lord Thum who came to her instead. Frowning, he said, "You have disappointed her majesty terribly."

Tashalya glared at him. "I don't understand her. I'll never understand her."

"I think perhaps because you do not try." He cocked his head to one side, the grimness in his hazel eyes belying his mild tone of voice. "You see, your mother brought the Ring of Solder with her. She hoped, we all did, that you would use it to take the Chalice back in time to save your father's life."

Tashalya gasped with astonishment. "You're joking."

"You alone of us know how to use the Ring. Even if you and the queen never come to terms, can you not find compassion for your father? Do you hate him so much?"

"Of course not. I—I do not hate the king."

"Dain is my oldest and dearest friend. I do not want him to die." Thum held out his hands, then dropped them helplessly to his sides. "Will you not spare him? Will you not try?"

"I don't understand this," Tashalya whispered bitterly. "I am the traitor, a thief and abductor. Why give the Ring and Chalice both into my keeping?"

"You are his majesty's only hope."

Still suspicious and bewildered, unable to believe him, she said nothing.

Wearily Thum pinched the bridge of his nose. "Very well. I shall attempt to lighten the charges which must be brought against you. Were there fewer witnesses, were the Prince of Mandria not involved, it might be possible to hush up some of the matter. Still, I shall see what I can do to sway the—"

"Stop!" Tashalya said in anguish, feeling torn in all directions. "How can you negotiate terms with me? Do you not—"

Impatience flashed across his face. "Your highness, to save the king's life I would grant you any terms within my power. Must I fall on my knees and beg you? Gladly will I do so. At the moment, your actions count as little to our desperation."

"And if I take the Ring and flee?" she asked.

He neither flinched nor hesitated. "Thod help you, if you can live with your father's death on your hands."

Fresh tears filled her eyes. "I can't touch the Chalice. It will kill me."

"Carry it in the saddlebag if you fear it. But in Thod's name, take it to him. Please. *Please.*"

All the men were watching her with a strange mixture of resentment and hope. The boys had returned from the woods. Syban and Guierre were making a point not to look her way, but Niklas was staring with open contempt. Tashalya stiffened her spine. She cared not if they all condemned her for what she'd done, but she did not want anyone doubting her courage.

"All right!" she said, the concession exploding from her. "I'll do it. I'll take the Chalice to the king."

Relief filled the faces of the men, and Alexeika closed her eyes for a moment, pressing her hand to her mouth.

Thum lit up. "Your majesty!" he called out.

Alexeika beckoned permission for Tashalya to approach her, but there was no gratitude to be seen her blue-gray eyes, no softening at all. In silence, the queen held out the Ring of Solder, and Tashalya slid it on her finger. At once the milky stone began to glow a little. She felt the metal band grow warm around her finger. It was too large, but she turned it around so that the big stone fit inside her fist, and held it tightly the way she had when she was a little girl.

I'll take the Chalice to Papa, she thought. *Then I'll flee with Truthseeker, never to return.*

Samderaudin emerged from the cave, sparks of *marzea* flying around him, and Tashalya shot him a guilty look, wondering if he'd read her thoughts. He ignored her, however, positioning himself near Callyn instead, and Tashalya drew a deep breath.

The saddlebag containing the Chalice was draped across her shoulder. Tense and afraid, Tashalya expected holy fire to destroy her on the spot, but nothing happened. Swallowing hard, she gripped Truthseeker's hilt securely. The powers of these three potent artifacts began lacing their energies around and through her until she could barely breathe. Without her lost *marzea* to shield herself, she would just have to endure it. But at the same time, she felt a rising sense of power and confidence. *At last,* she thought, *I am truly on the road to my destiny.*

"Wait!" Niklas shouted. Now mounted, he kicked his horse forward despite Bouinyin's attempt to stop him. "Mama, you mustn't trust her. She's planning another trick. She'll—"

"Hush, son," Alexeika said. "We have no choice."

"You can't let her go. She's done evil things. She—"

"I know what she's done, but I trust the princess royal to honor her word," Alexeika said formally, gazing straight at Tashalya with eyes like steel.

"Honor!" Niklas echoed in derision. "But, Mama!"

"That's enough, Niklas," Alexeika said with a snap.

Perplexed and angry, he fell silent and glared at Tashalya.

Unable to resist tormenting him one last time, she smiled a cold little smile, promising herself that he would never wear the Ring of Solder.

Alexeika reached out and gripped Tashalya's hand. Startled, Tashalya forgot about teasing her brother.

"Thod speed," Alexeika whispered to her. "I beg you— *beg you*—in the name of all Faldain's love for you, do not fail."

Sobered, Tashalya could not bear the naked pleading in her mother's eyes and pulled away. She focused her powers of concentration on the Ring.

Papa, Papa, Papa, she thought. And in a blaze of fire and trailing sparks, she was gone.

Chapter Thirty-two

❦

The Ring of Solder swept her so fast through the gray mistiness of the second world she could barely stay focused on her destination. She'd forgotten how powerfully dizzying it was to travel this way. Although she'd been able to slip inside the second world as an apprentice, she'd never gone more than a step or two across the threshold. This was much different.

And then she seemed to strike something solid, like a wall. With a jolt she crashed back into the first world and found herself in a heap on the ground, gasping and shuddering. Slowly she sat up, dazed and unsure of what had happened. She was in the forest, a dark gloomy section of it where sunlight barely filtered through the dense canopy.

Is my father here? she wondered. No, obviously not. Had she lost concentration, let her mind wander? How could the Ring have brought her to the wrong place?

Confused, still trying to catch her breath, she picked up Truthseeker and the leather bag holding the Chalice and crawled forward, instinctively moving to the center of the tiny clearing before she paused. Only then, as she pushed back her tangled hair and gazed around, did she realize she'd put herself inside an ancient Circle.

No saplings sprouted from the ground. No roots grew twisted and gnarled within the space. No vines and brambles overtook the Circle. Close by, she saw the primitive altar, weathered to a barely discernible lump of stone. Around her, almost hidden by drifts of old leaves, were the rocks forming the Circle.

What, she wondered in complete bewilderment, *am I doing here?*

A faint sound made her jump to her feet. "Papa?"

"Not exactly, good lady."

She spun around in surprise. "Kaon!"

He stood just beyond the Circle with silver fire arching over him. The passageway of glass yawned open at his back, and he was smiling.

She couldn't believe it. Tears stung her eyes, yet she was laughing, too. "You're all right. How can this be? I thought Samderaudin and Mama destroyed you."

His smile faded. "I am beyond the strength of a mere *sorcerel,* and your parent should have died."

The anger in his voice sobered Tashalya, steadying her over her shock. She realized that he must have somehow stopped her progress through the second world to bring her here, yet if he could do that—if his power was stronger than the Ring's—then how was she to withstand him?

"You've done well, good lady. I see that this time you've brought everything to me, as we agreed."

Instinctively her grip tightened on Truthseeker. "I'm taking the Chalice to my father," she said coldly.

Kaon scowled, his eyes flashing. "What need has a mortal for my Chalice?"

"It's not yours. And my father has great need of it."

"Lies, good lady. Lies!"

But Tashalya was thinking of how Kaon had changed himself to mist and attacked her. He would have engulfed her and smothered her the way he killed Guierre's two servants, had the queen not intervened.

"My lady mother has not lied to me," she said clearly.

"She had no reason to let me go, save for the purpose of saving his majesty's life."

"She has twisted the tenderness of your heart well," Kaon said, his voice growing warm and soft. "Come to me, good lady, and let me kiss away that frown. You know my feelings for you, how special you are to me. Bring the Chalice and Truthseeker unto me and fulfill our bargain. Now."

His voice was like liquid honey, warm and sweet. Dreamily, she opened the flap of the saddlebag and started to lift out the Chalice, but touching it broke Kaon's spell. Frightened, she jerked back her hand and dropped the bag so that the Chalice rolled out on the ground.

Tashalya stared at it, her heart pounding, and drew several unsteady breaths.

"Put aside your fear," Kaon cajoled her. "You touched it and stand unharmed."

Amazed, she thought, *Does this mean I am not evil after all?*

"Tashalya," Kaon said impatiently, "why do you hesitate? Give me the Chalice now."

"No," she said slowly, blinking against his attempt to hold her spellbound. "I dare not while Papa needs it."

"I told you this is a lie! Your father is well and has no need of you."

But the Chalice had cleared her mind. She frowned at Kaon. "Mama saved my life, and you nearly killed her. You stopped my progress home to Papa. You forced me here, despite the power of the Ring."

"I want you with me," Kaon replied with a smile. "There are few places where the worlds overlap naturally. The cave is one, and this is another. I cannot wait for you much longer. If we're to be together, come to me now."

Tashalya retreated a step. "No. You tried to kill me, too."

"What foolishness has seized your mind? Haven't I shown my love and given you pleasure enough?"

Thinking of her nights with him made her blush, and she felt a stirring of desire that she had to fight back. "Do you love me, Kaon?" she asked. "Or do you make use of me?"

"You are my good lady. I have granted you a place forever

beside me. I need not woo you with additional favors," he said impatiently.

"You want the Chalice, not me. And I'm taking it to Papa."

Anger flashed in Kaon's eyes. The silver fire above his head began to shrink, and no longer could she see the passageway stretching behind him. White mist began wreathing about his feet and legs.

"You dare defy me?" he shouted. "You dare break our bargain?"

"I swore to help my father."

"He needs nothing. It's a trick to force you to return the Chalice."

"Again you lie!" she shouted. "You, Kaon! You're the deceiver."

"Come to me, and I'll explain everything, but come now. If you love me, Tashalya, come."

The Ring was so hot on her finger it nearly burned her skin. She raised her fist aloft. "Release the Ring's power and let me continue on my way."

Kaon reached toward her. "Tashalya, no, no! Don't leave me, good lady! You are my heart and my life. We are bonded, and I want you with me forever."

"Is it me you want forever or god-steel?" She pulled Truthseeker from its scabbard. "Me or the Chalice?"

"All," he said, his eyes compelling her.

She flinched at the force he used in trying to mesmerize her. Pain spiked through her temples, and a memory came to her, of when she was very small and afraid, huddled on the stone floor of Tulvak Sahm's lair. The *sorcerel* was holding her chin in his taloned hand, and his eyes were boring into hers, as he said, "You will hunt Truthseeker, and when you have found it you will use it to unleash a potent force of destruction on all that is . . ."

"No!" she said with a gasp, blinking.

Realization flooded her, and for the first time she understood that the *sorcerel* had been manipulating her all these years by planting that command in her mind. Although he was long destroyed, she had been *obeying* him when she searched for Truthseeker. She'd been his dupe and Kaon's, and like a fool she'd destroyed so much in her life for this evil quest.

Repugnance filled her. Feeling befouled and dirty, she tossed down the sword.

At her feet, the Chalice had started to glow ever so slightly, and Truthseeker's blade shone white with power. The Ring had grown so hot it nearly burned her finger. *Warnings of evil's presence,* she thought. She could feel the Ring's power swelling against Kaon's, fighting him.

"Let me go!" she cried out.

Kaon didn't answer. She looked up in time to see him dissolving into mist. Only his face remained visible, but it was no longer handsome. Instead, it was the deformed, hideous countenance she'd seen in the cave.

Samderaudin showed me the truth, she thought, *and I refused to see it.*

"Tashalya, please come to me," Kaon said, his voice so heartbroken and imploring she felt the pull of his spell. "Do not fear me. We have known each other, you and I, as ancient and mortal seldom do. I have promised to share my power—"

"Promises, aye, and empty ones!" she interrupted. "Yet nothing did you give me. No powers have I gained to replace what you took."

"They will come. You must learn how to use them."

Fury swept her. "No! The visions have already faded. You are not an ancient at all, but just a *ciaglo*, as I was told from the first."

"Just a—" Rage contorted his face, and he bared his fangs.

"Ciaglo!" she shouted. "Demon ghost! Liar! Seducer! I won't be used by you. Never again! Begone from me!"

His misty form roiled before her. "All my promises have I kept. I gave you sufficient power to survive our union and pleasure beyond all mortal experience. I led you to Truthseeker. Now you will serve me by handing it and the Chalice forth into my world."

"I won't."

"Obey me!"

"Never!"

"Do you think I shall let you go?" he roared. "My power holds you here. And whether you obey me or take death as your punishment, to your father you will *not* go!"

How like Tulvak Sahm he was, in arrogance and temper. And she'd been blind to it all. She wondered how she could have ever loved him or believed him, wondered how she had never suspected she was serving both *sorcerel* and demon in turn. Her hatred for them swelled inside her, until she could not separate one from the other. And even worse, she hated herself for having been so stupid.

"Tashalya—"

"Here is the Chalice," she said, pointing. "And here is Truthseeker. If you want them, *ciaglo*, enter this sacred Circle and pick them up . . . *in my world.*"

"No!" Kaon roared, dissolving completely into mist. The demon flew right at her, veering off just before he entered the Circle.

She crouched low, her hands shielding her head, thankful for the old Circle's protection. The Chalice now blazed a fiery white, but she was too angry to be afraid. She picked up Truthseeker, intending to see if it could destroy Kaon as Severgard had not.

The mist came toward her, but more slowly this time, hovering just beyond the Circle. *Yes!* Kaon's voice said eagerly in her mind. *Yes, put Truthseeker inside me. With your hand on it, I can take it unto me.*

She felt the potent force of the weapon prickling and stinging her palms. It wanted to fight, she realized. It was drawing on her anger, focusing and intensifying her emotions, urging her to carry it into battle. Once she destroyed Kaon with it, she thought, she could gather her own army, then seek out . . .

With a start, she realized how terribly dangerous Truthseeker was. Although her father had used it for good, few possessed his strength of character. The sword could so easily compel someone to commit evil, yet within the close proximity of the Chalice, she put her temptations aside. Small wonder Faldain had surrendered it, she thought, for truly god-steel was not meant for mortals.

Tashalya knew that she was mortal, despite her ambitions

to the contrary. She understood that her dreams had been so grandiose they had led her to this place of extreme danger, where her life and soul could be lost. And if her father was truly dying, her father who had saved her from being forced to eat Ashnod's fire, how could she not sacrifice herself to save him?

No, Tashalya, no, Kaon's voice spoke to her mind. *You are wrong, so very wrong. Come to me, and I will give you immortality and more and all you've ever wanted.*

"You've taken from me what I've wanted," she said in a harsh, bitter voice. "You destroyed my *marzea*. You stole from me my future and my family's respect. You turned me into a common thief and caused me to jeopardize the lives of my brothers. And now you want me to ignore my father's peril, for what? To live within more of your lies? I won't do it!"

Then I must destroy you.

With tears streaming down her face, she lifted the sword, although she knew her defiance was futile. She lacked the physical strength and *marzea* required. Even Samderaudin, with all his skill and knowledge, had not prevailed against this creature.

Good, Kaon said warmly inside her thoughts. *Surrender the sword to me. Lift it higher, higher. Stand very still while I take it unto me. And afterward the Chalice.*

But Tashalya whirled around and slung Truthseeker into the bushes as far as she could, where no one would ever find it in this wilderness. No one could raid her thoughts for the knowledge of where it lay hidden, for she knew not where she was. These old Circles and altars were scattered across the land in numerous deserted sites. Truthseeker could rust away to nothing as far as she was concerned.

Kaon screamed with fury. He boiled and swirled at the edge of the Circle, threatening her until his voice was just a wild babble in her mind.

"I won't bring it back! I won't give it to you!" Tashalya shouted. "In the name of Thod I denounce you, demon! Go back whence you came. Die there and wither. For nevermore will I speak your name or summon you again. And never will you defile this sacred vessel with your evil."

He raged and gibbered, but she ignored him and instead stared down at the Ring of Solder on her hand. She understood that this would be her third and final use of it. Although she regretted that, she had a debt to repay.

Trembling, terrified, she knelt and gathered the glowing Chalice to her breast. Its power hummed against her, a force like nothing she'd known before. But as she tried to activate the Ring's power, Kaon came flowing into the Circle and engulfed her.

Caught entirely by surprise, for she'd believed herself safe, she felt the icy cold mist flowing through her body, smothering the air from her lungs as it drew her life away. Her heart was thudding wildly, and she began shaking uncontrollably from the contact with such evil.

They should have both been blasted by the Chalice's holy fire, yet nothing happened.

Kaon's mocking laughter filled her mind. *Fool! You protect me from the Chalice. While you hold it, you and it both are mine.*

"In Thod's name, I call on the Circle!" she shouted. "By the power of the Chalice of Eternal Life, by all that is good, I call forth your destruction!"

Flames shot from the Chalice all around her, dazzling her vision until she had to avert her eyes. Kaon screamed and was suddenly gone, his misty form burned away. Shuddering in the aftermath, Tashalya found herself crouching on the ground with the Chalice still in her arms. The rocks surrounding her were blazing and smoking, charring the leaves that had drifted over them. And the tree branch overhanging the old altar now looked withered and seared as though killed by too much heat.

Shocked by what had happened, Tashalya slowly straightened. All her life she had shunned the religion of her parents, knowing that the *sorcel*-magic she sought to learn was not compatible with it, not the way eld-magic was. Yet now she understood that Tulvak Sahm's influence had been responsible for keeping her from studying Writ with her siblings, for keeping her from swearing her vows or taking salt. All these years she had lived in a cage of his making, yet somewhere inside her had been faith when she most needed it. And this

small sacred place had responded to that need. As had the
Chalice itself.

She wanted to put the Chalice on the altar and kneel before it. She wanted to collapse there and weep for the wasted,
blighted years of her life. Yet it was all too much to assimi-
late at that moment. Her limbs were weak, and her head was
swimming, but she dared not let herself faint. Her task was
not yet finished.

Gazing down at the Ring of Solder, she thought, *Papa,
Papa, Papa,* and once again she was sucked into nothingness.

A heartbeat later she burst into the sacred grove near the
Tree of Life outside the walls of Grov. With sparks and fire
raining down on all sides, she gained a confused impression
of twilight being held back by faint little glowstones and the
fairlight flickering from the fingertips of eldin healers who
were singing softly. Her father lay on the big stone altar, surrounded by priests holding hands and chanting in weary
counterpoint to the eldin songs of life and endurance. Some
of the priests were on their knees, breathing hard. One lay on
the ground in complete collapse.

A strange filmy web covered the king like a shroud, but
although the sight of it scared her, she realized instinctively
that it must be part of the spell they'd woven to sustain him.

Beneath the web, her father's face was ashen, his lips
without color, his closed eyes sunk deep in their sockets.

That waxen look of death made her fear the worst. A sob
burst from her. "Papa!"

Her sudden arrival from the second world created havoc
on all sides. The circle of priests flinched at her unexpected
appearance, and the chanting faltered. The web covering the
king split, and one of the eldin healers came hurrying forward.

Tashalya could not hear what he said, for Lord Omas was
shouting louder than anyone with a voice like thunder. Turning to the lord protector, she said desperately, "Here is the
Chalice." Half-blinded with tears and panic, she held it out,
barely aware that it was still shooting holy fire from within.
"Take it and save Papa. Hurry!"

But the priests and healers drew back instead of helping

her, and when Omas tried to approach her, one of the eldin caught his sleeve to stay him.

"Princess Tashalya, hold the Chalice over your father," instructed a voice as cool and placid as a meadow pond.

Crying uncontrollably, she obeyed. She didn't understand anything as golden streams of fire fell onto Faldain. The web burned away, yet he was not harmed. Little squiggles of white fire flashed and raced across his chest and limbs; and then he began to glow all over with the same white pure light the Chalice emitted when it stood in its Chapel.

Tashalya watched a radiant, unworldly aura surround the king, and the Chalice abruptly stopped emitting fire. It turned cool and dark in her hands as the light glowing inside her father faded, too. Certain she was witnessing the departure of his soul for the third world, Tashalya could not believe she'd reached him too late. A tangle of emotions—chiefly horror and guilt—overwhelmed her, and she fell to her knees.

"No," she sobbed. "Oh, no! Papa, dear Papa, I am so sorry!"

The priests came up beside her, and gently took the Chalice from her unresisting hands. They removed the now-cold Ring of Solder from her finger and put it back on Faldain's. One of the healers stood on the other side of the altar and raised his voice in song.

The silvery notes, each one clear and pure, rose into the air. Believing it to be his requiem, Tashalya buried her face in her hands, rocking herself in grief. How could she have let herself be made a tool for her father's destruction? Never had he been unkind to her. All her life, he'd granted her whatever she asked for, forgiving her transgressions with a tolerance she'd never appreciated until now. His patience with her had been infinite, and she loved him with all her heart. She couldn't bear what she'd done.

"Look," someone said. "The king lives. He lives! Thod be praised!"

Tashalya thought she must be dreaming, but hands pulled her aside so that others could approach the king. As they lifted him gently off the altar, she saw his eyes flutter open.

Men were dropping to their knees, Omas included, making the sign of the Circle and murmuring prayers. The air was filled with awe, reverence, and thanksgiving.

Tashalya rose to her feet, heedless of the tears streaming down her face. Although she could barely believe her eyes, she watched her father revive. He seemed groggy and confused at first, but eventually lifted his head and looked around him.

A little choking sound came from Tashalya. "He's not dead," she said in a shaky voice. "He's all right?"

"Yes, child," a priest said to her. "All is well with him now, thanks to you and Thod's gracious mercy."

Fresh tears welled up in her eyes. She pressed her hands to her mouth to keep herself from wailing like a peasant.

"Tashalya?" her father said in wonder. He sat up, shaking off some of the blankets hastily swathed about him, and reached out his hand to her with a smile. "Daughter! Is that you?"

Something dark and terrible lifted from her heart, and she flung herself into his arms, sobbing uncontrollably.

Chapter Thirty-three

❦

Attired in gray clothing as somber as his eyes, with Miren-gard belted at his hip and a crown of silver and diamonds glittering upon his brow, King Faldain sat enthroned in the ancient Hall of Kings. Around him hung old tapestries and decorative arrangements of weapons and shields, representative of the violent history of his family. At his side, Queen Alexeika perched on a stool instead of her usual chair in accordance with the oldest traditions.

Alexeika's oval face was expressionless, her blue-gray eyes stony. Dain could see her hands hidden in her lap, white-knuckled and clutched together. Not once did she take her gaze away from the prisoner kneeling before them.

The Palace Guard lined both sides of the Hall and stood in front of the large doors. Another man guarded the rear private door behind the dais. Members of the king's Council stood closest to the throne, wearing their official robes and chains of gold. More of them were watching the king and queen than gazed at the prisoner. The courtiers—wide-eyed, curious, and silent—thronged the rest of that large, gloomy chamber.

The chamberlain stood beside the prisoner, his voice solemn and slow as he read the charges over her.

Ah, Tashalya. Regret squeezed Dain's leaden heart at the sight of his daughter kneeling before him on the hard floor. Her head, unveiled, was bowed beneath its smooth coil of black hair. No silver circlet of royal status did she wear. Her gown was plain and unadorned, fashioned from undyed linen. No jewels glittered at her ears or upon her white, slender hands. As the charges were read, a list of heavy offenses indeed, she did not move, did not look up.

Dain was not listening to them, for he knew them by heart. There had been no trial, for the accused had not protested her charges. But there had been wearisome days of listening to the furious arguments waged back and forth by his advisers, of listening to the criticisms and suggestions of the Kollegya, of consulting with the priests who had examined Tashalya, of questioning Samderaudin for the few answers he would give. Dain had spoken privately to Niklas, when Alexeika and the boys returned. He had also talked to Syban and Guierre in turn. Alexeika had been strangely reticent with him, but Thum had told him exactly what happened the day they caught up with Tashalya.

The court—wearied by the long campaign against the Grethori—feared that Mandria would declare war on Nether for having carelessly allowed Prince Guierre to be abducted. Thum's efforts to smooth that difficulty away by saying Guierre had gone off on a lark, as boys will, had been helped slightly by the fact that no harm had come to his highness. War, Dain knew, was unlikely, but whether Guierre would be recalled from fostering by Queen Pheresa was as yet unknown.

A far more serious offense was Tashalya's attempt on Niklas's life. No amount of diplomacy could smooth over such treason, nor should it. To attack the king's heir was to attack the king. Firstborn or last, Tashalya had no right to strike against the laws of succession.

Dain smothered a sigh. That one of his children could so hate another had shocked him deeply. Nothing excused it, nothing. The experience had changed Niklas, taken some of the trusting innocence from his eyes. And although, as a future king, it was necessary for Niklas to grow up seasoned and wary, Dain regretted that his son's first taste of genuine betrayal had come from a sister.

But the worst charge of all was one he also could not suppress, no matter how much he loved Tashalya and hoped for her possible redemption. Stealing the Chalice and indirectly endangering his life were transgressions that could not be forgiven by his subjects. Although she'd tried to rectify her mistake by returning with the Chalice in time, it was not enough to clear her.

He was under pressure from some members of the Kollegya to order Tashalya's execution. She had threatened the throne, the very future of the realm. She had brought Nether to the brink of possible war with its most important and powerful ally. She had profaned and committed sacrilege. Her royal blood could not excuse her, so they insisted, from these barbarous acts.

The recital of charges came to an abrupt end, and silence fell over the Hall, broken only by a faint cough at the opposite end and some restless shuffling of feet. Clearing his throat, the chamberlain folded the parchment containing the written charges, glanced around, and faced the king.

"Your majesty," he said, "such are the charges recorded. They have been entered and read officially, as is required."

Dain's mouth was dry, and his tongue seemed to be stuck to the roof of his mouth, but he forced himself to reply by rote. "Does the accused answer these charges?"

Tashalya did not move or look up. She made no reply.

A rustling murmur, swiftly hushed, went through the crowd.

The chamberlain drew a deep breath. "The accused does not answer, your majesty."

"Will her advocate speak for her now?" Dain asked.

Only silence answered him. He could feel the intensity of emotion in the room, thundering, overwhelming if he chose to listen. He closed his senses to it and focused on his daughter.

"Sire," the chamberlain said after a sufficient pause, "the accused has refused to name an advocate to speak for her. By custom, a refusal of advocacy is an admission of guilt."

Again the crowd stirred. The murmurs, this time, sounded louder.

Dain gestured, and guards assisted Tashalya to her feet. Still she would not look up. Whether she was ashamed or defiant, he could not tell. His heart grieved for her, this broken child who'd always been his favorite, whom somehow—despite his affection—he'd failed most of all.

Count Unshalin—fat, pompous, self-important, and merciless—stepped forward, making as deep a bow as his big belly would permit. "Your majesty, we call for judgment and sentencing of this traitor. We, your majesty's most loyal subjects, plead with you not to be swayed by familial ties or her royal blood, but to consider only her actions. Let those speak for her; let her admission of guilt, her confession through silence, speak for her."

Anger swept Dain. Unshalin had already made his position clear in Council. He had no business saying more than the simple call for judgment.

Rising to his feet, Dain's keen ears heard Alexeika's almost inaudible intake of breath. To his knowledge Alexeika had not spoken to Tashalya since the queen's return. Alexeika's anger remained a barrier between mother and daughter, and yet Dain knew how much his wife's heart was breaking. That, too, the girl must answer for.

"Tashalya," he said now.

His daughter glanced up, her pallor becoming more pronounced. As her blue eyes met his, he saw none of their usual arrogance and ill temper. Nor did he see any tears of contrition or shame. Her gaze was level and calm. It held no appeal for mercy. Although shattered in many ways, clearly Tashalya still possessed plenty of spirit.

Dain's own gaze narrowed. Was she trying to manipulate him now? he wondered.

On his left, he glimpsed movement among the assembly. Cardinal Velain of the Mandrian faction—most certainly a spy and troublemaker of the first order—was positioning himself closer, his sleek face avid for trouble as he watched the proceedings.

A wave of dislike passed over Dain, but he held his feelings in check. *I shall play no games of yours,* he thought to himself, well aware that Velain hoped to see him take a misstep here. He noticed the restiveness of the crowd but ignored it as he continued to stand without speaking. As their king, he could hold them indefinitely, spin out this judgment as long as he pleased, and none would dare complain. Yet to dally too long would be to appear weak, and he did not want to toy with his advisers at the expense of Alexeika's nerves.

"There are two possible sentences, based on the laws of this realm," he said at last, his voice stern and controlled. "Execution or exile."

An impatient rustle passed through the crowd. Tashalya's gaze dropped, and her mouth trembled slightly before she firmed her lips and forced herself to look up at him once more.

He met her gaze, hoping for more than that tiny display of nerves, even for a true sign of contrition. He did not get it.

So be it, daughter, he thought. *I shall not give you the easy way out.*

He lifted his head to gaze across the watching faces. "The king chooses . . . exile."

A babble of voices broke out, some rising in protest, others calling for his attention. Dain ignored them.

His daughter shut her eyes a moment and swayed on her feet before she rallied. A tide of color crept up her throat into her pale cheeks, then ebbed away. The tears had come at last, glistening in her eyes, but whether she was disappointed or relieved, he could not tell.

Betraying none of his own emotions, Dain said, "Let the accused be taken from Grov under armed guard, to a place of banishment. There, let her live without companions or visitation, separate from family and the court." He gestured curtly to the guards. "That is all."

The buzz of voices rose. Velain shot a look of furious disappointment at Dain and left. Unshalin shook his head and glared at Tashalya, who managed a curtsy to Dain and then Alexeika before being escorted through the hostile courtiers ranged on either side. She walked like a princess, her back straight, her head erect, but never again would her name be cheered by the people. No longer would she carry the title "princess royal," which had been hers since birth. He had deliberately not stated the duration of her term of exile, which could be taken by some to imply a lengthy, possibly permanent, banishment.

Dain watched her go, not knowing when he would see her again, unsure as to whether anyone could ever truly help her. According to Samderaudin, the influence of Tulvak Sahm remained deep inside her, and only Tashalya could eradicate it—if she chose to try.

Alexeika came to stand beside him. "Your decision has surprised no one," she said quietly. "But disappointed several."

He glanced at her, the wife he'd loved for so long, a woman of passions, contradictions, and long-held grudges. "You among them?" he asked.

She frowned, her gaze flicking up like a blow. "No," she said in muted annoyance. "How could you—"

He caught her hand and kissed it lightly, venturing a smile that calmed the storm in her eyes and made the stiff lines of her body relax.

"Where will she go?" Alexeika asked.

Dain drew her to the rear of the dais, away from listening ears. "The Castle Volvn."

Clearly that surprised Alexeika. She stared at him for a moment. "You will let her organize its restoration?"

"Don't you think our capable, headstrong daughter needs occupation?" he asked.

"Very much."

"Are you offended that I've chosen your estate?"

She shook her head quickly. "You've made it possible for me to visit her, under the guise of checking its progress."

He smiled, admiring how quickly she'd understood his purpose. "And will you visit her?"

Alexeika frowned. "Later, perhaps. Much later. I need time to forgive her, if I ever can. That she could have turned against her own brothers—"

He squeezed her hand to comfort her. "I know. Inexcusable, and yet she is driven by forces she cannot control."

"Sometimes, Faldain," Alexeika muttered darkly. "And sometimes by her own choice."

"At least she will be well guarded there, and safe," he said, thinking aloud.

"Safe? What mean you?"

Dain shifted his gaze away from Alexeika's sharp one. He hadn't told her about the *sheda's* final curse against their children, and he did not intend to. But one by one, he would find ways to guard and protect them, even if it meant scattering them across his realm and into Mandria. He would keep them far from the reach of old enemies, whether dead or still to come. *And Tashalya,* he thought, *is the bait to lure forth the Deliverer, if he exists.*

"Faldain?" Alexeika asked suspiciously.

He tucked her hand in the crook of his arm. "Tell me, dear wife, what are we to do about Guierre's clothing"

She smiled involuntarily, her eyes crinkling. They ducked through their private door into a passageway, alone for a precious moment where Alexeika could gasp, choke, and then laugh aloud.

"Oh, beloved," she said at last, wiping her eyes. "Does he not wear the worst garments imaginable? Those tight leggings . . . so indecent!"

"If my sons take up his example, I shall banish them all," Dain said with mock sternness.

"Your sons," she said with pride, smoothing back an unruly lock of his hair, "will never give you cause. They are good boys, brave and true. I'm so proud of them." She paused, sobering as she caressed his cheek. "Please don't grieve for Tashalya. Instead, take heart from the best of your children. We have to look forward, and leave the past behind us."

Dain took her hand and kissed her palm. "If we can," he said quietly. "If we can."

Epilogue

❧❧

Deep in the Dark Forest, Anoc climbed into a tree for the night. Predators were hunting; an owl sailed past him on silent wings to strike an unwary mouse and rise with it, great pale wings flapping. The sounds and restlessness of the forest at night no longer disturbed him, for he'd grown used to this land. He understood its savagery, avoided its pitfalls, and enjoyed its bounty.

Fed and content for the moment, he stroked the shining blade of the sword he'd found several days ago. It had been lying beneath a thicket of berry brambles, glowing with unworldly fire, its pommel stone a dark blue-green that seemed sometimes alive.

He would never forget the thrill of that first hesitant grasp of its hilt, or how its power jumped against his hand, welcoming rather than repelling his touch. Each time Anoc clumsily swung the heavy sword, he felt its responsive hum fill him with ideas and renewed ambitions. He seemed to hear She Who Made Him whispering her dreams and strategies, and the sword's voice mingled with hers.

"Truthseeker," he murmured now, not understanding why

he called it by that name. It was not a Grethori word, but he liked it.

Taking the small strip of blanket from his pouch, he began polishing the blade with great care, making sure there was no rust to be found anywhere. The gods had thrown him this weapon, he thought with suitable gratitude, and he had learned from the dwarves how to treat it with respect. Soon, he would hunt and gather hides. He would make a scabbard for it and a belt, the way the pale-eyes wore their weapons.

And in the darkness, he polished and smiled, dreaming of his future.

The Sword, The Ring, and The Chalice

THE BESTSELLING TRILOGY BY

Deborah Chester

"Entertaining" —*Starlog*

"Mesmerizing." —*Romantic Times*

The Sword	0-441-00702-3
The Ring	0-441-00757-0
The Chalice	0-441-00796-1

Available wherever books are sold or at
penguin.com

B150